SHATTERED

Janet Nissenson

Janet Nissenson
www.janetnissenson.com

Publisher's Note: This is a work of fiction. Names, characters, places, and incidents are a product of the author's imagination. Locales and public names are sometimes used for atmospheric purposes. Any resemblance to actual people, living or dead, or to businesses, companies, events, institutions, or locales is completely coincidental.

Book Layout © 2016 BookDesignTemplates.com

Shattered/ Janet Nissenson. -- 1st ed.
ISBN 978-11514384176

"I call him the devil because he makes me want to sin.
And every time he knocks, I can't help but let him in"

.

CONTENTS

Chapter One

Angela Del Carlo had just crested a hill – the one she'd nicknamed Coronary Peak – and heaved a sigh of satisfaction. From this point on, the terrain was mostly flat to gradual downhill, making the final four miles of her twenty mile route a little easier. She hadn't been pushing too hard today since she had a tough 50-kilometer trail race scheduled for next weekend, and didn't want to toe the starting line on tired legs.

She took a swig from her handheld water bottle, always careful about maintaining her hydration levels during these long runs, even when the weather was cold and blustery like today. Winters in San Francisco were relatively mild when compared to most of the country, but out here on the bluffs of the Marin Headlands the winds could be fiercely biting. She'd dressed accordingly in Lycra leggings, a long-sleeved windshirt, gloves and a knit cap, but the cold still permeated her ultra-thin frame. Angela was almost always chilled, regardless of the weather, a condition that wasn't surprising considering how skinny she'd become and with almost nonexistent body fat. But food had lost its appeal a long time ago, right around the same time her entire world had been shattered and she'd been cruelly left to try and pick up the pieces alone.

More recently, however, she'd finally begun to start picking up those bits of her life, albeit at a very slow pace and never more than one jagged section at a time. But for the first time for as long as she could recall, Angela was feeling – *something*. She wasn't quite sure what that something was – hope, optimism, or God help her, maybe even happiness – but all she knew was that she didn't feel quite as dead inside as she had for almost four years. She also didn't know if this newfound sense of hope was because of the new man in her life, or whether it was simply her own sense of survival that had finally kicked in. Whatever the reason, she was gradually getting to a point in her day to day life where she didn't have to drink herself to sleep every night, and where she didn't wake up each morning dreading the hollow emptiness that her life had become.

She gave a brief nod to the two mountain bikers who were headed up the trail in the opposite direction, ignoring the admiring glances they sent her way. It figured, she thought ironically, that most of the runners and cyclists she had met on her runs or at races didn't seem to think she was too skinny, unlike nearly every other person in her life did. Her mother and sisters, of course, never failed to make some sort of deprecating comment about her shrinking form every time they saw her – which was intentionally not very often at all these days. Her best friends – the McKinnon twins – also nagged her about the drastic weight loss, though Julia was kinder and more subtle about it than ballsy, in-your-face Lauren. And Cara – Angela's loyal, hardworking PA – seemed to be constantly trying to entice her to eat something – a candy bar, a piece of birthday cake, an egg roll.

Her fellow athletes, though, were nearly all as thin – or even thinner, in a few cases – than she was and didn't seem to think there was anything in the least bit unusual about her tall, emaciated body. It was one of the reasons she'd embraced the sport of ultrarunning in recent years, not having been content to merely run marathons or shorter distances. One of the reasons, but certainly not the only one. No, that would be the peace she seemed to find, the solace, from running these long, lonely distances. She would spend hours out on the roads and trails, running ten or twenty or more miles at a crack, and letting her sorrow, her despair, disappear for a time. The only other method she'd successfully employed to block out her brokenness involved drinking copious amounts of vodka, and usually waking up with a nasty hangover as a result.

Lately, though, she'd been laying off the booze. Whether that was due to Dwayne's influence, or just herself growing weary of waking up with a pounding headache and roiling tummy, it didn't really matter. Angela knew that drinking in excess like she'd done for so long wasn't healthy – mentally, physically or emotionally – and that its numbing effects were only short term at best. In the long run, nothing really seemed to work for any length of time.

She still had a couple of miles to go when it started raining. As it was, she'd been lucky to run this far without getting wet, given that the weather had been inclement for the past week. The trails she'd run on had been riddled with sections of thick, sucking mud, and she was glad she'd worn her sturdiest trail running shoes this morning.

Angela was soaked by the time she reached the parking lot, shivering from a combination of being wet and cold and a lack of calories in her system. Once inside her sporty Toyota 4Runner, she toweled herself off briskly before reaching for a pre-mixed recovery drink. She grimaced at the slightly chalky taste of the vanilla flavored beverage but forced herself to finish it, knowing she needed to replenish all the calories she'd just burned during her nearly four hour workout. Dwayne had given her a case of the drinks, along with a variety of protein bars, nutritional supplements, and other freebies he'd received from several of his sponsors. He'd claimed he had more of the stuff than he could ever use, and insisted she was doing him a favor by taking some of it off his hands. Angela gave a wry little smile, fully aware that this was Dwayne's own sweet, subtle way of getting her to eat more.

She cranked up the heater as she began the drive across the Golden Gate Bridge back into San Francisco, thankful that the traffic was light this morning. She was beginning to shiver and needed to get into a hot shower quickly. She'd come perilously close more than once now to full-blown hypothermia, and had been careful ever since the last near miss to watch for the signs. Maybe that was another indication that she was slowly returning to the land of the living. It had been a long time since she'd given a damn about her health or safety, not seeming to care very much about the potential consequences of not taking better care of herself.

The rain was coming down a little harder as she pulled inside the garage, and she found herself wishing yet again that there was an inside staircase leading to her flat upstairs. Instead, the only entrance to the flats was via the outside staircase, which meant she was going to get soaked again.

Angela had been thinking for a while now about moving, perhaps even buying a condo of her own. She made a healthy six-figure salary as a stockbroker, and had socked away a lot of money these past few years. Even with the outrageous cost of real estate in San Francisco these days, she could easily afford to buy a place. But she had never really liked making changes, especially the major one that moving would entail, and continued to procrastinate on making a decision. And since Julia had recently announced her intention to stay in the downstairs flat until her lease expired next January, Angela wasn't in a big hurry to move out. She would never admit it out loud, but it made her feel secure to know that one of her best friends lived close by. Or at least most of the time. Julia spent part of the week sleeping over at her fiancée's condo, but she and Nathan were almost always here at the Lower Pacific Heights flat at least three or four nights a week. They were currently building a custom dream home across the Golden Gate Bridge in Tiburon, and were keeping their fingers crossed it would be completed by the New Year.

As if on cue, Julia's brand-new silver BMW – an extremely generous Christmas gift from Nathan – pulled inside the two-car garage. Angela gave a wry smile as her almost perpetually perky friend alighted from the car, her face glowing. From her attire, it was obvious that Julia had just come from one of her daily yoga classes, and Angela thought it all a bit unfair that while she was a sodden, sweaty and mud-splattered mess, Julia looked as chic and put together as she always did.

"Hey, Angie. Looks like the heavens opened up on you during your run. This is why I prefer indoor exercise," said Julia as she began to unload several re-usable grocery bags from the trunk.

Angela shrugged. "It wasn't too bad, at least not until the last couple of miles. And it still beats running on a treadmill at some noisy, crowded gym. And, sorry, I know you've got this big love affair going on with yoga, but it's never really been my thing."

"I know. You and Lauren have always been these jock-girls," teased Julia. "Oh, thanks," she added, as Angela took two of the bags from her.

"Let's make a dash for it. Thank God you've got sensible shoes on for a change," commented Angela, glancing down at the vivid pink and orange athletic shoes on Julia's feet. It was an extremely rare occasion when she wasn't shod in four-inch heels.

Julia wrinkled her pert little nose. "I'm really not a sensible shoe kind of girl, you know. But I admit it would look weird to wear Jimmy Choo's to yoga. And at least these are cute."

Angela rolled her eyes as she closed the garage door and they dashed up the outside staircase to the landing. "Sweetie, I don't think anyone pays much attention to your footwear when you're wearing skintight yoga clothes."

Julia – and her identical twin Lauren – were both on the petite side but with curves in all the right places – boobs, hips, ass. Julia was wearing a cute little pink rain slicker over her yoga attire, but Angela knew that beneath it Julia's close-fitting pants and top would be clinging to every one of those eye-popping curves. And while Angela's running gear was equally as clingy – especially since it was soaked from the rain – whatever curves she might have had at one time had disappeared along with the twenty plus pounds she'd lost. Everything about her five foot eleven inch frame was flat now – breasts, stomach, butt. Her arms and legs were stick thin, her narrow hipbones protruding sharply, her cheekbones starkly pronounced.

Most of the time she didn't give a shit about how she looked any longer, rarely if ever bothering with makeup, going months without trimming her long, straight black hair, and paying little attention to her wardrobe. But every so often she'd get a fleeting urge to glam herself up like she used to – to spend hours fussing over her appearance in order to please –

Angela grimaced, forcing *those* kinds of thoughts firmly out of her head as she opened the exterior door to the flats. She helped Julia carry in the grocery bags, dumping them on the kitchen counter. Even Julia's re-usable grocery bags were stylish – in a variety of bright pink and purple prints – while Angela couldn't remember the last time she'd actually shopped for food, much less what sort of bags she'd used.

Julia smiled gratefully. "Thanks for helping. I'd have had to make two trips otherwise. Why don't I return the favor by inviting you over for brunch?"

Angela gave her friend a knowing little smirk, well used by now to Julia's not always subtle attempts to feed her. "Nice try, Jules, but I'll pass. Thanks all the same."

But Julia wasn't so easily deterred. "Come on, Angie, you need to eat something, especially after that long run you did. Have you had anything to eat today?"

Angela sighed, knowing she was incapable of lying to her friend. "A protein bar before the run. And one of these nasty tasting recovery drinks that Dwayne gave me. Maybe the chocolate one will be better than the vanilla was."

Julia shuddered daintily. "Ugh, neither of those items you just mentioned constitute a real meal. Look, Nathan's supposed to be here in a few minutes and I promised to make eggs Florentine. That used to be one of your favorites back in high school when Mom would make it."

"Maybe." Angela knew the poached egg and spinach dish covered in Hollandaise sauce would be delicious since Julia was every bit as good a cook as her mother Natalie had always been. And while she never seemed to feel actual hunger pains anymore, and food in general just didn't seem important, she realized that she did need to make more of an effort to eat.

Julia scented blood and went in for the kill. "I'm also serving home fries and fruit. Oh, and tangerine mimosas."

Angela laughed. "Actually, hard as it might be to believe, I've been on the wagon for over two weeks. In fact, the last time I had any booze was during our New York trip. But I love your tangerine mimosas so you've talked me into it."

Julia gave her a quick hug before wrinkling her nose delicately. "Oh, that's great news, Angie. Why don't you, uh, go catch a shower and I should have everything ready in about half an hour."

"I can take a hint, Jules," Angela replied drolly. "I've got wet dog stink and a hot shower that's calling my name."

After promising Julia that she would in fact return, Angela jogged upstairs to her own flat, and wasted little time getting into the shower. She almost wept as the blissfully hot water hit her chilled body, and she gradually felt the blood in her extremities begin to warm. Her hands and feet in particular were always cold these days, no matter how many layers she wore or how high she cranked up the heat.

She pulled on clothes without paying the slightest attention to what she grabbed, grimacing as she noticed her size zero jeans were a little looser than the last time she'd worn them. Her breasts were small enough not to need a bra but she pulled one on anyway for the extra layer. Over it she layered a white camisole, a long sleeved navy T-shirt and a gray thermal Henley. The three layers not only helped keep her at least a little warmer, but also added some bulk to her ultra-lean torso.

Angela pulled her almost waist-length hair back into a barrette, not bothering with makeup as was her norm these days. In fact, it was more than likely that any cosmetics she might still have lying about had long since dried up or expired.

As she pulled a pair of low heeled boots on over her thick wool socks, she fought off the temptation to call Julia and dream up some excuse to back out of brunch. Oddly enough it wasn't the idea of actually eating that was causing her reticence, but instead the thought of having to watch Julia cuddle up to her very affectionate fiancée Nathan.

It wasn't that she didn't like Nathan, even if his initial treatment of Julia had been more than a little on the douche-bag side. And so long as Julia was happy – which she evidently was in spades, being knee-deep in wedding plans at the moment – then Angela's own feelings about Nathan shouldn't matter. Part of it, she supposed, was that she had an inherent distrust of men in general these days. And the other part, she admitted ruefully, was that it bothered her to witness the frequent and rather blatant displays of affection that the besotted couple seemed to engage in almost constantly.

Angela had known little affection in her twenty six years, her childhood one of loneliness and emotional neglect despite growing up in a seemingly stable household with two parents and two older sisters. The few sexual partners she'd had during college had all been fleeting, casual encounters, all during a time in her life when she'd been angry, rebellious, and totally incapable of managing anything remotely resembling a relationship.

And then had come the time in her life she merely referred to as "the year" – though in actuality it had only been eleven months and five days. It had been the only time in her life when she'd felt truly alive, truly fulfilled, even though there had also been countless days during the same year when she'd felt helpless and out of control. And since then, she'd spent every day trying to claw her way out of the depths of hell that she'd fallen into when the ill-fated affair had ended so horribly.

But now, for the first time in years, she was beginning to find hope. That fleeting sensation of *something* that she'd felt earlier today during her run had been hovering on the outskirts of her emotions for a little while now, and she wasn't sure whether to embrace it fully and welcome it in, or shove it brutally aside so she could continue to wallow in her sorrow.

Not wanting to dwell any further on what might be happening to her, Angela headed downstairs. hoping she could find enough of an appetite to do justice to Julia's admittedly delicious eggs Florentine.

Chapter Two

April

As usual, she was the first one in the office, arriving well before the sun came up and most likely before the majority of her co-workers were even getting out of bed. She liked the quiet, preferred the solitude that she could enjoy before the intrusions of ringing telephones, loud voices, and client meetings demanded her attention. And despite her largely anti-social behavior towards her co-workers, Angela presented a much different persona to her clients. She was certainly businesslike and professional, but also engaging and personable, and her clients were extremely loyal to her. And of course that loyalty was further ensured by her unquestionable success in picking the types of investments that had performed exceptionally well over the past couple of years. She'd received a number of very lucrative referrals from those clients who'd been very pleased at the increase in their portfolio value.

Angela booted up her computer and sipped her coffee while she looked over her schedule for the day. She was meticulous about her daily to-do list, insisting on maintaining strict control over it as she had done for most facets of her life. It was somewhat ironic, considering the fact that no one had ever imposed any rules or controls over her as a child or teen, and that she'd been more or less free to do whatever she wanted for as long as she could remember.

Unfortunately, her unsupervised childhood hadn't been because her parents had been the sort of free spirits who believed in letting their children be themselves and make their own choices. In Angela's case, it had simply been because no one had really given a damn about her. So she'd made her own rules, controlled her own life, made her own decisions. Except for one all-too-brief period in her life – a time that had encompassed eleven months and five days. A period where she'd alternated between heaven and hell on a daily basis, but had still felt happier and more alive than at any other time in her life.

As she'd become so adept at doing these past few years, Angela firmly blocked out the memories that hovered so tantalizingly in the back of her mind. Instead, she focused her energies on the portfolio proposal she was finalizing for a prospective client – another referral from one of her largest accounts. Her ability to pick out suitable and well-performing securities gauged to the individual needs of each client was a large part of her success. Even in an office with over a hundred brokers, she was regularly ranked in the top fifteen percent for production credits.

Of course, most of the other brokers in the office would credit Angela's success solely to the good fortune that had come her way via an otherwise tragic event. She had been a very junior partner to Barbara Lowenstein, one of the top producers in the office and certainly the most successful female among them. And when Barbara had suffered a sudden, fatal heart attack, fifty percent of her very lucrative book of clients had automatically been passed on to Angela.

And while Angela never failed to be grateful for the opportunity she'd been given, the success she enjoyed today was almost entirely of her own doing. She'd taken the accounts she had inherited from Barbara and tripled that number, not to mention adding substantially to each client's portfolio value. But she continued to be subjected to professional jealousy from both male and female brokers in the office, and had learned some time ago to block out the catty, spiteful comments – much as she'd mastered the art of ignoring everything else in her life that caused her hurt or pain.

She was admittedly anti-social and a loner, but much of that was simply because she didn't have the patience to deal with people who either disliked or envied her. She hated playing games and pretending to like someone just because it was the polite thing to do. Angela figured she could count on one hand the number of people in this office she actually liked or tolerated.

One of those people was her administrative assistant Cara Bregante. Like herself, Cara was of Italian descent, though only on her father's side, and also like Angela, she was a finance major, still working on her degree at night school. Cara was usually one of the first to arrive in the office as well, nearly always at her desk before seven a.m.

"Good morning," greeted Cara's cheerful little voice from just inside the doorway to Angela's office.

Angela glanced up and couldn't help the answering smile she gave her very young assistant. She seldom smiled these days but resisting Cara was nearly futile. The twenty one year old was adorable, charming, and so sweet she could melt the hardest of hearts – like Angela's own. Cara was a tiny little thing, barely over five feet tall, and Angela always felt like a giant standing next to her. But unlike Angela's super skinny frame, Cara was curvy, with full breasts and hips, and always hovering oh so close to becoming plump. She had a cute heart-shaped face, enormous golden brown eyes, and a mass of thick, glossy dark brown curls that tended to overwhelm her small face.

"Hey, Cara," greeted Angela in return. "How was your class last night?"

Cara grimaced. "Gut wrenching. Sometimes I don't think I'm going to survive this semester. It's definitely the toughest one so far."

Angela frowned, noticing how tired her assistant looked this morning. She knew Cara had a rough time of it – working full time to support herself and then struggling to finish up her finance degree at night, all without a penny of support from her family. Angela knew that she could have easily found herself in a similar situation if she hadn't been lucky enough to receive an athletic scholarship to Stanford. Her mother would have never consented to paying for a college education, considering it a waste of good money, and her sweet but utterly spineless father wouldn't have dared to argue the case further with his domineering wife.

"If you want some help studying, just say the word," offered Angela. "And take it easy today, okay? Our schedule is pretty light and you look worn out."

Cara gave a small shrug. "I'm fine but thanks for asking. Do you want some more coffee? I'm headed over to the lunchroom for some."

"Sure, if you don't mind. And before you ask, little mother, I do not want a donut or a bagel or any other free food that might be lurking around."

Cara grinned. "Am I that predictable? Besides, I didn't see any breakfast meetings on the schedule this morning. Not with the new hire from competition who's supposed to be starting today."

Angela barely glanced up from the research report on tech stocks that she'd been studying. "What's so special about this one? It's not often that Corcoran doesn't pack the schedule full of meetings no matter what else is going on."

Jay Corcoran was the office sales manager, and one of the bigger pains in Angela's skinny ass. He was one of those overeager company men who did absolutely everything that management asked of him, and followed the corporate philosophy like it was religion. One of his responsibilities was to schedule meetings with the various mutual fund and annuity representatives, and he took that particular task to heart with a vengeance. It seemed to Angela that there was always one meeting or another going on, and the meetings almost always included some type of food service.

Angela despised meetings of any sort, and the ones with the sales reps were the worst. Her sentiments were wholeheartedly shared with most of the other top producers in the office, who shunned the meetings as frequently as she did. And of course this drove kiss-ass Jay crazy, making him fear that it would be a bad reflection on his abilities as sales manager if every meeting wasn't filled to overflowing with attendees. Thus, the hyperactive, annoying as hell sales manager – whom Angela had once likened to a Doberman Pinscher on crack – could be constantly seen trying to hustle one broker or another into attending one of the meetings. Angela just ignored him now, refusing to even look up when he popped his balding head inside her office, and tried unsuccessfully to entice, bully, threaten or beg her to attend.

Cara shook her head. "I think the new hire is a really big deal. Apparently he's moving into George Barnhart's old office."

That bit of news got Angela's attention. Barnhart had been the top producer in the office for almost two decades until he'd chosen to retire last year at the ripe old age of fifty-two. Most of the other brokers in the office had thought him crazy to call it quits when he was still at the very top of his game, but Angela had silently applauded his decision. The man had already accumulated tens of millions, and had wisely decided that life was too short not to start enjoying the fruits of his labors. Rumor had it that he, his wife, and their two teenagers were presently doing some sort of round the world trip on a sailboat.

Barnhart's former office – easily the largest and most ideally located in the place – had remained empty. Angela had heard via Cara that at least half a dozen of the top producers had been campaigning for it, but the rumor had floated around for a while now that management wanted to keep the spacious office vacant in hopes of luring in a big producer from a rival firm. And apparently their waiting game had finally paid off.

"He must be a pretty big fish to land Barnhart's office," mused Angela. "Any word on who he is or what firm he's transferring from?"

"Not yet, but I'll see what I can find out. Be back in a few and then we can go over today's schedule."

Angela gave her assistant a wave as she went off in search of coffee, thinking that if it wasn't for Cara she'd never know what was going on in the office. She rarely ventured out of her little corner office, the one she'd been given rather grudgingly soon after Barbara's death. But even though she would have been well within her rights to demand a larger office now, she was perfectly happy remaining in her secluded spot. Few people bothered her back here, and it was much easier to ignore the goings-on around her. Except for client meetings outside of the office or going to the ladies room, it was rare that she left her office at all during the work day.

What she *had* spoken up about, though, was having to share Cara with other brokers. For the first few months of Cara's employment, she'd been assigned to work for two other brokers in addition to Angela. But once Angela had achieved the required level of production to warrant a one on one assignment, she'd set her foot down quite firmly on the matter. And so, for the past eight months, Cara had worked solely for Angela, and worked very, very hard. Angela knew without being told that Cara was one of the best assistants in the whole office, and that she was damned lucky to have her.

And even though Angela was more than five years older, Cara was the one with the mothering instincts – the one who fussed over her boss, fretting when she didn't eat, telling her to take a break or that she worked far too hard. Most of the time Cara's ministrations either annoyed or amused Angela, but they also touched her at the same time. No one had ever really fussed over Angela very much, and certainly not in recent years. And while there were only so many ways she could politely refuse the muffin or the plate of Chinese food that Cara continually tried to tempt her with, deep down Angela was grateful that her little assistant cared enough to keep trying.

It was several minutes later when Cara returned, a cup of coffee in each hand, and her amber eyes sparkling with excitement.

"Omigod, Angela, I saw him," she said breathlessly. "McReynolds is showing him around the office as we speak, introducing him to everyone, and – wow! I didn't get a real good look at him, just from a distance, but – wow! Let's just say that every female in this place – and some of the men, too – are going to be very happy campers when they get an eyeful of our newest piece of man candy."

Angela gave her assistant a wry smile as she picked up her steaming hot mug of coffee. "That good looking, hmm? Better than the new Osborne Fund rep you were crushing on last week?"

Cara's perpetually rosy cheeks grew a bit pinker at her boss's teasing. "I know," she admitted with a laugh. "I've got a problem with hot guys. But new broker is way, way hotter than mutual fund rep. In fact, he might be off the scales hot. I'm not sure I've ever seen anyone quite as, ah, jaw dropping."

Angela had more or less learned to tune out the way Cara regularly gushed about one cute guy or the other, whether it was a broker in the office, the FedEx deliveryman, or someone she'd met at school. The irony of it all was that Cara was also super shy and never dated, though she claimed the latter was because she was way too busy with work and school. And it was probably a good thing she didn't date, thought Angela quietly, because Cara was so sweetly, adorably naïve that she'd be ripe for the plucking by some jerk who'd be all too happy to take advantage of her gullibility.

"So what does this magnificent specimen of manhood look like?" inquired Angela with feigned politeness. She'd brushed Cara's cheerful chattiness off a little too brusquely at times, and had recently vowed to try and be a little kinder, a bit more patient.

"Tall. *Really* tall. Like maybe he used to be a basketball player once. And huge. Oh, not like fat huge, I didn't mean that. More like bulked up, like he lifts weights eight hours a day or something. He must have to get his suits custom made to fit a body like that."

Angela's already cold hands suddenly felt completely bloodless, and a horrible sensation of dread began to slowly permeate her entire body from head to toe. Telling herself fiercely not to panic or jump to any sort of conclusions, she kept her voice deliberately neutral. "Sure doesn't sound like your typical stockbroker, does he?"

"I'll say. And I didn't get a good look at his face, darn it, but he's very dark. Oh, not his skin, he isn't African American or Latino. I meant his hair. It's – well, it's as dark as yours, I suppose."

Angela was grateful she was sitting, and that her legs were well hidden beneath her desk because they were starting to shake uncontrollably. "Did you – ah, catch his name? Or what firm he used to work for?"

Cara shook her head. "Not yet, no. Pretty much just saw him being introduced around. I can try to find out more details if you're interested."

"No, don't bother." Angela would have waved a hand in

dismissal if she hadn't been afraid it would start trembling as badly as her legs were. "I'm sure all the news will be forthcoming soon."

A wide smile made Cara's already glowing face light up like a Christmas tree. "And McReynolds will probably bring Mr. Hunky around to meet everyone soon enough. It definitely looked like he was making all the rounds."

Beneath the cover of her desk, Angela crossed her fingers. "I doubt he'll come all the way over here. One of the reasons I like this corner office is because so many people forget it exists."

Cara shook her head in dismay. "I'll never figure out why you squirrel yourself away all the time. Honestly, Angela, you're way too young to cut yourself off from the rest of the world. And I'm willing to bet McReynolds *does* bring him back here to meet you. After all, the new rankings came out yesterday and you cracked the top ten last month."

This bit of news startled Angela. She'd admittedly had a great production month in March due to the addition of several new clients, but hadn't even let herself hope it would be enough to catapult her that far up in the office production rankings.

She gave a careless little lift of her shoulders. "Last month wasn't typical and you know it, so I wouldn't get used to this state of affairs. By next month I'll have dropped down to reality."

"Don't be so sure. About the rankings or about McReynolds bringing Mr. Hunky over to meet you. My hunches about this kind of stuff are almost always right."

Angela was struggling mightily for control at this moment, fearful that she'd explode with a full blown panic attack otherwise. As she'd become so adept at doing for the past few years, she firmly shoved her anxiety to a place where she could turn it off, and forced herself to focus on something else.

"Let's go over our schedule for the day, okay?" she told Cara briskly. "Otherwise, we'll get interrupted by half a dozen phone calls."

Throwing herself into her work had been Angela's salvation these past few years, and when she couldn't be at the office she was usually running. So long as she stuck firmly to her routine, kept herself too busy and too exhausted to let her mind wander into places that were dark and dangerous for her to visit, she could cope.

And for the next couple of hours that was exactly what she did. She spoke to clients on the phone, made changes to several stock portfolios, read over some research, and emailed Cara with more than a dozen different tasks that needed taking care of. She allowed herself to get so caught up in her work that she temporarily forgot about the new broker in the office. The one she was absolutely terrified wasn't new at all to her; who had, in fact, been the reason she'd been inhabiting this ghost world of hers for the past few years.

Angela worried her bottom lip as she continued to wage a mental battle with herself. It couldn't be him, she reasoned. There was no logical reason why it would be. He'd been like a king over at Jessup Prior, with everyone in the place catering to his every need and whim. He'd been the George Barnhart of the office, except that he'd been even more successful and from a much younger age. Angela could think of no good reason why he'd give all that up to change firms at this point in his stellar career, to put himself through all the work involved in transferring his client base and getting used to a new way of doing things. No, none of it made sense and she was being completely irrational to even think that the man Cara had described could be – *him*. He wasn't the only tall, powerfully built stockbroker with dark hair and custom made suits in this city.

For that matter, she reasoned, the new broker could even be an out of town transfer – from San Jose or even Los Angeles. Reassured, she returned her focus to her work.

It was typical for her to keep both the door and the blinds to the outer window of her office closed, as they were this morning. Doing so helped her focus and blocked out any distractions, and since Cara was almost fanatically efficient at handling all the incoming calls and emails, they tended to communicate largely via instant messenger during the workday.

There was no way, therefore, when it happened, for her to

have ever seen it coming. And for all the times she'd envisioned how she might react should a situation like this ever actually occur, her response was nothing like her previous imaginings had been.

With a cursory knock at best, the office manager – Paul McReynolds – opened the door and strode inside her office briskly, followed by the tall, dark-haired, and thoroughly intimidating man who'd shattered her life and haunted her dreams for too many months to count. But instead of reacting in one of the many and varied ways she'd imagined over the years – scorn, tears, anger, indifference, outrage – or, God help her – joy – she'd never expected to just feel the same sort of blissful numbness she'd enclosed herself in for so long.

Paul McReynolds was speaking, but for all that Angela could care he might as well have been babbling in Klingon. And then *he* was stepping over the threshold, invading *her* territory, *her* corner retreat, and the perpetual iciness of her extremities seemed to spread through her entire body.

"Angela, come and meet the newest member of our team. Though you've probably already heard of the legend that's Nick Manning."

Looking back at that particular moment later in the day, Angela was never quite sure how she'd prevented herself from recoiling at the mention of *that* name. Or how she didn't faint dead away when she looked into those keenly intelligent dark brown eyes for the first time in almost four years. Or how she managed – by some inner, hidden strength she sure as hell wouldn't have thought she possessed – to hold out her hand as he took a few slow, precise steps towards her desk.

"Hello, Nick. It's been a long time."

Angela didn't know who was more shocked at that moment or why. She couldn't quite believe that eerily calm, almost disembodied voice had come out of her mouth, or that she could just stand there, cool as a cucumber, and offer to shake hands as though they'd been nothing more than the most casual of business acquaintances.

Nick, on the other hand, paled considerably beneath his

normally swarthy complexion, and he didn't even try to conceal the shocked look that crossed his compelling features. His big hand reached out instinctively to clasp hers, and she could see his very visible reaction when he felt how icy cold her skin was. But instead of hastily breaking contact as most people did, Nick only tightened his grip.

"Angela."

For one brief, tantalizing second she'd thought he would call her by the name no one else but he had ever used. But that had been another lifetime ago, it seemed, and she was no longer his "Angel", if in fact she had ever truly been so.

Paul McReynolds looked puzzled as his gaze flicked between the pair of them.

"You've met before?" he asked, and then answered his own question with a smile. "Ah, of course you have. I'd forgotten that Angela used to work at Jessup Prior. Though I'm surprised you remember her, Nick. She couldn't have been long out of college when she was there."

"I remember her very well," replied Nick in the deep, husky voice that Angela had once been enthralled by. "She's not a woman you'd ever forget meeting."

She should have fallen instantly back under his spell with those words, should have found herself staring back at him with an entranced look on her face, the way she'd done for all those months. After all, he'd always had that effect on her, from the very first time she'd seen him.

But, shockingly, she only felt anger now. Hot, vicious, aggressive anger, and if Paul McReynolds hadn't been in the room watching them curiously, she might have given in to the overwhelming urge to smack Nick as hard as she could across his devilishly handsome face.

Angela managed – just – to control her rising temper and jerked her hand out of his iron grasp before he could react.

"This is a – surprise," she told him in an amazingly serene tone. "I wouldn't have imagined you ever leaving Jessup Prior considering all the success you enjoyed there."

Nick gave a little shrug, the massive shoulders encased in a custom made charcoal gray suit as wide as ever. He'd played football – both in college and the pros – the great, revered defensive end for the San Francisco 49ers who'd retired well before his prime after suffering two concussions in one season.

"Circumstances have changed," was all he offered up by way of an explanation, "and even those of us most set in our ways have to adapt when necessary."

Angela frowned, not allowing herself to even contemplate any possible double meaning to his words. "I see. Well, I'm sure you'll settle in here just fine. Good luck to you, Nick."

Paul chuckled. "Nick won't need the slightest bit of luck. He *is* good luck, at least according to all of his clients. He's going to make everyone in this office forget George Barnhart ever existed."

Another careless shrug was the only acknowledgment Nick gave to Paul's praise. But then, thought Angela with a growing sense of rage, what more was there to say? Nick Manning's very name was synonymous with success, wealth, and power, the broker with the reputation of turning everything he touched to gold, and who had the extremely rare luxury of being able to pick and choose his clients, to actually turn business away.

Angela had to force herself to smile in response, enough that she feared her cheekbones might crack with the effort. "Well, if anyone is capable of a feat like that, I'm sure it's Nick."

Nick opened his mouth but before he could speak Paul was steering him out of the room. "Well, we won't take up anymore of your time, Angela. I know how you hate too many interruptions during your workday. Nick, you might be interested to learn that Angela is one of our most promising young brokers. She cracked top ten in production credits last month."

The smile Nick gave her was enough to make her knees go weak, enough to cause the blood to resume pumping hotly through her long-chilled body. "I am interested to know that, Paul," he drawled lazily. "But not in the least surprised. I always knew that Angela had great potential. I'm very glad to see that she's fulfilling my expectations."

Her jaw dropped open in shock, and she felt her cheeks grow warm. But before she could reply, Paul had shepherded Nick out of the office and she could hear Cara giggling nervously as Nick said something to her in a low voice. Angela rolled her eyes, easily imagining the sort of mildly flirtatious comment Nick had made to her adorably naïve assistant. Women had always been attracted to him, like bees to honey, and the jealousy she'd felt as a result had torn away at her, practically flaying the skin from her body, especially since she'd never dared to betray such feelings to him.

Like a dam that had just burst, all of the feelings she'd gotten so good at repressing – anger, hurt, bitterness, jealousy, desperation, sorrow – all came roaring back at the same time with a vengeance, flooding her mind and her heart until she was shaking again. Only this time it wasn't with cold or shock but with rage – utterly consuming rage – that burned through her. She wanted to scream and curse, to slap and kick and bite, to throw things and watch them break into tiny pieces. Instead, she paced frantically back and forth across the narrow width of her sparsely furnished office, digging her nails into her palms so hard it was a wonder they didn't draw blood.

Cara burst excitedly into the office, all ready to gush about the super hunky Nick Manning, when she froze in place. She stared at her boss, the always cool, always composed Angela who now looked about ready to burst a blood vessel. Angry color stained her normally ghostly pale cheeks, and her brown eyes were wide with emotion. A strand of glossy jet black hair had escaped the thick knot at the nape of her neck, and Cara jumped back in alarm when Angela slammed her clenched fist down on the corner of her desk.

"Um, are you – ah, okay?" ventured Cara timidly. "You seem – well, upset seems like too mild of a word. I've never seen you this way, Angela."

Angela's eyes were almost fever bright as she whipped her gaze towards Cara. "How is he – why is he here?" she murmured distractedly, almost as though she was talking to herself. "I don't understand how he's here."

The concern Cara felt at seeing her boss so unhinged was intensifying with each passing moment. "Do you mean Nick Manning?" she inquired gently. "Do you know him from somewhere?"

Angela nodded, then resumed her frantic pacing. "We – worked together. Years ago, when I first graduated from Stanford. But I never imagined he'd leave Jessup Prior. Never thought I'd see him again." She slammed her fist down again, this time on top of a bookcase. Her voice broke as she added, "And I especially never thought I'd see him *here*."

Angela's whole body was quivering in reaction now, and she clutched the corner of her desk to hold herself steady. Panic stricken, Cara pulled one of the guest chairs over and gently eased her boss down onto the seat.

"Geez, you look like you're going to pass out, Angela," Cara told her in alarm. "Let me get you a glass of water. Or, better yet, some sugar. Hold on. And don't faint."

It had been a long time since she'd had a panic attack, but she could definitely feel one beginning to start. Almost desperately, she closed her eyes, wrapping her arms around her trembling body, and forced herself to take long, calming breaths.

For the first few months after things had ended with Nick, these panic attacks had been a daily – if not twice or thrice daily – occurrence. But then she'd discovered how good she was at shutting off her emotions, blocking out the world around her, and the episodes of feeling like she was going to pass out or stop breathing or scream until her voice gave out suddenly faded away. Until a few minutes ago, that is, when the source of her long ago but never forgotten nightmares had strolled oh so casually through her office door.

As though he had every right to be here, she thought with a growing fury. As though she'd be *happy* to see him after all this time, would welcome the heartless bastard into the sanctuary she'd carefully constructed with open arms. As though the eleven months and five days she'd slavishly devoted to him had never existed or as if they'd only been the most casual of business associates. As though he hadn't ripped her still-beating heart out of her chest and crushed it in one of his massive hands into a million tiny pieces. As though he hadn't utterly and completely destroyed her, damaged her, shattered her.

"Here, drink some water. Then you're going to eat this, all of it, and you're not going to argue about it."

Angela almost laughed at the ferocious look on her assistant's little heart-shaped face, but rather meekly accepted the glass of water Cara shoved in her face. Her hands were still shaking as she drank, so some of the water dribbled onto her black Stella McCartney suit trousers. Cara whisked the glass away after she'd taken several sips only to plunk an already unwrapped candy bar in her hand.

And even though she hadn't eaten a Milky Way bar for as long as she could remember, Angela found herself consuming the entire thing in an astonishingly brief amount of time. The shock and panic she'd been experiencing was gradually giving way to an unusually calm, almost serene state, and when Cara began to hand her mini Famous Amos cookies she popped each one in her mouth automatically.

When she'd consumed the entire little bag, Cara breathed a sigh of relief. "There. You're finally getting a little color back in your cheeks and your breathing is returning to normal. God, for a few minutes there I thought I was going to have to call 911."

Angela shook her head. "I'm okay. It's just – been a shock is all. And I don't cope with change very well, as you've surmised. It'll just take some time to get used to the idea that Nick Manning is working in this office."

Cara perched herself on the corner of the desk. "Based on your reaction just now, I'm going to go out on a limb and guess the two of you weren't just co-workers."

Angela sighed. "You'd be correct. But it's not something I want to talk about, okay? And do *not* breathe a word to anyone else in this office, either. Nick – he's a very private man. He, well, he doesn't care to have his personal business discussed."

"I won't say a word," assured Cara. "But – geez, Angela – the way you're reacting after seeing him again. I can't say if you're pissed off or terrified."

Angela gave a hollow sounding laugh. "Both, I think. Pissed off that he thinks he can just waltz into *my* firm, *my* office, like he owns the place. And terrified because – well, that's the part I can't talk about." She glanced at the empty cookie wrapper in her hand like it was something slimy. "And what the hell did I just eat anyway?"

Cara grinned. "Chocolate chip cookies. And a candy bar before that. Probably more calories than you usually consume in an entire day."

Disgusted, Angela wadded up the wrapper and tossed it in the wastebasket. "You did that on purpose, didn't you? Took advantage of me when I was out of it and shoved sugar down my throat."

"You should eat sugar more often," Cara told her gently. "And pizza or a sandwich or some pancakes. Something besides black coffee and breath mints."

Angela shooed her well-meaning assistant off after assuring her three times that she was okay, but it was nearly an hour later before she could actually focus on work again. And even then she found it almost impossible to block out the image of Nick's devilishly handsome face or his big, powerful body encased in one of his expensive, handmade Italian suits. He'd aged a bit, evidenced by the occasional thread of silver in his raven hair and a few more lines radiating out near his temples. But he still looked damned fine for a man fast approaching forty, and would likely be the sort who would ooze sex appeal and charisma well into his seventies. And even though she'd convinced herself long ago that he no longer meant anything to her, she was beginning to realize all of that had been a pathetic sham. Just five minutes in his commanding presence had been more than enough to draw her back into his web, to fall under the spell he'd cast over her years earlier.

Angela gave her head an angry, determined shake. She couldn't – wouldn't – give that heartless bastard another thought. She'd blocked him out for all this time and she could continue to do so, despite his sudden, unwelcomed presence in her workplace. His new office was nowhere near her own, and assuming his work habits hadn't changed, he'd be likely to lock himself away in his lair for most of the day, delegating tasks right and left to the five-person staff he'd have undoubtedly brought along with him as part of the deal he'd struck with McReynolds.

Given her own tendency to bury herself in her work and her rabid anti-social behavior, the chances of them encountering each other would be infrequent at best.

'I can do this,' she told herself firmly. 'Nick Manning is a swine and you need to remember that, girl. Remember it and stay as far away from him as possible.'

But what she hadn't prepared herself for was Nick coming to seek *her* out, strolling into her office late in the day when Cara had already gone home and the rest of the office was nearly deserted. She felt his presence before she actually saw him, glancing up from her computer monitor in alarm as he shut her office door firmly behind him.

Angela fixed what she hoped was a ferocious scowl on her face as she glimpsed the somber expression on his own features. "What are you doing here?" she asked ungraciously. "Both at this firm and in my office. You have to know you're the very last person I want to see."

Nick ignored her question and asked one of his own. "What the fuck happened to you, Angela? You look like the walking dead."

She gave a caustic little laugh. "Gee, thanks. You never were one to dole out compliments very often, but I can't remember hearing direct insults either."

He shook his head. "I'm not trying to insult you. But for Christ's sakes, Angie, I barely recognized you earlier. You look – Jesus, exactly how much weight have you lost anyway?"

She shrugged, willing herself to remain calm and detached. "Don't you know it's not polite to ask a woman how much she weighs?"

Nick looked at her scornfully. "I think you and I are way past the point where we have to worry about being polite to each other. Christ – when I saw you earlier today – I can't remember the last time I had a shock like that."

Angela leaned back in her desk chair, regarding him coolly. "I don't believe you didn't know I worked here. For you to have made a move like this – to give up everything you'd built at Jessup Prior – you would have done a hell of a lot of research. You had to have known I worked here."

"I wasn't shocked to see you working here," he clarified. "Just at your appearance. You're – have you been ill? Is that why you're skin and bones and look like you've got one foot in the grave?"

She rolled her eyes. "And the compliments keep on coming, don't they? You, on the other hand, look as hale and hearty as ever, Nick. But then I wouldn't have expected anything less. After all, you always did devote a lot of time to putting yourself first."

Nick pointed a finger at her. "*I'm* not the one we need to be discussing right now."

"Well, we certainly don't need to discuss me, either. In fact, I can't really think of anything we have to talk about, Nick. So let's just agree to keep as much distance from each other as possible, shall we? You ought to be able to manage that just fine – in fact, I'd say you're the expert at cutting off contact with people."

He winced visibly at her very pointed barb. "I know I acted like a total bastard towards you. Both during and after our relationship. But you knew exactly what you were getting into, Angela. I was very, very clear about my conditions. As for cutting you off – you know exactly why I had to do that. You were – you got too close, let yourself care too much."

She clenched her fists tightly, sorely tempted to punch him in the jaw with one, even if it meant breaking every bone in her hand. "Well, rest assured that I don't feel a damned thing for you anymore, Nick. You made sure of that, didn't you? So if you're worried that I'm going to start stalking you or something, forget it. I'd have to actually care about you in order to do that, wouldn't I?"

Nick smiled slowly, the sort of sexy, seductive smile that had never once failed to gain her capitulation. "You tempt me to put all that newfound bravado of yours to the test. But I'm not here to lure you back into my bed, as intriguing as that sounds. I'm just worried about you. Paul McReynolds told me that not only are you the biggest workaholic he's ever known but that you shut yourself off from everyone else in the office, never socialize, never smile. And while he may not know any different, may never have seen you act any other way, *I* have, and I know damned well that this skeletal, pale and emotionless shell you've become isn't the Angel I knew."

Angela surged to her feet then, the color rising rapidly to her cheeks and her eyes blazing. "Don't you dare call me that," she hissed. "I don't want to ever hear that name on your lips again."

A satisfied look spread across his sinfully handsome face. "Ah, now you look at least half-alive. Maybe that's the trick – I should just keep finding ways to piss you off. Maybe that will wake you up from this catatonic state you've fallen into."

She glared at him. "Don't flatter yourself, Nick. Very little gets a rise out of me these days, and I've made damned sure that no one will ever have the sort of power over me that I so foolishly gave to you once upon a time."

His voice was deep and almost hypnotic. "But as I recall you liked giving me that power, Angel, liked having me control you. And you always, always obeyed me. So eagerly, so sweetly. I confess to missing that sort of blind obedience."

"I'll just bet you have, you bastard," she spit out. "I doubt there are many women in this world who are stupid and gullible enough to agree to your insane conditions the way I did. Too bad I had to screw it up, hmm?"

Nick stroked a thumb over his jaw, darkly shadowed as always by his rather disreputable two-day stubble. "Sometimes I wonder if I did the right thing, letting you go like that," he mused. "If I should have just ignored what you said, acted as though it never happened. But then I realize that it was the right thing to do – for both of us. You were too young, needed to get on with your life."

Angela was horrified to feel her eyes grow wet, and clutched her desk for support as she felt her legs start shaking again. "Except I never did," she whispered brokenly. "Does this – do I – look like someone who's really living? You said before I looked like the walking dead but you weren't exactly right. A more accurate term to describe me these days would be a ghost. Because that's just about all that's left of me, Nick, all that's managed to survive these past few years."

He stared at her, a horror-stricken look on his face. "Are you saying that *I'm* responsible for – for the way you look? That all of this – the weight loss, closing yourself off from the world, that dead look in your eyes – is because of me? Because you couldn't cope after I - "

"All I'm saying is that I don't want to have any contact with you ever again," she interrupted. "By some cruel twist of fate you've wound up working in my office but that doesn't mean we have to see or speak to each other. You're nothing to me any longer, Nick – friend, lover, and most definitely not my master. So why don't you go back to your life and forget I exist – just as you've obviously done such a good job at for so long now."

Nick's dark olive complexion had paled noticeably with each of her sharply uttered words. "Who says I forgot you?" he asked quietly. "I told Paul the truth before – you're not a woman a man could ever forget meeting. And just because I stayed out of your life – for your own damned good, I might add – doesn't mean I wasn't thinking about you."

Some unnamed little thrill – be it hope or joy or just awareness – shimmered up her spine at his statement. But Angela forced herself not to betray any sort of reaction, refusing to let herself look for any deeper meaning to his words. "Well, that's sweet, Nick, really it is. But you shouldn't have bothered, because there's really no point any longer. You ended things – very firmly, as I recall – and maybe you're right. Maybe it was for my own good. I'll admit it took some time but I can honestly say I'm well and truly over you now. And on the rare occasion I've thought of you over the years, I just felt – nothing. Just a rather peaceful sense of numbness."

She'd always forgotten how quickly Nick could move for such a big man. It was one of the reasons so many NFL quarterbacks had landed flat on their backs after getting thoroughly sacked by one of the hardest hitting defensive ends ever to play the game.

He'd been standing there – regarding her rather warily from the other side of her desk – and then the very next second he was beside her, grasping her almost brutally by the upper arms and she was half afraid he was going to shake her.

"I don't believe you," he bit out. "And you must know that saying things like that only tempts me to see just how quickly I could crack that protective shell of ice you've encased yourself in. To see," he whispered suggestively, "how fast I could make you come. As I recall, that used to happen with very little effort and practically no time at all on my part."

Angela bit down on the inside of her mouth so hard that this time she did feel a few drops of blood well up. She thought briefly of trying to push him away but knew it would be futile, like trying to move a steel plate. Instead, she forced herself not to react, willed her traitorous body not to betray her by swaying against him and letting him do whatever he desired. Just like old times, she thought bitterly.

"Go to hell," she replied in a voice dripping with venom. "And don't expect me to join you on the trip. I've spent quite enough time in that delightful place over the years and have no desire to ever visit again."

Nick shook his head. "I could change your mind," he bragged. "Very, very easily. All it would take would be – " he paused, his hands stroking over her arms beneath the severely tailored suit jacket as though belatedly realizing just how skinny her limbs were. "Fuck it all, Angela. You're so frail I could snap one of your arms like a twig if I chose to. What the hell have you done to yourself? Please don't tell me this is all a result of what happened between us."

If her mouth hadn't suddenly gone dry she would have gladly spit in his face. "Don't flatter yourself," she hissed. "I'm thin because I run a lot, that's all."

He eyed her toothpick-thin form dubiously. "You'd have to run a hundred miles at a crack to have lost this much weight."

"Not quite, but that's my ultimate goal," she replied. "So far my longest race has been a fifty miler, but I've got a hundred kilometer planned for later this year."

"An ultrarunner, huh?" Nick's voice held a grudging respect. "Still, to put in those kind of miles you have to eat. I know a couple of guys from my gym who do ultras, and while they might be lean they're far from skeletal. You - " he grimaced. "You need to pack at least twenty pounds on. For starters."

Angela somehow found the strength to wrench her arm from his grasp. "Thanks for your very unwanted opinion. But it's really none of your business, Nick. *I'm* none of your business."

He reached out to caress her cheek and she flinched from his touch, causing his full, sexy mouth to tighten in disapproval. "Maybe I want to make you my business again – Angel."

This time she did slap his hand away, fury giving her the sort of defiant courage she'd never dared displayed to him before. "Don't call me that," she growled. "You lost the right to do so when you cut me out of your life."

Nick's dark eyes, so much like her own, blazed furiously as he grabbed her left hand and squeezed it hard enough that she winced. "Tell me – does anyone else have the right to call you that – Angel?"

She glared at him, trying to pull her hand free of his iron grip. "None of your goddamned business. But I am seeing someone, yes. Someone who doesn't impose unreasonable restrictions on when and where I can see or call him, or dictate the sorts of things I'm permitted to talk about when we're together. In other words, Nick, an actual living, breathing human being who has blood in his veins rather than ice."

"Speaking of ice," he drawled in a deceptively casual voice. "Whoever this prince of yours is it doesn't seem as though he's been very successful at melting the deep freeze you've erected around yourself, does it?"

Very deliberately she gave him the sort of seductive little smile he'd always found irresistible. "Hmm, but then, as the saying goes, who really knows what goes on behind closed doors. Maybe what you see in front of you is just a façade, and I save the real me for my private life."

Nick chuckled, seeing right through her little pretense. "I can see you still like to play with fire, Angel. But don't forget that I'm the expert at that game. After all, who better than the devil himself to know his way around fire?"

He stepped back from her then as she only glared mutinously, refusing to further engage in their banter. He paused at the doorway of her office, and she recalled that somehow he always found a way to get the last word in.

"This is far from over, you know. The more I think about it, the more I realize just how much I've missed having you in my life. And how intriguing it would be to have you back. Fair warning, Angel. I always get what I want."

With a knowing wink, Nick left as silently as he'd arrived, leaving her to stare after him in stunned, frozen silence.

The sun was already setting in the mid-April sky by the time she could summon up the presence of mind to move again. Her hand closed briefly around her coffee mug, her fingers itching to hurl it against the nearest wall and watch the cold brown liquid remaining inside to trickle down slowly like streams of blood. Instead, she released her death grip on the mug and marched outside to Cara's neatly arranged desk. Telling herself that not only wouldn't Cara mind but would be jumping for joy instead, Angela slid open the top left drawer where she knew her assistant kept the stash.

Five minutes later she'd wolfed down a Hershey bar, a package of peanut M & M's, and a semi-stale, pre-packaged cinnamon bun without even being aware of her actions. And with each bite, each swallow, each increase in the massive sugar rush torpedoing through her bloodstream, she cursed Nick – for coming back into her life so unexpectedly, for being even more of a bastard than she'd remembered, and – damn it all to hell – for being every bit as sexy and irresistible as he'd been the very first time she'd seen him.

Chapter Three

She knew who he was the moment she saw him, even standing clear on the other side of the cavernous conference room. After all, there weren't many men who had his height – six feet six inches – or shoulders that were so wide his suits just had to be custom made to accommodate their breadth.

When she'd learned on her very first day on the job that Nick Manning – the famous football player for both the Stanford Cardinal and the San Francisco 49ers – not only worked in her new office but was among the highest producing brokers, she'd wondered when she might actually get a glimpse of the man.

It had taken almost two full weeks – and this mandatory-attendance meeting with the firm's CEO who was visiting from New York – to finally afford her the opportunity. But, she reasoned as she allowed her gaze to roam freely and thus far unobserved over the magnificent, manly specimen, the wait had sure as hell been worth it.

The impossibly tall, intimidatingly muscular body clothed in an impeccably cut charcoal gray pinstriped suit looked as though it was still in the kind of shape needed to play pro football tomorrow, if he so desired. And the to-die-for body was just part of the whole package.

From this angle she could only see his face in profile, but that was more than enough to form an impression of strong, ruggedly handsome features, darkly tanned skin covered in an irreverent two-day stubble, and thick, expertly styled hair as black as her own locks. She wondered briefly if he had any Italian or Latin blood in his background, or perhaps even some black Irish.

And then she was no longer capable of even a single logical thought, including her own name, because Nick Manning chose that particular moment to glance across the room, his sharp, dark-eyed gaze locking on her like a laser beam.

She would remember that exact moment for weeks, months, and even years later – the moment when time froze in place; when her heart was beating so fast she thought for sure it would burst right out of her chest cavity; when her palms grew sweaty and her breasts suddenly felt swollen and achy. And when she fell deeply and helplessly under his spell.

That intense, all-encompassing gaze performed a swift but thorough inspection of her face and figure, and Angela offered up a silent prayer of thanks that she'd taken some extra pains with her appearance today. She'd known that the CEO of Jessup Prior would be at the meeting, as well as several other high-level executives from the home office in New York. Not to mention all of the local office management staff, and every one of the brokers, including the very top producers. She'd worn the best of her five suits – the chic black Vivienne Westwood that had been purchased at an end of season sale at Neiman Marcus. Her girlhood friend Julia – who was mad about clothes and a would-be fashion designer – had helped her pick it out, insisting that it made her look both professional and smokin' hot at the same time. Angela wasn't totally convinced about the latter, though she had to admit that the slim skirt and short, form-fitting jacket made the most of her slender, five foot eleven inch frame. With the three-inch black pumps she wore, she topped six feet easily, making her not only the tallest woman here but probably taller than at least half the men present as well.

She'd left her long, stick straight raven hair loose today, instead of clipping it back into a ponytail or coiling it into a messy knot at her nape. Her makeup was minimal but still managed to accent her big, dark eyes, sculpted cheekbones, and the full-lipped mouth that was a tad too wide.

And it seemed that Nick Manning approved wholeheartedly of the pains she'd taken with her appearance, judging from the gleam in his eyes and the slow smile he gave her as their gazes remained glued together. She smiled back at him, sending him a silent message that 'yeah, you're hot, I'm hot, and we really ought to get together and let spontaneous combustion take its course'.

But then their office manager took the podium and announced that everyone should take their seats so the meeting could begin. And just like that, Nick turned and made his way towards the seat that had likely been reserved for him in one of the front rows of chairs, breaking not just eye contact but any hope Angela might have been harboring that he was actually going to approach her.

She should have known better, she scolded herself as she took her own seat with the other trainees – towards the very *back* of the room, of course. From all the office gossip she'd overheard the last two weeks, it was a certified fact that Nick Manning did *not* date co-workers. And from some of the stories Angela had listened to – some with horrified disbelief – an awful lot of women before her had done their damnedest to change his mind. He'd been ruthlessly pursued by brokers, administrative assistants, receptionists, and even by his own clients, and had spurned every one of them. And, if the gossip could truly be believed, a few of the women had become so aggressive in their pathetic attempts to get his attention that they had either been fired on sexual harassment charges, or, in the case of a client, her account had been transferred to a different branch office.

So, she realized with a sigh of resignation, that smoldering hot look of awareness she had just exchanged with him was all for nothing. Oh, she didn't doubt that maybe he had found her attractive – she wasn't all that experienced with men but she certainly wasn't naïve, either, and she knew quite well when a guy thought she was hot. But given Nick's reputation, Angela realized that looking was as far as he would take it.

Maybe she should quit her job, she thought in mild amusement. It would be worth it for the chance to date the most gorgeous man she'd ever seen. Worth it to have wild, screaming sex with him even one time, to experience the barely leashed passion she'd glimpsed all too briefly in that burning gaze of his. But even as she thought of doing something so rash, she knew it would still be pointless and futile, not to mention foolhardy.

From a practical perspective, quitting a job she'd just started two weeks ago would be the height of irresponsibility. The recession that currently had the country in a stranglehold had made finding a decent job extremely difficult, even for someone like herself who'd just graduated summa cum laude from Stanford with a finance degree. Under normal circumstances, she'd have had her pick of high-paying job offers, but times were anything but normal right now, with so many firms laying half their workforce off, or going out of business altogether.

And even if she hadn't worked at the same firm as Nick, any prospects of a long-term relationship with him were unrealistic, if not impossible. All the gossip she'd been unwillingly subjected to indicated that Nick went through women as often as he changed shirts. He was rarely if ever seen out with the same female more than once, and was extremely closed-mouthed about any of his relationships. He also, according to yet more gossip, favored blondes or occasionally redheads.

'So you've got two strikes against you,' she told herself in resignation. "Co-worker and brunette. Well, it was a nice little fantasy while it lasted.'

Angela forced herself to put the unattainable Nick Manning out of her mind and focused instead on what their visiting CEO was speaking about. None of the conference rooms back at the office had been large enough to accommodate everyone at once, so the meeting was being held at a hotel around the corner from the office. There was to be a cocktail reception after the meeting, where in theory she'd be able to meet the CEO and other executives. But she knew the chances of that actually happening would be highly unlikely, given the sheer number of people present, and of her lowly ranking in the office hierarchy.

One of her fellow trainees – there were a total of seven in the group, four men and three women – had joked that the office layout was just like the passenger decks on old-time cruise ships, where class distinctions had been very clearly enforced.

"The top floor is where all the big producers are," Noah Whitmore had related. "So that's like – I don't know – the first class cabins, the big suites. The middle floor is where all the manager's offices are located, plus some of the mid-level producers. I guess we'd call that the promenade deck. And the bottom floor – well, kids, that's where they've stuck us. The trainees, the junior brokers, the mailroom. We're in what they would have called steerage in the old days."

And while Noah had certainly been a bit dramatic about the whole thing, he hadn't been all that far off the mark. It had been made very clear to the new batch of trainees that they had no reason to venture to the uppermost of the three floors occupied by Jessup Prior in this high rise building smack in the middle of San Francisco's Financial District. But from various comments Angela had heard, it was rather like a different world up there. The offices were rumored to be huge, every one with a jaw-dropping view of the city, and each one more lavishly furnished than the next. The talk was that they had their own private lunch room, several spacious conference rooms, and an espresso cart available at all times of the day.

Angela contrasted those images with the one of her own tiny cubicle two floors below. The top of her desk had several scratches on it, and one of the drawers was constantly sticking. Her desk chair squeaked every time she rolled it back and forth, and whatever cushioning had once existed in the seat had been worn away a long time ago. Like the other trainees and very junior brokers, she pretty much had to beg, borrow or steal basic supplies like pens, paper clips, and notepads.

As trainees, they were also constantly getting stuck with what one of them had termed grunt work, another had labelled slave labor. In the two weeks she'd been employed here, Angela had already been required to man the reception desk, unpack and inventory office supplies, help one of the manager's PA's get caught up on a year's worth of filing, and bring some documents over to a client's residence for their signature.

In between the many and varied mundane tasks they were assigned, the trainees also had to study like mad for their upcoming brokerage license exams, complete a strictly prescribed series of training modules, and sit in on a never-ending schedule of podcasts, webinars, and conference calls. They were expected in the office by six a.m. – though Angela was typically the only one in quite that early – and required to remain until at least five p.m.

But as grueling as her schedule was, and as demeaning and

unpleasant as some of the tasks dumped on her were, Angela knew it was all a necessary evil. She'd be finished with the training program in just over three months' time, at which point she would take her exams – and hopefully ace them on her first attempt – and obtain her brokerage license. Then she'd be a full-fledged stockbroker, ready to start opening accounts, doing business, and making money – a lot of it.

And, she vowed to herself silently, she wouldn't remain stuck down in steerage for very long if she had anything to do about it. She had plans, ambitions, goals, and they all involved moving to the top floor within a relatively short amount of time. She had a knack for this business, she just knew it. Her professors at Stanford had told her more than once that she had a great analytical mind, and that she could be extremely successful in this business provided she worked very hard and didn't let anything stand in her way.

The meeting dragged on for over an hour, with the CEO fielding a dozen or so questions from the audience after a time. Predictably, the majority of the questions he answered were ones posed by the top producers and longest tenured brokers, and he all but ignored the few tentatively raised hands in the back of the room.

Angela tried valiantly to stifle a yawn, bored beyond belief with the predictable, pointless questions being raised. It was rather obvious that no one was going to ask anything that could be deemed the least bit controversial, and that everyone was sticking to topics considered safe.

At least until Nick Manning very leisurely raised his hand, lounging back in his chair as though he was attending a baseball game. The CEO obviously recognized him, and gave the tall, dark-haired broker a wide smile.

"Yes, Nick. What's your question? Knowing you, I'm sure it's going to be a good one!"

Like a great jungle beast unfolding itself from the crouching position it had been curled up in, Nick stood slowly, rising to his full, impressive height. Angela knew she wasn't imagining the collective sigh of feminine voices around her as every pair of eyes in the room fixed themselves firmly on the charismatic, devilishly handsome man.

His voice was deep, lazy, and held a hint of amused arrogance. "Thanks, Steve. And while *I* think it's a great question, and very relative to our current situation, I'm not so sure you'll agree. I wanted to ask about the rumors flying around that Jessup Prior is considering closing a quarter of their branch offices over the next year."

There was an immediate buzz of reactionary chatter around the room, with Noah, who was seated to Angela's right, muttering, "Dang, that guy's got a huge pair of *cojones*, doesn't he?"

Angela grinned. "Figuratively or literally?"

Noah laughed. "Probably both. But I meant the former in this case. Hey, nobody else has had the guts thus far to ask anything controversial. He's just a badass."

The CEO – Steve Schaeffer – was very visibly taken aback by Nick's forthright question, and stammered awkwardly as he tried to fob him off with an obviously lame reply. Nick looked anything but satisfied with the reply he received, but didn't seem inclined to pursue the matter further, merely shrugging casually before sitting back down.

Angela thought it was no coincidence that the Q & A session ended immediately after that, and then the meeting itself was adjourned mere minutes later.

"Thank God," breathed Noah in relief. "If that wasn't a totally useless waste of ninety minutes I don't know what was. At least there's free booze and food. C'mon, Angie, let's go grab a drink."

Angela didn't need to be asked twice. She admittedly liked to drink – sometimes quite a lot and more than she ought to. Her drinking had started as an act of defiance when she was about fifteen, sneaking alcohol none too subtly from her parents' liquor cabinet in a futile attempt to trigger a reaction of some sort – *any* sort – out of them. But she might as well have been drinking lemonade for all her disinterested mother cared, and the thrill of taking a forbidden swig or two from the vodka bottle had quickly lost its appeal.

In college, she'd liked to party as much as the next girl, but she'd had to be careful about not overdoing it. The athletic scholarship she'd been given came with a strict code of conduct that she'd been expected to follow. Not to mention that showing up to volleyball practice or a game with a hangover would have been completely idiotic. So she'd had to carefully pick and choose the occasions when she had overindulged, and there had admittedly not been *all* that many of those.

Angela maneuvered her way easily up to one of the bartenders, her superior height generally causing people to step out of her way automatically. She strolled away unhurriedly from the bar, cocktail in hand, as she looked around for her fellow trainees. A waiter passed by with a tray of hot hors d'oeuvre's, but she merely shook her head, not feeling in the least hungry.

"I don't blame you. Banquet food is notoriously bad. And *this* hotel's is exceptionally so."

She froze in place at the sound of that wickedly amused voice coming from just behind her. She'd only heard it once, just a few minutes ago when he had dared to ask the CEO a blunt, honest question, but she knew the sound of it would be emblazoned forever in her mind.

Forcing herself not to betray the rapid beat of her pulse, and definitely not to simper at him like some silly teenager with a massive crush, she fixed a casual smile on her face and turned around slowly to face him.

Up close, Nick Manning literally stole her breath away. He was one of the very few men she'd ever met that she had to actually glance up at, and when she did the gleam in his coffee dark eyes made her wish wildly for a chair or a wall or anything else she could lean against to keep her balance.

"I, ah, just wasn't especially hungry," she somehow found the presence of mind to stammer. "But thanks for the advice in case I'm ever tempted to eat here in the future."

Nick ran his gaze slowly from the tip of her head down to her black Ferragamo pumps and then back up again, and if he missed a single detail in between it would have shocked her. "Tell me –

are you easily tempted?"

Angela's mouth fell open in silent surprise and all semblance of rational thought instantly left the building. "Um, I don't - "

He chuckled, taking a sip of what looked like vodka – her own preferred drink. "Sorry, I didn't mean to render you speechless. And I'm usually not quite that direct. I'm Nick Manning by the way."

She placed her hand in the intimidatingly large one he extended to her. "Yes, I know. I'm pretty sure everyone in the office knows who you are. Not to mention the entire city."

He arched a thick jet black eyebrow. "Are you a football fan, then?"

Angela shrugged. "Somewhat. My dad's a huge 49er fan and I used to watch games with him all the time. Personally, though, I'm more of a basketball fan. No offense."

He laughed. "None taken, and thanks for being honest. Most people would feel the need to kiss up and blatantly lie about it. And do I get to learn your name at some point?"

She felt her cheeks grow warm. "Oh, sorry. It's Angela Del Carlo. I'm, um, one of the new trainees."

"Angela." The way he said her name felt like an intimate caress, one that she felt ripple through every nerve ending in her body. "I guessed you were Italian with your hair and eyes." He stroked his thumb over her knuckles, her hand still firmly clasped in his.

Her gaze remained locked with his, his dark, long lashed eyes so much like her own. "Are you? Italian, I mean. You're – well, your coloring is just like mine."

Nick grinned down at her. "Irish and English on my father's side, Greek on my mother's. In other words, no chance of us being distant relations of any sort. Which," he added in a hushed drawl, "is very, very fortunate because I draw the line at dating family members. Or married women."

The word "dating" instantly put all of Angela's senses on high alert. Surely he wasn't going to –

"And co-workers as well from what I hear," she blurted out.

His grin deepened. "Been listening to all the gossip about me, have you? Oh, don't worry, it doesn't take much imagination to figure out what's being said. But I confess to being a little surprised that you'd listen to much gossip – Angela. My initial impression of you was that of a cool, no bullshit kind of woman who doesn't particularly enjoy that sort of thing."

While some women might have interpreted his description of her as mildly insulting, she took it as a compliment. "It's a little tough not to overhear certain things when almost everyone around you is chatting about it. But," she added with what she hoped looked like a careless little shrug, "I don't always put a lot of store in gossip, or indulge in it much myself. I, ah, prefer to form my own opinions."

Nick's dark eyes gleamed with approval. "Good girl. I knew there was a reason you stood out from every other female in this room. And, no, I'm not talking about your height. So tell me, did you play basketball?"

His rather abrupt change of subject caused her to blink in reaction but otherwise she kept her composure – at least as much as she could reasonably expect to do under the circumstances.

"Not since high school. At college I played volleyball."

He finished off his drink, and somehow the sight of his strong throat as he swallowed was more intoxicating than the vodka in her own glass. "What college?"

"Stanford."

His grin returned. "Well, how about that? So we have more in common than just having the same coloring and being freakishly tall. When did you graduate?"

"Just this past June."

Nick's grin faded rapidly, and she thought she heard him curse softly beneath his breath. "So, you're like twenty-three, twenty-four, something like that?"

Angela hesitated, sensing his unease, but refusing to outright lie at the same time. "No, I'm only twenty-two."

"Shit." He set his glass down on a passing waiter's empty tray. "I'm thirty-three, closer to thirty-four."

She shrugged. "So? I happen to like older men."

He laughed, his good humor quickly restored. "Is that right? You got a daddy complex or something?"

She shook her head slowly. "I would never think of you as my father. Or the least bit old. And you're definitely not too old for me, if that's what you're suggesting."

His expression instantly grew deadly serious, his voice raspy. "Is that a fact, Miss Del Carlo? Well, you are just a whole lot of very pleasant surprises, aren't you? What's that you're drinking?"

Somewhat taken aback by the rather abrupt way he tended to segue from one subject to another so quickly, she glanced down into her nearly empty glass. "Vodka tonic. Though the vodka isn't my preferred brand."

"And what would that be?"

"Absolut Citron. On the rocks."

Nick smiled, taking the glass from her suddenly nerveless fingers and setting it aside. "The coincidences just keep piling up, don't they? That's almost always what I drink, too. And then, of course, there's the coincidence of our first names."

She gave him a puzzled look. "My name is Italian while yours is Greek. At least, I assume Nick is short for Nicholas."

"It is. But I wasn't referring to their ethnic origins," he corrected. "Has anyone ever called you Angel? As a nickname, of course."

Her pulse rate seemed to be jacking up another degree with each passing moment. "N-nno. Just Angie."

Nick shook his head. "Not Angie. That doesn't suit you in the least. But Angel definitely does. And, well, many people aren't aware of this but Nick is sometimes used as a nickname for the devil – Old Nick, to be precise. So, here we are then – the Angel and the Devil. Rather poetic, don't you think?"

She stared at him, too shocked and too enraptured in equal measures to think of anything remotely intelligent to say. Instead, she stammered clumsily, "But you – what about – I work here!"

He gave her a knowing smirk, as though he knew exactly how unsettled he was making her feel. "Are we back to that again? Very well, it's true. I've never dated a co-worker before. Too messy, too complicated, and way too invasive of the privacy I insist on having in my personal life. But this is different. *You're* different. Enough so that I'm going to break my ironclad rule and ask you to have dinner with me tonight."

She gasped and knew that her jaw must have dropped open in shock. "You – you are?"

"I am. I have. So, what's your answer?"

"Yes." She replied without the slightest hesitation, afraid that if she stopped to think about it too long that she'd wake up and realize this had all been a dream.

Nick looked pleased, satisfied, and maybe even a bit relieved. "Good. I hate when women play games. Unless, of course, they happen to be a particular kind of game."

But before she could even begin to think up a witty reply – hell, *any* reply – to that very deliberate taunt, Nick had pulled a business card and pen from the inside pocket of his superbly tailored suit jacket.

"Here." He handed her the card, on which he'd written a name and address in a bold script. "Meet me in half an hour. I'll leave first so that we don't give the gossip mongers in this place more fuel for their nosy little fires. God, how I hate that shit."

She took the card, unable to suppress a little shiver at the sound of disgust in his voice. "Are you – I mean, is it okay for you to leave so soon?"

Nick gave a hoot of laughter. "Let's put it this way. There's not a single person here who's got the balls to tell me otherwise. And that includes our spineless excuse of a CEO. In other words, Angel, I can do whatever the hell I please. Don't be late, hmm?"

And with that he walked out of the room without a backwards glance for anyone, flat-out ignoring those who attempted to approach him, including one of the higher-ups from corporate headquarters.

It was only after he was out of sight that she glanced down at the little card clutched so tightly in her hand. Even though she'd only been living in San Francisco a very short while, she still recognized the name of the restaurant – easily one of the best known and highly rated in the entire city. Talk was that it could take weeks to get a reservation there. And yet it appeared that the Nick Manning effect was wide reaching – to the extent that nabbing a table at the last minute would be the easiest thing in the world for him.

Angela slipped the card into her skirt pocket and wondered when she could make a discreet exit of her own. She was fairly sure it would be a ten minute walk or less to the restaurant, but from the commanding tone of Nick's voice she wouldn't dare risk being late.

By rights, she really ought to be bristling right about now at the arrogant, take-no-prisoners sort of way he'd maneuvered her into meeting him. Normally, men wouldn't even think of trying to intimidate or boss her around, since most of the men she'd met were more than a little daunted by her height. Only a handful of boys in her high school class had actually been taller than her, and even then not until their senior year. As a result, she hadn't dated at all back then, except for a rather embarrassing arranged date to her senior prom with her older sister's brother-in-law. It had been ten different kinds of awkward, and Angela wasn't sure which of them had been more relieved when the very uncomfortable evening had finally drawn to a close.

Fortunately, college had been different, and she'd dated several athletes – basketball and volleyball players, and swimmers and water polo players among them. But they had still very much been boys – immature, awkward, hardly more experienced than she was. Nick was most assuredly the first *man* she'd ever come close to going on a date with, and she doubted he'd been awkward – or inexperienced – for a very, very long time.

But even as she steeled herself for the approach of her obviously curious co-workers – swarming around her, she thought in mild disgust, like a school of fish around bait – she wondered if this dinner with Nick was even a real date. Maybe he just wanted to talk about their mutual alma mater. Or sports. Or one of a dozen different subjects.

But no, she thought, as a satisfied little smile tugged at the corners of her mouth. It was very obvious what Nick wanted with her. Drinks, yes, and dinner, of a certainty. But there was little doubt in her mind that a man like him would also expect sex at the end of the evening. Probably a lot of sex, and she doubted there'd be much intimacy or romance involved. And judging by how tight and swollen her breasts felt at this moment, not to mention how damp her black silk thong was getting, her body liked the idea of that particular outcome. A lot.

Her fellow trainees all seemed to be talking at once, at least those who weren't still shocked speechless by the fact that the unapproachable Nick Manning had actually, well, *approached* her. The others were noisily asking her what he'd talked about, why he'd singled *her* out of every other woman in the room, was he as hot up close and personal as he was from a distance.

Angela instinctively sensed that Nick would not want her sharing even the smallest detail about their conversation, and thus fobbed off her co-workers with some barely believable tale about how they'd merely discussed Stanford and sports. She knew no one believed her, didn't particularly give a shit whether they did or not, and was quick to extricate herself from the group with the excuse of having to visit the ladies room. Two minutes later she was exiting the hotel out onto the sidewalk, and walking at a brisk pace towards her rendezvous with the most exciting, stimulating man she'd ever met.

A block away from the restaurant she regretted not having taken an extra few minutes to actually pop into the ladies room to check her hair and makeup. Hastily, she dug a lipstick from her bag and reapplied the dark berry gloss without benefit of a mirror. She was lucky that her stick straight hair was naturally shiny and required little in the way of styling.

She was almost five minutes early, but Nick was already there when she arrived, having commandeered the most private table in the softly lit, intimate bar area at the front of the restaurant. He stood up the moment he spied her in the doorway, a knowing smile on that rakishly handsome face. It didn't escape Angela's notice that every female in the bar was staring at him longingly, and she couldn't help the added little swagger in her step as she walked over to him.

But nothing could have prepared her for the way he took her hand and tugged her in close against his hard, unyielding body just before bending his head to capture her mouth in a searing, domineering kiss. Her free hand fluttered up limply to rest against one of his broad, steely shoulders, bracing herself as her knees grew weak from the continued onslaught of his kiss – the kiss that felt as though he was branding her, claiming her. His tongue was making lazy but bold sweeps through her mouth, letting her know that he was in charge, and that he expected not just her participation but her complete and total enjoyment as well.

And then he lifted his head, gazing down at her in satisfaction. She knew her eyes must be glazing over by now, her cheeks flushed, her freshly applied lipstick all for naught. Her lips felt swollen and bruised, and she'd never even come close to being this highly aroused before. She would have done anything at that point for him to whisk her off to bed, to cup her achy breasts in his big hands, and she had to resist the urge to pull his head back down to hers for another deep, dirty kiss.

"Sit. Your drink's already here."

Rather than object or rebel at the commanding tone of his voice, something deep within her responded to it instead, recognized it, even liked it, and she sat down obediently in the chair he pulled out for her.

Nick took his own seat, his long legs brushing against hers very intentionally as he picked up his glass. "Here's to what will hopefully be a very interesting evening to come," he toasted in a deep, seductive voice that seemed to reverberate throughout her entire body.

Angela gave him what she hoped was an equally seductive smile. "I'll drink to that," she replied, clinking her glass against his before taking a sip of the lemon flavored vodka. "But it's already been a very, very interesting evening for me."

He lounged back leisurely in his chair, stretching his extra-long legs out and crossing them at the ankles. "Is that right?" he drawled. "Well, why don't we see how much more interesting it can get. Are you on birth control?"

She coughed and sputtered as the mouthful of vodka she'd just swallowed went down the wrong way. She raised watery eyes up to him, observing the amused look on his face. "I'd, ah, ask what business that is of yours but I'm having a little trouble speaking at the moment," she croaked.

"Bullshit." He took a leisurely drink from his own glass. "To both statements. You're talking just fine and you know exactly why it's my business." Without any warning he captured her hand and brought it to his mouth, his tongue tracing a wicked little circle around her palm. "After dinner I'm going to fuck you, Angel. Probably more than once. So answer my question like a good girl, would you?"

Angela felt her entire body suffuse with heat, felt a fine sheen of perspiration begin to cover her skin. "Yes. I use one of those long lasting implants – Mirena, to be exact."

"Good. Not that I won't use a condom, too. That's non-negotiable. But they aren't a hundred percent foolproof so I like to know what I'm getting myself into. Ah, no pun intended."

"O-okay," she answered slowly, more than a little dazed "Are you always this, um - "

"Forward? Outspoken? Ballsy?" He nodded. "Always. I shoot from the hip, hate bullshit, won't tolerate lies or dishonesty. And I especially despise playing games. At least outside of the bedroom."

Some inner, unnamed little demon taunted her to reply teasingly, "Now, that's the second time tonight you've mentioned – ah, bedroom games. You're not one of those guys who's into kink, are you? Because even though I've got a pretty high pain tolerance, I generally reserve that for playing sports. *Outdoor* sports."

Nick laughed heartily, clearly amused. "And what does a twenty-two year old Stanford grad know about kink, honey? You must have lived in a very different sort of residence hall than I did."

She ran an index finger very deliberately around the rim of her glass before taking a small sip. "Actually, what I know about kink I learned back in high school. But not in the way you might be thinking."

He pulled his chair in closer, resting his elbows on the table. "Now, this is getting very, *very* interesting. I knew there was a lot more to you than what I'm guessing you let most people see. So tell me, Angel. Exactly what do you know about kink and how did you acquire this so-called knowledge?"

Angela grinned. "Nothing first hand, if that's what you're thinking. God, I never even dated in high school. Except for a very awkward arranged date for my senior prom."

Nick returned her smile, brushing his knuckles over her cheek. "Now *that* I have a very difficult time believing. Especially if you had all of this beautiful hair back then - " he picked up a long, silky strand and sifted it through his fingers. "Not to mention these long, gorgeous legs."

She couldn't stifle the gasp that escaped her lips as he very unexpectedly slid a hand up beneath the hem of her skirt to caress a silk covered thigh.

"I, ah, had both," she managed to reply somewhat breathlessly. "I was also five eleven and taller than almost every guy in class. For a long time the only one who was taller was this huge geek who wore oversized glasses and kept walking into walls."

He chuckled. "I'm assuming that all changed for you once you got to Stanford. But that's another story. Let's get back to the original topic, shall we?"

She nodded, finishing her drink. Nick signaled to a cocktail waitress for refills, pointedly ignoring the woman's very interested, inviting smile.

Angela took a sip of her fresh drink before continuing. "I played soccer in high school, as well as volleyball and basketball. It was – well, let's just say I looked for excuses to stay away from home as much as possible. Sports were one way I had of escaping – stuff. Anyway, one of my soccer teammates – Erika Lyman – her house became the unofficial after-practice gathering place on Friday nights. Especially since her parents always went out then."

"Any particular reason why it was always her place?"

"Sure. " She took another swig of her drink. "The Lymans had a huge estate out in Pebble Beach – pool, tennis courts, gym, game room, you name it. Plus the fridge was always overloaded and the bar stocked with nothing but top shelf stuff. And then of course there was the locked room. The one Erika's parents had no idea she'd copied a key for."

Nick's eyes were twinkling with mischief. "Go on. What was behind this locked door?"

Angela glanced around, making sure no one was eavesdropping, before leaning in a little closer and murmuring softly, "I guess you could call it their – ah, adults only game room. Only this one didn't have an Xbox or a foosball table inside. More like shackles, floggers, paddles, chains, and a whole lot of X-rated DVD's."

"Ah." He nodded in understanding. "*That* kind of game room. So tell me, Angel, were you shocked when you saw this little playroom for the first time?"

She lifted her shoulders in a casual shrug. "I'm not sure if shocked is the most accurate description. I think when Erika tried to describe what *she* thought went on in there, it was more of the "eew" factor than anything. It was kind of cold and creepy in there, all red leather and no windows, like something you'd see in a Halloween chamber of horrors. It wasn't until we watched some of the more, er, explicit DVD's that it became pretty clear exactly what went on in that room. Though Erika was convinced her parents were way too uptight to actually *do* most of that stuff, that they just liked to - "

"Watch?"

She nodded as Nick finished the sentence for her. "Pretty much, yeah."

He was grinning at her. "I assume her parents never found out that their daughter and her very naughty friends discovered their little playroom? Or furthered their sexual education by invading their stash of porn?"

"I'm not sure about that. But they did catch Erika in there one night with her boyfriend, um, trying out some of the equipment. They changed the locks right after that."

Nick gave a hoot of laughter. "And cut off your Friday movie nights in the process. Though I'm guessing you'd already watched your fill by then."

Angela wrinkled her nose. "That's for sure. You can only watch so many of those – God, calling them a movie is

SHATTERED 51

something of a stretch, isn't it? – before they get awfully repetitive. Like my friend Lauren used to say – when you've seen one blowjob you've seen them all."

Without warning, he slammed his glass down on the table and cupped the back of her head, his long fingers tangling in her hair. "I suggest we change the subject," he bit out. "Because when you start talking about blowjobs all I can think about is that sexy mouth of yours wrapped around my dick. Later on you can show me some of the dirty things you learned from watching porn, hmm?"

She was wide-eyed and slack-jawed, unable to think of a reply, and merely nodded.

"Finish your drink, then we'll have dinner."

She picked up her glass automatically and took a sip before regarding him warily. "You do like to dole out the orders, don't you?" she asked caustically.

Nick chucked her almost playfully on the chin, the smile returning easily to his sinfully handsome features. "Absolutely. And I'm not used to anyone refusing me, either. Not for a very long time anyway. Does that bother you, Angel?"

She was about to tell him yes, but was shocked to realize that she actually – God! – *liked* him ordering her around. Without stopping to consider how completely fucked up that sounded, she answered truthfully. "Surprisingly, no."

"I didn't think it would. On the outside, you give off this cool, calm and collected Independent Woman air. But on the inside – ah, it's just the opposite, isn't it, Angel? You want someone to boss you around, bend you to their will. You want to submit."

"Jesus." She gulped down the rest of her drink, shaken to the very core at what he had just told her in such a matter-of-fact manner. "No. Not like that. I'm not – no. I won't - "

"Shh. Relax." Nick was gently massaging the nape of her neck. "I don't mean like the bondage games your friend's parents played around with. Or like the BDSM movies I'm guessing you and your horny little friends watched. I'm not into whips or punishments or that kind of shit. That's a little too much on the kinky weirdo side for me. But there are many different forms of submission, Angel. And if I decide that's what you really want, we'll talk about it some more. But not tonight. Tonight's about getting to know each other a little better. Or maybe even a lot better."

He stood then, drawing her to her feet, and signaling to the host that they were ready for their table. And just like that a waiter materialized to show them to what was definitely the most private and desirable spot in the place, set back in a semi-secluded alcove.

Nick didn't bring up the subjects of submission or sex or anything that could even remotely be considered intimate for the duration of the meal. Instead, he kept her entertained with stories from his college and NFL football days, discovered that they had both been finance majors at Stanford and taken classes from several of the same professors, talked briefly about his meteoritic rise to success in the brokerage business, and managed to pry a considerable amount of information out of her as well.

"I confess to knowing very little about volleyball," he admitted. "Why did you choose that particular sport to play in college?"

"Easy. It's the one I got offered a scholarship for. There's no possible way I could have afforded to attend Stanford otherwise. My parents – correction, my mother – would never have even considered the possibility." She took a drink of the excellent Cabernet he'd ordered to go with their steak dinners – a huge Porterhouse for him, a petite filet mignon for her.

"You must have been a hell of a player to win a scholarship," he acknowledged. "Stanford has extremely high standards, after all, both academically and athletically."

Angela nodded. "I was pretty good, yeah. I was a starter even as a freshman. We fell just shy of winning the national title that year, but came back with a vengeance the next three."

Nick looked suitably impressed. "Three successive NCAA titles, hmm? A pretty impressive feat. You must cherish those trophies."

"I do. Though not quite as much as my Olympic medal."

He set his knife and fork down carefully, staring at her with an expression resembling awe. "You were on the Olympic volleyball team?

"Yes." Her cheeks flushed at his continued regard. "I was chosen for the national team at last summer's games. We, um, won."

"The gold?" He was incredulous at her nod. "Jesus, I'm sitting across the dinner table from an Olympic gold medalist? That's just – wow."

She laughed a little, pleased beyond belief at his tone of near reverence. "Come on, look who's talking. I'm sure between college and the pros you've racked up a ton of MVP, All-Pro, and Hall of Fame honors. Plus a Super Bowl ring. Nobody gives a rat's ass about Olympic volleyball or probably even remembers who won the gold medal last year."

Nick shook his head. "But I never won an Olympic medal, hell, never even had an opportunity to participate in the Olympics. And that's probably every athlete's dream, you know? Your family must be incredibly proud of you. Do your parents have some sort of shrine erected to you in their house?"

Her smile faded abruptly as she reached for her wine glass. "No. They – it's not like that with them. They don't – let's just say that I've got all my trophies and medals stored at my place. What about you?"

Nick apparently got the message that the subject of her parents was a sore one, and tactfully didn't press the issue further. "The same. All of my awards and other sports memorabilia are displayed in a room in my house. But that's largely because both of my parents tend to move around a lot. Separately, of course. They divorced when I was still a kid."

Before she could quiz him further, he changed the subject, but Angela sensed that he – like herself – hadn't had the happiest of childhoods. It was one more thing they seemed to have in common.

Nick refilled his wine glass but set the bottle aside without offering any to her. When she looked from him to her empty glass quizzically, he shook his head.

"No more booze for you tonight, Angel. You've had more than enough. And the very last thing I'd allow you to do tonight is get drunk."

She stared at him like he'd just sprouted horns, turning into the devil he'd jokingly compared himself to. "You're kidding, right? I mean, you've had just as much to drink as I've had."

He sipped the fine Cabernet with slow deliberation, his coffee colored eyes narrowing dangerously. "I rarely joke, Angel, and definitely not about something like this. You've had enough booze and that's that. As for me, I'm estimating I've got a good seven inches and maybe as much as seventy, eighty pounds on you. My tolerance for alcohol is a lot higher than yours."

She thought briefly about protesting again, or telling him about the drinking contests she and Lauren had often engaged in, but then thought better of the idea. She could sense he wasn't prepared to negotiate on the matter, and she absolutely didn't want to risk pissing him off. At least not until he'd fulfilled every one of the sexual promises she could see glittering in his eyes.

'Besides,' she consoled herself, 'he's probably right. I've had quite a bit to drink already, and I want to make sure I remember every single second of this night.'

Because she had a niggling fear that this was destined to be a one and done kind of affair. Nick might have already broken one of his rules by going out with a co-worker, but it was highly unlikely he'd break a second by seeing her again after tonight. So she really ought to make the best of it – enjoying this fabulous dinner at one of the best restaurants in town, and then have as much wild, raunchy sex with the impossibly gorgeous man seated across from her as she could handle. She wondered dizzily how many times a barbarian of a man like Nick would be capable of getting it up in one night, how long it would take in between, just how huge –

"Eat your dessert. You could stand to put on a little weight, you know. I like it – a lot – that you keep things nice and toned, but five to ten more pounds would look really good on you."

Once again, Angela opened her mouth to protest, but Nick merely used that opportunity to shove a huge forkful of Meyer lemon tart in her mouth. He was grinning at her wickedly, her mouth now too full to offer up any sort of protest.

"I'll have to remember that little trick when it looks like

you're getting ready to sass me," he chuckled. "Just stick some food in your mouth."

She glared at him while frantically chewing her food, then washed it down with a few sips of coffee. "Maybe not such a big bite next time, okay?" she croaked. "I almost choked."

"Sorry." He offered up a falsely apologetic smile before turning his attention to his own plate.

Angela toyed with the rest of her dessert until Nick placed a hand over hers, stilling her motions.

"Don't pick at your food," he told her firmly. "Eat it. Please."

It was that last, rather unexpected word that did the trick, and she somewhat reluctantly managed to eat at least half the tart. She tried to take another bite but shuddered instead, pushing the plate away.

"I can't," she confessed. "I don't usually – what I ate tonight is way more than I normally do at one sitting."

"Okay," he assured her. "After all, not only don't I want you drunk tonight, I sure as hell don't want you getting sick, either."

He beckoned their server over, handing over his credit card – an AMEX black card she noted, not surprised that he'd be one of the select group who'd been issued one. Nick didn't even glance at the total when the bill was presented, merely writing in a tip and signing his name with a bold flourish.

He stood then, and pulled her to her feet. "Let's go. The night isn't getting any younger, and I hate wasting even a minute of my day. Especially," he murmured as he pulled her close against his side, "when I could be putting those minutes to a much more pleasurable use."

She knew he felt the shiver that trembled through her body because he smiled down at her knowingly, looking very much like the devil he'd likened himself to back at the meeting. She knew that this was it – the point of no return at it was – and that if she was having even the slightest doubt about going with him she'd have to speak up now. Otherwise, he would take everything she had to give him – body, mind, and soul – and she knew that nothing would ever be the same for her again.

Nick seemed to sense her uncertainty as they waited for the valet to bring his car around, and gave the nape of her neck a sensuous little massage.

"Are you sure about this, Angel?" he asked, tipping her head back as his dark eyes bored into hers. "All of a sudden you seem a little nervous."

She bit her bottom lip, belatedly aware that once again she hadn't taken a moment to duck into the ladies room to freshen up her lipstick and hair. "Maybe a little," she admitted. "It's – I'm not all that experienced, and I guess I'm sort of afraid that - "

"What? That I'll be disappointed because you haven't fucked a dozen other guys before me?" Nick shook his head. "Or that in spite of some porn you watched back in high school you don't know a lot of different naughty little tricks?"

She shrugged. "Maybe. I'm not exactly sure what I'm afraid of. The others – four, if we're keeping exact count – they were all boys. College guys. I've never – you're so much more – *everything* than they'll ever hope to be. And I guess what I'm really afraid of is that I can't handle you."

"Ah, so that's it." He nodded in understanding. "Come here, Angel."

She went into his outstretched arms willingly, leaning her head gratefully against his shoulder as he held her gently. She breathed in the scintillating smell that was a blend of his discreet cologne, the crispness of his white dress shirt, and the overpoweringly masculine scent that clung to his skin, the scent that was simply Nick.

Nick stroked her hair with long, soothing motions. "Look, if I'd thought for one minute that you'd screwed your way through college, I doubt I'd have been attracted to you. I like a woman who's confident and cool but not to the point where she's overly aggressive or feels she has to impress me with how hot she is in the sack. If you haven't already figured it out, I like things done my way, according to my rules, and that definitely includes sex. So relax, Angel, and just follow my lead, hmm? Ah, here's my car."

His car was a fire engine red Ferrari, an ultra-luxe vehicle that she knew had likely cost several hundred thousand dollars. As he held the door open and she slid inside, she couldn't help but think of her own tiny, well-used Ford Fiesta – the one she'd bought off her brother-in-law Joe back in high school. She doubted Nick's six foot six bulk would even be able to squeeze inside the sub-compact.

"What's your address?"

Nick had slid behind the wheel and was powering up the car's sophisticated, built-in GPS system. A bit hesitantly, she recited her address – a quiet little residential street on the outskirts of Noe Valley. The tiny studio apartment had been all she could afford on her trainee's salary, and she'd been lucky that her other brother-in-law – Marco – was closely related to the owner of the building and had been able to snag her a modest discount on the rent. It had surprised Angela that her sister Deanna would have even bothered to help her out to that degree, but then she'd realized how relieved her family probably was that she was finally living on her own way up in San Francisco, and officially out of their hair.

"You don't have a roommate, do you?"

Nick's sudden question startled her, as lost in thought as she'd been, but she shook her head in reply. "No, it's just me. The place is sort of a shoebox, I'm afraid. You might have to duck your head to get through the doorway."

He frowned. "You do have a bed at least? And I don't mean a frigging sofa bed or a futon."

Angela grinned at the hint of irritation she heard in his voice. "Yes. It's a real, honest to goodness bed. It's even king sized. Takes up almost half the floor space but it's worth it."

"Good." The gaze he sent her way was positively smoldering, and she was left speechless by what he said next. "Because if the answer had been no, we'd be heading to the closest hotel right about now. The way I intend to fuck you tonight Angel – well, let's just say that bed of yours had better be up for the task."

Chapter Four

She'd been prudent to warn him about ducking his head upon entering her tiny studio apartment, for he definitely wouldn't have cleared the doorway otherwise. Angela intentionally didn't look at him once he shut the door and began to inspect the small space, likely with the same eagle-eyed attention to detail that he'd looked her over with earlier this evening. She didn't particularly want to see the expression on his face when he took in just how small the room was, noticed how sparsely furnished it was, and that except for the bed – which she'd insisted on buying new – the other few pieces of furniture were well-used hand-me-downs culled from a variety of family members.

But when her curiosity couldn't be contained any longer, she glanced over at Nick as he continued his slow, careful inspection of her place. He stopped and gave a very thorough look at the one quality piece of artwork she owned – the seascape somewhat small in size but beautifully framed and exquisitely painted.

"Is this really a Benoit?" he asked incredulously. "I'm not sure I could even begin to estimate how much it's worth if it's the real thing."

"It is the real thing," she assured him. "And I've got a pretty good idea of what it would sell for. But that was given to me as a gift – by the artist herself – and I'd never consider selling it."

Nick blinked in surprise. "How do you know an artist like Natalie Benoit?"

Angela smiled softly at the mention of the woman who'd treated her like a daughter for so many years. "Natalie is the mother of my two best friends. We all grew up together in Carmel, and I've known Lauren and Julia since we were in the fourth grade. I've probably spent more time at their house than I have at my own."

He regarded her quizzically. "That's the second time this evening you've made some reference to not spending much time at home. Were things that bad for you there?"

She shook her head in amazement at his brazen question. "Wow, you really do shoot from the hip, don't you? And subtlety is definitely not one of your better traits in case you weren't aware."

Nick grinned. "Oh, I'm very well aware. I told you back at the restaurant that I'm ballsy. Trust me, Angel, there's no topic that I won't dare to ask you about. And you'll always give me the answers I want, too."

Angela frowned. "Is that part of this so-called submission you mentioned?"

"Yes." He answered without the slightest hesitation. "Honesty always."

She lifted her chin stubbornly. "Does that go both ways? If I ask you a question, will you always answer it honestly?"

Nick's gaze narrowed dangerously. "Angel, it's way too soon for us to start talking about – ah, let's call them conditions for now. When and if I think you're ready, we'll have ourselves a nice long chat. Until then, show me that gold medal of yours."

She thought about pressing the issue further, asking him what these so-called "conditions" might be, but decided not to push her luck. Instead, she merely indicated the rather dilapidated bookcase that she'd pressed into service as her trophy case.

Nick glanced over the various trophies, plaques, medals, ribbons, and framed certificates that she'd earned over the years, in half a dozen different sports, but it was the Olympic medal that he honed in on.

"May I?"

Angela nodded in assent as he picked up the protective plastic case that held the medal. "You can open it if you like."

He did, running his long fingers over the raised inscription, shaking his head in awe. "I've never seen one of these close up, you know. And I'd still rather have one of these than my Super Bowl ring."

"You don't wear your ring?"

He shook his head. "I'm not a jewelry kind of guy, except for a watch. I wear the ring occasionally, if I'm attending a Hall of Fame induction or some other NFL event. Otherwise, it just stays with the rest of my collection. Speaking of which."

He closed the medal case and placed it back on the shelf. "You should take better care of your awards, Angel. Especially this medal. You don't live in the safest of neighborhoods, after all. And the lock on your door is pathetic. Don't your parents have any space in their house for you to keep all this stuff?"

"They do. That's not the issue." She hesitated, not really wanting to discuss her messed-up relationship with her family at the moment.

"Then what is?"

Angela huffed, trying not to display the agitation he was causing to rise up with his persistence. "It's a really long, boring story, Nick, and I'd rather not get into all that shit right now. Let's just say that my mother didn't want a lot of mementoes of me laying around the house once I left for college."

"Hmm." He was leaning negligently against a wall, his arms crossed over his midsection as he studied her carefully. "You're right. It already sounds way too complicated to get into now. But one day you'll tell me all of it, Angel, even though I sense it's the last thing you want to talk about. In the meanwhile, come here."

He sat down on the edge of the bed and held a hand out to her. She walked over to him slowly, alarmed to notice that her hand was shaking as she placed it in his. But Nick only tugged her closer, until she was standing between his spread legs, his hard, muscular thighs imprisoning her. His hands held her in place by the hips, making sure she couldn't back away even if she'd wanted to.

It was suddenly very, very hard for her to breathe – small wonder considering how hard her heart was pounding and how rapidly her pulse was racing. But if Nick was aware of her agitation he gave no clue about it. Or, at the very least, wasn't allowing it to rush him. And he seemed to be in no hurry whatsoever to get to the main event of this evening – namely getting naked and then giving her brand new mattress one hell of a workout.

His voice was deep and deliberate as he wrapped his arms around her hips, his hands splayed over her buttocks. "When I went to that pointless meeting today – and, by the way, I don't go to many of those things no matter who the special guest might be – all I could think about was how fast I could make a discreet exit. I don't especially enjoy listening to people spout all that corporate bullshit, nor do I need pep talks from higher-ups who don't know their ass from third base. But, as it turned out, I wound up being very thankful that I attended. Do you know why that is, Angel?"

She tried desperately to lighten the mood by cracking a weak joke. "Well, it certainly wasn't for the great food and top shelf booze."

He smirked. "Very observant, Angel. But you and I both know the real reason."

She gasped as he unexpectedly shoved a hand up beneath her skirt to squeeze one of her ass cheeks, the skin bared by the skimpy cut of her thong.

"Ahh." Her eyes fluttered shut as he continued to caress her bare skin. She was already wet and ready for him, quivering with need at each bold, confident stroke of his hand.

"Look at me."

Her eyes flew open as she gazed down at him obediently. Nick was unsmiling, his dark gaze silently warning her not to look away again.

"That's better. It was your eyes, you know, that did it for me. Made me realize that for once I didn't give a damn if you worked at the same firm, that I was willing to take the risk so that I could have all of this for myself – the big eyes, that sexy mouth, all of this gorgeous hair – " he paused to wrap a long, shiny strand around his hand, giving it a sharp tug that made her wince a little. "And especially," he added in a husky voice, "this very, very fuckable body."

Before she could respond or protest or even move, Nick had begun to strip her with swift, precise movements. In less than a minute she was left standing in just her lingerie and shoes – all of it black – and trying valiantly to stop herself from quaking all over.

He stroked her hip soothingly. "Relax. I'm not going to rush this so you don't need to tremble like a frightened bunny. Hold still now, that's a good girl, and let me look at you."

She wanted desperately to close her eyes, or cross her arms over her breasts, but she knew instinctively that Nick wouldn't allow her to do either of those things. His dark gaze inspected her with precise scrutiny, and she could almost feel his eyes boring a path along her skin.

Without warning he deftly unhooked her black lace bra, tossing it carelessly away as his massive hands began to shape her bare breasts. She whimpered as he pinched both of her nipples, plucking the pale mocha peaks until they were hard and throbbing.

"Your breasts are perfect, Angel," he told her in a husky voice, his hands pushing the twin mounds up until they were closer to his eye level and his tongue could easily flick out to circle each nipple. "Not too big but beautifully shaped and very firm. Firm enough that you don't really need a bra, provided you're wearing the right sort of clothing and at the right sort of occasion." He sucked one already tender peak into his mouth, the sensation of half-pain, half-pleasure rippling all the way down her body, her pelvis starting to tilt forward in reaction.

Nick lifted his head from her breasts, watching her face carefully for a reaction as he skimmed a palm down her torso to her quivering belly.

"Nice toned abs, Angel. I can see you work out a lot, take good care of this sexy body. But you're a little too thin, just like I guessed. Ten more pounds, I think. That would still keep you nice and trim but with a few more curves in the right places. We'll work on that."

Angela was so turned on, so consumed with excitement and heat, that she could neither argue nor protest at his arrogant declaration. Her hands dropped to his shoulders to steady herself as he toyed with the flimsy band of her tiny black lace thong.

"As little as this thing covers, you might as well not have bothered," he drawled, as he began to work the miniscule garment down past her hips. "In general, I'm not a big fan of the thong, don't find it especially sexy. More of a panty man, actually. Or nothing at all. Are you making note of all this, Angel?"

"Wh-what?" she stammered, her voice no more than a wisp. His words were hypnotizing her, drawing her deeper and deeper into his web, and she wasn't sure she could remember one damned thing he'd said at this moment.

Nick smiled knowingly. "Never mind. This probably isn't a good time to be asking you to pay attention. Time enough for all that."

He returned his attention to her body, in particular the narrow strip of black hair that was all that remained of her otherwise bare pubic area.

"Now *this*," he rasped, his index finger tracing along the neatly shaved little patch, "I like. Your little landing strip here is a lot sexier than a full Brazilian would be. We don't need to change this at all."

Angela couldn't suppress the moan that rose up from her throat as Nick's clever – and no doubt very experienced – fingers began to slowly trail through the outer folds of her labia. She was wet, God, so wet, and had never come close to feeling this sort of overwhelming physical need, a need that was all she could think about. But still he continued to tease her, to merely flutter his fingers around her clit or glance them across her slit before withdrawing.

"Please."

She barely recognized her own voice, that raw, hoarse sound. Her hips kept thrusting forward, seeking his touch, her body already so highly stimulated that she felt like screaming if she didn't find some sort of satisfaction very, very soon.

Nick sounded amused. "Please what, Angel? You're an impatient one, aren't you? We'll have to work on that, too, teach you some control. But in the meanwhile, let's see what we can do for you."

He'd barely slid his middle finger halfway inside her soaking wet pussy, had only rubbed two slow circles around her clit, when the orgasm ripped through her. But rather than back off at that point, Nick just kept at her, adding a second finger, both of them pumping in and out of her wildly responsive body with increased aggressiveness.

And when she was already crying out with pleasure, was already mindless with sensation, he bent his dark head and sucked her clit between his lips. A second, even more intense orgasm pulsed through her, until she lost the ability to think or speak or move, and all that remained was pure sensation.

Dimly, she was aware of Nick gently laying her down on the bed, the amusement in his voice now touched with something that sounded an awful lot like awe.

"Well, you're an easy one to please, aren't you, Angel?" he asked with a low, purring laugh. "I barely had to touch you and off you went like a skyrocket. Tell me, are you always so easy to get off or do I just have magic fingers?"

"Hmm?" She stared up at him, watching as if in a trance as he began to undress, removing his suit jacket and tie before starting on the buttons of his shirt. "Sorry, I – um – can't - "

"You heard me. Tell me what I want to know now. Is it typical for you to have an orgasm – no, make that *two* orgasms – with such little effort?"

Angela felt her cheeks flush hotly, not used to such behavior from a lover, or to such deeply intimate questions. But she knew Nick was waiting for her answer, and none too patiently, either.

"No." She ducked her chin in embarrassment. "It's – it's usually just the opposite. I just figured it was me, you know, that I wasn't one of those women who could - "

He shook his head, unbuckling his belt and then pulling his shirt free. "Well, you figured wrong, Angel. In fact, I'm not sure I've ever seen another woman who could come that fast. Or that hard."

She propped herself up on her elbows, her big eyes wide as he stripped the shirt from his body. "Maybe I just needed the right partner," she told him huskily.

And then she could only stare in slack-jawed disbelief at the sight of his naked torso, not sure what part of his heavily muscled body was more droolworthy – the massive breadth of his shoulders; the powerful, chiseled circumference of his biceps; the six-pack abs that could only be the result of thousands of hours spent in the gym or great genetics or both. And what made that mouthwatering upper body even more eye-popping was all that smooth, darkly tanned skin and the narrow ribbon of black hair that bisected his chest before tapering down below his waist.

"Like what you see so far?"

Nick's sinfully full mouth was quirked up at the sides in a confident, knowing grin.   He knew, damn him, she thought darkly, just how beautiful he was – how buffed and ripped and strong.   And he also had to know exactly the sort of affect he had on women, knew just how much she was enthralled by the sight of him right now.

"Yes." Her voice was barely above a whisper.

The rasp of his zipper seemed to echo around the small, confined space of her apartment, and her eyes felt like they were bulging out of their sockets as he shucked his pants, dealt with his socks and shoes.   The form fitting gray briefs that were his only remaining garment seemed barely able to contain the enormous bulk of his erection.

He gave a low, deep laugh as he began to peel his underwear off.   "Angel, I hope you never play poker because you'd lose your shirt.   That saying about a face being an open book – honey, I can read every single word on yours clear as a bell right now."

Angela's brain felt like mush, her vocal cords seemingly paralyzed, and she could only stare – and keep on staring – at the sight of his splendidly nude body.   Especially the intimidatingly huge length and girth of his fully aroused cock. The thick, dark red tip seemed to throb with a life of its own, and she swallowed with a great deal of difficulty as she tried valiantly to imagine how she could possibly take all of him inside her body at once.

"We're going to fit together perfectly, Angel," he assured her confidently, as though he'd just read her mind.   "Even with that tight little cunt of yours, you'll take all of me, won't you?"

Her big, dark eyes were transfixed as he removed what looked at first glance to be half a dozen or so foil packets from his suit jacket.   "I – I'll try," she promised faintly as he rolled one of the condoms over his pulsing cock.

He sat down on the bed, gripping her chin between his long fingers as he tipped her head back.   His eyes were gleaming, his mouth unsmiling.   "You'll do it, Angel.   I knew the minute I saw you that you were made for this, that your body was made for *me*. You're going to take everything I have to give you, and you're going to fucking love every minute of it."

He took her mouth in a brutal kiss, his tongue possessing her with a ravenous hunger that made it very, very clear who was in charge. She groaned, her head starting to spin dizzily beneath the harsh demand of his mouth, and her arms drifted up of their own volition to wrap around his neck.

Nick hauled her body further up the bed, until her head butted up against the pillows.

"No headboard, I see," he muttered, almost as if to himself. "Something else to work on. Until then, this will have to do."

He removed her arms from around his neck and drew them up and over her head, shackling them in place easily with one of his big hands. He then began to trace a slow, deliberate path down her body with his mouth, alternating between delicate, butterfly-like kisses on her eyelids, cheeks, the tip of her nose, and then becoming more aggressive the lower he went. She let out a yelp as he bit down on one of her earlobes before laving the same spot with his tongue. He tore a gasp from her throat as he sucked the side of her neck in a possessive love bite. His tongue licked a bead of sweat from the hollow at the base of her throat before moving in a straight line down between her heaving breasts.

He lingered over the taut, swollen mounds for a long while – his tongue circling each nipple over and over before sucking it into his mouth. With each long, hard pull of his lips at her breast, she could feel the sensation shimmer all the way down her torso, past her belly, and directly to her womb.

Nick lifted his mouth, his strong fingers still plucking at one of her fully engorged nipples. "Ever come this way, Angel? Just from having your tits sucked on?"

"Ahh." Her upper body bowed off the bed as he twisted one taut peak hard. "No. I didn't - "

"Didn't know that you could have an orgasm that way?" he finished. "It isn't all that easy, but I think given how damned responsive you are that it will be for you. But we'll have to try that another time, Angel. Because right now there's something else I really, really need to do."

He released his grip on her wrists, sliding down her body and prying her thighs apart as he did so. Then, as his intent became clear to her, she bucked her hips up in protest.

"No." She tried desperately to pull her legs closed but his grip was like a steel bar holding her in place. "Please, don't. I – I don't like that."

Nick chuckled. "*That*? You mean oral sex, Angel? Having your cunt eaten out, your clit sucked? Tell me why you don't like it."

She shook her head, feeling her face flame with mortification. "I – I can't. Please, Nick. It's just not something I like."

"Tough. Because I do like it. A lot. And I think I'm going to really like eating up your sweet, juicy cunt. Now tell me why you don't enjoy it."

She whimpered as his fingers dug deeper into her thighs and she knew there'd be bruises there tomorrow, as well as in a number of other places on her body. "It just doesn't feel good, that's all. Only a couple of the guys I've been with ever tried it and it just felt – icky."

"Icky?" He threw back his head and laughed heartily. "Oh, that's a good one, Angel. And you know what? If some fumbling twenty year old college boy tried to go down on you and didn't know what the hell he was doing, then that very, uh, vivid description probably isn't far off the mark. However," he added in a low, sexy voice, "*I* know exactly what I'm doing."

And before she could protest further, he'd buried his face between her widespread thighs and began to run his tongue with deliberate precision all around the moist folds of her labia.

"Oh, God!" she cried out, her hips rearing up off the bed as her hands threaded into his thick black hair, pulling him in even closer.

It took only those few clever, arousing licks for her to realize he'd been quite right. Not only did he know *exactly* what he was doing, but he seemed to be an expert in the art. The pathetic attempts her previous partners had made at this were laughable now in comparison. Except that laughing was the very last thing she felt like doing at this moment.

Nick lifted his head, only to replace his tongue with two long fingers, and she quivered each time he would thrust them deep inside of her body before sliding back out. He repeated this action far too many times for her to count, until she was writhing against his fingers, her pelvis thrashing around wildly, seeking, needing, begging.

"You're a greedy little bitch, aren't you?" he rasped. "You want it real bad, don't you, Angel? How many orgasms do you think you can handle in one night, hmm? I'm betting an awful lot."

"Yes," she cried out frantically. "I – I do need it. Please, oh please, just - "

He pinched her clit between his thumb and forefinger, pulling on it hard, and then bent his head and flicked his tongue across it twice, thrice, until she came apart, her nails digging into his scalp as she clutched his head to her. The orgasm went on and on, causing the bed to shake as her legs seemed to flail around uncontrollably.

Her whole body was still throbbing with sensation, and she badly needed a few minutes to come back down to earth, to remember how to breathe. But Nick was at her again, this time with his tongue thrusting up boldly inside her vagina, mimicking the motion his fingers had been making just minutes ago.

"Ah, no more. I – I can't, " she pleased weakly. "So – so good, but I need - "

"You need to be prepared for me, Angel," he told her firmly, his fingers spreading the lips of her inner labia apart. "You feel as tight as a virgin and I'm admittedly a big guy. If I don't get you wet enough, relaxed enough, I'll hurt you. Not intentionally, of course, but I am, ah, considered very well hung. So trust me on this, hmm? One more time and then I'll fuck you."

That promise was enough to make her heart begin to race in mingled fear and excitement, even as his mouth got busy again. It took very little time and not a whole lot of effort on his part to bring her over yet again, the climax causing her vaginal muscles to convulse around the pumping motion of his fingers, to shudder against the talented mouth that kept sucking on her over-sensitized clit.

When he finally moved away, Angela could only let her arms and legs sprawl limply in a weirdly contorted position. The blood was pounding in her ears and she was half-afraid she was going to pass out from the sensory overload. Dimly she realized that Nick was speaking to her as he ran a hand almost absently up and down her leg, still covered in its sheer black thigh-high stocking.

"I like these," he murmured in a low voice. "Very sexy, even more than a garter belt. Not that I won't look forward to seeing you wear one of those as well. Or a corset. But for tonight I think I'd prefer these long, gorgeous legs of yours to be bare."

Nick removed one of her shoes, inspecting it as though he were an authority on women's footwear. "Hmm, I suppose you have to wear something conservative like this to the office. But I'd love to see you in stilettos instead, in a really high fuck-me heel." He began to roll her stocking off. "That kind of shoe would make your legs look as though they went all the way up to your armpits."

As he removed the other shoe and stocking, Angela gasped as he ran his hands assertively up along her bare legs, caressing their long, pale gold length.

"Your skin is so smooth," he purred, his caresses growing bolder. "Do you wax your legs, too?"

"Yes." She was quivering in anticipation as he slowly spread her thighs apart, rising up to kneel between them.

"When I saw you standing across that room – all long hair and big eyes and these gorgeous legs," he told her, his voice deep and enthralling, "the first thing I imagined was having them wrapped around my neck while I fucked you so deep and hard that both of us passed out from the pleasure." He took hold of his intimidatingly huge erection and began to slowly feed it inside of her an inch at a time. "But not this first time," he murmured against her mouth, nipping at her bottom lip sharply with his teeth. "I want both of us to remember every second."

Angela was dizzy with sensation by now, already overwhelmed by how big he was, how deeply he filled her, and she fought off the panic when she realized he was barely halfway in. "I can't – you're – it's too much," she whispered helplessly.

"Hush. That's a good girl." He took her mouth in a long, leisurely kiss while his fingers plucked at her nipple. "You just need to relax, Angel. Give yourself over to me and let it happen. Don't think. Just feel."

"Okay." Her voice sounded rusty as she took a deep breath, willing herself to relax, to allow her body to open further to him.

Nick continued to murmur in her ear – words of praise and encouragement, soothing her, calming her, seducing her. And as she did as he commanded and let herself go, he took advantage of her compliance and slid all the way inside of her, buried to the root.

Angela couldn't suppress the little sound of alarm she made as he completed his possession, as she felt every hard, throbbing inch of him tightly sheathed within her. Nick propped himself up on his elbows, gazing down at her intently, and simply remained still.

"I told you," he whispered, brushing long strands of hair off her face. "I knew you could take me, Angel, knew that you were made for me. Not many women can handle all of me, you know."

"I'm not so sure I can, either," she breathed, firmly pushing aside the thought of how many women he must have been with in his lifetime. That was the very last thing she wanted to dwell on right now.

"Yes, you can. I told you – we fit together perfectly. I'm going to move now, Angel, and I'll try to take it easy this first time. But you feel fucking amazing, like a fist around my dick, so holding back isn't going to be easy."

Angela could tell by the way he clenched his jaw, at how tightly bunched the huge muscles of his biceps were, that Nick was struggling mightily to do as he'd promised. But even with the long, slow strokes, the tremendous effort he was making to be gentle, she still feared he might split her in two. And then her inner muscles finally began to relax and she opened to him a bit more with each controlled thrust.

"Okay there, Angel?"

She nodded, placing her hands on his shoulders. "Yes. It's –

it's good. You can, um, you don't have to keep - "

His dark eyes were gleaming as a slow smile broke across his face, beads of sweat dampening his forehead. "You sure?"

"Yes."

Nick made a low, feral sound deep in his throat as he began to pick up the tempo, sliding his hands beneath her ass as he tilted her pelvis to the angle he wanted. As his movements grew faster and faster, his thrusts deeper and deeper, she bit down on her lip to keep from crying out. He was too big, she thought wildly, too much. But the protest she was about to make froze in her throat as she felt the orgasm start to build, felt the broad head of his cock hitting that sweet spot deep inside of her over and over, the angle of his thrusts perfectly positioned to stimulate the G-spot. And, as if that wasn't more than enough to send her spiraling into oblivion, Nick worked a hand between their tightly joined bodies to find her clit, and the very second he rubbed his thumb over the distended little nub she went soaring – soaring so high that she was scarcely aware when he began to fuck her even harder, faster; when his breathing grew rough and when he came and came and came, his head thrown back as he let out a ferocious yell.

She thought perhaps that she did faint then, at least for a few seconds, because the next thing she was aware of was Nick walking out of her miniscule bathroom, having disposed of the condom. Her limbs – not to mention her brain – felt like jelly, so weak and drained that she could only let him draw her into his surprisingly tender embrace – surprising because she sensed that Nick was not by nature a tender or gentle man.

"You doing all right there, Angel?" he asked, his lips brushing her hair.

"I'll let you know when I can feel my legs again," she murmured weakly.

Nick chuckled. "Believe it or not, mine are a little shaky, too. But you're okay otherwise? I wasn't too rough on you?"

She wrapped her arms around his rock hard torso, burying her face against his throat. "Not too rough, no. I'm pretty tough after all."

"Is that right?" He wrapped a hunk of her long hair around his hand and tugged her head back, forcing her to gaze into his eyes. "Well, Angel, that's the best news I've heard for a good long while." With his free hand he traced a path down between her heaving breasts, over her quivering belly, and then cupping her between her thighs. "Because I'm nowhere even close to being through with you tonight."

Chapter Five

"You seem to be walking okay today, Angie. That muscle you pulled the other day all healed up now?"

Angela paused by Noah's cubicle on the way back to her own desk, a bit taken aback by his question. "Uh, yeah. It's a lot better, thanks."

Noah patted her on the arm with a reassuring smile. "Well, take it easy with those workouts from now on. I should hit the gym with you one of these days, have you show me some stuff. I'm admittedly a lazy bum but it sure looks like you keep yourself in great shape."

She forced herself not to give a little eye roll as her co-worker rather openly ogled her. It was a warm Indian summer day so she'd worn her lightweight gray linen suit and a sleeveless white blouse that was a bit on the semi-sheer side.

"I actually don't spend all that much time at the gym these days," she acknowledged, taking a careful step or two away from Noah. "As you know, working twelve hour days is sort of draining, and the last thing I feel like at the end of one is going to the gym."

Noah shrugged. "You take all of that stuff too seriously, Angie. I've heard that the exam isn't all that tough, and as smart as you are I'd be shocked if you didn't ace it on the first try."

"There's a lot more work involved than just studying for the exam, Noah," admonished Angela. "In fact, I've got to finish the next training module so I'd better head back to my desk."

He grinned. "All work and no play makes Angie a very dull girl. We ought to go out for a drink after work tonight, maybe dinner. You like Thai food?"

"Not especially, no. And thanks for the offer but I can't. I'm, uh, busy tonight."

Noah raised a brow. "Hot date, huh? Who's the lucky guy?"

Angela was suddenly very anxious to end the conversation. "Uh, just someone who went to school at Stanford."

He brightened. "So, like, an old college friend, something like that? Maybe there's still hope for me, huh? Why don't we get together this weekend then?"

She bit her bottom lip to stop herself from laughing or making some sort of sarcastic comment. Noah had more or less been hitting on her since they'd started working here, which was rather laughable considering he was a good five inches shorter than she was – in stocking feet – so with the added three inches from her shoes she towered over him rather noticeably.

"I never plan that far ahead these days," she told him casually. "Now, I've really got to get back to work."

"Killjoy. But I am glad to see you're not walking funny anymore. You must have had a hell of a workout the other day."

'You have no idea, pal,' Angela was sorely tempted to add. 'But it was more a case of getting worked over than working out.'

Even as she sat down somewhat gingerly on her lumpy desk chair, she couldn't suppress the shiver than ran up and down her spine as she recalled exactly what had caused her sore muscles. And it certainly hadn't been from running too many miles or a particularly strenuous spin class. More like way too much sex in one night.

Nick had been insatiable, using up nearly all of the condoms he'd deposited on her bedside table. He'd pushed, pulled, bent, contorted, stretched her body into a variety of positions, some of which she hadn't known existed, and he'd kept at her for hours. It had been close to two a.m. before he'd finally had enough, leaving her bed to get dressed, and she'd been too wrung out, too physically spent to do much more than lift her head limply from the pillow when he'd told her good night.

"Give me your phone number," he'd instructed, and had tapped it into his cell as she'd weakly recited the numbers. Nick had pulled the duvet up over her naked body, and then pressed a kiss to her forehead before murmuring, "And I *will* call you again, Angel. If you've been listening to the sort of gossip I imagine you've heard, then you're probably figuring that this is it – another notch on Nick Manning's bedpost, another woman he fucked and forgot. But not you, Angel. I promise. I'll call you, okay? It might take a few days but I *will* call."

He'd let himself out and she had fallen asleep instantly, so wiped out by the multiple bouts of sex – each one more physically demanding than the last – that she couldn't even think about moving. Her alarm had gone off far too early, and she'd groaned at the very idea of dragging herself into work after such little sleep. And then, as she'd very tentatively gotten out of bed, she'd groaned for a whole different reason – namely the soreness and stiffness of just about every muscle in her body. The bed – and her body – had reeked of sex and sweat and Nick – but she'd been reluctant to take a shower and thus wash his scent off her skin.

The spray of the shower had caused her to wince as the hot water beat down on a dozen different assorted bruises and love bites, not to mention the bumpy red whisker burn that covered a good part of her skin. And she'd barely been able to tolerate washing her private parts, for they'd been incredibly sore and tender, her battered insides feeling like mush.

Walking had been difficult for the past few days, her gait resembling that of an old arthritic woman, and she'd had to fob everyone off with the story about pulling a muscle during an especially strenuous workout. Which, she'd realized with a grimace, wasn't exactly a lie.

It was Friday afternoon, almost a full three days now since that fateful office meeting where she'd first met Nick and wound up having the sort of wild, screaming sex she'd never really believed existed. It had been much dirtier, more physical, and definitely more stimulating than any of the porn she'd watched back in high school. And as for the orgasms – so many that she'd lost the ability to count them after a time – they had been nothing, *nothing* like the pathetically simulated moans and groans that the actresses in the X-rated films had so obviously been faking. The way Nick had made her feel – the reactions he'd coaxed so easily from her body – well, there was just no way to fake something like that. Certainly none of her previous partners had possessed even a smidgen of his skills, had never been able to rouse the tiniest fraction of response from her. Nick had seduced her, enthralled her, and now she craved more, needed more, like a brand new junkie who'd had her first taste of smack and was immediately greedy for more.

And despite his whispered promise to call her, Angela wasn't permitting herself to really believe it would happen. A man like Nick – with his face and body, his wealth and power, his mind-blowing sexual expertise – could easily have any woman he wanted and as many as he could handle. So why would he want to see *her* again when he'd always enjoyed a wide variety of women in the past, had avoided commitment in any shape or form, and had a reputation as the ultimate love 'em and leave 'em kind of guy.

Oh, she knew he'd found her attractive, had enjoyed her body and her fiery response to him. But she'd never considered herself especially beautiful or sexy, and she had realized first hand on Tuesday night just how sadly lacking her sexual experience really was. Was it possible that it was her inexperience that Nick was attracted to? She would admittedly be something of a novelty for him, quite a bit younger and far more impressionable than the women he usually dated. Maybe she was just a change of pace for him, someone different from the undoubtedly sophisticated and sexually adept others who'd shared his bed.

But she had refused to set herself up for disappointment, to hope for what was extremely unlikely to occur, and hadn't allowed herself to believe he would actually call her again. She'd kept herself busier than ever with work, throwing herself into studying and going through the training modules, and had actually been grateful when she'd been assigned the task of filling in for the sales manager's PA's yesterday. Filling her days with work had kept her mind off of Nick and wondering if and when he would call, had stopped her from checking her phone every fifteen minutes for a missed call or text, had helped ease the secret disappointment she'd felt as each hour and then day had passed without hearing from him.

But while she managed to keep herself fully occupied during the day, the nights had been a very different matter. Normally she would have gone out for a run, not much caring that the days were getting shorter now and that a good part of her workout would be in the dark. But she was way too sore for running right now, Christ, could barely walk a straight line after Nick's nonstop sexual marathon the other night. So that left her with a few hours to kill in the evenings, and it was all but impossible not to remember in bold, living Technicolor everything that had taken place in her apartment three nights ago.

One of the pillowcases had still held a lingering trace of his scent, and she'd wrapped her arms around it each night, imagining it was his body instead. Twice she'd become so aroused while reliving Tuesday night's torrid romp that she'd been mightily tempted to touch herself, to rub her fingers against her clit, to make herself come. But both times she'd stopped – and not just because her private parts were still way too sore for any sort of intimate contact. Angela knew it was because she'd never come close again, no matter who her partner might be, of climaxing that hard, of feeling so much, or of falling so hard as she'd done with Nick. He'd already ruined her for any other man, had set the bar so impossibly high that no one else would ever be able to even attempt to scale its height.

She'd just completed the training module – an incredibly boring one about treasury investments that she'd struggled mightily to pay attention to – when her phone buzzed. Conscious of the close proximity of her co-workers, she answered it immediately, even though the caller ID was blocked.

"Can you talk or are you surrounded by nosy-ass employees?"

Angela almost dropped the phone as a feeling of shocked elation pulsed through her body, the sound of the amused, lazy drawl not one she'd ever expected to hear again.

"Um, no and yes," she murmured in hushed tones.

Nick sighed. "That's what I figured. I'll need to text you in future when you're at the office. Are you able to leave your desk for a few minutes?"

She knew she was at least two training modules ahead of everyone else, and hadn't taken much of a lunch break, so she didn't feel in the least bit guilty replying readily. "Yes, not a problem."

"All right. There's a little conference room on your side of the floor if I recall correctly. I'm guessing on a Friday afternoon it's not being used so walk over there now and tell me if you can talk."

"Okay." She stood and walked the short distance down the hallway to the conference room. It was dark inside and thankfully unoccupied. Once inside she shut the door but left the lights off. "I'm here now. Alone."

"Good. The last thing I want – or need – is for anyone in this office to overhear our conversation. Or worse – to suspect we're seeing each other."

She was both puzzled and thrilled at his statement – puzzled because she wasn't quite sure why there was such a need for secrecy, and thrilled to hear Nick imply that they would be seeing each other again.

"Um, not that I've told anybody about the other night – or plan to, for that matter – but what's the big deal? I mean, I know there can't possibly be a rule about employees not being allowed to date each other. From what I hear, people in this place hook up with each other all the time. You almost need an organizational chart to keep track of who's slept with who."

Nick's voice was biting. "There's no office rule, that's true, but then I have my own set of rules, Angel. And I've already broken at least two of them for you already. My need for privacy is absolute, especially here at work. Nothing pisses me off more than to know people speculate behind my back about who I'm dating or banging. So that's rule number one with me – not one single word mentioned to anyone in this place that we've had any involvement. Clear?"

"Yes." She took a seat, suddenly aware that her legs were wobbly. The undercurrent of anger in his tone was threatening to send her into panic mode, and she forced herself to take a deep breath.

"Well, now that we've got that out of the way, I'll tell you why I'm calling. I want to see you. Tonight. I'll pick you up at seven-thirty, we'll go have some dinner, and then we'll – talk."

She waited briefly for him to ask if those plans were okay with her, then sighed when she realized he wasn't actually asking her but simply telling her the way it was going to be. "I'll be ready."

"And there'll be a package waiting for you when you get home," he told her briskly. "Wear everything you find in the box to dinner tonight but not another thing more."

Angela opened her mouth to protest but realized from his tone that it wouldn't do her any good at all to argue. "O-kay," she agreed slowly. "How, um, do I know it will fit?"

He chuckled. "I'm a pretty good judge of that sort of thing. But in your case I actually checked all of your sizes before I left, easy enough to do since all your stuff was still just laying around. Size ten shoes, the skirt was a four, your bra size is a 34B. I couldn't find a tag on that piece of dental floss you were wearing between your ass cheeks so I had to guess at the panty size. So if they don't fit just leave them off."

She was speechless at his bold, careless manner and could only mumble, "Um, sure."

"See you at seven-thirty, Angel. Be sure you're ready."

And then, abruptly, the call ended and she found herself staring dumbly at her phone. It was almost five minutes later before she could stimulate enough functioning brain cells to propel herself back to her desk.

It was a good thing, she thought about half an hour later, that she was so far ahead in her training program. Because there was no possible way she was going to get one damned thing more done today.

***

Angela stared at the garments she'd laid out on her bed in mingled alarm and admiration. Everything in the exact right size – even the panties Nick had had to guess at – and everything of the finest quality from the very top designers. Angela knew that if Julia was here right now she'd be squealing in delight over everything, while her twin Lauren would be shaking her head in dismay and saying something caustic along the lines of "you're actually going to let a guy dress you up like some sort of sex toy?"

But while the outfit laid out in front of her certainly shrieked sexy siren, it was also classy and sophisticated, and were certainly the nicest things she'd ever been given to wear.

The black jersey dress looked conservative from the front, with its long, tight-fitting sleeves and boat neck, discounting, of course, the short, narrow hem. But the low, plunging back instantly transformed the dress from demure to daring. It would be impossible to wear a bra with such a dress, and she wasn't in the least surprised to discover that particular item of clothing had not been included in the box. In fact, the only article of lingerie was a pair of sheer black lace Agent Provocateur panties that to her mind were nearly as skimpy as the thong that Nick had professed a dislike for. But she knew from shopping trips with Julia that this single pair of undies had likely cost over a hundred dollars – the same price she would have normally been able to buy a dozen pair for.

Angela typically shied away from very high heels – her nearly six feet of height already cause for extreme self-consciousness. But Nick would still have a few inches on her, even when she donned the black suede Prada sandals with their sexy ankle strap and the buckle detail across the forefoot.

There were three other items in the box that had been delivered from Barneys – a small black Fendi clutch, a gorgeous pair of gold and diamond drop earrings, and a tube of Nars lipstick in a vivid crimson shade.

Angela wished Julia was here instead of back in Manhattan where she'd moved after college. Her fashionista friend would be able to add up in her pretty little head in a few seconds how much all of this stuff had cost. But Angela had a fairly good idea herself, and was aghast at how much Nick had casually dropped on an outfit for her to wear out to dinner.

As she stripped off her work clothes and headed for the shower, Angela tried – really tried – to feel some level of annoyance or anger or another suitable emotion at the very high handed way Nick was arranging everything. After not hearing a word from him for days, he had called without warning and informed – not asked – her that they were having dinner tonight. It was the same – worse, actually – with the dress and shoes.

And even a lipstick, for God's sake, she thought wildly as she began to wash her hair. She'd never worn red on her lips before, had always considered her mouth too wide and full for such a bold shade. She wondered a little defiantly what Nick would do if she wore a different color. He was strong-willed enough, she feared, that he'd make her wipe it off and reapply the lipstick he'd sent.

She waited until practically the last minute before actually applying the lipstick. Everything else was done – the dress that bared her entire back and most of her legs had been pulled and tugged into place; the sexy stilettos were buckled around her bare ankles – no stockings tonight, apparently. She'd fastened the earrings into her pierced lobes, stuffed a few necessities into her new clutch. Her long, straight hair shone with the application of clear glaze she'd applied, and the rest of her makeup had been artfully applied.

The lipstick was her one holdout, and she kept glancing back and forth between the sultry fire-engine red and the more subtle berry shade she normally favored. Should she acquiesce to one more of Nick's demands, or defy him by wearing the color she preferred?

It was the buzzing of the outside doorbell that jerked her out of her contemplation, and even as she was depressing the buzzer to admit Nick into the building she was hastily slicking the red gloss over her mouth before dropping the tube into her clutch.

Angela took a deep breath before rather slowly opening the door, and then gasped as Nick's intimidatingly huge body filled the door frame. He looked – like the devil, she thought helplessly. Like the sexiest, most tempting, and most irresistible devil one could ever conjure up. He wore another superbly tailored suit – this one of solid black – paired with a dark gray shirt and a black and gray striped tie. With his raven hair, dark eyes, and deeply tanned skin, the almost satanic image he projected made her feel like swooning.

And from the wide, knowing smile on his face, he apparently liked what he saw, too – his sharp gaze taking in every detail about her appearance, from the top of her silky head down the long, long length of her legs to those fuck-me stilettos on her feet.

"I knew that you'd look like this," he told her confidently. His long fingers gripped her chin, tilting her head from one side to the other. "That dress could have been made for you, those shoes are practically screaming sex, and that mouth of yours – I think I'll nearly always want you in red lipstick when we're together."

She felt her cheeks grow warm beneath his regard. "Thank you – for all of this. Everything is gorgeous, but you shouldn't have spent so much money on me."

He shrugged carelessly. "Why not? I wanted you to have a particular look tonight so the best way of ensuring that was to hand pick the outfit. Including the undies. I take it they fit okay?"

Angela was flabbergasted at the forthright way he demanded answers. "Uh, yes. Just fine."

"Pity. I was almost hoping they'd been the wrong size so you would have had to go commando. After all," he added in a husky voice, "it would be so damned easy to just cop a feel while you're wearing this dress, wouldn't it?"

Without warning, he banded an arm around her waist and hauled her against him, at the same time inserting his hand into the low back of her dress and sliding it down to fondle her buttocks.

"Next time," he murmured in her ear.

Before she had a chance to respond, he was taking her key and locking the door, then dropped the key into his own pocket. As usual, she wasn't given the opportunity to protest his high-handed behavior as he grabbed her hand and tugged her along in his wake, taking the stairs so briskly she was half-afraid she'd stumble and twist her ankle in the high heels she wasn't quite used to.

Expecting to see the scarlet Ferrari, she was surprised when Nick led her instead to a much more conservative silver gray Jaguar.

"Do you collect cars or something?" she asked half-jokingly as he opened the passenger door.

Nick smirked. "I don't know if collect is the right word. Besides the Jag here and the Ferrari, I have an SUV and a classic

Corvette – a 1963 with the split-back window. Now my friend Dante, he's what you'd call a collector. Last count I think he had more than a dozen."

"Wow." She shook her head in disbelief as she eased herself into the car. The tight fitting dress slid even higher up her thighs, almost to the crotch, and Nick's eyes gleamed at the sight.

"Yeah, definitely commando next time, Angel," he told her with a wink. "The only sight more erotic than these long, gorgeous legs would be your bare, pretty pussy."

She gasped as he ran a hand up her leg from the knee to the very top of her thigh, his knuckles brushing over the crotch of her new panties. Panties, she realized with a gulp, that were already wet.

Nick drove across the city with an almost careless skill, somehow knowing the best route to take to avoid the worst of the evening traffic. She was puzzled as he pulled up in front of an elegant, multi-storied, Georgian-style mansion that had no visible signage.

"This is a restaurant?"

He shook his head at her question. "Not exactly. It's a private club – a very discreet, exclusive club – that happens to have an excellent dining room for its members. Come on, you'll enjoy it. Some of the best food you'll ever eat."

Nick got out of the car as the valet assisted Angela, and then they were walking inside the most beautifully appointed, discreetly extravagant building she'd ever seen. The doorman and the receptionist both knew Nick by name, calling him "Mr. Manning" in awed, almost respectful tones.

He ushered her over to the elevators, his hand on the small of her back. His fingers seemed to be burning an imprint into her bare skin and she couldn't help the little frisson of excitement that rippled through her.

He smiled down at her knowingly. "Cold, Angel?"

She shook her head slowly. "Not in the least."

As they stepped inside the elevator, Nick bent his head to murmur in her ear, "No, I agree. You're hot as hell, Angel. I haven't been able to stop thinking about you since Tuesday night. And that's not something I ever tell a woman."

Angela smiled up at him. "I'm flattered then. And the feeling is mutual. I've thought about you a lot, too."

"Have you?" His hand slid from her back to clasp her hand in his. "And yet you didn't try to get in touch with me to let me know how you felt."

Her spine stiffened in alarm at the somewhat sarcastic tone of his voice. "I wasn't under the impression that you expected me to," she replied carefully. "And from the little I know of you I just assumed you're the sort of guy who prefers to make the moves."

Nick gave her hand a squeeze. "You assumed right, Angel," he replied gently. "And you're one of the very, very few women I've known who's both realized and respected that. I can't tell you the number of others who've pestered me with phone calls or texts or who just happened to be in the neighborhood where we'd be sure to run into each other."

She shrugged. "Not that I would have tried contacting you anyway, but you never gave me a phone number or email address."

"When there's a will there's a way, Angel. You do know where I work and how to contact me there. You could have easily obtained my extension from the employee directory, or just stopped by my office."

"No." She shook her head. "You've made it very clear that you like to keep your private life private, so there's no way I would have done something like that. Besides, you told me you'd call and whatever else you might be it isn't a lying dickwad."

Nick gave a shout of laughter. "Never forget that, Angel. Honesty always, that's my motto. And," he added in a low voice. "the fact that you didn't make any attempt to contact me is one of the reasons I *did* call you again."

Angela arched a brow at him. "Oh? And what exactly would the other reasons be?"

He whispered to her. "I still need to fuck you with these incredible legs wrapped around my neck. Soon, Angel, very, very soon. And you'll wear those fuck-me shoes while I'm doing it. If not this particular pair then another."

Once more she was left with her jaw dropping open, but seemingly lacking the inability to utter a coherent response. Still holding hands, they walked off the elevator directly to the hostess stand where a slim, exquisitely dainty Asian woman greeted Nick by name.

"A pleasure to have you dining with us this evening, Mr. Manning," she told him, her accent vaguely British. "Please follow me to your table. It's the one you requested, sir."

Angela thought of asking him why he'd reserved a particular table, then thought better of the idea. She was fairly certain Nick wouldn't like being questioned too often, and she realized that even this early on in their – relationship? acquaintance? – that she'd need to carefully pick and choose her battles.

The petite hostess – who made Angela feel like a brawny Amazon in comparison – led them smoothly through the dimly lit, dark wood paneled dining room. From her peripheral vision she caught glimpses of other couples or small groups seated around tables or booths, and at first glance everyone seemed to be exceptionally well dressed. The whole place was giving off a vibe of old money – lots of it – and she was glad now that Nick had sent her the dress and shoes. She had some nice things of her own, of course, but nothing even in the neighborhood of what she was wearing tonight.

They were ushered to a high-backed, very secluded booth with thickly padded brown leather seats. Located in a corner of the spacious dining room, the booth would afford them the privacy she sensed Nick insisted on having wherever he went.

The smooth leather was cool against the backs of her bare legs, and she couldn't help shivering just a bit as she sat down. A busboy appeared almost immediately to fill water glasses and set out a basket of assorted rolls and breadsticks.

"So what do you think?"

She looked at Nick and blinked. "About what?"

"The club. The dining room. What's your first impression?"

Angela took a sip of the ice cold water, wondering briefly if she ought to couch the truth, but then decided to throw caution to the wind by telling him bluntly, "It's classy and expensive but it's also stuffy as hell.   Someplace you'd expect to see your grandparents eating at."

Nick chuckled. "I knew you wouldn't bullshit me, Angel. The women I've brought here in the past have all oohed and ahhed about it, probably because they knew how exclusive the place is. But not you. And you're right, it's the epitome of class but not exactly the most happening place in town."

"So why do you come here?"

His answer was succinct. "Privacy. No one here would dare to gossip about who they saw at dinner or an event. The staff has to sign all sorts of non-disclosure agreements, and there's something of an unspoken pact among the members to mind their own business."

She couldn't resist teasing him a bit. "So what you're saying is that what happens in – uh, whatever the name of this club is – stays here? Though, honestly, I can't imagine anything too controversial or even exciting going on."

He smirked. "Exactly. And this is the Biltmore Club. Very, very elite, extremely expensive to join, and nearly impossible to gain admittance to."

"Hmm. So how did you get in? Was it because you were a former football player or is it your current position at Jessup Prior?"

A closed-off expression crossed Nick's features, his mouth tightening in displeasure. "Neither one. I got admitted here courtesy of a family member. My father, to be exact. And before you ask, I don't discuss my family. Ever."

"I wasn't going to ask," she whispered, more than a little intimidated by the dark look on his face. "But it seems that we have one more thing in common, though. I really don't like discussing my family, either."

She could sense he was about to ignore her statement and start asking her about them anyway when he was interrupted by the arrival of their waiter. Like the hostess had done, he greeted Nick by name before handing them menus and asking for their drink order.

"Absolut Citron on the rocks. Make that two."

Angela waited until the waiter left before daring to frown at Nick. "Aren't you making assumptions here? What if I'd wanted something different tonight?"

"Did you?" he asked casually, reaching for a roll and starting to butter it.

She gave a little huff. "Well, no. At least I don't think so. But it might have been nice if you had thought to ask first."

He gave a careless shrug. "I'm rarely nice, Angel. And you told me the other night that was your drink of choice so I just took the initiative and ordered. But if you really want something else, I'll get it for you. Easiest thing in the world."

She shook her head. "No, it's fine. I just – well, I'm not used to someone taking charge the way you do."

"Yeah, I sort of get that feeling. But you secretly want someone to do just that, don't you, Angel? "

Her gaze flew up to his in alarm. "What?"

Nicked chewed on his roll slowly. "You heard me just fine. And you know it's true. You might deny it, most people would, but deep down you know you actually like it when I get bossy. Were your parents strict with you?"

"No." The reply slipped out automatically. "Not in the least."

"Hmm." He finished the roll and picked up a long, thin breadstick, tapping one end on the table before taking a bite. "So you were a spoiled, indulged little brat then?"

"I wouldn't say that either. In a nutshell, my parents – mostly my mother – just didn't give a rat's ass about me. I was – an accident, one that my mother rarely failed to remind me about."

She was saved from further questioning by the arrival of their drinks, which she suddenly felt in dire need of. She took an ungainly gulp and then promptly opened up the leather bound menu, very intentionally hiding her face from Nick.

"We won't talk about it again tonight," he told her quietly. "I can already tell it isn't your favorite topic of conversation. But we will have a conversation about it one of these days, Angel. Now, what looks good to you on the menu? I can recommend a number of things, especially the sea bass or the pan seared scallops."

She wrinkled her nose. "I'm not a big fish eater actually."

She didn't add that her distaste stemmed from childhood memories of watching her father gutting and cleaning some freshly caught fish, and her mother cooking it up with garlic, tomatoes and olive oil before rather resentfully plunking a plate in front of her, not especially caring if the strong taste was appealing to a five year old's picky palate.

"You're something of a fussy eater, aren't you? I could tell the other night by the way you pushed the food around on your plate. You know, you'll never gain those ten pounds I mentioned if you keep doing that. Here, I want you to eat one of these rolls – with butter – and then humor me by letting me order for you tonight, okay? I promise if you don't like what I choose you can get something else."

Reluctantly she selected a roll and began to spread butter over it. "Fine. But nothing too fishy tasting." She swallowed a bite of bread before glaring at him sulkily. "And I don't really agree about the ten pounds. I've always been a little on the slender side but it's not like I'm skinny or anorexic looking."

Nick set the menus aside and regarded her carefully, as though he was mentally stripping off her dress down to the bare flesh he was already very familiar with. "You're not skinny, I'll agree with that. But you are too thin. For someone of your height, you should be more like a size six instead of a four. Those ten pounds will fill you out a little in all the right places."

And it seemed as though he was intent on having her gain nearly half that number of pounds in one sitting, judging by the meal he ordered up. They dined on lobster bisque, a huge wedge salad, and the pan seared scallops with rice pilaf and sautéed vegetables, all accompanied by a crisp Chardonnay. She was conscious throughout the entire meal of Nick's watchful gaze, making sure she didn't push her food around, and that she ate what he considered an adequate amount.

They didn't talk much during dinner, and when they did it was mostly small talk about such mundane topics as an economics professor they'd both taken class from at Stanford, or the 49ers chances this season of making the playoffs, or Nick quizzing her in more detail about her Olympic experience.

She had nearly cleaned her plate before setting her fork down with a sigh. "I can't eat another bite. The scallops were delicious but I'm really getting stuffed."

He eyed her mostly empty plate assessingly. "All right. That's enough for now. After all, there's still dessert."

Angela stifled the little groan she longed to make, her flat belly already starting to bloat up a bit from the rich meal she'd just consumed. But Nick was ruthless, ordering her some mile-high concoction of chocolate cake layered with mousse, ganache, and whipped cream, plus a frothy cappuccino served in a cup the size of a soup bowl.

She could only stare at the monstrous piece of cake. "I don't even know where to start."

Nick grinned, already digging into his own bowl of apple cobbler. She had noticed that his appetite for food was just as big as it was for sex, and she guessed that a man of his height and weight would need to consume several thousand calories a day.

"Take your time, Angel. We've got this table reserved for the entire evening so there's no rush."

She took a bite of the fabulously rich dessert and almost sighed with bliss at how delicious it was. "This is amazing. I'm still not sure how much of it I can actually eat but I'll give it the old college try. And why," she added with a little frown, "is the table reserved for the whole evening? There is *no* way I can eat anything else after this."

"No worries on that count. After all, we can't have you getting sick, can we? No," he continued calmly, "the reason I asked to have the table all evening was so we could talk. And we'll be assured of our privacy here. "

"Okay." Her senses immediately went on high alert, not at all sure what he really meant by "talk" or exactly what he planned to discuss.

He sipped his coffee leisurely. "You're not going to ask what I want to talk about?"

She pushed another forkful of cake/mousse/ganache into her mouth and shook her head. "No. Because I've got this feeling it wouldn't do me any good. You'll tell me when you're ready."

He clapped his hands together lightly in mock applause.

"Very good, Angel. You catch on quickly. Yes, I have a real good feeling about this. Glad I trusted my instincts with you. So, you finish at least half that cake and then we'll talk. Or at least *I* will. You're going to listen – very, very carefully – and when I'm done you can ask questions. Sound good?"

She nodded, already eating another bite of dessert. And even though her stomach was beginning to protest having more food crammed inside of it, she continued to dutifully pick away at the cake, barely tasting it now but anxious to eat enough to satisfy Nick so that he could tell her – what?

Angela tried hard not to make assumptions while she kept working on her dessert. If Nick didn't plan on seeing her again after tonight, he would have zero compunctions about coming right out and telling her, so she honestly didn't think it was that. But what else –

"Okay. I think that's enough dessert if you're full. Would you like to have the rest wrapped up so you can take it home?"

She shuddered as she pushed the plate away. "No, thank you. I don't think I'll be able to eat again for a couple of days."

"Ah, but that's where you're wrong, Angel. You *will* eat tomorrow, and every day after that. You seem to get full rather quickly, so it will have to be small, frequent meals, but healthy ones, too. I'll have you draw up a meal plan with a nutritionist I know of. And work with a personal trainer as well."

"Huh?" She stared at him in bemusement.

"Guess I'm getting ahead of myself a bit. Let me start at the beginning, all right? And pay attention, because there's going to be a lot of shit for you to consider. Here goes."

Nick took another drink of his coffee before setting the cup down and reaching across the table for her hand. All hint of teasing or laughter was gone from his expression, his eyes dark and deadly serious.

"As you probably gleaned from overhearing all the lousy office gossip I despise so much, I don't do relationships," he began. "For me to even date the same woman more than two or three times is extremely rare. And that isn't because I enjoy having a reputation as a player or because I go out of my way to avoid any sort of commitment. It's largely because I find it very, very difficult to meet a woman I feel will suit my needs. And I'm not talking strictly about sexual needs here. It's far more about my need for control – total and absolute control of everything. And I can almost always tell – from the very beginning – if I think a woman has any chance whatsoever of fulfilling that need. In the past eight years or so, I've met less than a handful I considered even worth taking a chance on. And I strongly believe that you, Angel, are exactly what I'm looking for."

He was briefly interrupted by the busboy who refilled his coffee cup, leaving Angela to stare across the table at him in complete bemusement, not at all sure where he was going with all this.

Nick smiled briefly. "Ah, I can tell you already want to start asking questions. But bear with me, Angel, hmm? I'm really just getting warmed up here. First, let me tell you that the other women I tried to form this sort of relationship with – three, to be exact – didn't last very long at all. Two of them less than a month while the third stuck it out for nearly two months. And that was almost three years ago. I'd almost given up hope of ever finding someone else when I met you on Tuesday. And I just had this feeling about you, right from the beginning, even before we'd spoken one word to each other, that you'd be perfect, that you'd last much longer than any of the others. That you," he lowered his voice huskily, "would obey."

She gulped, hastily reaching for her cappuccino even though it had already turned lukewarm, and took a long drink anyway. "Obey? But I thought you said - "

"I said I wasn't into any kinky BDSM shit and I meant it," he insisted. "Inflicting pain or doling out punishments does nothing for me. Not that I've ever tried that stuff, mind you, but just the thought turns me off big time. But I also told you, Angel, that there were different kinds of submission. Mine doesn't involve you calling me Master or wearing a collar or not allowing you to look at me without permission. That kind of thing is completely fucked up in my book. No, my reasons for wanting control don't have anything to do with boosting my ego or satisfying some pent-up need for power. Basically, Angel, I'm just a self-centered, selfish bastard who's completely set in his ways and doesn't know the meaning of the word compromise. That's how I live my life, how I run my business, and I'm not prepared to apologize for it and definitely not willing to change my ways for anyone."

She continued to stare at him, equally repelled and mesmerized by what he was telling her. She opened her mouth to speak, only to have Nick press two fingers over her lips.

"Shush. I'm a long way from being through here," he admonished. "In fact, I've barely begun." He reached out and picked up a long, shiny strand of her hair, sifting it through his fingers. "Don't cut your hair, not unless I ask you to. Not even a trim, understand?"

Angela winced as he gave her hair a brief, sharp tug. "Um, Nick, I'm not sure you really have - "

"But I do have the right," he corrected. "Or at least I will if you agree to my terms. If you want to continue our relationship, Angel, there are many things you'll need to agree to, things you'll have to, well, obey. And your appearance is one of those, at least when you're with me. There will be times when I tell you what to wear, or send you things like I did tonight. That will probably be one of the easier conditions for you to go along with."

With each word he spoke, her unease grew and she wondered wildly if she ought to just get up and run as fast as she could in her four-inch heels, run away from this darkly compelling man who was pulling her deeper and deeper into his web with each seductively spoken word.

"Don't leave yet, Angel," he drawled in amusement. "You have that look on your face – like you're getting ready to bolt at a moment's notice. Hear me out, don't panic, and know that I won't be the least surprised if you tell me to go fuck myself at the end of it."

He released her hair and propped his elbows on the table, chin in hand as he continued. "If you decide that you want to keep seeing me, there are – conditions, rules, restrictions. Probably far too many for any sane person to agree to but let's give it a shot. First rule – the relationship is private. Completely, one hundred percent private. You don't talk to your family or friends about me, and especially not to anyone at work. You don't mention my name on social media, don't post photos of me anywhere. I value my privacy like a fiend, Angel, and if it's breached I get pissed off. Big time. So that's rule number one, and probably the most important one. Got it?"

She nodded solemnly, wondering if her eyes were as wide open as they felt.

"Okay, next rule. I'm not the sort of guy you're going to bring home to meet the parents. Or double date with your friends. Holidays, weddings, office Christmas parties – those aren't part of the deal, either. Don't ask me, don't throw hints, and don't hope that I'll have a change of heart someday."

He took a sip of coffee, ensuring he still had her full attention before continuing. "Next, I'm the one who calls all the shots. When I want to see you, I'll call or text. I decide the time and place, and it will usually be somewhere I know our privacy will be ensured. I'll give you a phone number to contact me at but it will be for emergencies only, if you have to cancel a date at the last minute. Otherwise, I call you, not the other way around. No texts, no emails, and especially no dropping by my office. I keep erratic hours at work, have a very strict schedule I stick to, and I definitely don't appreciate interruptions. But I also won't be one of those pricks who says they'll call and then don't, and I won't go more than a week without contacting you. But I'll also expect you to be available when I call, sometimes on very short notice. You getting all this, Angel?"

She gave a slight inclination of her head, feeling completely incapable of speech, totally flabbergasted at what she was hearing and unable to believe this was really happening right here, right now.

"Good. Moving on. Because of the need for privacy that I keep harping on, I'll usually prefer to make the decisions about where to go. But if there's a particular restaurant or movie you really want to see, ask. I can't promise I'll agree but at least I'll consider it. You'll get to know my likes and dislikes pretty quickly. Speaking of which."

He trailed a forefinger over her lips, which she realized were trembling in reaction.

"One place where I'm always, *always*, in charge, Angel, always the one calling the shots, is in bed. That's non-negotiable. I'll get to know your body very, very well, probably better than you'll know it, in fact. I'll teach you, show you what I like. And I'll give you the sort of pleasure that you've only fantasied about until now, and that you'll never come close to feeling with anyone else ever again."

Nick slid his finger inside her mouth, smiling when she swirled her tongue around it. "That's nice, Angel. Very nice. In fact, I'd like you to do the same thing to my cock when I slide it inside your mouth. One of the many things I'll teach you is how to relax your throat enough to take me all the way in." At her wide-eyed expression of alarm, he smiled. "Trust me, you'll do it, Angel. Now, what's next? Ah, yes."

He removed his finger. "I understand you have to dress a certain way at the office, adhere to codes and all that crap. And what you wear outside of work when we're not together, that's your business, too. But I wasn't joking before about telling you what to wear. Depending on my particular mood on a given day that could run a pretty wide gamut of different looks. Tonight, for example, I almost chose all white for you, knowing that I'd be in black, a little play on this angel/devil relationship I mentioned on Tuesday. But after I thought about all the things I needed to say to you, I reconsidered. Because if you were in white right now it would just remind me how damned young you are. And inexperienced. And that was the very last thing I needed to think about tonight."

Angela lifted her chin in a meagre attempt at defiance. "I'm not that in- "

"You are," he interrupted arrogantly. "I don't give a crap if you fucked four other guys in college. They were boys, probably morons, with no finesse and definitely no skill. Trust me, I know exactly what type I'm thinking about. Most of the guys I went to college with fit that description."

"But not you."

His eyes gleamed at her whispered observation. "No, not me. By the time I was seventeen I knew pretty much everything I needed to know about sex. It was just a matter of getting in plenty of practice after that."

She squirmed a bit, feeling her bare thighs sticking to the leather seat, and trying very hard not to start mentally calculating just how many women Nick had practiced with over the years.

"But we're getting off the subject now, Angel. As I was saying, I'll want you to wear certain clothes, create a particular image, most if not all of the times we see each other. We'll go through your wardrobe together, see if you own anything that meets my approval, something I'm doubting will be the case. So you can expect to start receiving lots of packages from me, and get dragged along on some shopping trips."

"I can afford - " she began hesitantly.

"No, you can't." he stated bluntly. "Not on the crap salary I know you're getting paid. That outfit you're wearing now – not even counting the earrings – would be a couple of months' worth of paychecks for you. So you'll accept what I give you, wear what I choose. And none of this garbage about how that makes you a kept woman or some other bullshit. Keep in mind that I'll be buying you things that will be for my pleasure, and not necessarily yours. It'll be the same with your hair, makeup, jewelry. After a while you'll get a better idea of what I like and expect so I might not have to dictate to you all the time."

She shook her head, thinking wildly that this was sounding more and more like some crazy, bizarre dream she was going to wake up from at any moment. What other possible explanation could there be for why she was still sitting here listening to this man – this undeniably hot, incredibly powerful, but possibly insane man – listing all of the ways he planned to control her, the unreasonable demands he would make of her, and taking for granted that he had every right to do so.

"Ah, don't shake your head that way, Angel," he chided. "Remember I asked you to reserve judgment until you'd listened to everything I had to say? I'm almost finished now, so indulge me for a few more minutes, hmm? Then you can tell me to go screw myself if that's what you decide."

Angela hesitated before giving a short, sullen nod. He took one of her hands back in his, stroking his thumb over her knuckles soothingly.

"Your hands are always so warm," he murmured. "Now, one last thing. I started off this conversation by telling you that I don't do relationships, or at least not the conventional kind. I don't believe in marriage or falling in love or even having a long term relationship. I won't sleep over, and we go to your place or a hotel or sometimes away for the weekend, but never to my house. And when I decide it's over, Angel, then it's over. No regrets, no tears or angry scenes, no post-relationship stalking." He released her hand and lounged back leisurely against the high-backed booth. "Now, are you ready to tell me to shove all this up my ass or do you have any questions?"

She swallowed with some difficulty. "I think – I need a drink," she croaked hoarsely.

"Of course." He motioned their waiter over and ordered two glasses of port, raising a brow at her inquisitively "That sound okay to you?"

She nodded, secretly pleased that he'd bothered to ask this time. She forced herself not to glance across the table at Nick, her thoughts tumbling over and around in her head at a dizzying speed, more confused and distraught than she had ever felt before. She didn't need the added complication of staring into his hypnotic eyes or studying his arrestingly handsome face.

The waiter arrived with their port and she drank half of hers down in one gulp, ignoring Nick's frown of disapproval. The silence continued to stretch between them, but she knew he'd said everything he intended to, and that the ball was now squarely in her court.

"Two questions." Her voice was less raspy but still whisper soft. She lifted her gaze to his, relieved to notice he was looking at her impassively and not trying to seduce her into agreeing with his eyes and smile.

He gave a short nod. "Ask as many questions as you like. So long as they concern the – ah, conditions. One other thing I didn't mention before – no personal questions. If I think you need to know something, or feel like sharing information, then I will. Otherwise, don't pry."

"Yeah, I sort of figured that would be the case," she replied wearily. "But relax. The two questions do concern the – conditions, as you call them. First, can I assume that this relationship will be – well, that for as long as it lasts there won't be anyone else? For either of us?"

Nick took a slow sip of his port. "Do I look like a man who likes to share, Angel? I don't let anyone sleep over at my house or drive my cars or even borrow a book. So you can be damned sure that I'll be the only man fucking you while we're together."

Angela bit her bottom lip uncertainly. "I just assumed that. And, well, I couldn't do something like that anyway – sleep with two different men at the same time. *You* were the one I was really asking about. I mean, I realize you'll be calling all the shots but I just – I couldn't do it if you were with - "

"Relax, Angela." His voice was uncharacteristically gentle, his use of her full name letting her know how serious he was. "I'm ten different kinds of a bastard but I've never cheated on a woman in my life. For as long as it lasts, you'll be the only woman in my life. What's your other question?"

She fidgeted a bit, not quite sure how to phrase it. "You've told me about all your conditions, all your rules, and it's pretty obvious that this would be a mostly one-sided relationship. So my second question is – what would I get out of this? What in the world would compel me to agree to something this crazy?"

He picked up her hand again, entwining their fingers as he smiled at her wickedly. "You already know the answer to that question, Angel. You get me. And you've already experienced how explosive we are together, how good I can make you feel." He brought her hand to his lips. "I've barely begun to teach you everything I want you to learn, or to show you just what this beautiful, sexy body of yours is capable of feeling. In other words, Angel, what you get out of this is as much mind blowing, earth shattering sex as you can handle. Does that sound like a fair exchange to you?"

Angela closed her eyes, far too overwhelmed with everything

he'd thrown at her tonight to even begin to think clearly. "I don't know," she whispered shakily. "I do want to be with you, Nick, you know I do. But I'm not sure I can be who you want me to be."

"Angel." His big, warm hand cupped her cheek tenderly. "Don't you know? You already are that person. I knew it within the first few minutes of our meeting, knew that your need to be controlled, to have rules imposed on you, was every bit as great as my need to do the controlling. But I don't expect your answer tonight. I wouldn't accept it this soon, anyway, no matter what it was. You need time to think everything over, to consider all the conditions, and then decide if you want to give it a shot."

"How much time?"

He shrugged. "What sounds reasonable to you? A few days? A week? More? Less?"

She slid her hand over his, needing the physical contact badly. "Less. I can let you know by tomorrow."

"All right, then. If you're sure, this is how it will happen. You take tonight and all day tomorrow to consider everything we've discussed. In the meanwhile, I'm going to have another package delivered to you, along with instructions about when and where to meet me. If you decide to accept my offer, you meet me at the designated time and place. And if you don't show up, that will be your way of telling me to fuck off and we both forget this ever happened and move on. Sound reasonable?"

"Yes. That's – I'll know by then."

"Good. I like a decisive woman. Another thing that drew me to you. Now, no more discussion about this tonight. I'm going to settle up the bill and take you back to your place, where I'm going to leave you – alone – to start thinking this over."

She stared at him in surprise. "But, aren't you – I mean, I thought - "

"No sex. Not tonight. Oh, I had every intention of fucking you senseless again, Angel, especially when I saw how you looked in that dress and those shoes. But I've changed my mind. You need to make this decision without any additional influence, so I'm willing to wait. So let's get you home so you can have plenty of time to sleep on all this.

But as Nick took care of the bill and then guided her outside to his waiting car, Angela knew she'd get precious little sleep tonight, no matter what her decision wound up being.

Chapter Six

She stood on the sidewalk for a full five minutes after the cab let her out, still not sure why she was here and certainly lacking the nerve to walk inside. She ignored the curious, interested stares from the people who passed by, especially the men's, as she continued to wage a fierce internal struggle with the decision she needed to make within the next few minutes. Because if she did decide to listen to the bold, impulsive side of her nature and go through the door, she didn't dare be late. And if she chose instead to run for the hills and try to forget any of this had ever happened, thereby giving in to her practical, sensible side, then that also needed to happen very quickly before she saw him and began this mental debate all over again.

And even though she'd been cautioned not to discuss the situation with anyone, she'd taken out her cell phone half a dozen times over the last twenty-odd hours, her finger poised on the speed dial button for her best friend Lauren. She'd told herself that Lauren didn't have to know names or all of the specifics – just the basics, enough to help her make this decision. But she knew that wasn't a realistic assumption, for Lauren McKinnon was rather like a bulldog at times – or was that a pitbull? – when it came to digging up information. She'd joked with her girlhood friend more than once that Lauren should have pursued a career in investigative journalism instead of photography, for she had the tenacity and boldness needed to succeed in such a demanding profession.

But even if she hadn't belatedly remembered that Lauren was currently half a world away on one of her very first assignments with National Geographic – somewhere in Malaysia – she knew she'd be too chicken to actually put the call through. For one thing, there was no way Lauren would have been able to remain impartial, would have told her flat out how insane this idea was, and that she'd be a complete idiot to even consider it. And then there was the matter of disobeying his orders. Somehow, she wasn't at all sure how, but she'd been terrified that he'd find out, that he had ways of discovering such things, and would be very, very angry that she'd so blatantly disregarded his cardinal rule.

So she'd spent a largely sleepless night instead, going over everything she'd been told so many times that her head had ached by the time she'd finally fallen into an exhausted, troubled slumber. Upon waking, she'd forced herself out for a five mile run, hoping that the exercise would clear her mind, but fearing that such a hope was futile. After showering and forcing down a bowl of cereal, she'd made the weekly, perfunctory call home that both she and her mother dreaded, but still put themselves through out of some twisted sense of obligation.

And then she'd been alone with her thoughts for hours, pacing back and forth along the narrow length of her apartment, even going so far as to make a list of the pros and cons, only to tear the stupid list up when she saw just how unbalanced the two sides were.

The arrival of the package – this one from Neiman Marcus – only served to confuse her further. A sheet of paper rested on top of the tissue, and was short and to the point, written in the bold script she was already familiar with. The name and address of a restaurant was included, along with the meeting time of 8:00pm. Nothing else, not one single word that might try and persuade – or dissuade – her one way or the other.

Tonight's outfit was white, though in her opinion the color was the only thing the least bit virginal about it. The Herve Leger bandage dress was V-necked and sleeveless, and she already knew the fabric would cling tightly to every curve of her body. The shoes were Christian Louboutin – towering white snakeskin stilettos with their signature red sole. A white leather Coach clutch made up the rest of the outfit. No underwear at all, not even a tiny pair of panties this time, and she'd been grateful to note that the dress was fully lined. The Dior lipstick that had been included was of a pale, virginal pink, a world apart from the brazen red from last night.

There had been one other item, wrapped separately in its own box, and her hand had shook while opening the lid. Inside rested a necklace, a simple gold choker that she still knew must have cost a tidy sum, and that, in her mind, greatly resembled a collar. It was his way, no doubt, of asserting his ownership of her, his mastery, even though he'd told her he didn't expect to be addressed by that particular title. By wearing this necklace tonight, it would be an acknowledgement that she was agreeing to all of his conditions – that she was ready and eager to obey him.

She'd procrastinated until there was just enough time left to dress and catch a cab, and even as she applied her makeup, zipped up the dress, stepped into the shoes, she still didn't know what her decision would be. She applied the shell pink lipstick, dropped it into her clutch, and picked up the necklace. She couldn't help flinching as she fastened it, the metal cold against her skin, and then stared at herself in the mirror for an unknown length of time. She looked – expensive, like the pampered, indulged mistress of a very rich, powerful man, and it occurred to her that was exactly what she would be if she went through with this. She'd be showered with clothes and jewelry like these, be taken out to five-star restaurants and fed the very best foods and wines, perhaps be whisked away on indulgent weekend trips to locations she couldn't even imagine right now. The sex would be frequent and demanding, and oh, so incredible, and she quivered in anticipation at the mere idea.

But what would the price be for all of that? Her body, yes, but that she would give willingly no matter what. She wasn't the least bit afraid or hesitant to give him that. What terrified her, held her back, was the realization that what she'd really be sacrificing up was her soul. After all, wasn't a person's soul what the devil craved most of all?

Like most Italians, she'd been raised a Catholic, and had been forced into attending Sunday mass every week with her family. She'd hated it, not so much because of the service itself, but because of the hypocrisy that surrounded her there – that her mother and sisters could act like such devout Christians while inside the confines of the church only to become cold, bitter, and distant as soon as they left. It was because of her disgust with this blatant two-faced behavior that she'd stopped going to church at the age of sixteen, flatly refusing to participate any longer in what she considered a mockery of values.

But her refusal to attend mass didn't mean she had stopped praying. She'd always said a little prayer, for example, before each of her collegiate volleyball games, and prior to every final exam she'd ever taken. And right now, even though it might be considered blasphemy under the somewhat sordid circumstances, she prayed for some form of divine guidance to make the decision she now had only about three more minutes to make.

As if on cue, the streetlights switched on at that particular moment, and she took a deep breath before crossing herself briskly and striding inside the restaurant.

If Angela had harbored any chance of sneaking inside the place unobserved and thereby buying herself an extra minute or two, those hopes were quickly dashed as she stood poised at the entrance of the cocktail lounge located at the front of the restaurant. Nick was already there, larger than life, and had very obviously been watching for her. He was sitting at one of the high, raised tables, a half-empty glass in front of him. His sinfully seductive mouth curled up at the corners as he extended a hand to her while remaining seated. He was not going to make this easy for her, was forcing her to come to him of her own free will, and asserting his dominance over her at the same time. This, she knew, was now the point of no return, that with each slow, tentative step she took in his direction she was sealing her fate, agreeing to his proposal, and that once she placed her hand in his there could be no turning back.

"Your hand is shaking, Angel. Are you afraid?"

She nodded, knowing it was pointless to lie to him for he would only need to look into her eyes to see the truth. "I'm terrified."

He chuckled. "I know. I watched as you got out of that cab and waited out on the sidewalk for over five minutes. A few times I swore you were going to start running down the street, though how in hell you would have pulled that off in those shoes is beyond me." He tugged her in closer, whispering in her ear, "And I will definitely fuck you with those shoes on tonight."

Angela trembled, resting a hand on his broad shoulder to steady herself. "Oh, God. Nick – I'm not – I should go – this isn't - "

"*This* is what was meant to be, Angel," he assured her gently. "Don't be frightened, okay? And the only place you're going right now is to our table, where I've got a bottle of very expensive champagne waiting for us."

She gave a nervous little laugh. "You already ordered? Wasn't that a little presumptuous?"

"Nope, not a bit." He shook his head. "I knew you'd show up, knew you wouldn't be able to stay away."

Angela lifted her chin defiantly. "You're that sure of yourself, are you? So sure that I wouldn't be able to resist the thought of going to bed with you?"

He brought her hand to his lips with a grin. "No, Angel. Because I was positive you couldn't resist the need to be controlled. Now, let's go celebrate."

She wasn't the least surprised to find that their table was located in another darkened, private corner of the restaurant. She'd heard of this place, an elegant French bistro with a Michelin star and a weeks' long wait for reservations. Obviously the Nick Manning Effect was in full force once again, given the relative ease with which he'd managed to secure a table here.

The champagne was perfectly chilled and had a fancy French name she didn't even attempt to pronounce. But it tasted delicious and she bolted half the flute down at once, needing the liquid courage she knew it would provide.

Nick frowned, clamping his hand around her wrist hard enough to leave a bruise. "Easy there, Angel. That's not apple juice in your glass, after all. You don't guzzle pricey French champagne, you sip it, savor it."

"Sorry." She set her flute down carefully. "I'm pretty nervous, after all."

He clasped both of her hands in his, and the look on his face was actually kind, something she sensed would be a very rare occurrence. "I know you are. And I get that. This is new for you, and frankly it sort of is for me, too. We'll take this one step at a time, Angela, okay? And you won't need to get yourself tipsy or half-drunk to hasten that process along. I've noticed you like the booze, Angel, a little too much for my liking. We'll need to keep an eye on that, make sure you don't overindulge. Now, let's try this again, but slowly this time." He bent his head close to her ear, his breath sending shivers up her spine. "The same way I'll have you suck me off later tonight," he purred in a low, suggestive voice.

Her hand was trembling as she picked up her flute, careful this time to only take a small sip. "Um, I – yes, okay."

Nick chuckled. "You'll need to start getting used to me saying things like that, Angel. Especially when we're alone. I'm very direct when it comes to what I want and expect in bed. So stop looking so shell shocked because what I just said is actually pretty tame compared to some of the things I'll be telling you."

Angela was saved from thinking up a response by the arrival of their waiter. This time she didn't even blink when Nick ordered their entire meal, multiple courses, with each one sounding like it contained a thousand calories per serving. And while he ordered himself a glass of Pinot Noir to accompany his braised short ribs, she was presented with plain mineral water instead.

"Three flutes of champagne before dinner was enough," he told her. "I want you wide awake and sober when I take you to bed tonight. And eat up, Angel. We're going to be burning a lot of calories later on. Good thing tomorrow is a Sunday, because it's going to be a very, very late night."

She couldn't help giving a little gulp just before picking up a forkful of her chicken coq au vin. She'd just barely recovered from the hours long sexual marathon they'd engaged in on Tuesday, and the thought of another night of equally rough, demanding sex made her body quiver in anticipation and need, and maybe just a bit of fear, too.

Nick took a leisurely sip of his wine, smiling carnally as he observed the way she reacted to his declaration. "It'll be easier on you this time, Angel," he assured her. "The other night – it had been a while for you, hadn't it?"

She shrugged and pushed a tiny potato around with her fork

until she stilled the motion, knowing he'd disapprove. "Not since February. My classes during the final semester were incredibly tough. It seemed that all I did was go to class, study, write papers, take tests. There wasn't time for – er, dating."

He nodded in acknowledgment. "I get it. That explains why you felt so tight. Was I too rough?"

She kept her eyes downcast, not wanting to confess the truth, until he tipped her chin up to meet his gaze. Angela gulped again, knowing that she'd never, ever, be able to lie to him.

"Maybe a little," she whispered. "I was, um, pretty sore for a couple of days, had a little trouble walking."

He reached over and pressed a kiss on her cheek, a tender gesture that startled her. "I'm sorry," he told her gently. "I knew I should have shown more restraint, left you alone after the first time or two. But I wanted you too damned much, Angel. It's been a very long time since I've felt that way, you know. So forgive me, even though it was really your fault for looking so fucking sexy."

It was exactly the right thing for him to have said, she thought wildly, just what she'd needed to calm her nerves a bit and make her feel more confident about being with a man as experienced and demanding and overwhelming as Nick.

"If you didn't want me to look sexy, I could have worn one of my work suits and a pair of flats," she told him with a smirk.

He grimaced. "You mean like the outfit you had on a couple of days ago? Navy blue pant suit, low-heeled pumps, and your hair all scraped back into a bun?" He shook his head. "Not a good look for you, Angel, trust me."

She stared. "How did you know - "

"I saw you, of course. You were hurrying out of Starbucks on your way back to the office, while I was across the street heading out to lunch with a client. I made sure you didn't see me since interacting at work isn't part of our arrangement. I don't like you in pants," he told her abruptly. "New rule – when you're with me it's dresses or skirts or nothing at all. Maybe a bikini or a pair of shorts if I decide to take you away someplace warm. And none of those ugly ass flat shoes either."

She thought of protesting but belatedly realized she wasn't

permitted to do such things any longer. "Speaking of which, I didn't thank you for tonight's outfit. It's beautiful, Nick. Especially the necklace. It, um, reminds me of - "

"A collar." His fingers shot out and slipped beneath the gold choker, tugging on it. "Yes, that was the general idea. Though of course it's more symbolic than anything. I won't require you to wear it all the time, especially since you'll be getting plenty of other jewelry from me."

Angela set her fork down, relieved to notice she'd managed to eat all but a few bites of her admittedly delicious dinner. "About that. I'm really not all that comfortable with you - "

"Tough. Get used to it." His voice was stern. "I told you that there will be a certain way I want you to look, depending on my mood, and I expect you to do as I ask. And the easiest way to make sure you do that is to hand pick what I want you to wear. Jesus, most women I know wouldn't think twice about accepting expensive gifts."

She shrugged helplessly. "I guess maybe it's just going to take a little getting used to. Most of the guys I dated at Stanford expected me to pay for half of the meal even if we just went out for pizza. I've never been to even one restaurant this nice, much less three in under a week. As for the clothes and jewelry – until I started work a few weeks ago I pretty much lived in jeans or track pants and sneakers. I'm surprised I haven't tripped and broken my neck in these heels yet."

He laughed, his good humor restored. "You'll get used to them, Angel. After all, those long, gorgeous legs of yours were made to wear stilettos. Now, not surprising that your idiot college boyfriends never sprang for a nice meal but why didn't your parents? Is money an issue for them?"

She immediately felt a part of her shut down inside, like it always did when she was forced to discuss her family. "No. To both questions."

Nick trailed a long finger down the bridge of her nose, over her lips and then to her chin, which he tipped up to meet his searing gaze. "You know that's not going to be anywhere near enough to answer my questions. More details. Please."

It was on the tip of her tongue to tell him to go fuck himself, but then Angela realized that if she did so Nick would refuse to fuck *her*. Or even see her again. She sighed, already regretting the foolishness of her decision in coming here tonight, but reluctantly gave in to his demands.

"My parents are comfortably off. Not rich, definitely not mega-rich. My father was a contractor, built a bunch of multi-million dollar homes in Pebble Beach and Big Sur, including our own house in Carmel Highlands."

"Hmm." Nick finished off his wine. "So sounds like they could have easily afforded to take you to a nice restaurant once in a while. And aside from an annoying tendency you have to pick at your food – which I commend you for trying very hard to improve on this evening, by the way – you don't have atrocious table manners or anything. So why didn't your parents ever go to fancy restaurants? Especially since Carmel and Monterey are chock full of them."

She eyed his empty wine glass longingly, wondering if she could somehow lick the dredges off the bottom. If she was going to be forced to talk about her family, she would have really, really preferred to be stinking drunk first.

"I never said they didn't go to nice places. They just didn't bring me with them. Before I was old enough to stay at home alone, I got dumped off with my grandmother or an aunt or one of my sisters. Or practically anyone my mother could pawn me off on."

He gave a careless lift of his shoulders. "It's not unusual for parents to want a date night every now and then."

"Agreed. But they would go out to dinner and a movie at least once a week. Plus bridge nights, ballroom dance classes, Italian American lodge events, Junior League meetings, and probably half a dozen other groups or clubs they belonged to. Mostly my mother, though she dragged my father along most nights. Basically," she summarized, "my mother refused to let the arrival of an unplanned baby interfere with all the plans she *had* made for her life. And I never got invited out to dinner with them because I would have been an unwanted reminder of how she'd had to put her life on hold for me." She looked around the table frantically. "I really, really need a fucking drink right now."

Nick didn't argue, didn't say a word, and merely beckoned the waiter over to order two glasses of the Pinot.

"Thank you," she whispered, closing her eyes and trying desperately not to start crying. She hated talking about her cold, distant mother; hated remembering how unloved and lonely she'd always felt growing up; hated – her mother. And hated the fact that she'd always known the feeling was mutual.

"Here's your wine, Angel. Drink up."

She opened her eyes and accepted the glass, resisting the urge to bolt the whole thing down at once. Instead, she forced herself to take small, almost dainty sips.

"I'm sorry."

Angela gave a little shrug at his apology. "I'm not the first person who had a fucked up childhood. I'm not sure which of us was happier when I left for college – me or my mother."

"What about your father?"

She smiled faintly. "My dad's a sweetheart, wouldn't hurt a fly, but he's – well, not to be incredibly crude, but he's totally pussy whipped. He's tall, like me, while my mom is almost a foot shorter, but he's terrified of her, does whatever she says."

This time she did bolt the rest of her wine, shuddering as it hit her stomach. Nick quietly took the glass from her.

"No more family horror stories tonight," he declared. "I shouldn't have pushed, Angel. Especially since the last thing I want to do tonight is upset you."

"I'm just not used to talking about it," she admitted. "The only people I've ever discussed my family with are my best friends."

"The twins."

"Yes." She'd mentioned the McKinnon girls to him the other night. "They were more like sisters to me growing up than my own sisters. But that's not so surprising considering mine are so much older than I am."

Nick cocked his head. "I guess I didn't realize that. How old are they?"

"Marisa is thirty-eight, Deanna is two years younger. They

were sixteen and fourteen when I was born, and really not thrilled with the idea of having a new baby in the house. Or seeing their forty-something mother pregnant."

"And now we're talking about them again. Time to change the subject. What do you want for dessert?"

She made a little face. "Gee, you mean I actually get to choose?"

He pinched her cheek, a little too hard to be considered teasing. "Smart ass. Yes, you can choose. And speaking of your ass."

Angela gasped as one of his big, warm hands slid up beneath her tight fitting dress until it reached her bare buttocks. She was grateful for both the dark, private corner their table was situated in as well as the heavy, opaque tablecloth that hid their lower bodies from view.

"Your skin is so soft," he murmured close to her ear, his hand caressing her ass cheeks persuasively. "This is why I like the no-panty rule, so I can touch you this way whenever the urge takes me. And no matter what we might have for dessert, it won't be the sweetest thing I'm going to eat tonight."

"Ah, God." Her head fell back weakly as he slowly thrust two fingers deep inside her wetness. A whimper escaped her throat as he continued to pump his fingers in and out of her body, his thumb rubbing circles around her clit.

"I could make you come right here, Angel," he whispered seductively. "You're already close, I can tell. I could have this tight, juicy cunt convulsing around my fingers in less than a minute."

She gasped in protest as he slowly removed his fingers, only to bring them to his mouth and very deliberately lick them dry. His dark eyes were gleaming and the smile he gave her was devilish.

"But I like to savor my dessert," he purred. "To save the best for last. And you're the most delicious thing I've ever tasted. Now, have you ever had cherries jubilee? They serve it here for two and it's incredible."

Angela's whole body was quivering in reaction, having been brought tantalizingly close to orgasm, only to have it deliberately denied. Meanwhile, Nick had once again smoothly changed the subject, was even now beckoning the waiter over to order his damned cherries jubilee and coffee. He smiled at her knowingly as the waiter left to get their order.

"Something wrong, Angel? You seem a little fidgety."

She glared at him. "And whose fault is that? Couldn't you at least have finished what you started? Now I'll be - "

"Anticipating how good it's going to feel when I fuck you in less than an hour?" he asked rather matter-of-factly. "Sometimes when you have to wait for something, Angel, you appreciate it more. Not to mention we still need to do a lot of work on your control. Or, more accurately, your complete lack of it."

"I could just go into the ladies room, you know, and take care of the, ah, situation by myself," she challenged, lifting her chin bravely.

"Don't you dare." He clamped his hand around her upper arm ferociously. "One more rule I forgot to mention, Angel – you don't get to have an orgasm unless I give it to you and not until I say it's time."

"Fine." She crossed her arms across her chest sullenly and tried to ignore the throbbing between her thighs. "Tell me, how many other rules did you forget to mention last night?"

Nick gave her an unholy grin. "Oh, I'm sure there'll be plenty more. Maybe I should have just told you the truth – that I expect you to obey everything I ask of you. In fact, if I had just told you that to begin with, we could have saved ourselves a lot of time last night. Ah, here's our coffee."

Angela honestly didn't think she needed the extra stimulation the caffeine would provide, not when she was already so tightly strung that she felt like screaming. Some calming herbal tea might have been a better choice, but then she hadn't been given the opportunity to actually choose. Part of her felt like defying Nick and asking the waiter for some chamomile, but another part remembered the bit about picking and choosing her battles, and in the overall scheme of things this one was awfully small.

By the time they finished dessert and he'd paid the bill, it was over an hour later, and she was a virtual bundle of nerves by then, small wonder considering how often Nick had touched and caressed her teasingly, deliberately. His long, talented fingers had brushed over almost every inch of exposed skin on her body, and hadn't been content to stop there – sliding his hand beneath the short hem of her close-fitting dress to caress her thigh or hip or buttocks. She'd been shocked speechless when he'd leaned over her, shielding her body from anyone who might see them, and slipped his hand inside the low neck of her dress to cup her breast and rub his thumb over the nipple.

"Let's get out of here," he'd whispered after putting his credit card away. "I really, really need to fuck you, Angel. It's all I've been able to think about since I left you on Tuesday, and I'm not a man who's used to denying himself."

There was very little traffic en route to her apartment, a fortunate state of affairs since Nick drove fast enough that she couldn't stop herself from clutching the seat in fear. At one point he glanced over at her and grinned.

"Relax. I'm not about to get us killed. Or get pulled over for a speeding ticket. But I am – let's call it *anxious* – to get you upstairs. By the way, I'm going to buy you a frame for that bed of yours. Headboard and footboard. I'll let you know when it will be delivered."

"What?" She stared at him in bewilderment. "I mean, why?"

The smile he gave her was satanic. "So I can spread you out and tie you up, of course. Oh, did I forget to mention the frame will have slats? Gives us more flexibility, so to speak."

Angela was equal parts alarmed and aroused at the images his lightly teasing words invoked. "Um, you're kidding, right? Because we talked about that stuff and you said - "

"I said I wasn't into pain and punishment or humiliation," he corrected. "But there's a lot to be said for some light bondage and a blindfold once in a while."

"Define light."

Nick's laugh was wicked, maybe even crossing over the line into evilness. "Ah, interested, are we? Well, my naughty Angel, my definition of light would include silk ropes or scarves, maybe some leather cuffs – lined, of course. In other words, no chains or ropes or anything else that could chafe this beautiful skin."

He picked up her hand and drew it to his mouth, his lips caressing the tender skin of her inner wrist. "Trust me, hmm? Tying you to the bed – binding your hands and feet so you can't move, then blindfolding you – it's more than just giving me control over you. It's about you giving me your trust so that I can give you pleasure, can focus solely on you."

She closed her eyes, too overcome with everything that had happened in the last twenty-four hours to cope with even one more thing right now. "Maybe," she whispered.

He squeezed her hand reassuringly. "No rush, Angel. We'll get there. Speaking of which, here's your place."

They were barely inside her apartment, had just closed and locked the door, before Nick shoved her up against the wall almost violently, her head falling back against the hard wood surface. Almost before she could take a breath, he'd sunk to his knees and pushed her dress up above her waist, sucking her clit between his lips.

"Ah, God."

She clutched his head desperately, her pelvis thrusting frantically in sync with the hungry, ravenous motions of his lips and tongue. He thrust two long fingers as deep inside of her as he could reach, and she came instantly, convulsing around his hand uncontrollably.

Her legs were unsteady, shaking in the high heels, and she was afraid they would give out from under her at any moment. But Nick either didn't notice or didn't care, because he kept at her, this time thrusting his tongue up inside her body, his thumbs spreading the lips of her inner labia apart so he could go even deeper. The second orgasm felt twice as strong as the first, and if she hadn't been clutching handfuls of his hair like her life depended on it she would have certainly collapsed this time. She kept her eyes tightly shut, afraid she might faint otherwise from the waves of pleasure that continued to quiver through her body.

Nick took her hands in his, removing them gently from his hair. "Another minute there, Angel, and I think you would have pulled a few hunks out by the roots." His voice sounded both amused and awed as he stood, pulling her into his arms.

She flushed, her cheeks as hot as the rest of her highly stimulated flesh. "Sorry," she mumbled, burying her face against his neck as she clung to him. "I thought – I was afraid - "

"I've got you, Angel. I won't let you fall. And," he added huskily, "I was right at the restaurant, you know. You taste sweeter than any dessert in the world. See for yourself."

He kissed her long and hard, his big, hard body pressing hers into the wall, the huge, intimidating swell of his erection rubbing against her naked vulva. The musky sweet taste of her feminine juices was all over his lips and tongue, and she groaned beneath the bruising pressure of his kiss.

She gasped as he unexpectedly hoisted her over his shoulder and carried her the short distance to her bed where he dumped her onto the mattress with very little finesse. He didn't waste even a minute as he pulled the dress up and over her head, baring her body to his hot gaze.

"Even more beautiful than I remembered," he rasped as he began to undress. He took a handful of condoms from his pants pocket and left them on her bedside table. "I need to keep a box of these here. Maybe a few of them."

Angela's eyes widened as he finished stripping, his ripped, muscular body proudly naked, his cock appearing even bigger and more terrifying than it had the other night. She moistened her lips, her mouth falling open in anticipation.

"Later," he told her as he rolled a condom on. "In fact, I'm going to spend a real long time tonight teaching you how to blow me the way I like it. But for now, this is what I want, Angel. What I've wanted since the first time I saw you."

One by one he lifted her legs up and over his shoulders, her feet still shod in the towering white stilettos.

"Lock your ankles around my neck and keep them there," he ordered. "Don't move them unless I tell you to."

She could only nod, her eyes huge and her body tense as Nick slid his hands beneath her ass, angling her to his desired position.

"Easy, Angel," he soothed. "Just relax and let me in. Nice and easy now."

He took hold of his penis and began to guide it inside of her with almost maddening slowness. Still, she couldn't contain the little gasps that escaped her throat with each gradual, careful thrust, as he filled her a little more each time.

And when he was somehow – miraculously – fully sheathed, every long, throbbing inch of his cock buried inside of her – she stared up at him in wonder.

"God, that's so – " she breathed.

"Good. So fucking, incredibly good," he hissed. "I knew you'd be able to take me this deep, Angel, knew you'd be a perfect fit for me."

"Ohh, ohh." She moaned long and low as he began to increase the tempo of his thrusts, as he lifted her lower body even higher off the bed. Her moans became pants that swiftly became screams as he slammed into her with increasing boldness, the heavy weight of his balls slapping against her buttocks.

"That's it, Angel," he crooned. "That's what I want. Scream for me, let me hear how much I make you feel. Come and get fucked, baby, yeah, just like that."

Angela clutched the bedcovers desperately as he fucked her almost brutally, the broad head of his cock butting up repeatedly against the very tip of her womb, making her wonder wildly if it was possible for him to literally rip her apart. She grew dizzy, even with her eyes tightly shut, and her breathing grew more and more shallow as she frantically struggled for air.

"Open your eyes, Angel. Watch me."

Her eyes flew open at the commanding tone of his voice, already so deeply under his spell that she couldn't even begin to fight it off. His dark eyes were like a burning thing, scorching her with their intensity, and his skin was darkly flushed beneath his tan. They were the only signs that he was beginning to lose control, that he was every bit as swept away by their shared passion as she was.

And it was this realization – that she could make him feel as much as she did – that brought her over the edge, that triggered the spasms that racked her lower body as she came and came and came.

"That's it, baby. I love feeling that tight, juicy cunt of yours squeezing my cock, love feeling you come around me so hard.

Yes, just like that, that's my girl."

With the added stimulation of his dirty talk, Angela not only plummeted over the edge but kept falling and falling, falling so far down that she feared she'd never stop, or that the tremors that racked her body would keep on going until she passed out – or died – from the pleasure.

And she knew then, even as Nick was finding his own release, his head thrown back as he shouted his pleasure, that while she'd been falling into bliss she'd also been falling in love at the exact same time. The realization filled her with mingled joy and terror – joy because she'd never, ever come close to feeling this way before, and terror because she'd already broken one of the most important rules she'd promised to obey. She was grateful that she had just enough presence of mind to keep her emotions bottled up, and that instead of whispering her true feelings the only words that escaped her lips were, "That – that was incredible, Nick."

He nuzzled his face into the side of her neck, his body still joined with hers, both of them hot and sweaty from their primal mating. "That it was, Angel," he whispered back. "And that was just the warm-up."

She winced as he slowly withdrew, his cock still semi-hard. "I, ah, might need a little while to recover. You, um, sort of have this way of overwhelming a girl."

Nick grinned and dropped a quick kiss on her lips. "No problem, Angel. Because while you're recovering, I've got another way to keep you busy. Wait here a minute."

He disappeared briefly into the bathroom to dispose of the condom and clean himself up before re-emerging with a dampened towel. As he sat down on the bed beside her, she couldn't resist running her hands up and down his arms and shoulders, across his chest, marveling at how hot his skin was, how hard his muscles were.

"God, you're a beautiful man," she murmured in awe. "Is it all right for me to, well, touch you? I know you said that you always like to be in charge but - "

He captured one of her hands in his, but rather than pull it away he merely stroked it further down his chest to the chiseled planes of his abdomen. "It's more than all right, Angel," he rasped. "You can touch me as much as you want. I might like to control what position we're in, but the only times you can't touch me will be when I decide to bind you. Here, let me."

He'd rinsed the washcloth in hot water, and the heat felt blissful and soothing as he gently sponged her off. Nick tossed the cloth to the side as he laid back against the pillows.

"Come here," he beckoned. "Time for your lessons to commence."

And his teachings were extremely detailed, his particular preferences very carefully imparted, as he told her exactly how he liked to have his cock sucked. She was in awe at the control he could exert over his body, even after she'd been sucking, licking, stroking him for nearly an hour. He was hard as marble, his erection long and thick and throbbing, the broad head so dark a red it almost looked purple. At his hoarsely muttered instructions, she learned how to relax her throat enough to take almost all of him inside her mouth without gagging; to run her tongue up and down the length of him, sometimes slowly, other times with rapid flicks; how to draw just the tip between her lips and then thrust her tongue into the slit. At one point he took her hand in his, bringing it to his hugely swollen balls, and taught her precisely how to fondle them, what the right amount of pressure to apply was. His hand covered hers as she stroked him from tip to root, showing her the motion until she learned it to his satisfaction.

And then his iron control finally shattered, as his breathing became unsteady and his lower body began to buck up off the bed with each pull of her lips or stroke of her hand.

"Finish me off now, Angel," he commanded hoarsely. "Take me inside that sexy mouth and show me everything you've learned tonight."

Eager to please him, to prove what an apt pupil she was, she did exactly as he bid, her mouth and jaw working frantically as she bobbed her head up and down along his cock. Nick's hands grabbed fistfuls of her long hair, pulling on it painfully as she continued to focus diligently on pleasuring him, on bringing him over the edge. She lost herself in her efforts, using her hands, lips, tongue, mouth to coax him into orgasm, the blood roaring in her ears as she focused entirely on giving him pleasure. She barely heard the short, guttural curse he uttered before his hands clamped down firmly, holding her head in place as he emptied himself into her mouth, flooding her with hot, sticky bursts of cum, far more than she could swallow at once. Nick gave one final shudder, one last bellow as he finished, his torso flopping back limply onto the bed.

Still focused on pleasing him, she licked him up and down like a little cat, cleaning away every last bit of semen from his body, until his grasped her chin, tilting it up to meet his gaze.

"Enough, Angel," he said firmly. "I think you've sucked – and licked – me completely dry. Now, come here."

He hauled her up alongside him, wrapping her up close against his body, and she gloried in the feel of his hot, damp skin next to her. He kissed her then, a long, deep kiss, his tongue tasting the saltiness of his cum that still lingered in her mouth, much as she'd tasted her own musky essence against his lips earlier.

Nick's hand caressed her from shoulder to hip and back up the side of her ribcage until he reached her breast. As he pinched a nipple, he whispered to her wickedly, "You're an excellent pupil, Angel. You learned that particular lesson very quickly and very thoroughly. But that was just the beginning of what I'm going to teach you. So pay attention, now, because your next lesson is about to begin."

Chapter Seven

"And what exactly would this be?"

Angela heaved a sigh as she turned yet again to face Nick. He'd been ruthlessly plundering her admittedly sparse wardrobe and tossing aside just about everything he'd found, from her favorite baggy sweatpants with holes in both knees and paint stains splattered in a haphazard pattern, to a pair of navy slip-on shoes that he'd declared were ugly as a troll's ass, to the plain white cotton underwear that he'd just shook his head at in silent disgust before tossing it onto the ever growing discard pile.

She recoiled in a panic when she spied the white T-shirt in his hands. "Hey, no, not that! That's my lucky shirt."

He grimaced as he noticed the ripped neckline, half a dozen holes, and a stain that looked suspiciously like pizza sauce or ketchup. "I don't know what kind of luck you think it brought you, but I can tell you one place you sure as hell didn't get lucky when you wore it."

She made a face at him and tried futilely to snatch the shirt away. "Please, Nick. My – my dad bought me that when I signed my letter of intent to Stanford. It was the only acknowledgment I ever got that anyone in my family was proud of me for getting in."

The white shirt had the Stanford name and emblem emblazoned in red on the front and looked not only well used but well loved. Nick studied it a moment longer before reluctantly handing to back.

"Well, it's probably a hell of a lot more than my father gave me when I signed on, so keep it. As long as you never wear it in my presence," he warned.

She gave him a cheeky grin and took the shirt from his outstretched fingers. "I promise I'll only wear it on laundry days, or when I'm scrubbing the floor."

Nick glared. "It looks like something you'd scrub the floor *with*."

She folded it away in the back of a dresser drawer. "I'd wear that shirt during warm-ups before every collegiate volleyball game. And if I started the game we never lost. That's why it's my lucky shirt. Didn't you have any sort of good luck charms you wore before or during a game? Or at least a routine you stuck to, some sort of superstition?"

He shook his head as he continued to rifle through her clothes. "My routine, as you call it, was to show up on time, always prepared, and then go and hit people as hard as I could. If you train hard enough, prepare the right way, you don't need good luck charms or superstition or routines. Just skill and dedication. Now, looks like you've got quite a pile of stuff to donate, Angel. Though I'm really not sure some of it is even thrift shop material. More like rag bag material."

She sighed again, even as she fetched the box of heavy duty trash bags he'd told her to buy. "I told you I wasn't into dressing up until now. In fact, if I had a class that started before ten a.m. I'd usually stumble in wearing pajamas and slippers. Which I see you found," she added in resignation as she surveyed the pile.

"Angel – beautiful, sexy twenty-two year old women do not wear flannel pajamas with cartoon characters printed on them. Or moth-eaten slippers that look like – what the hell were they at one point anyway?"

"Monkeys, of course. How can you not see that? And I love those slippers. Can't I - ?"

"No. I think they have mold. I know they smell bad. Out they go."

Angela gave a little huff. "I'm not even sure why the pajamas and slippers matter to you. After all, it's not like you're actually here to see me in them when I fall asleep or wake up, is it?"

She regretted the words the moment they left her mouth, and she stared at him in horrorstruck remorse. His eyes narrowed dangerously, his mouth a thin line of irritation.

"Complaining already, Angel?" he asked in a low, unpleasant voice.

She shook her head frantically. "No, no, not at all. I – I'm sorry. I'm not even sure why I said something like that."

"Forget it." His voice was flat, emotionless. "Why don't you start putting all of these things into the bags? Have you decided what you're going to do with them?"

She kept her gaze downcast as she started filling up the trash bags, not wanting to see the anger she knew would be visible on his face. "Throw out the really gross stuff and then bring the rest to the Goodwill store a few blocks from here."

"Good. And since we've made room in that ridiculously tiny closet of yours we can get to work on filling it up again. I'm taking you shopping tomorrow afternoon."

Angela didn't dare even think of protesting, knowing she'd already pushed too many of his buttons tonight, and merely replied, "Okay. Just let me know when and where."

Nick threaded a hand into her hair, pulling her head back so their eyes could meet. "I like it when you're agreeable like this, when you let me call all the shots. What's more, I think you like it, too. Don't you, Angel?"

She gave a little gasp as he gave her hair a hard tug, one of the many ways he used to assert his control over her. "Yes," she whispered, alarmed to notice how easily she agreed with him, and that her affirmation was shockingly true.

He released his grip on her hair and took a step back before inclining his head towards the bed. "Get on the bed. Clothes off."

Angela trembled at the barely disguised passion in his voice, at the look of dark possession in his eyes, and was quick to obey him. Even in the very brief time they'd been together, she'd learned to heed his instructions quickly, and that patience was definitely not one of his better virtues.

She undressed swiftly, the outfit she wore another new one he'd bought her, and a surprisingly conservative one given most of his previous choices. The gray wool pencil skirt and ivory silk blouse would have been entirely suitable for the office, though the towering gray pumps might have been a bit over the top. He'd actually selected underwear for her this time, too – to a degree. Beneath the clothes she wore a seriously sexy push-up bra of ivory lace and a matching garter belt that held up ultra-sheer silk stockings, but no panties. She shivered as she recalled the numerous times during dinner tonight when Nick's big hand had slid up beneath the tight fitting skirt to stroke a silk stocking, to snap one of the garters against her thigh, or to cup her damp, aching sex, his long fingers merely teasing her but never going any further.   She'd been a bundle of quivering, frustrated sensation for the remainder of the meal, and had crossed and uncrossed her legs constantly in a futile attempt to calm her wayward body's needs.   And Nick, damn him, had merely sat next to her with a smug, knowing smirk on his ruthlessly handsome face, casually eating his dinner and drinking his wine as though nothing at all was wrong.   She'd longed to return the torment, to slide her hand up his thigh and stroke his cock, only to teasingly retreat time after time.   But she'd known he wouldn't have allowed it, wouldn't have permitted her to touch him unless it was his idea.

She'd been certain that he'd fuck her the minute they walked inside her apartment – up against the wall or on the floor or maybe they'd make it as far as the bed this time.   But, instead, Nick had decreed this would be an excellent time to filter out her wardrobe, and they'd spent the last hour or so doing just that.   By now, her body was almost convulsing with need and she silently cursed him for inflicting this sort of emotional torture on her.

She was reaching behind her to unhook the bra when Nick shook his head.

"Change of plans, Angel.   You look like one of my best ever wet dreams like that – your tits spilling out of that bra, those stockings making your legs look like they go on forever.   And you know what it does to me when you wear those fuck-me shoes.   Don't you?"

She nodded, spellbound by his deep, seductive voice.   "Y-yes. It makes you want to – to fuck me."

"Lay back, Angel.   I want to fuck you for hours, maybe all night.   Starting like this."

Angela closed her eyes as he tugged her arms up over her head.   He slid open the drawer built into the bottom of the bedframe, and removed the lengths of black silk cord he kept there.   She welcomed the feel of the silk around her wrists as he tied her to the slats of her new headboard, then repeated his actions on her ankles until she was spread-eagled. The silken bonds were loosely tied, and she could have easily wriggled free of them if she so desired. But after the first time he'd tied her up this way – the very same afternoon the new bedframe had been delivered – she'd quickly overcome her initial fear and uncertainty at being bound, and allowed herself to surrender to the pleasure.

"My beautiful, sexy angel," he purred in her ear as he finished securing the cords. Then she could hear the sounds of him undressing, his clothes being tossed to the floor heedlessly. "Open your eyes now, Angel. You know it pisses me off when you don't look at me."

She opened her eyes then, just as Nick was easing his big, hard body onto the bed and looming over her intimidatingly. The smile he gave her was nothing short of demonic.

"Got you just where I want you, Angel," he murmured. "You're completely at my mercy, so that I can ravish you a dozen different ways if I want to."

Angela stared up at him, her breathing already jagged in anticipation of what would come next. "Only a dozen?" she asked unevenly.

Nick threw back his head and laughed. "That's the attitude, Angel. Now, no more talking, hmm? But moaning is definitely allowed."

"Ohhh." Her back bowed as far off the bed as possible, given that her limbs were tied down. His lips sucked hard on the side of her neck, hard enough that she knew there would be a dark purple bruise there in the morning. At the same time his hands groped her breasts roughly, squeezing them as his thumbs brushed over the nipples. He delved a hand inside the shallow bra cup, lifting her warm, swollen flesh out and she whimpered as his touch became more aggressive.

"Your tits have gotten bigger, Angel," he whispered wickedly. "My plan to fatten you up is working. This is bigger, too." He squeezed her ass cheek. "A few more pounds and you'll be exactly the weight I want you at. And you're going to keep that weight on, too."

She groaned as he bent his head and sucked her exposed nipple into his mouth, while his hand shoved the other bra cup down and pinched the nipple hard.

He took his time with her, lingering over her for what felt like an hour or more, kissing and caressing every inch of her body, taking full advantage of her bound state and the fact that she was utterly helpless to resist anything he might do to her. She cried out plaintively as he thrust two long fingers up inside her vagina, hooking them over her pubic bone.

"You're not wet enough. As hard as I am right now, we need to get you wetter so I don't fuck you raw."

Angela could already feel the moisture of her arousal trickling down her inner thighs, but she knew that mentioning this fact to Nick would be pointless. Instead, she greedily welcomed the first lick of his tongue along her labia, trying in vain to spread herself wider to give him full access. He pinched her clit between his fingers, pulling it taut while his tongue stabbed inside her slit, fucking her with the sort of expertise she knew had only been attained with a great deal of practice. But she was too far gone now, the pleasure too consuming, to start fretting over how many other women he'd done this to. He was with her now, his mouth and tongue devouring her like a rare delicacy, and she would cherish each moment with him, commit it to memory for all time.

He wasn't satisfied until he'd made her come three times, until she was so wet that his thick, throbbing cock made little slurping noises when he finally surged fully inside her. Tears trickled down her cheeks as he fucked her steadily, longing to wrap her arms and legs around him, not liking this aspect of being bound and helpless. But she knew better than to plead with him for her release, knew this sort of domination over her was what aroused him more than anything else, made him harder and fiercer and more demanding.

He kept at her for a long time, amazing her with the control he could assert over his body. With such God-like stamina, she knew that she'd be bruised and tender tomorrow, would have to soak in a blisteringly hot bath of Epsom salts to soothe away the worst of the soreness. But it was all worth it – God, so worth it –

to feel him plundering her body over and over with that huge, hard cock, to be brought so tantalizingly close to the edge with each savage thrust. Nick seemed to know exactly when she was ready to come, when she was oh, so close, only to pull back just enough to deny her fulfillment. She was almost ready to scream with frustration, to beg him to stop toying with her, until she'd recall in a haze what he'd done the one and only time she had pleaded with him in that exact same manner – he had very deliberately pulled out of her and stroked himself to orgasm, spurting streams of hot, thick cum all over her breasts and belly. He had dressed after that, all without uttering a word, then tossed her a towel before letting himself out, leaving her still bound and unsatisfied. It had been an easy enough task to free herself of the silk cords, but she hadn't dared to get herself off for fear that he would find out somehow.

So she didn't dare beg him now, no matter how badly she needed to come, knowing that he wouldn't hesitate to leave her unsatisfied again. Instead, she bit down on her lip so hard that she broke the skin and tasted the coppery rush of blood in her mouth.

"Easy, Angel," he soothed, bending his head and licking away the drops of blood. "You need to come, don't you? Answer me."

She felt a fresh rush of tears well up behind her eyes but knew he wouldn't like it if she didn't keep looking at him. "Yes," she whispered brokenly.

He caressed her cheek, even as he continued to fuck her without mercy. "Blood and tears," he murmured in wonder. "Is there anything you wouldn't endure for me, Angel? Anything you wouldn't do for me?"

She shook her head weakly. "No, nothing. I'll do whatever you want. Always."

His fingers dug almost harshly into her cheekbone, holding her head still, and his voice was raw and dangerous. "Then come for me, Angel."

This time he didn't deny her, didn't pull back when the spasms began deep within her, consuming her until she screamed and sobbed, her entire body thrashing wildly as she tugged on her bonds. Then and only then did he allow himself to climax, his powerful body shuddering repeatedly. But still he kept himself in check, held something back, while in contrast she was a complete and utter wreck, unable to speak or think and certainly totally incapable of moving a single muscle.

Nick was relentless, not giving her even five minutes to recover before he was at her again. She was limp and drained, her limbs numb and aching, and he must have sensed her discomfort for he gently untied the silken cords before flipping her over onto her stomach.

"I want you on your knees this time, Angel," he rasped, as he rolled on a fresh condom. "Hold onto the headboard and keep this sweet ass up in the air."

She yelped as he gave her a swift, sharp slap on one of her buttocks but complied, gripping the slats of the headboard as he positioned himself behind her. She couldn't stifle a low whimper as he slammed into her, his arm banding around her waist as he resumed his relentless fucking, as though the powerful orgasm he'd had just minutes before had never happened.

Angela lost track of time, lost count of how many times he made her come, how many condoms he used up. By the time he finally left, she was almost comatose from exhaustion, her nude body sprawled out limply on her bed. She barely twitched when Nick pulled the duvet up over her and pressed a quick kiss to her temple. He let himself out, locking the deadbolt with the key he'd demanded she give him, and she slipped immediately into a deep, dreamless sleep.

***

She winced as she slid out of bed the next morning, sore and stiff, and knew she was kidding herself by thinking she could somehow manage a quick run. Not to mention the fact that it was already late morning and she had no idea of what time Nick would summon her to meet up for their shopping excursion. Knowing him and the way he liked to exert his control over her, he could very easily call within the next five minutes and demand her presence somewhere within a very short period of time.

Moving as quickly as possible, given her somewhat battered body, she turned on the taps in the bathtub, spooned coffee into a filter and began brewing a pot, and snatched up her phone. She kept it close by as she bathed, not daring to miss his call, and breathed a sigh of relief when it didn't ring just yet. She kept her fingers crossed that she'd have enough time to finish her bath, bolt down some coffee and food, and get dressed before the call came in.

This was probably one of the more difficult and frustrating parts of the relationship for her – never knowing exactly when Nick would call, not being allowed to contact him, and having no idea where he was or what he was doing at any given moment. She didn't even know where he lived, for he'd never mentioned it and she knew better than to ask. Given his familiarity with San Francisco – all the restaurants and shops he seemed to be recognized in, how smoothly he navigated around the streets – she assumed he lived here in the city and most likely in one of the most exclusive neighborhoods – Pacific Heights, the Marina, Nob Hill.

As for how he occupied his time when he wasn't at the office or with her, Angela could only guess. He was in such incredible physical condition that she knew he'd have to spend a great deal of time at the gym. She assumed he had close male friends, people he knew from football or work, but he'd seldom mentioned any of them by name. Of his family she knew absolutely nothing, just that his parents were divorced. She had no idea if he had siblings or kept in close touch with his family or even where he'd grown up. She had come very close on a number of occasions to researching him online, figuring there had to be at least some basic information about his background from his NFL days. But she'd always resisted, partially from the fear that Nick would find out somehow and be annoyed at her for prying, but mostly because she wanted *him* to be the one to tell her about himself, instead of reading some statistics about him on Wikipedia.

In the few short weeks they'd been seeing each other, Angela had more or less been living on tenterhooks. She was constantly afraid she'd break one of Nick's rules, whether by asking him a question on a forbidden topic, or innocently mentioning him to a co-worker, or, worse, betraying her ever-increasing feelings for him. And because she never knew when he would call and want to see her, she'd stopped making plans of her own and was never without her phone. He'd called once when she'd been out on a run, and she had had to swiftly turn around and almost sprint the rest of the way back to her apartment. If she had to do laundry or go grocery shopping, it was usually on a day after she'd been with him the previous evening, for he hardly ever saw her two days in a row. And while it was still too soon in the relationship to establish any sort of pattern, at least for now Nick usually saw her two to three nights a week.

Thus far there hadn't been any family events she'd felt obliged to attend – and thereby find a way to blow off - but the holidays would be here very soon, followed by a slew of birthdays – her father's, sister's, niece's, brother-in-law's – and the pressure would be exerted on her to be present. Even though her mother and sisters still shunned her as much as possible, the three of them lived by some ridiculously outdated sense of protocol that called for keeping up appearances and maintaining the farce of a close, happy family. How many times had she heard her mother tell her briskly. "What would your aunts think if you didn't attend Uncle Aldo's retirement party? I'd never hear the end of it, Angela." Or it would be Marisa whining that "Of course you have to be here for Samantha's eighth grade graduation. It would look terrible to Joe's family if my own sister didn't show up."

Angela rarely bothered to point out that the three of them didn't even acknowledge her presence at any of these events, that they didn't really want her there but that it was *expected*, that it would look bad to the rest of the family if she wasn't in attendance. And so she'd gone, every single time, with the futile hope that her willingness to be part of the family would finally make them accept her, make her feel wanted. But of course it never had, and she had yet to wise up and realize that her relationship with her mother and sisters would probably always be fucked up.

She applied her makeup in between sips of coffee and bites of buttered toast, her phone in easy reach as the time crept gradually past the noon hour. She didn't dress yet, in the event that Nick had a specific outfit in mind, but mentally chose a dress, a pair of shoes, a jacket, some jewelry. Her closet had been ruthlessly stripped bare after his clean-out project last night, and just about the only things left were her business suits and the clothes Nick had bought for her.

She paced around anxiously after that, willing the phone to ring, and feeling too unsettled to pass the time any other way. She was so far ahead of everyone else in her training class at work that studying or reading seemed pointless. Desperate to find ways to occupy herself when she couldn't be with Nick, she'd been spending ridiculously long hours at the office, and was only one module away from completing the entire training program. She'd studied for the licensing exam until her head hurt, and had already assembled a sizeable list of potential clients to contact once she was approved to do so.

But she couldn't work all the time, and running or other forms of exercise weren't always an option given that a night in bed with Nick usually left her too wrung out and achy in too many places to count. She didn't have many friends yet in San Francisco, since most of her old college chums had scattered all over the country after graduation. Julia was living in New York, and Lauren seemed to be constantly flitting between her cabin in Big Sur, staff meetings in Manhattan, and assignments in every corner of the globe. Not that she was overly anxious for either of the twins to call more often, or worse, to pay a visit. The McKinnon girls knew her far better than anyone else ever had, certainly much more so than the family she was like a virtual stranger to, and Angela wasn't entirely confident around her best friends about her ability to keep her relationship with Nick the carefully guarded secret it had to remain.

Wistfully she couldn't stop herself from hoping that one day soon things would change – that she and Nick could have a normal relationship, one where she knew exactly when they would see each other every week, where she was free to call or text or email him when she felt like it, where she could proudly introduce him to her family and friends. It was hard, much harder than she'd thought it would be, to abide by all of his rules. Already there had been numerous occasions where she'd had to force herself not to call the emergency only number he'd given her, or to ask him when they would see each other again, or drop hints about him spending the night or taking her to see his home. And she was constantly having to restrain herself from blurting out how she felt about him, biting her lip in the throes of orgasm not to cry out how much she loved him.   Any of these transgressions – and especially the latter – would be the end of it. She knew all this instinctively, and also knew she'd have to continue to wage this internal battle for as long as their tenuous relationship lasted.

She consoled herself with the fact that she'd lasted longer than any of the other women he'd dated in the past, including the three he'd fleetingly mentioned the night he'd first set down his list of conditions. She didn't fool herself into believing that Nick might actually have feelings for her. He was too tightly controlled, too set in his ways to be the sort of man who'd ever admit to loving or needing someone. And no matter how intense the sex was – she wouldn't permit herself to think of it as lovemaking since any semblance of love between them was strictly one-sided – Nick never, ever lost control. Whereas she was a quivering, emotional basket case each and every time they fucked, he remained cool, detached, always holding part of himself back. And it was that aspect of their relationship that bothered her the most – that she could feel so much, could be so deeply affected by their physical closeness, while it seemed to have little to no effect on him.

Angela closed her eyes, forcing back the tears she so desperately wanted to shed, and told herself firmly to be grateful for what she did have. She reminded herself of how many women would kill to trade places with her, that what she'd shared so far with Nick was much, much more than he'd ever give to another woman. And that if she wanted to remain in his life in any sort of fashion, she would have to accept things as they were and stop wishing for what couldn't be.

Her phone rang and she snatched it up immediately, the caller ID telling her it was a blocked call and most assuredly Nick.

"Angel." His voice was a throaty purr that made her knees weak and her nipples hard even as she listened to his instructions about where and when to meet him and what he wanted her to wear.

***

Lauren McKinnon was very seldom caught by surprise, and could count on one hand the number of times in her twenty-two years that she'd gone so far as to be shocked. But as her best friend walked inside the funky Noe Valley café where they'd arranged to meet for brunch, Lauren's jaw dropped open and she realized she'd have to start using her other hand to keep the tally up to date.

She'd known Angela for more than half their lives, had grown up with her, considered her another sister. They had played sports together, shared confidences, pulled some admittedly evil pranks on girls they had hated at school, and given each other advice on a wide array of subject matter. Lauren had felt more than a little guilty these past few months over the lack of contact between them, given the demands of her new job. She'd hardly been home at all what with the time she spent in New York attending planning and follow-up meetings, and actually being on location for assignments. Communication with her best friend had been infrequent and brief. And, based on the startling physical changes she observed now, a whole lot had happened to Angela in the interim.

"Wow." Lauren stood and gave her a fierce hug, noting that Angela had to bend down even lower than usual, given the four inch heels she was wearing. "Who are you and what have you done with my best friend?"

Angela laughed and took a seat at the cozy corner table Lauren had secured for them. "Sometimes when I look in the mirror I think the same thing. Does this mean you don't approve?"

Lauren inspected Angela thoroughly, taking in the shiny smoothness of her jet black hair; the tasteful but dramatic way she'd applied her makeup; the new curves to her formally wand-thin body – the fuller breasts, hips and ass that Lauren had to admit looked fantastic on her. And the way she was dressed – in a close-fitting V-neck sweater of cream cashmere, a short, tight skirt of dark brown wool, ribbed tights, and sexy brown ankle boots with those stiletto heels – was a far cry from the laid-back jeans, T-shirt and flip flops Lauren was used to seeing her in. Her classy, fashionable outfit was the exact same sort of ensemble Lauren's twin sister Julia favored.

And while Lauren was nowhere near as fashion obsessed as Julia, she was savvy enough to recognize Angela's attire as being designer from head to toe, including the diamond and gold jewelry that adorned her ears and throat, and the exquisite gold watch that circled her wrist.

Lauren grabbed hold of that same wrist and raised a brow. "Holy crap, where the hell did you get the money to buy a Piaget? Julia was looking at these watches in Barney's when she dragged me along the last time I was in New York. When she noticed the price tag she started to wonder if she ought to snag some rich old sugar daddy to buy her pretty things. Looks like you had the same idea, Angie."

Angela's cheeks flushed beneath their expert application of bronzer. "I don't have a sugar daddy. It's – er, not like that."

"Ah, so there is someone," exclaimed Lauren triumphantly. "Okay, girlfriend, spill. I want all the details – name, age, occupation, net worth, and most important how big his equipment is."

"Lauren!" Angela admonished her in hushed tones, looking around the crowded café to make sure no one had heard her.

"What?" Lauren grinned. "Come on, Angie, it's me. We watched enough porn together back in the day that nothing should be able to shock you. Tell you what – you can save all of the juicier details for after we eat and just fill me in on the basics now."

Angela's full mouth – glossed over in a shiny mocha – tightened into a thin line and an expression that looked an awful lot like fear appeared in her eyes. She shook her head regretfully. "I can't, Lauren. I'm sorry, I know I've never kept anything from you before but this time – no."

"Huh?" Lauren stared at her best friend in utter bewilderment. "I mean, forget about how good this guy is in bed for a minute. Why don't we start with something simple like – oh, I don't know – his name?"

But Angela only gave another stubborn shake of her head. "Not even that. He – we – want to keep this private. I shouldn't even be telling you I'm seeing someone."

"Are you shitting me?" Lauren was incredulous. "What's up with that load of bull? Is this jerk married or something, and you're just his booty on the side?"

"No, he's definitely not married. And, well, he has his reasons. He's just a very private person and doesn't want me talking about us to anyone. Even to you, Lauren," she added contritely.

Lauren was primed and ready to launch into another tirade when their waiter appeared with menus and a pot of coffee. Lauren, who'd already had a cup while waiting for Angela to arrive, eagerly proffered her mug for a refill. She'd only arrived back in San Francisco less than two hours ago after a multi-stop seventeen hour journey home from Chile, where she'd been doing a feature on Torres del Paine National Park. Most people would be in a zombie-like state right about now, but Lauren had never been like "most people" in any aspect of her life, including the uncanny ability to fall asleep anywhere and with very little effort. She was the envy of her fellow crew members and figured that she'd probably slept for a good nine hours on the flight. Even so, she had an unapologetic caffeine addiction and was rarely without a heavily creamed and sugared, extra-large cup in her hand.

After the waiter took their orders – crème brulee French toast with a side of bacon for Lauren, a veggie egg white scramble with whole wheat toast for Angela – Lauren was right back in attack mode.

"Now, I don't know if this is some really bad joke you're trying to play on me, but if so I'm definitely not laughing," Lauren told her sternly. "I cannot think of any other *reasonable* explanation why you can't at least tell me this guy's name. The only other reason that comes to mind is that he's some sort of international spy, or works for the CIA or Interpol or something."

Angela laughed. "Nothing quite that mysterious. And I think you've been watching too many of those espionage movies you love. Tell me the truth – what movie did you watch on your flight home?"

Lauren had the good graces to look sheepish. "Okay, I admit it. The latest Bourne movie was playing. And on the flight out I watched Bond *and* Mission Impossible. But you're trying to divert the subject here, Angie. Why can't you tell me anything about your mysterious – and apparently filthy rich – new man? I mean, I'm no fashionista like Julia or my aunt Maddy but I've had my ass dragged along on enough shopping trips to know that outfit you're wearing is probably worth two grand – not counting the watch or the jewelry. And – Jesus – is that a Fendi bag down there? Add another thousand – at least – to that total."

Angela fidgeted, clearly discomfited by the direction their conversation was headed, and stared down into her coffee mug. "Julia would be pleased to learn that you actually paid attention during all those shopping excursions."

Lauren scowled. "Julia would be as pissed off – and worried – as I am about this whole mess. Or she would, if she wasn't involved in a questionable relationship of her own. You know I was never the biggest Sam fan all those years they were together, but he's a prince compared to this asshole Lucas she's dating now. There's something fishy about that guy, I knew it from the first minute I met him. And it sounds like he's not the only bad smelling boyfriend I need to worry about. At least I know his name and met him face to face. Unlike your mystery man. So, come on, spill the beans, Angie. You know you want to, I can see it in your eyes."

"I can't." Angela sighed. "I'm sorry, Lauren, I really am, but this is one time in our lives when I can't share with you. Just know that he's a great guy, he treats me well, and, most importantly, I'm happier right now than I've ever been."

"Hmmph. Sounds to me like you've been brainwashed. Or drugged. Let me see your arms."

Angela gaped at her in shock. "No! I am *not* doing drugs,

you idiot, and you are *not* checking my arms for track marks. I admit all of this sounds a little suspicious, but you're going to have to trust that I know exactly what I'm doing."

"Famous last words, Angie. I'll reserve judgment on that, if it's all the same to you. Has he met your parents yet?"

"Are you high? Smoked something wacky down in South America?" inquired Angela in disbelief. "Even if I wasn't supposed to keep all of this hush hush, my parents are probably the last people I'd want him to meet right now. As usual, they have no idea about what goes on in my life and are quite content with that state of affairs."

"Well, *I* want to know," insisted Lauren. "Sorry, but this whole situation sounds creepy to me. I mean, you can't even tell me his fucking name? What's it like – Beetlejuice – where you say his name too many times and bad stuff starts happening?"

Angela shook her head in frustration. "God, you are just like a pitbull sometimes, you know? The main reason he wants to keep it quiet is because we work together. Not directly, but at the same firm, and the gossip mill in that place grinds round the clock."

"I guess I can understand that," admitted Lauren grudgingly. "But that doesn't explain why you can't tell your family and friends."

Angela looked decidedly ill at ease, her agitation becoming more apparent the more Lauren continued to push her. "He's just – private, okay? And I don't want to mess this up, Lauren. I feel – alive when I'm with him. More alive and happier than I've ever come close to feeling before. So please don't push, okay? Can't we just enjoy our meal and catch up? Please?"

Lauren blew out a breath, not in the least bit willing to drop the subject. But she sensed that Angela would really start to clam up if she continued to probe right now, so she merely shrugged and allowed the subject to be changed.

However, it wasn't in Lauren's nature to ever give up on anything. There had only been one time in her entire life, in fact, when she'd backed away from something and moved on, too hurt and disillusioned to pursue it further. This situation with Angela's mystery man was definitely not something she was prepared to let go quite so easily.

"Are you going home for Thanksgiving?" she asked casually as they tucked into their meal. She noticed that Angela was eating more than she normally did, and wasn't pushing the food around on her plate. Lauren guessed that Mystery Man was responsible for this, as well as the ten pounds she'd packed on in all the right places.

Angela grimaced. "What do you think? I hate the very thought of going there, and you just know my mother and sisters are secretly wishing I won't show up."

"You could always go to New York with us. We'll see Julia, go out drinking and dancing, hopefully convince her not to drag Lucas the Loser along for the ride."

"As awesome as that sounds, you know I'd never hear the end of it if I didn't go home. Marisa's cooking dinner this year and half of Joe's family will be there, so of course we have to keep up appearances, don't we?"

Lauren played her next hand very carefully. "Why don't you just go away for a nice long weekend with your new man? I mean, if being with your family just makes all of you miserable, why not do something to make you happy for a change?"

Angela closed her eyes, her hand trembling as she picked up her coffee mug. "Don't, Lauren. I thought we just agreed we weren't going to talk about this anymore."

Lauren pointed an accusatory finger. "*I* never agreed to anything. All I did was table the discussion to humor you for a little while. Honey, I've just begun to hound you."

Angela glared at her darkly. "Hound all you want but I'm not answering your questions."

"Does he beat you? Is that why you're scared shitless of him? If you're in an abusive relationship, Angie, just say the word and I'll give the asshole some real abuse."

"Jesus." Angela sounded disgusted. "Always the badass, aren't you? But, no, he doesn't beat me and I am not in a physically abusive relationship. Can't you just leave it alone? I'm happy, I'm safe, and I know what I'm doing."

"I'm not so sure about that," muttered Lauren. "What other

ridiculous rules does this guy have for you? Not that keeping his identity a big ole secret isn't already mega disturbing."

Angela sighed wearily. "Okay, I'll make you a deal. I'll tell you a few juicy tidbits – nothing too detailed – and then you drop the subject. Agreed?"

Lauren scowled, but sensed her suddenly reticent best friend wasn't prepared to offer up anything more. "Fine. But they had better be really juicy tidbits."

"I see him two to three times a week. I never know exactly when but when he calls I go. He picks out all my clothes, bought me a wardrobe that Julia would stab me in order to steal, tells me how to dress, orders my food at restaurants. He fucks like a wild beast, is hung like a horse, and I have trouble walking the next day after a night with him. And I'm crazy in love with him but don't dare let him know for fear he'll break things off. And that's all you're getting."

For the second time that day, Lauren was shocked – utterly and completely shocked – and she stared at her best friend in total disbelief.

"Wow," was all she could think of to say. "That's, um, not exactly what I was expecting to hear, but – wow. Can I ask you just one more question and then I promise I'll leave it alone?"

Angela looked wary. "You can ask. Can't promise to answer, though."

"These rules – this control he has over you. Do you actually *like* it?"

"Yes. I know it sounds crazy but I do. When he first laid it all out for me – what he would expect if we kept seeing each other – I wanted to tell him to go fuck off. I stayed up almost all night weighing the pros and cons, came real close to calling you and asking for advice."

Lauren smirked. "Betcha you can guess what my advice would have been. It would definitely not have been to tell you to become this – this little subservient slave girl you've turned into. Why in the hell did you ever agree to something so ludicrous, Angie?"

Tears shimmered in Angela's huge brown eyes. "Because it was the first time in my life that anyone ever tried to impose rules on me," she whispered unevenly. "And even though I know he doesn't love me – will probably never love me – at the very least he cares enough about me to set down those rules. In his own way it feels that he cares more about me than my own family ever did. I don't expect you to understand, Lauren, and certainly not approve, and I know this is all sorts of fucked-up. But he makes me happy and that's not something I've been able to say too many times in my life."

Lauren nodded, sliding a hand over her friend's and giving it a squeeze. "Okay, then. As long as you're happy and safe and it's enough for you, I'll back off. But if you ever need me to kick his ass, I'll wrap one of my three black belts on and wipe the floor with his sorry ass."

Angela chuckled. "Now that I'd pay good money to see. After all, he's more than a foot - "

Whatever she was about to say was interrupted by the ringing of her cell phone. Lauren had noticed that Angela had kept the phone on the table next to her place setting during the entire meal, and had checked it at frequent intervals. She answered it now on the first ring and turned away slightly, speaking in a low, hushed voice.

And then, for the third time in less than two hours, Lauren was shocked speechless again as Angela ended the call, pulled out some cash from her wallet and set it on the table as she stood.

"I hate to eat and run, but, well, I've got to go," Angela told her briskly. "You're heading back to Big Sur this afternoon, aren't you?"

Lauren continued to stare as Angela dropped the phone into her satchel. "You're leaving? You're just fucking walking out on me this way? I thought we could hang out awhile longer, get caught up, maybe see a movie."

"I'm sorry. I just saw him last night and honestly didn't expect to hear from again this soon. But I've got to go, Lauren, so please understand. And don't worry, okay?"

Lauren stood reluctantly and gave her best friend a fierce good-by hug. "Okay. I'll call you in a couple of days. Hey, I know you can't give me any details but how about a rating? Like, on a scale from one to ten, is he – "

"A twenty. At least. Gotta go. Love you."

"Love you, too, Angie."

But Angela was already hurrying out of the café like the place was on fire. And, despite the half-hearted reassurances she'd given her, Lauren couldn't help but have a very, very bad feeling about the situation her girlhood friend had gotten herself into.

Chapter Eight

Late November

Nick propped the pillows up against the headboard and lounged back, regarding Angela with barely concealed amusement. "Well, now that we've taken the edge off, Angel, why don't you tell me what's been on your mind all night? And don't try to deny it, because you're strung tighter than a brand new tennis racket right now."

Angela smiled a bit sheepishly. "Good thing I followed the advice you gave me that first night about never playing poker. There's really nothing you don't miss, is there?"

He ran a hand over the curve of her naked hip, then to her buttock. Less than a minute after they'd arrived at her apartment after dinner he'd promptly stripped her, bent her over the side of the bed, and fucked her hard from behind, holding back his climax until he'd made her come twice. Only then had he finished undressing and only then had he spoken a single word.

"Nothing," he agreed matter-of-factly. "And I knew you were wound up about something the minute you walked inside the Biltmore tonight. So let's not waste any more time, hmm? What's bothering you, Angel?"

She worried her bottom lip between her teeth, having dreaded this particular conversation for weeks now, but knowing she couldn't put it off any longer. After all, Thanksgiving was less than a week away and she had to get answers now.

"I, um, well, that is, " she stammered. "My, uh, family will be expecting me to see them next weekend. For Thanksgiving, you know. And I know I'm not supposed to ask about your schedule, or when we're going to see each other, but - "

"Relax." His hand moved to her nape soothingly. "I just assumed you'd be seeing your family for the holiday weekend. And I, very unfortunately, will be spending my weekend with my father and stepmother. One of the very few times I see them all year."

"Oh." The relief she felt was like a huge weight being lifted off her shoulders. "Okay, well, I'm glad. I mean, glad that we got that out in the open," she added hastily. "I'm *definitely* not glad to be spending Thanksgiving with my family."

Nick lifted a brow at her inquiringly. "Then why the hell are you going?"

She sighed, rolling onto her side to face him. "Duty. Obligation. Bad habit. It's expected, you know? My oldest sister is cooking this year and a bunch of her husband's family will be there, so it would look odd if I didn't show up."

He snorted in derision. "What a load of bull. Do you really give a shit what your sister's in-laws think?"

"No, not really." She trailed her fingers up and down his bare, sinewy arm. "It's just – well, I'm already so alienated from my mother and sisters that I don't want to intentionally do anything to make it worse, you know?"

Nick shook his head. "Can't say that I do, Angel. Especially since I have no idea why you have such a fractured relationship with them. Maybe it's finally time for you to spill the beans about that."

She immediately felt her chest tighten at the very idea and shook her head emphatically. "No, Nick. I've told you before that I don't like to talk about them."

He reached out and brushed his thumb over her bottom lip. "All the more reason for you to unload. Hey, I never talk about my family, either, so I get it. But I've learned to deal with all that shit, sure as hell don't let it bother me, and you can be damned certain they never try to guilt trip me into spending time with them. Not that I don't feel a certain sense of obligation like you do, but it sounds like it goes a whole lot deeper than that for you."

"Yes." She scooted up to sit beside him, shoving a pillow behind her and pulling the duvet over their lower bodies. He wrapped an arm around her shoulders and she cuddled up against him eagerly. It was rare for Nick to indulge her with this sort of behavior, this uncharacteristic affection. On a typical night with him in her bed, he was insatiable and demanding and it usually took two or more rounds of aggressive, domineering sex before he took even a short break. His powers of recovery had to be the stuff of legends, how quickly he could get hard again, and his stamina was undoubtedly record setting. She was surprised, therefore, that he was evidently putting his satisfaction on hold for a bit to initiate this very unwanted conversation on her part.

He kissed the top of her head. "Tell me. All of it. Maybe if I understand it all a little better I can help you find a way to deal with it, and not have it make you an emotional wreck all the time."

Angela shrugged. "I usually deal with it by keeping my distance. I make the obligatory phone call home once a week to check in – provided my parents aren't away on yet another vacation, of course – and that very awkward conversation lasts five minutes or less. And I only go home when I absolutely have to. Though with my family, every holiday, birthday, anniversary, graduation, etc. seems to require my presence. To keep up appearances, of course, because it would be too embarrassing for my mother to explain my absence to my aunts."

"I can't believe that's all of it," soothed Nick. "I mean, your parents must miss you, look forward to your visits."

She shook her head. "My dad, yes, though he's pretty much told what to say or think or feel most of the time. My mother – aside from keeping up those appearances to the family, I can honestly say she wouldn't give a damn if I ever came home again."

He frowned. "Something pretty major must have gone down between you and your mother at some point for her to feel that strongly. What the hell happened?"

Angela closed her eyes, but couldn't prevent a single tear from tracking down her cheek. "I was born," she whispered."

***

"My mom was forty-one when she had me. Not all that unusual for women to have babies at that age nowadays, but back then it wasn't quite as common. But that wasn't even the issue.

After having my sisters so many years before, she'd figured her family was complete. And with Marisa and Deanna both in their teens, my mother was already starting to enjoy more freedom, to make plans for when my sisters would be eighteen and she could get on with her life, pursue her interests."

"What sort of interests?"

"The stuff I mentioned to you at dinner that one night – traveling, joining clubs, taking classes. She was even thinking about going back to college and getting her degree. All the things she had to give up when she got married and started a family."

"Hmm." Nick regarded her curiously. "Why did she have to give it up? Your mother's in her early sixties, I'm guessing? It certainly wasn't unheard of for women of her generation to go to college."

"Not for good Italian girls raised by very old-fashioned immigrant parents," corrected Angela. "My mom was one of seven children, four of them girls. Her parents – especially her mother – were very strict, very set in their ways. It was drummed into my mother from an early age about what was expected – get a good steady job somewhere like a bank or the phone company, marry a nice Italian boy, and have babies. And as much as my mother wanted to rock the boat and have a different sort of life, she gave in and did what her family pressured her to do."

"Your mother told you all of this?"

She gave a short, bitter little laugh. "Hardly. My mom speaks to me as little as possible, ignores me as *much* as possible. No, I heard all of this – and a lot more – from her cousin Carla. She and my mom are the same age and grew up together, were even closer than sisters at one point in their lives. It was at my grandmother's funeral – I was around twelve at the time – and Carla could see how unhappy I was, how much my mother and sisters shunned me. So she tried to explain a bit about why that was, about the things that made my mother the way she was."

She drew her knees up to her chest, wrapping her arms around them as if for comfort before continuing. "When my mom and Carla were in high school, they started to make all sorts of plans for what they were going to do with the rest of their lives. And while Carla actually followed through with hers, my mother gave up her dreams and caved into family pressure instead. Carla said at one time my mom talked about going away to college – as far away from Monterey and the family as possible – and working as an interpreter since she spoke fluent Italian – like at the U.N. or an embassy. She wanted to travel, have fun, enjoy herself for awhile before settling down and starting a family. Instead, she got a job at my uncle's insurance agency, married my dad when she was only twenty-two, and got pregnant two years later."

"I take it Carla followed a very different path?"

"Absolutely. She got her degree from UCLA and settled in southern California. She works in the movie industry, some sort of film editor. She's been divorced twice, has no kids, no obligations, and in her own words, 'does whatever the hell she wants whenever she wants'."

Nick's mouth quirked up at the corners. "I get that. Sounds like a woman after my own heart. So is that what your mother wanted for herself when your sisters turned eighteen?"

"Not exactly. I mean, as much as she pushes my dad around, she'd never consider a divorce. I think she just wanted the freedom to do her own thing and have more time to herself. What she definitely *didn't* want – or plan on – was getting pregnant again. It was a very, very unwelcome surprise. She, ah, wanted to have an abortion, didn't even want to think about having another baby at that point in her life. In fact, she'd already made an appointment to have the procedure done. And then my dad found out what she was planning."

"And the shit hit the fan, did it?"

"That's a gross understatement. My dad is a quiet man, doesn't say much or speak up for himself very often. But he refused, absolutely refused, to let my mother go through with it. Told her if she had the abortion he'd divorce her, get custody of my sisters, and cut her out of his life for good. It was probably the first and only time he ever stood up to her but it scared her enough to go along with his wishes. As it turned out," she added sorrowfully, "we would have all been better off if he'd just let her go through with the abortion."

"Angela." His voice was reproachful. "Don't say things like that, hmm? Why would you ever say such a thing?"

She closed her eyes, the lashes wet with tears. "Because it's true," she whispered huskily. "My mother gave birth to me but she resented the hell out of that fact my entire life. I've spent twenty two years being ignored by her, pushed away, unloved. To make things worse, my sisters resent me, too.   It was mortifying for them to bring friends or boyfriends to the house and have them see their forty year old mother was knocked up again. And then, of course, they got stuck with the bulk of the babysitting duties and taking care of me because Mom couldn't be bothered. Marisa and Deanna have never let me forget that, always harp on the fact that they missed out on all sorts of stuff as teenagers because they had to stay home with me."

"Didn't your father help out or notice what was going on?"

"He worked a lot back then. A *lot*. I know there was a huge building boom for several years, but I think part of the reason he stayed away so much was because my mother was even more of a bitch to live with than usual. She never, ever let him forget that it was his idea to have another baby, that he forced this on her. I think he stayed away as much as possible because he didn't want to fight with her constantly."

Nick shook his head in disgust. "I can maybe understand your mother feeling resentful at first about having another baby at her age, about being angry at your dad for forcing the decision on her. But to take her anger and frustration out on an innocent child – Christ, she wasn't a first time mom, after all, or a young girl. She should have been able to put aside her own needs and take care of her baby, for God's sake."

Angela gave him a sad smile. "That's almost exactly what Carla told her when I was about three years old. They had a huge falling out about it, though they'd already been drifting apart for years. My mom was resentful of the fact that Carla had been brave enough to defy her family and live the life she wanted. And when Carla dared to criticize the way I was being brought up, that was the final straw and things have been completely strained between them since."

"Sounds to me like your mother is a very unhappy woman. A jealous one, too."

"Yes." Angela nodded. "In fact, Carla was convinced my mom was jealous of me. First because my father would have chosen me over her – would have divorced her if she'd gone through with the abortion. And second because – well, because I looked so much like my other grandmother – my father's mother. Apparently Mom did not like Nonna Isabella at all."

"Dare I ask why?"

"I don't remember much about her – she died when I was around six – but I know from what I was told that she didn't like the way Mom treated my father – how she bossed him around, belittled him, would never let him speak up for himself. There was always tension between the two women and my mother refused to have much to do with her."

Nick squeezed her shoulder. "And you look like her? Your grandmother?"

"A lot. She was tall, like I am, like my dad. And beautiful, really, really striking. I have a picture of her somewhere around, where she was all dressed up, her hair and makeup all glam, and she looked almost exactly like Sophia Loren."

"I'd like to see that picture sometime. I can just imagine how much you must resemble her." He brushed his lips against her cheek tenderly. "In fact, that's how I want to dress you one of these nights – like a sexy, voluptuous Italian screen goddess."

She grinned. "I'd need another ten pounds on me – at least – before I could be considered voluptuous. But don't get any ideas. This is the most I've ever weighed in my life right now and I really don't want to gain another pound."

"Okay, we'll settle for sexy Italian screen goddess only. Does this mean your sisters didn't take after Isabella?"

"Not even a little. They look exactly like my mom – short, kind of plump, wavy brown hair – the three of them could be triplets. So of course I really stick out like a sore thumb when I'm with them. By the time I was nine years old I was already taller than they were."

"Did your sisters play sports like you did?"

Angela snorted. "God, no! Marisa would have had a fit if she got dirty or her hair got mussed, while Deanna would have cried if a ball hit her or someone shoved her too hard. Plus, my mother didn't think it was ladylike for girls to play sports, so they got pushed into taking ballet instead. My sisters got bossed around just like my dad, and now history is repeating itself because they're treating their husbands and kids the exact same way." She shuddered. "It's an awful thing to see unfold. And there is no possible way I'll ever have that messed up kind of marriage. If I ever get married at all, that is."

Nick fell silent for long moments and she mentally kicked herself for even mentioning the evil "M" word – marriage. But he didn't seem annoyed or angry, just thoughtful.

"What about kids?" he finally asked. "Do you want a family someday?"

"Honestly, I don't know," she admitted. "I had such a screwed-up childhood – dumped off at daycare or with a sitter or at a relative's – and then virtually ignored by my mother when she couldn't find anyone else to leave me with – that I don't have much of a role model to emulate, you know? I don't think I'd know the first thing about raising a child. And given my lousy genes, I'd probably screw things up big time."

"I doubt that," replied Nick somberly. "I think you have a great capacity for love and compassion, Angel. I think you'd be the complete opposite of the cold hearted bitch your mother was to you."

"Maybe. But it's not something I even want to consider for a long time yet. Unlike my mother, I haven't let anything stand in the way of realizing my dreams. I went to college, played on an Olympic team, got a job in my chosen field."

"Are they proud of you?"

"I doubt it. Oh, my dad probably is, but he keeps everything bottled up inside, isn't very good at expressing himself. But none of them ever gushed when I got into Stanford, or called to congratulate me when the team won the gold medal."

He frowned. "Called you? Weren't they there at the Olympics to watch the games in person?"

She shook her head, glancing away so he wouldn't see the hurt she knew would be so evident in her eyes. "No. I'm not even sure any of them watched it on TV. My parents had already booked a cruise to the Greek Islands, and there's no way either of my sisters would have made the trip to the games without their husbands and kids in tow. Lauren wanted to go but she got offered this once in a lifetime internship that summer and I forced her to accept it."

Nick slid a hand into her hair, tilting her face up as he kissed away her tears. "If I'd known you then," he whispered, "I would have moved heaven and earth to be there, cheering you on, celebrating with you. You would have been far more important than a stupid vacation."

Angela clung to him then, burying her face against his neck as the tears began to fall unchecked. "I wish I had known you back then, too," she breathed. "These past two months with you – they've been the – well, they've been amazing."

She'd been about to blurt out that her time with him had been the absolute best two months of her life. But she knew that, despite his uncharacteristic kindness and tenderness this evening, that he wouldn't appreciate hearing such sentimental drivel, and so, as usual, she kept her feelings tightly bottled up.

He rubbed the back of her neck. "Yeah, it's been a good time, Angel, no complaints here." He sifted a long, silky strand of her hair between his fingers as he fell silent again for a time. She closed her eyes and tried to quell the turbulent emotions that all this talk had stirred up. She'd never spoken to anyone this way about her family, not even the twins. Lauren and Julia knew that her mother had always been a cold, distant bitch, but she'd never actually confessed the real truth to them – that Rita Del Carlo had been within twenty four hours of aborting her youngest daughter, stopped only by the threat of divorce. It had been too shameful, too hurtful, to admit to anyone, even her best friends. After all, Lauren and Julia had been blessed with two warm, loving parents and they would have been horrified at the very idea that Angela's own mother had been so eager to get rid of her.

But Angela had sensed that such a revelation wouldn't bother Nick the same way, and the words had poured out automatically And even though he'd never chosen to confide even one personal fact about himself to her, even though he continued to keep these impenetrable emotional barriers up between them, and that she knew it would only be a matter of time before he left her for good, she also knew he would be the only person in her life that she would ever entrust these secrets to. Perhaps it was simply because she suspected that his own childhood had been as equally screwed up as hers, even if he'd never spoken about it.

He was quiet so long that she had almost begun to fall asleep. When he spoke again, his words seemed stilted and carefully chosen.

"So, I'm curious," he began. "Everything you told me about your mother – how she didn't want you, didn't pay attention to you, how she pawned you off on everyone else. When she *was* with you, was she strict? Did she discipline you, enforce rules?"

Angela gave a rather undignified snort. "Hah! You have to actually pay attention to someone in order to do that, and when my mother was forced to look after me herself she never seemed to give a damn what I did. And, naturally, to get her attention I acted out all the time – breaking things, getting dirty, refusing to eat, disappearing for hours at a time when I got older. She never even blinked, never even seemed to notice. After awhile I stopped trying. I mean, where's the fun in being a brat or breaking rules if nobody even bothers to react?"

Nick nodded. "That's sort of what I thought. And it explains a great deal."

She turned her head to gaze up at him, puzzled. "Like what?"

He tumbled her back onto the pillows, rising above her as he drew her arms over her head, shackling her wrists in one hand. "Like why you agreed to obey me, follow my rules," he murmured. "It was the first time in your life that anyone even tried to do so, wasn't it? And it's why you like it so much."

She thought of denying it, was almost ashamed to admit he was right, but knew she was incapable of lying to him. "Yes," she whispered. "That's exactly why."

Nick ran his tongue along the side of her neck, then bit down sharply on her earlobe. "Lucky me," he purred.

And then he was securing her wrists to the bedpost with a pair of fleece-lined leather cuffs, and whispering exactly what rules he expected her to obey tonight.

Chapter Nine

March

"Well, Angela, I have to say you're certainly doing your best to light the world on fire. I see you opened ten new accounts just last week, and brought in almost twenty million in new assets. Not only are you the star of your training class but you've even surpassed other brokers who've been in production for two years. You're more than fulfilling your potential, young lady, you're sending it to the moon. Keep up the fantastic work now, okay?"

Angela beamed at Lloyd Raskin, the office sales manager and her direct supervisor. "Thanks. I'm just trying to do my best. And while I have been working hard, I have to admit to catching a few breaks, too. Three of those accounts I opened last week were actually unsolicited, apparent referrals though none of them actually came out and told me from who. I, ah, suspect they were sent my way via a fellow Stanford alum that I've, um, kept in touch with."

She conveniently left out the part that the aforementioned alumni was most likely Nick Manning. She'd suspected for several weeks, in fact, that he was quietly sending business her way, though she didn't dare ask him directly and knew he'd deny it even if she could work up the guts to inquire. They rarely discussed business, and definitely not his own practices or methods, but she'd heard via the office gossip mill that Nick had very strict standards when it came to accepting new clients. Any potential new accounts were required to have a minimum net worth in the multi-millions, and be willing to invest a good portion of those assets. In addition, word had it that Nick demanded total and absolute control over each client's investment strategy, and unless a client was willing to give him almost complete discretion over their portfolio, then he wouldn't take the account.

Ever since she'd passed her exam and been granted her brokerage license in December, Angela had not only met all of the goals she'd set for herself up to this point, but had exceeded them well beyond her wildest expectations. She'd already moved to a much larger and better furnished cubicle, and Lloyd had very recently promised that if she continued to exceed her goals he would move her into the next available private office. Angela knew these sorts of perks were almost unheard of for someone as young and inexperienced as she was, but also knew how hard she had worked to earn such rewards – albeit with some unconfirmed help from her uber successful lover.

Lloyd waved a hand in dismissal. "Does it matter where the accounts came from or who may or may not have referred them? There's no denying how hard you work, Angela. I know you put in far more hours than any of your contemporaries, and it certainly shows. And let's not forget that getting the client is one thing. Keeping them happy and investing for them responsibly and successfully is all up to you. So if these accounts did come to you as a little bonus from an old friend, that's no reason for you to look a gift horse in the mouth."

She nodded, even though in all honesty she wasn't terribly comfortable with the idea that Nick was very likely acting the part of puppet master with her career, and without either her knowledge or consent.

"You're right, Lloyd," she agreed quietly. "And whoever might be referring these clients to me, I'm definitely grateful. *And* extremely committed to taking very good care of their accounts. Especially," she added with a grin, "since I plan on asking all of them for referrals when the chance arises."

Lloyd grinned. "Now that's the kind of attitude your co-workers need to adopt more often!" He sighed. "Unfortunately, more than half of your training class is already falling well short of their thresholds. But I guess it's not really fair to compare you to them. I've rarely seen someone as young as yourself who has such an intense work ethic."

She gave her watch a discreet peek – not the horrendously expensive Piaget that Nick had casually presented her with but a much more affordable Anne Klein that she kept for everyday use. She and Nick had agreed months ago that it would be unwise and indiscreet for her to wear any of the pricey designer clothing or jewelry he'd given her to the office. The very last thing she wanted was to have to dream up an explanation to her co-workers about how she could afford an Armani suit or Manolo Blahnik pumps.

"Speaking of which, I'm supposed to be calling a client in about ten minutes and I want to review my notes first. That is – if we're done here for now?" she inquired politely.

Lloyd nodded. "Yes, of course. I'm just happy there's at least one of you I don't have to worry about or keep pushing. Oh, by the way, Angela."

She paused, one hand on the doorknob of his office. "Yes?"

Lloyd winked at her conspiratorially. "That office I mentioned to you recently – please don't say a word just yet, but I think you should start preparing for another move within the next week or so."

Angela couldn't hold back the answering grin she gave him. "Wow. I never thought it would be this soon. But I'll try not to get my hopes up just yet. You know, the old 'I'll believe it when I see it' attitude?"

Lloyd chuckled. "I get it. Though in this particular case you should really start believing. Go on now, we'll talk again next week. And keep batting a thousand there, slugger."

She resisted the urge to roll her eyes as she walked back to her desk. It was very obvious from all of the San Francisco Giants memorabilia cluttering up Lloyd's office that he was a diehard baseball fan. As if that wasn't enough, he frequently talked about the sport to anyone he could get to listen, even those who had no real interest in the game. And he often used baseball metaphors when he was making presentations or giving pep talks. Still, he was a good manager – supportive without being smothering – and Angela knew he was extremely impressed by the success she'd had thus far.

Even without Nick's covert maneuvers to sweeten the pot for her, Angela was confident she'd still be at the top of her training class just with the accounts she'd brought in on her own. She knew the others from her class were all struggling, some of them barely hanging on to a job at this point, and she felt badly for them. But she also knew that most of them didn't arrive in to work until almost two hours after she did, took well over an hour for lunch each day while she brown bagged it at her desk, and were usually done for the day before five p.m. while she continued to plug away. This realization helped to assuage some of the guilt she felt about the accounts she knew – just *knew* – that Nick had sent her way.

But Lloyd was quite right, she told herself firmly. Getting the account was one thing – retaining it, keeping the client happy, and making sure their investments paid off – well, that was all up to her now and she would only have herself to blame if things didn't work out. On the other hand, when the clients were happy and chose to send even more business her way – well, then she'd have only herself to credit. Besides, she consoled herself, it certainly wasn't as though she'd ever asked Nick to help out. In fact, doing so would have been the very last thing she'd have dared to do.

As she began to look over the notes she'd prepared to discuss with her client, Angela paused for a moment to contemplate the current state of her relationship with Nick. She continued to be in disbelief that they were still together at this point – more than six months after that first night. She had never allowed herself to hope that he would still be interested in her, wouldn't have moved on long ago or grown tired of having a steady relationship with the same person for this amount of time.

Though to call what they had a relationship would be a stretch of anyone's imagination. What they had, in brutal honesty, was far more of a master/slave relationship, though not the sort generally thought of in BDSM circles. Instead, it was more a case of Angela being at his beck and call, of permitting him to call all the shots, and of molding herself into the sort of woman he wanted her to be at all times. He continued to choose her clothes, though by now she had an extensive wardrobe and knew exactly how he liked her to dress. Nick accompanied her when she got her hair cut – at a salon he'd picked out – and actually oversaw how much the stylist trimmed at one time. She had a thrice weekly session with a personal trainer that Nick had selected for her, at a very private, exclusive gym that he'd also chosen. He ordered her food and drinks when they dined out, and always chose the restaurant. And he kept a very diligent eye on her weight to make sure she didn't lose any of the twelve pounds she'd packed on at his insistence.

After six months together, they had gradually fallen into an informal pattern of when they saw each other. Nick never called her on Tuesdays or Thursdays, and she guessed he spent those particular evenings working out, entertaining clients or hanging out with his friends. Friday and Saturday nights were always spent together, as well as most Wednesdays. And he'd surprised her more than once by calling on a Monday or Sunday and demanding to see her. Since he had a key to her place, there had also been numerous occasions when she'd arrived home from work or the gym to find him inside waiting for her, often with dinner waiting and always in the mood for sex.

She lived for the times they were together, often counting the hours until she knew she'd see him again, and always wishing she could have more. She longed for him to finally open up to her, to tell her about himself, and to admit he had feelings for her. The nights without him were pure torture, as she would find herself imagining – or trying *not* to imagine – what he might be doing or who he might be with. Angela knew him to be a man of his word, and one who valued honesty above all else, so she wasn't overly worried that he was cheating on her with another woman. However, even though having dinner with a female client, or casually flirting with a woman at the gym, or giving one a onceover at a bar wasn't precisely cheating, the thought that he could be doing any or all of those things filled her with an almost obsessive jealousy. But of course she had to keep her feelings well hidden, would never dare admit to Nick that she fretted over such things. And it was far more than her unwarranted jealousy that she had to keep to herself.

It was becoming increasingly difficult to hide her relationship with him, especially since he expected her to be available whenever he wanted to see her. She was hesitant to make any sort of plans these days, continually refused to go out for drinks with her co-workers, made sure she ran errands and did chores on Tuesdays and Thursdays. She'd made a variety of excuses to several old college friends about why she couldn't meet them for dinner or attend their parties. She'd even ignored more than a few of Lauren's phone calls in recent months, not wanting to deal with her best friend's increasingly nosy questions about her relationship with Nick. Or, worse, to try and come up with an excuse for why she couldn't spend time with Lauren when she happened to be in the city.

And then, of course, there were the increasingly frequent occasions where she'd backed out of one family event or another. There was no way she could make the two and a half hour drive each way to Carmel for her brother-in-law's birthday dinner or her niece's dance recital or her cousin Lisa's twenty-fifth wedding anniversary party – not when all of those events occurred on a Saturday, one of the days she always saw Nick.

She hadn't told her family the truth, of course – that she was head over heels in love with the sexiest, most exciting man in the entire world and needed to keep her weekends free for him; that he was a man she would walk over broken glass for, just to hold his hand; would give away her Olympic gold medal in exchange for one night in bed with him; would choose him over her family almost every single time. Instead, she'd fobbed her mother and sisters off with a variety of excuses – a meeting with an important prospective client, a flat tire or dead car battery, a terrible cold or severe food poisoning. She didn't care any longer about making her family angry or pleasing them, or whether any of her excuses were believable or not. Not when she was so completely obsessed with Nick, to the point where nothing else was important – where *nobody* else was important.

And obsessed she was. In the span of half a year, he'd become her whole world, the one person she'd willingly do anything for and would gladly do everything he asked of her. She adored him, body and soul, and devoted herself entirely to satisfying his every need. She never even considered disobeying one of his rules, and was fanatical about doing everything exactly as he liked.

The way she obeyed him almost slavishly reminded her of a movie she'd seen once on late night TV about a sexy, compelling vampire and the beautiful woman he'd cast a spell over. Angela realized she was just like that woman – held in Nick's thrall and totally incapable of resisting him in any way.

In bed he was unquestionably the master, and she was more than eager to let him dominate her. Over the months he'd become extremely inventive and more than a little kinky in their sexual encounters. More often than not he seemed to enjoy tying her up in some way, liked to blindfold her and had even gagged her on occasion. He constantly surprised her with new and varied sexual positions, and of course his strength and stamina in bed continued to astound her. She often felt bruised and battered after a romp in bed with him, but the weight training and intense cardio workouts she did several times a week had helped a lot to make things easier on her physically. She never said no to anything he wanted to do, would have gladly given him carte blanche over her sexually, and found it impossible to hold back her wild, consuming reactions to him. In truth, it was Nick who held himself back at times and not her.

She'd asked him once why they had never tried anal sex, given that it was just about the only type they hadn't engaged in. He touched her there frequently, after all – kissing and caressing her buttocks, sliding a well-lubricated finger inside her anus while he licked her pussy at the same time, pressing a thumb on the small, puckered hole as he fucked her hard.

Nick had shaken his head firmly. "Uh, uh. I don't do anal. And you should have your head examined to even be asking me that question."

She'd looked at him quizzically. "I mean, given some of the other stuff we've done, it's hard for me to believe you think that's taboo or something."

"That's not it at all. Come on, Angel. You've seen what a big guy I am – and that's just pure and simple fact, not ego talking. If I fucked you in the ass, I'd break you in half, rupture at least a couple of internal organs. At the very least it would be excruciatingly painful for you, even with a whole tube of lube.

So, no, thanks for the offer but I'll be keeping my dick out of your ass."

She'd grown used to his very frank way of speaking by now and hadn't even blinked an eyelash at his forthright explanation. With Nick, she had learned to shed pretty much every inhibition she might have had, something he'd been insistent on. If he told her not to wear panties or go braless or both, she did so without even thinking about it. When they were together at her apartment she walked around stark naked, not in the least bit shy or modest any longer. Nick had taught her to be proud of her body, to be as comfortable in her skin as he so obviously was in his. From the very beginning of their relationship he'd strode around her place in the nude, without the slightest bit of self-consciousness. And she had loved every second of it, of course, nearly drooling each time she got to feast her eyes on his spectacular male beauty.

Angela gave her head a firm shake, rather appalled to realize how lost in thought she'd become, and was alarmed to see that she had less than three minutes now to review her notes before calling her client.   Fortunately, she had something of a photographic memory and this certainly wasn't the first time she'd studied the information.

An hour later, she was feeling on top of the world after finishing the call. The client – a youngish tech firm employee who was flush with cash – had been enthused about the proposed investment portfolio she'd put together for him, and had given her the green light to go forward.

As she made some additional notes, Angela couldn't help the smile that teased the corners of her mouth. If Lloyd had already all but guaranteed that the next available office on this floor would be her, she couldn't wait to see his reaction when he learned about her newest account. And her client had already promised to refer several of his equally affluent co-workers to her. At this rate, she thought somewhat smugly, Lloyd might not wait for an office to become available by natural attrition and decide instead to demote one of the brokers who hadn't been toeing the line in order to create a spot for Angela.

Life was undeniably good these days. She loved her job,

loved her gorgeous, sexy lover, loved being alive. For the first time in her twenty two years she was learning to distance herself from her family, and therefore from all the years of feeling left out, unloved and unwanted.

Of course, life could be even better were Nick to suddenly change his ways and make a real, lasting commitment to her. But she had never been a greedy person and wasn't about to become one now. She was grateful for what she did have with him, and determined not to screw things up by wanting more.

As if on cue, her cell phone rang, and she knew it had to be Nick. Even though his number continued to be blocked, she always had a certain feeling, could always sense when it was him calling.

"Angel. Got any plans for the weekend?"

Today was only Monday, and she rarely allowed herself to think more than a day or so ahead as far as Nick was concerned. She glanced briefly at her calendar and stiffened in mild alarm when she noticed what day it was on Saturday – Deanna's birthday. She vaguely recalled getting an email from Marisa sometime last week about a birthday dinner for their sister at a restaurant on the Monterey Wharf, but she hadn't bothered to reply just yet. Knowing Marisa and her almost OCD organizational skills, Angela guessed there were at least two follow up emails from her, each one sounding increasingly irritated because she hadn't replied yet.

It would be nearly unthinkable to blow off her sister's birthday. She'd never dared to do anything like that before, and knew there'd be serious hell to pay as a consequence if she did. But then she remembered how snotty Deanna had been to her during a recent visit, and how Marisa had barely even acknowledged her presence, and Angela's hackles rose up something fierce. Why should she care what her family thought anyway, when they clearly didn't give a shit about her? It was well past time that she started thinking about herself, considering her own feelings and wants. And what she wanted, more than anything else, was Nick.

She deliberately flipped the cover to her desk calendar shut as she told him, "No plans whatsoever. What did you have in mind?"

***

Angela took a long drink of her icy cold margarita before setting the glass down and reclining back on the chaise lounge. After an exceptionally cold and rainy San Francisco winter, relaxing out here in the hot Mexican sun felt like heaven. And spending a long weekend with her devilishly handsome lover was beyond her wildest dreams.

Nick had convinced her to take a couple of well-deserved days off, and once she'd told Lloyd the news about her new account – the one that came with the promise of several referrals – he'd actively encouraged her to take a little break. She sensed she could have asked for two full weeks off and he would have agreed without hesitation.

She wasn't sure if Nick had made previous arrangements for the trip and just arrogantly assumed she'd accept his invitation, or if he'd simply thrown it all together on short notice. Whatever the case, he'd dazzled her with the opulence of it all – the chauffeur driven limo ride to the airport, first class flight to Cabo San Lucas, another limo drive to the hotel. They were staying in a detached casita at the ultra-luxe Gregson Resort, and Angela hadn't known it was possible to be so pampered. The casita boasted its own private butler who was at their constant beck and call; spacious, airy, beautifully decorated rooms equipped with state of the art electronics and every amenity she could have ever dreamed of; and the private patio where they were sunning themselves now, complete with its own pool and hot tub.

During the flight down on Thursday evening, she had decided against telling him about blowing off Deanna's birthday this weekend. After that night when she'd opened up to him about her family, Nick had seemed completely disinterested in hearing anymore about them and so she generally kept such things to herself. She'd conjured up a weekend seminar that her bosses at work "absolutely insisted" everyone had to attend, and made her excuses to Marisa via a rather brief email. She'd known it wouldn't be that simple, of course, and hadn't been all that surprised when her mother had called her the very same day. Rita had been scathing and irate, telling her she should be ashamed of herself for choosing work over family, and it had taken every ounce of self-control Angela possessed not to yell back at her mother that she'd learned that sort of thing as a very young girl, time and time again as Rita had chosen her social life and independence over the child who'd needed her desperately. But she'd lacked the courage to pick that particular fight, and had merely told her mother that she didn't have a choice in the matter, that her job required it, and that Deanna wouldn't even notice her absence.

To assuage her guilty conscience, she'd sent Deanna a gorgeous floral arrangement and a gift card to a restaurant in Carmel, as well as an email apologizing for her absence. But apparently Deanna was good and pissed off because thus far there had been zero acknowledgment of either the gifts or the email.

She forced herself now to stop dwelling on it, reminding herself that neither of her sisters or her mother had even once made an attempt to drive up to Stanford and watch one of her volleyball games. Gino had tried to attend as many games as possible, which usually amounted to one or two each season, since Rita kept their social calendar chock full of events. With another swig of her margarita, Angela firmly resolved to stop thinking about her family and to focus instead on the remaining time she had here with Nick.

They were due to return home on Monday evening, two days from now. Nick had already insisted she indulge in a massage, a mani-pedi, and a facial, and they had worked out both mornings at the resort's world class fitness center. She'd barely been able to focus on her own workout, however, mesmerized instead by the sight of Nick lifting weights and doing chin-ups and push-ups. His powerfully sculpted body was like a work of art, and it hadn't escaped her notice how many other women – and men – had openly ogled him

They'd slept in, had brunch delivered to the casita, sunned themselves out by the pool. Last night he'd taken her to dinner at one of the resort's four-star restaurants, and tonight Nick had made reservations for a twilight dinner cruise on a sleek Catamaran. Tomorrow they were going on a snorkeling expedition and having another massage in the late afternoon.

He'd bought her several new outfits from the resort's designer boutiques, including three bikinis, one of which she wore now. The two scraps of white fabric that bared a great deal of her smooth olive skin had cost an obscene amount of money, just like everything else Nick had picked out for her with an offhanded, careless regard for prices. Though she honestly didn't know why he had bothered to buy her anything, since she'd spent more than half of their time here thus far naked. And she knew it was only a matter of time before she would shed the pricey white bikini – along with a few more of her inhibitions.

Nick had just laughed when she had timidly expressed concern about sunbathing in the nude, waving a hand arrogantly in dismissal.

"Relax, Angel. No one can see us here, or hear a thing. I made sure of that when I booked this particular casita. Several of the top level managers at the Gregson Group's U.S. headquarters are my clients, including the facilities manager. The guy has a memory like an elephant, knows the layout of every hotel the group owns in North and South America. He assured me that next to the owner's suite this particular casita was the most private accommodation in the place. So the only Peeping Tom you have to worry about is me. Speaking of which."

Angela gulped as he removed his aviator sunglasses and his dark eyed gaze traveled over her barely clothed body with great interest. The way he smiled made her nipples peak instantly, her breasts feel full and achy, and her pussy was suddenly wet and needy.

Nick reclined back on his chaise, the really magnificent display of his bare torso making her mouth water. But it was what he did next that caused her heart to race triple time, and her legs to feel incapable of supporting her much longer.

He crooked one long finger at her, his grin unholy. "Come here, Angel."

Mesmerized, unable to look away from his compelling gaze,

she walked the few steps from her chaise over to his, stopping in front of him as he swung his long legs over the side.

Nick's big, warm hands caressed the curve of her hips, bared by the tiny string bikini bottoms.

"You should live in a bikini," he rasped, bending his head to lick her navel. "Or be a swimsuit model. But as hot as you look in a bathing suit, Angel, I prefer you wearing just your birthday suit."

She gasped as he deftly undid the ties at either side of her hips and drew the swimsuit bottoms away. He splayed his hands over her naked ass and pulled her forward, burying his face between her legs.

"Ah, Nick," she breathed in surrender. Her hands clutched thick strands of his hair, still damp from a recent swim in their private pool.

He took his time, ignoring her plaintive whimpers, running his tongue along her slit, sucking her swollen clit between his lips, feasting on her like she was the sweetest, most succulent dessert ever created. God, he was so good at this, so immensely skilled, an expert at wringing one orgasm after another from her quivering body. He pumped two fingers deep inside her wetness several times before replacing them with this tongue, and then slowly, carefully, inserted one lubricated finger up her ass.

She bit down on her lip to suppress the scream he would have otherwise torn from her throat, the dual stimulation of his tongue deep inside one opening and his finger in the other more than her overloaded senses could take. He gripped her fiercely by the hips as the orgasm rippled through her, his lips caressing the moist, sweat dampened skin of her belly.

Nick swiftly divested her of the bikini top, squeezing both of her bare breasts before running his tongue over the nipples.

"Hmm, another day or so of sunbathing au natural and your tits will be the same skin tone as the rest of your body," he murmured wickedly. "Your beautiful ass, too. And as soon as you take care of me, Angel, I'll be very, very happy to rub plenty of sunscreen into every inch of your skin."

He pushed her gently but firmly to her knees as he stood and shoved his dark blue swim trunks down his legs, baring his intimidatingly huge erection.

"You know what I want, Angel," he crooned. "And exactly how I want it."

She was thrilled to hear the sharp intake of his breath as she slowly ran her tongue up and down the full, throbbing length of his cock. Nick always kept such a tight rein over himself, rarely showing any reaction during their sexual encounters, no matter how hard she tried to provoke him. But that brief, betraying indication that she was, in fact, giving him pleasure was all it took to spur her on. She was determined to get a real reaction out of him this time, to make him lose control, and began to use every trick he'd ever taught her. She speared the tip of her tongue deep inside the slit of his cock head while stroking him with a steady, unceasing rhythm. She relaxed the muscles at the very back of her throat and then worked her mouth a little further down his cock with each devouring pull. And then, when she'd taken all of him, every inch of that spectacular cock as deep into her throat as possible, she reached back to lightly squeeze his balls. Even with the blood pounding fiercely in her ears, Angela could hear him groan, felt his hands fisting in her hair and pulling it taut. Knowing he was still holding back, was still in control, she became more determined than ever to make him lose it for once, to make him be the one shaking uncontrollably. Impulsively, before she lost her nerve, she carefully inserted her index finger inside his anus and pressed down hard, hoping wildly that what'd she read once in Cosmo about this particular little trick was accurate.

"Fuck, Jesus, fuck!" yelled Nick as his hips began to buck frantically, the head of his cock butting up against the back of her throat and threatening to gag her with each violent thrust.

He came hard, much harder and longer than she could ever recall, even as she continued to stimulate his prostate gland. The hot, sticky bursts of cum flooded her mouth, shooting down her throat faster than she could swallow, and she could feel rivulets of it trickling down her chin. She winced in pain as his grip on her hair grew even tighter, holding her head still as he continued to empty himself. Her jaw was sore from swallowing, the back of her throat tender from taking him so deep, and thick white beads of his semen clung to her cheek and neck and even her breasts. But it was all worth it to hear his grunts of pleasure, to feel him continue to shudder in reaction, to know that he'd finally lost control and just allowed himself to feel. She felt an almost giddy sense of triumph, especially when she finally dared to glance up at him from beneath her lashes and saw the way he was gasping for breath, his skin darkly flushed and his eyes tightly shut.

Nick released the death grip he'd had on her hair, sliding his cock out of her mouth, and then turned and stalked over to the pool. Without a word he dove into its crystalline depths and began to swim laps with focused precision. She knew he was deeply shaken by what had just happened, and cursed herself for having made him lose control, knowing how pissed off he must be right now. She carefully got to her feet and grabbed a towel from the neatly folded stack next to the pool. She wiped off her mouth and upper body before glancing over at Nick as he continued to swim with steady, purposeful strokes. Conscious of her nudity and the hot Mexican sun beating down on her, she wrapped the oversized towel around her body and began to pick up the discarded pieces of her bikini.

"Get your ass in this pool. Now."

Gulping, she looked over at Nick who was treading water at one end of the pool. His dark eyes were stormy and his mouth a taut line of disapproval. She didn't dare protest, dropping the towel where she stood before easing herself into the water.

He was on her in an instant, wrapping the long length of her hair around one big hand and jerking her head back to meet his burning gaze. She swallowed with some difficulty and was grateful when he wrapped his other arm around her waist to support her.

"I don't especially care for surprises," he growled in a dangerous voice. "So the next time you feel like experimenting with something new – don't. And that little trick you just pulled – unless I specifically tell you, don't try it again. Clear?"

Incapable of speech, and terrified that she'd messed up big time, she could only nod.

"Good."

His mouth crashed down on hers, kissing her brutally. She clutched the brawny muscles of his biceps desperately as he made her grow dizzy with his punishing kisses. She whimpered when he bit down deliberately on her bottom lip, not hard enough to break the skin but she knew it would swell up within a few short minutes.

Without warning he hoisted her up to sit on the edge of the pool, her long legs still immersed in the water. He was rock hard again, his incredible powers of recovery never ceasing to astound her. But as he spread her thighs apart, she glanced around apprehensively.

"Nick – should we – I mean, are you sure - "

He snickered and shook his head in disbelief. "Angel, you have got to be kidding. Just a few minutes ago I was shoving my cock as far down your throat as you could take it, and a few minutes before that I had my tongue in your cunt and my finger up your ass. And *now* you're worried about someone overhearing us?"

His eyes darkened as he lowered his head, his mouth sucking at her nipples until she was groaning. He gripped his cock and positioned it at the slick entrance to her body.

"Relax," he murmured. "No one is going to hear us. Besides, what's the worst that could happen? Even if they did hear us, you'll never see any of these people again."

"Ah, God." She cried out in a low, startled voice as he rammed himself inside of her with one savage thrust. She wrapped her legs around his hips, her arms around his neck, and held on for dear life as he fucked her hard and deep.

She had just enough presence of mind to gasp, "C-condom."

"Tough. You're protected, I'm clean, and it feels too fucking good to pull out now. In fact," he bit her shoulder, lifting her legs even higher up until they circled his waist, "doing you bareback is something I should have done a long time ago. And definitely something I'm going to do a lot more of in the future."

He screwed her roughly, almost brutally, and without any of his usual finesse. He was wild and frantic and Angela knew she'd crossed a line, pissed him off, by making him lose control earlier. And this, now, was her punishment, his way of letting her know in no uncertain terms that he was still in charge, would always be in charge. But it was the sweetest kind of punishment, she though shakily, the sort he could dole out for hours or days at a time, the sort she'd welcome with open arms.

It was almost unheard of for him to climax before he'd gotten her off at least once, but she knew this, too, was part of her punishment – the denial of her pleasure – and he came quickly and silently deep inside of her. But, as though he instantly regretted his selfishness – not to mention his brutality – he lifted her back into the water and held her close as they floated in place. She couldn't hold back the hot rush of tears that spilled from her eyes, and buried her face against the side of his neck as her shoulders shook with quiet sobs.

"Shh. It's okay, Angel," he soothed her. "I can be a mean bastard sometimes, I admit it." He pressed a kiss to her forehead. "I'm sorry."

She shook her head. "No, it's okay. And I'm – I'm sorry, too. For what I did. I know you need to be in control and - "

"Hush. Let's not talk about that now. And I'd have to be a real asshole – or a moron – to be pissed about having the best orgasm of my life, wouldn't I? Come on, let's get dried off and then we're going to have some real fun with that bottle of sunscreen."

She shivered in anticipation as he murmured in her ear, "Good thing I bought an extra-large bottle, because when I'm through with you it will be your turn to return the favor."

Chapter Ten

June

As she looked around at the three hundred or so guests assembled inside the church, Angela thought yet again that if it wasn't Gabriella who was getting married today she would have definitely found a way to blow this off. She'd never been a big fan of weddings, having been dragged to an indeterminable number of them since childhood. And since she had at least thirty cousins on her mother's side of the family alone – all of whom were now married – that added up to a lot of these affairs over the years.

Gabriella, in fact, was her second cousin. Gabriella's grandmother was Angela's Aunt Paula, who was a full fifteen years older than Rita. Paula's oldest child – Marta – was Angela's first cousin, and the mother of Gabriella. And since the bride was herself a year older than Angela, the two of them had spent a lot of time together as children, playing at all the various family events and parties. It was only because of their closeness growing up that Angela had given up a weekend with Nick to attend the wedding today.

She'd fretted for weeks over telling him about the wedding, knowing there was zero chance he'd actually offer to go with her, and worrying that he'd be annoyed about her decision. But she'd given up so much for him already – blowing off *both* of her sisters' birthdays plus a handful of other family events – that she'd hoped he would be understanding.

She had told him about the wedding over dinner three weeks ago, her words halting and unsure.

"And you know how much I dislike all these family functions but this one – well, this one is special. I mean, a birthday is one thing – you have those every year, after all. A wedding – you'd like to think it's once in someone's lifetime."

Nick had rolled his eyes. "Try telling my mother that. I've lost track of how many husbands and boyfriends she's had. My father as well, considering he's on wife number three right now."

"I'm sorry." She'd reached over to squeeze his hand, sensing from his caustic tone that his parents' multiple relationships were a source of considerable emotional distress for him.

"Forget it." He'd moved his hand away to pick up his wine glass. "So which cousin is the one being stupid enough to get hitched?"

Angela had sighed. "Gabriella. Second cousin, really, maybe even a third. I'm not exactly sure how that works. Her mother is my first cousin but because of all the various age differences that I won't confuse you with Gabby is a year older than I am. We were pretty close growing up, hung out together as kids at all the family doings."

Nick had shook his head in disgust. "And she wants to tie herself down like that at age twenty-three? Hasn't anyone told her this isn't the nineteenth century we're living in?"

"Actually, I think most of my female cousins were right around the same age when they got married, some even younger. The Italians are like that, at least in my family – get married young, have babies young, and then watch the next generation repeat it all over again."

"Is that what you want, Angel?"

She'd glanced up at him, startled by the question and the serious manner in which he'd asked it. She had recovered quickly, shaking her head emphatically. "No. God, no. At least not for a long time. We've had this discussion already, Nick. You know my feelings on the subject."

He'd shrugged and refilled his wine glass. "Feelings can change, Angel. People can change. Here's the girl you grew up with, played with as a child, and she's tying the knot. It's only natural that you might be feeling like you suddenly want the same things as – what was her name?"

"Gabriella. Gabby. And, no," she'd insisted. "I don't want that for myself. You're absolutely right that twenty-two, twenty-three is way too young to get married. And the very last thing I ever want to do is be like the rest of my family."

He had seemed mollified after that, changing the subject without really saying for sure if he minded her being away for the weekend of the wedding. It was only as they were getting ready to leave the restaurant that he brought the subject up again.

"You go to your little cousin's wedding, Angel. I'm guessing they'd all be pretty pissed off if you missed it."

She'd nodded, touching him lightly on the arm. "Okay. You – you don't mind?"

He'd chuckled then. "I didn't say that. Of course I'll miss not having you at my beck and call for two whole nights. You'll just have to think of some very creative ways to make it up to me."

She had thought about asking how he'd spend the weekend without her, then abruptly decided not to push her luck. And then he'd startled her anew by declaring he was taking her shopping the next day for a new outfit to wear to the wedding.

"And I'll expect pictures to prove that you actually wore it," he'd warned her. "No chickening out at the last minute. I'm going to pick out an outfit for you that makes a statement. The sort of statement that will have everyone staring at you instead of the bride."

And the stares had definitely been obvious, beginning with the startled looks she'd received just a short while ago from her parents as she'd descended the staircase at their house.

"My God, where did you get that dress?" her mother had gasped. "It's – isn't it a little short for an afternoon wedding?"

Angela had shrugged, trying valiantly to appear nonchalant. "It's not that short, Mom. Don't forget that I'm so tall everything is automatically a few inches shorter on me."

Rita had looked down at her feet disapprovingly. "And why such high heels? You already look like a giant compared to all the other girls. With those shoes you'll be even taller than the men. You won't get asked to dance even once."

Angela had rolled her eyes. "So what? I'm not fifteen and going to a high school dance, after all."

Rita had thrown up her hands in frustration. "As usual you have to be difficult, have to be different from the rest of us. No one else is going to be wearing that color or such a short skirt. I can just imagine what your aunts are going to say about you."

It had been on the tip of Angela's tongue to reply that she didn't give a flying fuck what her annoying, gossipy aunts had to say. Over the years they'd undoubtedly said plenty, and she could just imagine some of the mean, catty things they'd whispered about her.

But this weekend was already proving to be difficult enough, and since the last thing she wanted to do was start a big fight with her mother, she kept her mouth shut. Fortunately, her sweet, soft spoken father came to the rescue as he'd done so often over the years.

He'd given her a gentle kiss on the cheek, ignoring the look of displeasure Rita sent his way at the gesture. "You look beautiful, Angie," he'd assured her. "Like a movie star. Nobody's going to be looking at the bride because they're all going to be staring at my little girl instead."

Rita had snorted. "Little? In those slutty shoes she's taller than you, Gino. And stop filling her head with nonsense. Of course everyone is going to be looking at Gabriella. She's going to make a gorgeous bride. Such a sweet girl, and what a nice boy she's marrying."

Angela had been sorely tempted to correct her mother about the so-called "slutty shoes" – to tell her that the strappy cream sandals were in fact Christian Louboutins that had cost a thousand dollars, and had been purchased at Neiman Marcus, the classiest store in San Francisco. But she'd continued to keep her mouth shut, not wanting to alert her parents to the fact that her entire outfit had cost Nick more money than either of them could ever imagine spending on clothes.

The short aqua lace sheath dress was a Valentino, the cream quilted shoulder bag Chanel. At her throat she wore a new choker-style necklace – this one of cultured pearls with a diamond clasp in the center – and matching drop earrings. The dress admittedly bared an awful lot of her long, deeply tanned legs, but it was one of the loveliest, most exquisite things she'd ever seen.

The wedding was as carefully orchestrated and elaborately planned out as all of the others she'd been to over the years. Her cousins tended to be very competitive, much as her mother and aunts had always been, and they were constantly trying to one up each other, with each birthday party, bridal shower, baby shower, more elaborate and over the top than the one before. As Angela took in all of the tableau – the whimsically printed wedding programs; the soprano crooning "Ave Maria" from the choir loft as guests continued to arrive; the lavishly beribboned floral bouquet that adorned the end of each wooden pew; the seven bridesmaids with their frothy, petal pink gowns and wreaths of pink roses in their identically coiffed hair.

Rita had fretted for weeks when Angela hadn't been asked to be a bridesmaid. "I don't understand. I mean, the two of you were so close growing up. Gabriella ought to be ashamed of herself for not asking you. But part of this is your fault, too, Angela. You should have made more of an effort to keep in touch with her instead of spending all your time with your college friends or those McKinnon girls."

When Rita got on a roll, very little could pacify her. So Angela hadn't bothered to point out that she and Gabby had begun to drift apart years ago, when they'd attended different high schools, made different friends, developed vastly different interests. She hadn't blamed Gabby in the least for wanting those closest to her now – her own sisters, best friends, her fiancé's sister – to be her bridesmaids.

And, thought Angela as she wrinkled her nose in distaste, it was actually a very, very good thing she wasn't one of Gabby's bridesmaids because there was no *possible* way she would have ever willingly consented to wear that ridiculous spun sugar confection of a dress. Not to mention the fact that she was at least four or five inches taller than the next tallest of the bridesmaids, and would have looked and felt horribly awkward standing next to all of them.

Instead, thanks to the exquisite things Nick had bought her, and the self-confidence he'd instilled in her over the past months, she felt poised and beautiful for the first time in her life.

Angela stood with everyone else when the bride began to walk up the aisle, and she could feel the stares of her sisters from the pew just behind her as she did. She just hoped that neither of her rather dowdy siblings would recognize the telltale red soles of the Louboutins, and that they thought the signature Chanel emblem on her bag was a knockoff. She could hear them whispering to each other even above the sound of the processional music, and just assumed they were saying something unkind about her as usual.

But she forgot all about her snotty sisters the moment she glimpsed Gabriella's happy, glowing face. Of all the weddings she'd been to over the years, Angela didn't think she'd ever seen a lovelier, more enchanting bride than her cousin. And, quite unexpectedly, it made her long for what Gabby had, made her wish that *she* was the bride today and that Nick was the one waiting up at the altar instead of Gabby's rather nerdy – in her opinion, anyway – husband to be.

She was alarmed at her very unexpected – and very unwelcome – reaction. As the wedding Mass began and she took her seat, Angela told herself firmly that she was just getting caught up in the silly sentimentality what with so much lace and flowers and overblown romanticism surrounding her. She did *not* want to get married – at least not for a long time; did *not* want to float down the aisle in a big, poufy white dress and veil; did *not* want to exchange vows and rings with Nick and promise to love and honor each other for the rest of their lives.

But she did, she realized in something of a panic, and, if she was being really honest with herself, probably always had, from the very first time she'd seen him. She'd done an admirable job of convincing not just Nick but herself that she was perfectly happy with the state of their relationship, that she didn't want or expect anything more. But it was all a big, fat lie and deep down she'd always known it. If Nick were to ask her to marry him – or even to move in with him – she'd be over the moon, the happiest woman in the universe. She'd agree instantly, would willingly and happily accept whatever small scraps of attention he might toss her way. She'd allowed herself to become his slave, his doormat, who was pathetically grateful for every minute she could spend with him.

She should, by all rights, be feeling disgusted with herself right now, should be hurt and angry that Nick could treat her with so little regard. But in the next breath Angela knew that if she'd had to do it all over again, nothing would be different. She'd accept Nick's conditions over and over again, no matter how much pain she'd endured over the last months. It had all been worth it, she thought despairingly, even for just one hour with him. She would sacrifice anything – her family, her friends, her pride – to be with Nick for however long it lasted.

**

The wedding reception was being held at one of the numerous country clubs on the Monterey Peninsula, and was thus far turning out very much like all the others she'd attended over the years. The champagne was of a mid-range quality, the chicken marsala a tad on the rubbery side, the slightly undercooked vegetables rather bland. Without Nick on hand to watch what she ate, Angela picked at her food but made sure to keep her wine glass full. She ignored the frown of disapproval Marisa sent her way as she reached for the bottle of barely palatable merlot for the third time. Being with Nick all these months had definitely spoiled her, for she was now used to drinking eighty dollar vintages, dining at Michelin starred restaurants, and wearing an extensive assortment of designer clothing similar to what she had on now.

She tried to picture Nick here at the wedding, surrounded by her family and their friends, and shook her head. It would never happen, she realized. Even though he'd been upfront with her from the start, she was honest enough with herself now to admit she'd always secretly hoped he might change. She wanted him here beside her now, to show him off and feel immense pride at being able to introduce him as her boyfriend. She was just about the only one here without a spouse or date, and certainly the only one here at their table of seven – Marisa, Deanna, their cousin Valerie and the three husbands. The place on Angela's right was glaringly empty, a continual reminder that she was alone, and would always attend these sort of events alone as long as Nick was in her life.

Soon after the entrees were cleared away, Marisa's oldest daughter Samantha ventured over to their table and plopped down next to Angela. The kids that had been invited to the wedding – teenagers, really, since no one under the age of fourteen had been included – had been seated at separate tables from their parents, presumably because someone had thought it would be more fun for them that way. In actuality, thought Angela with a smirk, it was because their parents were glad for an opportunity to eat a meal and get tipsy without having to deal with all that teenage angst for a change.

Samantha, the oldest of Gino and Rita's grandchildren, had always been a sweet girl, and Angela had felt sorry for her considering the way Marisa had bossed her around since birth. Lately, however, with the onset of adolescence, Samantha had become something of a brat. Marisa fretted constantly about how sassy her oldest had become, how impossible to deal with, and blamed her behavior on the new group of friends she'd met since starting high school. Angela guessed it was more a case of raging teenage hormones combined with finally standing up to her bossy, domineering mother.

Marisa frowned as her daughter took the empty chair between her and Angela. "What's the matter? Why aren't you sitting over with the other kids?"

Samantha rolled her eyes. "They're all a bunch of dorks, Mom. God, I am so bored right now! And I hate this dress. Why couldn't we have got the black one that I liked?"

Marisa sighed. "You know why. You're fourteen and much too young to wear black. Plus, that dress you liked was way too low-cut and tight. You look beautiful in this dress, honey. Ask your Aunt Angie if you don't believe me."

Personally, Angela thought the yellow and white floral print dress was too fussy and at least three or four years too young for her niece but wasn't about to get in the middle of a disagreement between mother and daughter. She'd made that mistake before, only to have Marisa fly off the handle and tell her to butt out of things she couldn't possibly understand.

Angela picked up one of Samantha's long, golden brown curls, and smiled at her moody, petulant niece. "You look really pretty, Sam. And black probably wouldn't have been the best choice for a summer afternoon wedding." She bent her head to whisper conspiratorially, "But it would be awesome for the homecoming dance in October."

Samantha giggled, ignoring the irritated scowl her mother sent her way. Marisa and Deanna hated the fact that their kids always seemed to flock to their Aunt Angie, and especially when it was Samantha, who was, after all, only eight years younger than Angela.

"Ooh, I just noticed your dress, Aunt Angie," gushed Samantha. "Omigod, I swear this is the exact same dress I saw in *InStyle* magazine last month. I think Cameron Diaz was wearing it to some premier. Or maybe Gisele Bundchen. Hang on, I'll check."

"No, don't bother, Sam. It's not – " Angela's protest fell on deaf fourteen year old ears as her niece began to tap on the keyboard of her cell phone.

"Here it is," exclaimed Samantha triumphantly. "Hah, I knew it! It's the exact same dress."

Marisa peeked over her daughter's shoulder at the phone and gasped. "That can't be the same dress. I mean, it looks exactly the same but Angela's has to be a copy, a – a knockoff. I mean, this one in the magazine – it's what – a Valentino – and costs – how much?" She pressed a hand to her heart. "Thirty five hundred dollars? For one dress?"

Before Angela could stop her, Samantha impishly peeked at the tag inside the dress and squealed, "It *is* the same dress! It's a Valentino! Wow, Aunt Angie, way to go! And – Omigod, are those real Louboutins? Mom, did you see her shoes? Those are the ones JLo wrote a song about."

By now Deanna and Valerie had joined in on the conversation, all of the husbands otherwise occupied in a heated discussion about the NBA playoffs.

Valerie, who worked part-time at a consignment shop in Carmel, honed in on the cream quilted shoulder bag that Angela had draped over the back of her chair.

"And that's a real Chanel bag," murmured Valerie in awe. "Definitely not a knockoff. God, Angela, that's something like a three thousand dollar purse."

Deanna just stared. "How in the world can you afford all this? I mean, Marco had to call in a favor to get your rent reduced on that apartment in his uncle's building. Where did you get this kind of money all of a sudden?"

Angela took a much needed sip of wine and tried desperately to shrug the matter off. "I make good money now. I brought in a really big account last month and decided to treat myself to a new outfit."

Marisa shook her head. "I don't believe it. You can't make *that* much money, you haven't even been there a full year. And if you got that big of a bonus why didn't you buy a new car instead of an outfit like this?"

Valerie was inspecting Angela's jewelry now and she damned the bad luck that had resulted in her snoopy cousin sitting at her table. "These are real diamonds. And cultured pearls. The necklace and earrings must have cost a pretty penny, too."

Samantha giggled. "I'll bet Aunt Angie has a rich boyfriend who's buying her all this stuff. Hey, does he have a younger brother? Or a nephew or cousin?"

Angela fought back a rising sense of panic at her niece's innocent but potentially disastrous comments. "No, no. There's no one."

Marisa scowled. "You always were a terrible liar, Angela. Now fess up – who is he?"

"More importantly," chimed in Deanna, "why didn't he come with you today?"

Angela hoped she sounded casual, nonchalant. "Because it's just not that serious. It's a very low key, very informal kind of thing."

Deanna snorted. "He's dropping – what – like ten grand on what you're wearing and it's not serious? Marisa's right – you're a lousy liar. We always knew it was you when our stuff went missing or something got broken when you were little."

"What's his name? And how long have you been dating? I can't believe Mom never told us about him," lamented Marisa.

Angela took another swig of wine, reaching for the half empty bottle to refill her glass yet again. "Mom doesn't know. Because it isn't serious and there's nothing to talk about. So let's drop the subject, shall we?"

But the others weren't so easily dissuaded and continued to ply her with questions about the new man in her life. Angela either kept her answers short and non-committal or ignored the question altogether. She was very, very careful not to give the slightest hint that Nick was someone she worked with, and certainly not even the tiniest clue as to who he was. Both of her brothers-in-law were huge football fans, perhaps even more so than her father, and the name of Nick Manning would instantly ring all sorts of bells.

Marisa made a horrible face at her. "Oh, God, this is why you stood us up for our birthdays, isn't it? You were seeing this man, weren't you? Why didn't you just tell us? And if things aren't serious why are you choosing him over your family?"

Angela was thankfully saved from having to dream up a response by the announcement that the cake cutting was about to commence. Samantha returned to her own table while her sisters and cousin hurried to gather round the bride and groom to snap photos as they playfully fed each other slices of wedding cake. But she knew this temporary distraction wouldn't last long, and that her sisters would be quick to resume their interrogation of her any minute now.

She desperately wanted to get the hell out of here, to just get in her car and head back to San Francisco – to Nick. But she'd made the unfortunate decision to drive here with her parents and was now dependent on them to get back to their house. And, knowing her mother and the importance she placed on family and keeping up appearances, she'd be stuck here until nearly the bitter end.

And she knew, just knew, that her sisters wouldn't waste any time in telling their mother all about her new boyfriend and the fact that he was showering her with expensive gifts. She cursed her gossipy, jealous sisters for taking a very untimely interest in her affairs. They nearly always chose to ignore her, rarely asked about her life, and generally didn't give a crap about her. But, she realized sourly, they also relished any opportunity to make trouble for her, to paint her in an unflattering light to Rita – as though they needed any help to accomplish that.

And she cursed herself, too, for having accepted such an admittedly extravagant gift from Nick. It was one thing to wear expensive clothes when they were out together, especially since the restaurants, clubs, and parties they frequented were patronized by equally well dressed individuals. But she'd never suspected her rather frumpy sisters would even notice what she was wearing, much less figure out how costly it was. And if Samantha hadn't chosen to venture over to their table, no one would have been the wiser.

She managed to avoid any further discussion about either her outfit or her boyfriend for the remainder of the wedding, though it wasn't an especially easy task. She alternated between slipping away from the table to chat up other guests or to hit the bar, and simply ignoring her sisters' more persistent questions.

But there was no avoiding her mother's demands for answers that started the moment her father began to pull out of the parking lot. She couldn't very well fling herself out of a moving vehicle – though she was sorely tempted to do just that in order to avoid what she knew was going to be an extremely unpleasant conversation.

"Why didn't you tell us you had a boyfriend?" demanded Rita. "And why didn't you bring him to the wedding?"

Angela once again attempted to sound relaxed and totally unconcerned about the matter. "Mom, he's not really what you'd call a boyfriend. We go out once in awhile, that's all. Nothing serious at all."

"Not serious? Marisa said this man – whoever he is – bought you that outfit you've got on and that it cost thousands of dollars. "

Angela sighed. "Marisa needs to mind her own business. Or go back to ignoring me like she has all my life."

"Your sisters are worried about you," chided Rita. "If you're accepting expensive gifts from a man you aren't even serious about, then I would say that's cause for concern."

"Well, that would be a first, wouldn't it?" retorted Angela caustically. "I can't remember a single time in my life when either of them worried about me."

Rita shook her head. "You know that's not true, Angela. Why do you always say such awful things about your sisters? Of course they worry about you. Now, who's this man you're dating? Someone from work, I suppose?"

Angela looked out the back window, knowing things were going to get unpleasant very quickly. "I'd rather not talk about him, Mom. And we're not really dating, just hanging out once in awhile."

"And yet you chose him over your own sisters, your family? You skipped your sisters' birthdays to be with this man and yet you still don't bring him to meet us? Are you ashamed of us or something?"

Angela closed her eyes, feeling the beginnings of an all too familiar tension headache beginning to throb at her temples. "No, Mom. I'm not ashamed of you."

"Oh, God, are you seeing a married man, Angela?" Rita demanded. "That's why he gives you expensive gifts, isn't it? And why you didn't bring him today to meet your family. Gino – for God's sake – your daughter is fooling around with a married man. Say something to her."

Calm as ever, Gino merely asked gently, "Is that true, Angie?"

She reached out and squeezed his shoulder. "No, Dad. He's not married. But it's just not that serious between us to bring him to something like a big family wedding. It's really not a big deal."

Rita snorted. "No big deal? You let this man – we don't even know his name – buy you expensive presents and it's not a big deal? Are you turning into some sort of whore – sleeping with men so they'll buy you nice things?"

Angela gasped at her mother's vicious accusation while Gino – ever the peacemaker – made a futile attempt to diffuse the escalating unpleasantness.

"Rita, don't say those things to Angie," he pleaded. "She just told us everything's okay."

"And you believe her – just like that?" asked Rita incredulously. "Well, why would it be any different than when she was a child? You always believed whatever lies she told you, how she always tried to turn you against me and the girls. Wise up, Gino. Angela is lying to us both. I'll bet you a hundred dollars this man she's sleeping with is married and has a family. And he buys her designer dresses and jewelry because she's his *puttana.* God, I thought I taught you better than that, Angela."

Furious at her mother's insults, Angela lashed out almost without thinking. "Taught me? What the hell did you ever teach me? How to ignore and neglect your own child? How to make her feel unwanted and unloved? Well, you did a damned good job teaching me all that, Mom."

Rita moved too fast for Angela to turn away, and the crack of her mother's palm against her cheek sounded like gunfire within the closed confines of the car. Even in the dark she could see the blazing anger in Rita's eyes, the way she was trembling with rage.

"How dare you!" hissed Rita. "You know nothing – *nothing!*"

"I know *everything,*" corrected Angela. "How you got knocked up again by accident at age forty, how you were a day away from getting rid of me until Dad stopped you. And how you've made me pay for that every day of my life."

"Angie, no," pleaded Gino. "That's not how it was. Who told you such terrible things?"

Rita's eyes were cold, and Angela shuddered in revulsion at the low, horrible sound of her voice. "No, Gino. She's got it exactly right. And I don't know who told her but whoever did left out one fact – I shouldn't have listed to you back then, shouldn't have given in. I should have gotten rid of this ungrateful *puttana* when I had the chance."

Angela wasn't sure who was more shocked by Rita's outburst – her or Gino. Her father paled, his jaw dropping open soundlessly, but somehow he managed to maintain his focus enough to drive the remaining mile or so back to the house safely. Angela, meanwhile, was numb, even though the angry words that had tumbled forth from her mother's lips were ones she'd always known to be true.

Angela had never been so grateful to see the house – the one she'd always hated coming home to – as she was now. Before Gino had even turned off the engine she was out of the car like a shot. She sorely regretted having had so much to drink, far too much to consider driving even a few miles, much less making the long drive back to San Francisco. She was stuck here in Carmel for the night, and wished desperately that Lauren's parents weren't out of town right now. Otherwise, she would have run next door, as she had so many times over the years, knowing that Natalie would have found a way to make everything all right. But the McKinnon's were in New York right now visiting Julia, which meant that Angela would be forced to stay the night in her parents' house, a thought that made her want to vomit profusely.

"Angie, wait. Talk to me, honey. It's not like she said," Gino called out even as she strode inside the garage.

Angela turned and faced her father, shaking her head even as she recognized the sorrow on his dear, sweet face. "No, Dad. It's exactly like she said. And, sorry, but there really isn't anything more to talk about. I mean, Mom pretty much said it all, didn't she? I'm going to bed now and I'll be leaving early in the morning. And don't expect to see me back here for a long time."

***

It would have been glaringly obvious even to a five year old child that Angela was deeply upset. Given that Nick was just about the most observant, intuitive person she'd ever known, he barely had to glance at her to realize that something was wrong – major league wrong.

He was waiting in her apartment – why she wasn't quite sure because she'd returned to San Francisco several hours earlier than originally planned – but suddenly being in his arms was more important than breathing. Within seconds of being enfolded in his warm, crushing embrace, she burst into tears – huge, wracking tears.

"Shh. It's okay, Angel," he soothed. "Hey, I know it's

traditional to cry at weddings but this is ridiculous."

But his rather lame attempt at humor failed miserably and she only clung to him tighter as her sobs escalated. She was far too upset over everything that had gone down with her mother and sisters to realize that this was the first time she'd ever really broken down this way in front of Nick, the first time she'd ever been so in need of his comfort. The night when she'd told him about the circumstances of her birth had certainly been emotional, but even then she hadn't sobbed her heart out as though it was breaking into a million tiny pieces.

Gradually her weeping began to cease, though her entire body was trembling in reaction. She'd barely slept a wink last night, as upset as she'd been, and had consumed way too much coffee this morning to compensate. She hadn't eaten a thing, her stomach a gnarly mess, and as a result she was shaky and exhausted and extra emotional.

Fortunately, Nick didn't seem to mind her overwrought state and merely continued to hold her, his embrace making her feel warm and protected and even loved – though she knew the latter was a truly dangerous thing for her to hope for.

"You going to tell me what happened?" he asked quietly.

"Yeah." She nodded and began to recount – haltingly – what had occurred, starting with her niece's well-intentioned but ultimately devastating comments about her dress and shoes. By the time she'd finished, culminating with the really dreadful truths her mother had lashed out with, her voice had diminished to a hoarse croak, too wrecked with tears and lack of sleep to go on.

Throughout the re-telling of the clusterfuck of events, Nick had remained silent, his expression blank and carefully controlled. When she finished, he didn't say a word, merely stood and walked into her tiny excuse of a kitchen and began to brew her some tea.

"Do you have any honey? Or whiskey?" he asked as the water boiled. "Preferably both."

"No whiskey. I think there might be some packets of honey in one of the drawers along with the ketchup and soy sauce. But I can do it, Nick," she offered tiredly.

"Forget it. Ah, here they are. Jesus, what *don't* you have in this drawer?"

She accepted the steaming mug of tea from him gratefully, the hot, honeyed brew instantly soothing her scratchy throat. "Thanks," she whispered.

She was alarmed to realize her hands were trembling and she clutched the heavy mug with both hands to steady it.

"No problem." He sat on the bed beside her, tucking a loose strand of hair behind her ear. "It's the least I can do, considering it's largely my fault this whole fucked up mess went down."

"What?" She glanced up at him in surprise. "How is any of it your fault? You weren't even there."

Nick shook his head. "No, but I was the one who insisted you wear that dress and those shoes. And it sounds like this whole thing started when your niece honed in on what you were wearing."

Angela shrugged and took a sip of tea. "I blame myself, actually. I should have known better than to provoke my mother. I should have kept my mouth shut, just acted like nothing had ever happened, and let her continue to sweep everything under the rug."

He stared at her in disbelief. "You can't mean to say that this was the first time you ever admitted to your mother that you knew the truth?"

She stared down into her mug. "You don't get it, Nick. My mother isn't the sort of person who talks openly about her feelings. She keeps it all bottled up, puts on an act most of the time. And since she barely talks to me at all, it makes perfect sense that she'd try to act like none of that stuff ever happened. In her mind, she probably believes that she's been an ideal mother to me, and that I'm the ungrateful brat who makes up stories."

"That's fucked up, Angel," he muttered darkly. "Really, deeply fucked up. You should have walloped her back when she slapped you." He took her chin between his fingers and tilted her head from side to side. "Doesn't look like she hit you very hard. At least, I don't see any sort of mark."

"No, she didn't hit me all that hard. Or maybe I just ducked in time and missed the full impact. I got pretty good at that over the years."

Nick's mouth tightened grimly. "She made a habit of wailing on you, did she?"

"Not exactly. Especially since I was already taller than she was by the time I was nine. But every so often I'd do or say something to really piss her off and she'd give me a swat on the ass or slap my face. As long as my father wasn't around, of course. He didn't always stick up for me like he should have but he wouldn't have stood for her hitting me."

Tenderly he caressed her cheek and pressed a kiss to each side. "I'm sorry your weekend was such a disaster."

She rested her head on his shoulder. "Me, too. I should have blown off the stupid wedding, just like I skipped my sisters' birthdays. None of this would have happened if I'd done that."

The hand that had been caressing her shoulder stilled. "When did you miss their birthdays?" he asked quietly.

Angela strove to sound casual and unconcerned. "Deanna's was back in March when we went to Mexico. And Marisa's was in May, the same weekend as Dante's big party."

"Why didn't you tell me?"

She gazed at him in bewilderment. "Because I would have much rather gone to Mexico and the party than attend some boring birthday dinner. Besides, it wasn't like they were special birthdays or anything. Not to mention the fact that no one would have paid any attention to me if I'd gone."

Nick covered her hand with his. "Angel, I never intended for you to choose me over your family. Especially when it sounds like that's been causing problems for you."

She set her mug aside and wrapped her arms around his waist. "I don't care," she declared firmly. "And I know you'd never ask me to make that sort of choice. It was *my* decision, Nick, and I don't regret it one bit. Besides, I thought you told me that I needed to gain some independence from my family and not care so much about what they think."

"I did tell you that," he agreed. "And I meant it. But not to the point where you alienate them. You should have told me about the birthdays, Angel. We could have gone to Mexico another weekend. And Dante has parties all the time. Promise me that from now on you'll tell me if it's something significant, okay?"

"All right." She heaved a sigh. "Though as strained as things are between my mother and me right now, I'm not sure if I'll be welcomed back anytime soon."

He squeezed her hand reassuringly. "I wouldn't worry about that. If your mom is as good as you say she is at sweeping things under the rug, she'll probably act like none of this ever happened."

"Unfortunately, you're probably right," she agreed tiredly. "And how fucked up is that?"

He slid an arm around her shoulders and lowered her head to rest against his. "You look exhausted, Angel. Did you get much sleep last night?"

She shook her head. "Too wound up and upset. If I hadn't chugged a full bottle of wine plus pre-dinner cocktails I would have driven home last night."

"Tsk, tsk. Sounds like someone was a very bad girl," he chided. "You know you're not supposed to drink that much. I should tie you up just for that. However," he added, brushing a kiss on her forehead "what I should really do instead is let you get some sleep."

"No." She rose up on her knees, twining her arms around his neck. "I don't need to sleep. What I need now is to forget. So, please, Nick," she whispered, "make me forget. Everything but this, that is."

She swiftly began to strip before his intense, watchful gaze until she was naked and reclining back against the pillows. Wordlessly, his hand trailed down her throat between her breasts to her belly. She was already quivering in arousal and gasped when his fingers slid deep inside of her body where she was wet and needy.

"Your wish is my command, Angel," he murmured in her ear, just before his mouth closed over hers demandingly.

Chapter Eleven

Within days after that fateful Sunday morning at her apartment, things began to change – or rather, deteriorate – rapidly in her relationship with Nick. It wasn't any one thing, or anything too obvious, but Angela sensed that he was gradually beginning to put more and more distance between them. He didn't see her as often, for one thing – no more than twice a week, if that – and when they were together he seemed distant, distracted, and said little. She longed to ask him what was wrong, to beg for his reassurance that everything was still okay between them. But with a horrible, hollow feeling deep in the pit of her stomach, she began more and more to fear that the end of their relationship was inevitable.

Her fears began to consume her, and soon she found herself hanging onto him almost desperately when they were together. She tried harder than ever to be as accommodating and adoring as possible, to do everything in her power to please him. At the same time, though, she also became clingier, silently begging him with her body to stay in her bed just a bit longer, to pull him close for one more kiss, for five more minutes in his arms.

More than once she'd actually pleaded with him to stay with her, to not leave quite so soon. He'd hesitated each time but had given in to her pleas more often than not, holding her until she'd fallen asleep before slipping out of her apartment as was his norm.

Sleep itself became more and more elusive. She'd have trouble falling asleep, tossing and turning as she fretted and worried about how much longer it would last with Nick. Or, if she did manage to fall into an exhausted slumber, it rarely lasted more than a couple of hours and she'd wake up abruptly, unable to fall back asleep.

She was nervous and on edge all the time, and the only thing that distracted her even a little was work. Ironically, she was receiving more referrals than ever, and she wondered wildly if this was Nick's parting gift to her. Her appetite began to fade rapidly, though she was careful not to let him notice when she lost a few pounds, and would force herself to eat in his presence.

And she began to drink – a lot. She found that having a few glasses of wine or several shots of tequila seemed to take the edge off and calm her down, and helped her to fall asleep. Again she was careful not to let Nick know, kept any liquor bottles well hidden, and only drank sparingly when he was with her.

She consoled herself with the fact that the sex at least was every bit as hot and passionate as ever, that Nick hadn't seemed to tire of her between the sheets. If anything, the sex was even more intense, more satisfying than ever, and there was an almost savage desperation about the way he took her nowadays. It was the one thing that continued to give her hope that things weren't falling apart in their relationship, that made her believe that she might just be imagining the distance between them, or that Nick might be preoccupied with work and nothing more serious.

But it became increasingly more difficult to convince herself that nothing was wrong as the weeks passed, and she saw less and less of Nick. She knew, however, that coming right out and asking him what the matter was, or to beg him not to leave her, would be the final nail in the coffin. So she kept her fears and insecurities hidden, as she always had, and, as a result, lost a little more of herself with each passing day.

Her twenty third birthday was in late July, but thus far she hadn't even begun to make any plans to celebrate. Her relationship with her family these days was strained – to put it mildly – and she knew better than to expect her mother or sisters to organize any sort of celebration for her.

The weekend after Gabriella's wedding – and the huge, nasty scene with her mother – Angela had reluctantly made her usual phone call home. Predictably, Rita had acted as though their fight had never happened, once again sweeping all the unpleasantness under the carpet. Their phone call had been brief and impersonal as it always was, and Angela knew her mother would never willingly bring the subject up again.

And Rita had evidently not shared the details of their blow-up with Marisa and Deanna, for Angela knew she'd have heard all about it from her sisters otherwise. But they were rather obviously still pissed at her for skipping both of their birthday celebrations because neither of them had made any mention of getting together for her own birthday. Their parents were leaving on a two-week Mediterranean cruise a few days before her birthday, and Angela couldn't help but wonder if her mother had planned their departure date intentionally. Her father, clueless as he was, never seemed to remember important dates like birthdays so he would have willingly gone along with whatever Rita told him to do – as usual.

By the day before her birthday, Angela had more or less resigned herself to celebrating the occasion alone. There'd still been no word from her sisters, not even a card or an email greeting; her parents were cruising somewhere in Italy; Lauren was on assignment in Nova Scotia; and because she was so paranoid about keeping her schedule free in case Nick called and wanted to see her, she'd more or less alienated all of her friends and co-workers by now, so she certainly couldn't count on any of them to celebrate with her.

And it had been more than a week now since she'd seen or heard from Nick, a state of affairs that concerned her far, far more than the idea of spending her birthday alone. She wasn't even sure if he knew it was her birthday tomorrow, given his overall dislike of all things sentimental. She'd never dared to bring the subject up, and didn't know when his own birthday was.

On the actual day, she received email greetings from Lauren, Julia, and their mother Natalie, and Angela found it both sad and ironic that the McKinnons had remembered her when her own mother and sisters hadn't – intentionally or otherwise. She received several other emails from college friends, volleyball teammates, and other family members – including her cousin Gabriella and niece Samantha. But the one person she longed to hear from the most – quite frankly, the *only* person she ached to hear from – continued to remain incommunicado and she was beginning to sink a little deeper into despair with each day that passed without a word from him.

She left work earlier than usual, not because she was anxious to get home and spend another lonely evening by herself – and on her birthday, to boot – but because she was too depressed and unfocused to get any work done. She stopped en route and bought a very pricey bottle of champagne, a red velvet cupcake, and a takeout order from her favorite Chinese restaurant. She'd settle in and get caught up on the last season of *The Big Bang Theory* while enjoying her dinner, and wouldn't permit herself to dwell on the fact that she was alone and forgotten on what should have been one of the best days of the year.

But as she approached her apartment building, she recognized the scarlet Ferrari parked in front, and her spirits and her step picked up considerably. She took the stairs at an almost breakneck pace, forcing herself not to burst into the apartment.

She found it impossible, however, to contain the joy that filled her as she saw Nick standing in the middle of the room, a huge bouquet of lush, showy red roses in his hand and a sexy smile on his sinfully handsome face.

"Happy birthday, Angel," he drawled, holding his arms open.

She rushed to him, never having been so happy to see anyone in her entire life, and never having needed anyone as badly as she did at this exact moment. Heedless of the huge bouquet in his hand, not to mention all of the parcels she was clutching, she flung herself against him, burying her face against the strong, tanned column of his throat.

Nick held her for long seconds, pressing a kiss to the top of her head before gently easing her away. "Why don't we get the flowers into some water, hmm? And what's all this?"

He nodded approvingly at the bottle of champagne. "I see that you've managed to acquire an appreciation for fine wines, Angel. Glad that my influence has finally rubbed off. But," he added with a frown of displeasure, "greasy Chinese takeout isn't a fitting meal for your birthday. And I have a very different dessert in mind tonight than a cupcake." He bent his head and whispered to her wickedly, "I'd take a taste of that sweet, juicy pussy of yours over cream cheese frosting any day."

She gasped as he slid a hand past her belly to her crotch, cupping her through the fabric of her skirt. "God, yes," she breathed. "It's been so long. I need - "

His hand slid to her ass, pulling her flush against his fully aroused body, his hugely swollen cock rubbing against the notch of her thighs. "I know exactly how long it's been, Angel," he rasped. "And exactly how much I need to be inside of you right now. But," he added as he stepped back, releasing his hold on her, "not until after dinner. And we can't leave for dinner until you change into your new dress."

As she hurried to change clothes and touch up her hair and makeup, she realized that he'd offered no explanation – much less any sort of apology – for why it had been nearly ten days since he'd contacted her. Ten days during which she'd suffered the agonies of hell while wondering if he would ever call again or what she'd done to anger him. But of course she couldn't ask him why, couldn't even hint about the fact that she'd been so upset. Emotional attachment had never been part of their relationship, and she shuddered to imagine the consequences if she betrayed her feelings to him now.

An hour later they were seated at the best table at her very favorite restaurant, drinking an even more expensive champagne than the one she'd bought earlier. She was wearing her gorgeous new dress of scarlet silk, paired with the sexiest shoes she'd ever seen – ankle strap stiletto sandals of scarlet satin. Angela had been thrilled to note that Nick was wearing her very favorite suit – a dark gray pinstripe teamed with a crisp white shirt and a dark red silk tie. She knew he'd worn it for her, that he knew it was her favorite, and she almost giggled with delight at how he seemed to be going out of his way tonight to please her.

In addition to the dress, shoes, and red satin Fendi clutch, Nick had given her a gorgeous set of ruby and diamond jewelry – another choker-style necklace, drop earrings, and a dainty bracelet.

He reached across the table and trailed a finger along the deep V neckline of the seriously sexy dress. "Red is your color, Angel," he observed lazily. "Ironic, isn't it, given that's typically a color associated with the devil."

She tugged playfully on his tie. "Maybe you've succeeded in corrupting me."

He grinned, pinching her cheek. "So you're a fallen angel now, are you? Or more of a scarlet woman? Hmm, no, I don't believe it. To me you'll always be my angel, no matter what color you're wearing."

She slid her hand over his, turning her face to press a kiss to his palm. "I'll be whatever you want me to be. Always."

Nick squeezed her hand. "Tonight I just want you to be the birthday girl. The pampered, totally spoiled birthday girl."

Angela laughed happily. "I can totally be her. In fact, I'm pretty sure I already am being her."

He drew her hand to his lips, sucking the index finger into his mouth, and she was glad they were seated – as usual – in a darkened, secluded corner. "You ain't seen nothing yet, Angel. I've got plans for you once we get back to your apartment. And, no, it doesn't involve sharing the cupcake you bought."

She giggled, even as a shimmer of desire rippled up her spine and she felt her unbound breasts swell within the fine silk bodice of her dress. Fortunately the garment was fully lined so that the pointed tips of her nipples weren't glaringly obvious.

Nick had even arranged for a birthday cake, beautifully decorated with her name written across the top, and lit by more than a dozen candles. Several of the wait staff gathered around their table to sing "Happy Birthday" and Angela's own heart sang with happiness. She was head over heels in love with the gorgeous, compelling man seated across the table from her, the man who had gone to great lengths to arrange this fabulous evening for her, who had hand-picked the stunning outfit and jewels she wore. And she was convinced that he cared for her far more than he would ever admit, for how could he have gone to this much trouble to make sure her birthday was something special if he wasn't at least a little in love with her?

She was filled with renewed confidence that everything was just fine in their relationship, that they were as solid as ever. The sense of relief that washed through her was incredible, and she told herself firmly that she'd been worrying for nothing, that things were exactly as they should be.

In the eleven months they'd been together, Angela couldn't

think of a time when they'd gone more than a few days without having sex, and she could tell that Nick was as highly strung and needy as she was. Their awareness of each other grew and grew as the evening continued, but he only touched her very fleetingly and casually – a brush of his knuckles against her cheek, a squeeze of her hand, a light touch of her arm. In spite of the privacy their table afforded them, he didn't attempt even once to touch her more intimately – to slide his hand up her bare thigh and higher, to where she'd been wet and ready for him all evening; or to not so subtly cup her breast, his thumb flicking over the tight bud of her nipple through the silky fabric of her dress. She squirmed impatiently, aroused just from being near him, from inhaling the scent of his soap and his skin, and she almost whimpered aloud with need.

Nick gave her a knowing smile, almost a smirk, as he very deliberately lingered over a post-dinner glass of port. "How well I know that look on your face, Angel," he told her in an amused voice. "But it won't do you any good. I'll fuck you when I decide the time is right. And you're not quite ready."

She bit down on her bottom lip as she crossed and uncrossed her legs, struggling not to fidget. "I'm always ready for you, Nick," she whispered.

"Hmm." He took another leisurely sip of his drink, regarding her with that maddeningly cryptic smile that both enthralled and infuriated her at the same time. "And here I thought we'd made so much progress on teaching you control, Angel. Perhaps someone needs a refresher course. Like, for example, tonight I could spread you out, tie you to the bed, and then make you wait for a couple of hours in that position."

Her pulse rate accelerated rapidly and she felt beads of sweat form between her breasts. Her breathing grew uneven as she visualized the erotic picture he'd just painted for her. "But what about – how can you wait - " she asked hesitantly.

Nick grinned wickedly. "I never said anything about waiting. In fact, I can't think of a bigger turn-on than watching you that way." He leaned in close, his hot breath tickling her ear. "Watching you spread and bound while I come all over your belly and breasts, and then rubbing my cum into your skin. Next,

I'll flip you over and come on your back and your ass. The third time," his teeth bit down on her earlobe and she shivered as his voice grew huskier, "I'll fuck your mouth, come so hard down your throat that my cum will be running down your chin. And then, finally, I'll give you what you want so badly." He slid a hand up her thigh to cup her crotch. "I'll ram my cock inside this hot, tight pussy so hard you'll scream, fuck you so long and so deep you won't be able to walk straight for a week."

Angela was shaking, so turned on that she thought wildly if he kept talking to her in that deliberately seductive voice she could have an orgasm just from listening to him.

He must have sensed her distress, for he quickly summoned their waiter over and settled the bill, then hustled her out of the restaurant. She could sense his own impatience now, could feel the way his big, hard body throbbed with need as they waited for the valet to bring the Ferrari around.

He drove with his usual precision and control, but also at a faster than normal speed. Angela breathed a sigh of relief when he found a parking space close by her building, fearful that he would have rammed another car out of the way otherwise.

He didn't speak as he tugged her along in his wake, not breaking stride until they were inside her apartment. He wasted no time in unzipping her dress, the red silk sliding to the floor like a pool of blood around her feet. She was naked except for her towering high heels and the tiny scrap of her red lace thong.

Nick's hard, fully aroused body pressed up against her back, his hands cupping her breasts as his lips caressed her throat. "I want you to get on the bed now, Angel," he rasped. "This is going to happen exactly as I described to you in the restaurant." He pinched her nipples hard enough to draw a startled gasp from her throat. "However, if you're a very, very good girl I might be persuaded to improvise every so often. Like right now, for example."

She cried out as he penetrated her soaking wet slit with two long fingers, hooking them inside her pubic bone while his thumb rubbed over her clit. She came instantly, her hands clutching his muscular forearms desperately as her whole body shook.

He'd barely given her time to recover before giving her a hard smack on the ass. "Back on track now, Angel," he growled. "Get on the bed."

Angela complied instantly, too accustomed to his domineering ways by now to even think of hesitating. He tied her to the bedposts with red silken cords, the binds feeling tighter than usual to her for some reason. Nick ran a hand over her still quivering belly, his heated gaze inspecting her body carefully, critically.

"You've lost weight," he told her with a disapproving frown. "At least five pounds, I'm guessing. Why haven't you been eating, Angel?"

She thought briefly about denying the fact, then considered fobbing him off with a story about working too many hours or having upped the amount of cardio she'd been doing, but knew he'd see right through any lie she could dream up. So even if hearing the truth angered him, she had no other option but to tell him.

"I missed you," she whispered. "I worried that you weren't going to call again."

Nick shook his head, his fingers plucking at the narrow, lacy band of her thong. "That's no reason to stop eating, Angel," he told her quietly. "I'm sure as hell not worth you risking your health over. I want you to promise me now that you'll never do that again."

She nodded, too mesmerized by his dark gaze boring into hers to deny him anything. "I – I promise."

He bent and kissed her cheek softly, his hand sliding around to squeeze her ass. "Good girl. Always so obedient. And always so sexy."

Nick kissed her mouth then, with long, deep swoops of his tongue, kissed her until she groaned beneath his lips and her hips began to lift off the mattress involuntarily. His deep, drugging kisses went on for long minutes, but aside from his fingers holding her jaw in place he didn't touch her.

By the time he lifted his mouth from hers and stood up to begin undressing, she was panting – breathless from his devouring kisses, and with every nerve ending in her body so tightly strung she knew she'd be able to come long and hard with the most subtle of touches.

But Nick was intent on following his game plan to the letter – undressing without the slightest bit of urgency, smiling carnally as he watched her reaction to the sight of his bare skin. His cock was enormous, so long and thick and hard that she whimpered at the sight of it, longing to feel its heavy girth thrusting deeply inside her body. Instead, he began to stroke himself, his hand moving slowly and deliberately up and down the considerable length from root to tip, over and over again, until he began to breathe a little harder with each stroke. She licked her lips as her pelvis thrust up off the bed, almost as though she could feel him inside of her already, as if each time his hand stroked his penis it was her pussy engulfing him instead.

A low shout was the only sound he made when he came, the thick, hot streams of semen landing all over her body – belly, breasts, thighs. As he'd tantalized her with back at the restaurant, he took his time rubbing every drop of his essence into her skin, bathing her in his scent, and the experience was so erotic, so deeply personal, that tears streamed from her eyes and she had to choke back a sob.

"Shh."

He kissed each eyelid, his thumb prying her bottom lip open until she sucked on it. His mouth moved hotly down her throat to her breasts, and she yelped in surprise as he bit down hard on one of her nipples. He squeezed both of her breasts roughly as his mouth moved from one to the other, suckling on her over-sensitized nipples until she was squirming in renewed arousal. Her arms strained at their bonds, and she longed for her hands to be free so that she could clutch his head closer to her swollen, aching breasts.

Without warning, Nick slid down her body and swiftly drew her clit between his lips. Her body was already so highly stimulated that it took mere seconds for her to shatter again.

Afterwards, he returned to the script he'd recounted for her back at the restaurant – flipping her onto her belly; stroking himself to another climax and coming on her back and buttocks;

then turning her again to lay on her back as he straddled her head, guiding his insatiable cock between her eagerly parted lips. Without the use of her hands she had to rely solely on her lips and tongue to bring him pleasure, and on Nick himself to control the depth and frequency of his thrusts. She took him willingly, opening up her throat to accept every hard, throbbing inch he gave her. He murmured to her in a low, guttural voice what it was he wanted, and she complied instantly, desperate to please him. And when he came, her jaw was too sore from the endless minutes of sucking him off to swallow, and the hot, sticky streams of semen overflowed her mouth, running down her jaw to her breasts.

He untied her then, and had to lift her arms and legs to wrap around his body since she was too wrung out, her muscles too sore, to do it herself. Nick pressed a kiss to her bruised, bee-stung lips.

"You've pleased me well, Angel," he crooned. "As always. But I'm forgetting that this is *your* birthday and that tonight should be about *your* pleasure."

She cupped his cheek in her hand. "But your pleasure *is* my pleasure," she murmured huskily. "Pleasing you is what I live for, Nick."

His eyes darkened at her words, but he was unsmiling as he trailed a finger between her breasts. "I've taught you well, haven't I, Angel? Sometimes I think too well."

She shook her head. "No, never. I want - "

Her protest was swallowed up by the incessant demand of his kisses, his tongue taking renewed possession of her mouth. And then her protests were forgotten as he lavished attention on her body – kissing, caressing, licking, squeezing. It seemed there wasn't even an inch of her body he didn't touch or kiss, and he kept it up until she was writhing in arousal, her hips thrusting up at him frantically, and she was begging him plaintively.

"Please, ah, God, Nick, please," she panted. "God, I need you so much, need to be fucked so badly. Do it now, please!"

Angela screamed as he wrenched her thighs apart and rammed inside her body with one commanding thrust. He'd aroused her to the point where she came immediately, her body so primed and ready that it had only needed the feel of him sheathed deeply inside her to start the convulsions. And as he began to stroke in and out of her, the tremors only grew in intensity until it felt as though the orgasm was never going to stop. She wasn't able to discern if there were multiple orgasms happening one after the other, or if the bliss she was feeling was simply one long, continuous climax. Either way, she had no choice but to hang on tight and enjoy the sweetness of the ride, her arms wrapped around Nick's neck, her face buried against the side of his throat. Her long legs were entwined around his pistoning hips, her heels digging into his buttocks as she urged him on. He was wild, more out of control than she'd ever recalled him being, and he continued to drive into her relentlessly, fucking her until she was limp and sobbing from the demands he was making on her body. She was so far gone, so caught up in the wildness, that she wasn't even aware of the cries she emitted, or that his body suddenly stiffened and went still at the words that slipped out from between her lips, as naturally as breath.

When she looked back on it afterwards, she thought perhaps she might have passed out for a bit, for she honestly had no clear recollection of uttering the words. Either that or it had simply been a case of having had to suppress her true feelings for far too long, and her emotions finally reaching the breaking point.

When he withdrew from her, she was barely aware, too weak and drained to murmur even a feeble protest. She fell into a deep, dreamless sleep, almost a state of unconsciousness, and it wasn't until she awoke late Saturday morning – alone, of course – that she finally realized what she'd done.

"Oh, God, no," she gasped, her long hair falling around her like a curtain as she buried her face in her hands. "Please, God, tell me I didn't actually say it, that I didn't tell Nick I love him."

But even as she bolted for the bathroom, her stomach revolting violently at the realization of what she'd said, Angela knew it had really happened. In the very height of passion, she hadn't been able to suppress her feelings any longer and had cried out her love for him. And as she vomited into the toilet, shuddering with the effort, she knew it was as good as over between them now –

her punishment for having broken one of his most steadfast rules.

***

When the better part of a week had already passed without a single word from Nick, Angela lost a little more hope each day that she would ever hear from him again. So when the text pinged on her phone late Friday afternoon, she had to re-read it several times just to make sure. It was brief and to the point, as most communications from him usually were, and she tried valiantly to tamper down the sense of relief she felt as she read it for the fifth time.

"Dinner tonight. Biltmore Club at seven."

He hadn't told her what to wear, but over the past two or three months he'd done that less and less. She knew now what he liked, what he expected, and since they were dining at the rather stuffy private club he belonged to, she'd make sure to wear something on the conservative side. She was also going to make damned sure that she looked as stunning as possible, that she pulled out every trick she knew to make herself irresistible. Because even though she'd been filled with dread all week, had been a walking basket case, convincing herself that she'd totally ruined any chance she had of keeping Nick, she was now filled with renewed hope. As she mentally ran through the contents of her extensive wardrobe, she vowed that she wasn't going to let him end things without a fight. She'd find a way to convince him that the words she'd uttered in the heat of passion had been completely unintentional, had just slipped out unthinkingly, and that of course she wasn't really in love with him. She was just like him, after all – not believing in love or commitment, being way too focused on her career right now to even think about the future, being more than content to keep things casual and low key between them, just as they had done so successfully for almost a year now.

She left work earlier than normal, needing the extra time to get ready for what could very well be the most important dinner of her life. She tried on nearly a dozen outfits, rejecting one and then the other as being too short, too sheer, too innocent, too sophisticated. She fretted over the sort of image she wanted to project tonight, not wanting to come across as too young or vulnerable, but also not wanting to seem too much the experienced, mature woman of the world.

In the end, she chose a simple white sheath dress, its starkness relieved by the black button detail on the yoke and a thin black patent leather belt. She left her hair long and straight, the way she knew Nick preferred, and her makeup was all smoky eyes and dark red lips. The only jewelry she wore were diamond stud earrings and a gold and diamond cuff bracelet, both gifts from him, of course.

He had left instructions for her with the club's receptionist to head directly up to the dining room, an action that made her feel a bit uneasy since it wasn't his usual way of doing things. Typically when she met him at a restaurant he would be waiting for her in the bar or at the entrance. Now, as she followed the hostess across the dining room floor towards their usual corner table, Angela kept her fingers crossed that her suddenly shaky legs would continue to hold her upright, or that her wobbly ankles wouldn't cave in on her towering black patent stilettos.

Nick was already seated, a heavy crystal tumbler of what looked like whiskey in his hand. She frowned, for he rarely drank whiskey, preferring vodka as she did, or wine, and she tried not to make anything of it. He wore a light gray suit, unusual for him since he typically favored dark colors. He stood as she arrived but he was unsmiling and there was a strained look about his eyes.

A waiter brought her drink, her usual Absolut Citron, and she took a long swallow, not caring for once if Nick chided her. But he remained almost morosely silent, finishing off his whiskey and signaling to the waiter for a refill.

"I hardly ever see you drinking whiskey," she commented, her voice sounding hollow to her.

He shrugged, glancing away. "I just wasn't in the mood for vodka tonight. Seemed more of a Maker's Mark evening."

"Oh."

The tension was heavy in the air and grew increasingly thicker as the meal dragged on. She let Nick order for her, but she had no appetite and no real idea of what she was even eating. For once, he didn't harass her about picking at her food, and he himself ate little. Angela's stomach was churning, as it had been all week, and she wondered distantly if she was developing an ulcer. Or acid reflux. Or IBS. Or –

"Do you want dessert?"

She shuddered at his question. "No. Maybe some tea, that's all."

"Okay."

He skipped dessert, too, and even declined coffee in favor of a glass of port. It seemed to Angela that he'd had quite a bit more to drink than usual tonight, but she didn't dare bring up the subject. They'd barely said a word during the entire meal, and Nick had been broody and unsmiling throughout. She'd wondered despairingly why he'd even bothered asking her to dinner, why he hadn't just broken up with her over the phone or via text. Or just not contacted her at all. Anything would have been better than this ominous silence, this awful, menacing quiet.

She took a sip of her tea, though she really longed for another vodka. "Nick," she ventured timidly. "Is something wrong? Why are you - "

"Not here, Angel," he interrupted, holding up a hand. "We'll talk in a bit, but not here. Finish your tea and then we'll go for a drive or something."

He was driving his SUV tonight, something he rarely did when he was with her, yet another difference in what had been an evening filled with unsettling changes. The uncomfortable silence continued as he drove with uncharacteristic care – no doubt because of the amount of alcohol he'd consumed – across the city until they reached the Presidio. Nick parked at Crissy Field, cutting the engine before getting out of the car. He helped her out, keeping a grip on her elbow as they slowly began to walk along the beach promenade. It was mostly deserted at this time of the evening, the sun having set almost three hours ago, but the weather was still balmy. It had been hot in the city today, reaching into the 80's, but Angela had felt cold for days now and shivered a bit as they continued to walk along in silence.

"Is it too cold out here for you?" he asked abruptly. "We can go back to the car. Or find somewhere to get coffee."

She shook her head. "I'm fine."

Nick let go of her elbow then, shoving his hands into the pockets of his suit trousers, almost as if he didn't trust himself to touch her. He stopped suddenly, staring out at the bay where the waves lapped gently at the shore. The silence continued to hang between them, growing heavier and more uncomfortable with each passing second, and Angela felt like screaming to relieve the unbearable tension. But when he finally spoke, his voice sounding rusty, she longed for the silence to return – for the words that came out of his mouth were the very ones she'd hoped to never hear.

"It's over, Angel," he said quietly, almost matter-of-factly. "I'm ending this – whatever it is we've shared for the last year. Tonight. I won't be contacting you again and I trust you'll respect my decision and accept that it's done."

She couldn't speak, couldn't move. She felt frozen in place, her entire body engulfed in ice as she began to shiver uncontrollably. She tried to say something but even her throat felt frozen over, and she couldn't seem to open her mouth. A single tear began to track its way very slowly down her cheek, hovering near the corner of her mouth, but her hand didn't seem capable of moving enough to brush it away.

Nick shut his eyes, shoving his hands even deeper into his pockets as he continued to speak in that deep, raspy voice. "I never, ever, expected things would last this long, you know. In my entire life I've never been with a woman more than a few weeks at best, and most of them a hell of a lot less time. So this – you – was definitely a first for me, Angel. But it needed to end sometime and that time is now."

"No." She was finally able to speak, though the sound that escaped her throat was barely a croak. "Please, Nick. Don't – don't leave me."

He turned to her then, one of his big hands threading into her hair as the other wiped the tears from her cheeks as they fell more rapidly now. "I have to, Angel," he muttered roughly. "I should have ended this weeks ago, months even. But I was too weak to do it then, couldn't make myself say the words."

She wrapped her arms around herself in a futile attempt to stop shivering. "Why?" she whispered on a sob. "Why now?"

"Because you've gotten too close," he told her flatly. "You've allowed yourself to feel too much, feel things you weren't supposed to feel for me. Things I can't – don't – feel in return. And you deserve someone who *can* return your feelings, Angel. Someone who can love you. Someone who'll offer you all the things you know deep down you really want – love, marriage, kids."

"But I don't want that stuff!" she protested wildly. "You know I don't! Nick, please. When have I ever asked you for anything, ever once hinted I wanted more from you?"

"You haven't," he replied gently. "But that doesn't mean you don't want them. And you're lying to both of us when you keep denying the truth. I've probably known all along that you really weren't this modern, independent woman you try so hard to be. But it was after your cousin's wedding – when it was so obvious how much your family's behavior had affected you – that I finally recognized the real truth. And I knew then the time had come to let you go."

"No! No!" She flung herself against him desperately, clinging to him fiercely. "You can't let me go, Nick. Please! I need you in my life, I can't bear the thought of not being with you. I don't care how it has to be, I never have. All I've ever cared about is just being with you, on your terms, no matter what. Besides, I'm way, way too young to even think about getting married, that's not even close to what I want right now. All I want," she sniffled, twining her arms about his neck, "is you."

"Angel." He held her close, stroking her hair soothingly. "You say that now, but I know differently. Even before you told me last Friday night, I knew you were in love with me, knew that you'd felt that way for a long time. And I should have ended things the moment I realized the truth, should never have let things last this long. You might not agree right now, but one day you'll see that I'm doing you a favor. Because as long as you're mixed up with me, you'll never be truly happy. I told you from the very first time that I was a selfish, fucked-up bastard and that's never going to change."

"I don't care." She was weeping openly now, the tears streaming down her face faster than she could wipe them away. "It doesn't matter, nothing matters as long as you don't leave me. Please, Nick. I'll do anything, but please don't end this."

"Stop." His voice deepened, became less raspy and more commanding. "You have to stop this now, Angela. Nothing you say is going to change my mind. And seeing the way you're reacting now, how emotional you are, makes me realize that this is the right thing to do. We need to end this before I hurt you even more than I already have. Now, come on. You're shaking like a leaf. Let's get back in the car so I can take you home."

"No. No." She shook her head, refusing to budge, refusing to accept what he was telling her. "It can't be over, it just can't. I love you, Nick, it's true. I've loved you from the beginning. But that doesn't mean I won't put my feelings aside. I'll never say the words again, will never, ever expect you to say them back. I just want you in my life, on whatever terms you're willing to give me."

"No." He took her firmly by the arm and began to propel her back towards his car. "I'm not willing to go along with those terms. While I've never apologized for being a selfish, cold-hearted prick, even I have my limits. And I refuse to go on hurting you intentionally, Angel, refuse to let it last even one more day. Because I'm finding it a little bit harder each day to live with myself. So it has to end now. For both our sakes."

Angela was limp and unresisting as he practically hefted her inside the car, even buckling her seat belt when she was too unresponsive to do it herself. When she continued to shiver almost violently, Nick quietly switched on the automatic seat warmer but she barely noticed. The chill she felt was coming from deep inside of her, and she knew that nothing would help warm her. Nothing except Nick's declaration that everything he'd said tonight had been a lie, that he hadn't meant a word of it, and that nothing had changed between them.

The SUV pulled up outside of her building before she knew it, the drive having taken a revoltingly brief amount of time. Nick kept the engine idling and made no move to come around and assist her out.

"You should go now." His voice was soft but firm. "There really isn't anything more to say. All the things I've given you – the clothes, jewelry, furniture – obviously it's all yours to keep."

She couldn't – wouldn't – move, was stubbornly prolonging this, making it as difficult for him as possible. "Don't do this," she began to plead.

"It's already done." He cut her off brutally. "And there's nothing more to say. Let's just say good-by and go our separate ways."

She clutched his arm. "No. We can make it work. Please give me another chance."

His fingers were almost crushing hers as he forcibly removed her hand. "It's over, Angela. Don't humiliate yourself any further by begging. It won't make a damned bit of difference. And don't try contacting me, either. The phone number I gave you – the one you've been so diligent about not using – it's been disconnected. And if you try to enter my office, my staff will be given very specific instructions to stop you. You'll only embarrass yourself if you try. So let's just finish this now and part with some semblance of dignity."

"Nick." Her voice broke as she began to weep again.

He reached across her with barely concealed impatience and flung her door open before unlatching her seat belt. When she didn't budge he gave her a slight shove. "Get out, Angela. It's over and I don't want to see you again. Now, go, before I have to come over there and lift you out by force."

He gave her another little push and she half-stepped, half-fell out of the vehicle, teetering wildly as she landed on the sidewalk. Without another word Nick closed the passenger door and drove off.

Had he bothered to glance back, he would have witnessed her crumpling to the ground right there on the sidewalk, her legs buckling underneath her, and sobbing as though her heart was breaking.

Chapter Twelve

Having been brought up a Catholic – and thereby subjected to more than a decade of religious education classes – Angela had always thought herself familiar with the concept of hell. But any of her previous images of that dark, evil place didn't even begin to compare to the torturous depths she'd plummeted into over the past two weeks. Ever since the night Nick had broken things off between them, each waking moment had been far worse than her most vivid imaginings of hell had ever been. And since she hadn't been able to sleep more than a couple of hours each night, nearly every moment in the day had been a waking one. Moments where she lived in constant agony, where she existed in a state of dazed disbelief, and where her body took over when her mind shut itself off.

She operated on auto-pilot round the clock, somehow managing to get dressed and off to work and go through the motions there. Except for her clients, she rarely spoke to anyone at the office, didn't notice the looks of concern her co-workers sent her way, and she'd often spend half an hour or more at a time simply staring numbly into space.

She had no appetite whatsoever and was subsisting on power bars, black coffee, and booze – a whole lot of the latter. Most every morning since the break-up she'd woken with a hangover – bloodshot eyes, pounding headache, roiling stomach. Over the course of two weeks she'd already lost six more pounds, and her clothes hung loosely on her frame. She'd stopped paying attention to how she looked, not bothering with makeup, scraping her hair back into a messy ponytail, and not especially caring if her clothes were wrinkled.

She checked her phone almost obsessively for the call or text from Nick that never came, no matter how hard she willed it to happen. More than once she'd actually taken the elevator up to his floor and paced around the foyer for almost half an hour, hoping that he'd walk by. She was still too much under his control to outright disobey him and go directly to his office.

She kept telling herself that this was just a temporary break, that any day now Nick would realize what a terrible mistake he'd made and call her up, begging her to take him back.   She imagined any number of different scenarios where this reconciliation took place – where he told her he couldn't live without her, confessed he'd always loved her, promised to always be with her.

Her daydreams, her hopes, were the only things that kept her from snapping completely.   Some part of her recognized that she was a complete and utter fucked-up mess and was barely hanging on to reality, but she couldn't summon up enough strength to roust herself out of her stupor.

And after so many months of letting Nick control every aspect of her life, of organizing her schedule to accommodate and always be available for him, she was suddenly at loose ends – lost and adrift without any idea of what to do with herself.   She was alienated from the family she'd never really been close to anyway; had pushed Lauren away so many times that she was good and pissed off by now; had basically cut off contact with nearly every friend she had.   She had no one to talk to about what had happened, no shoulder to cry on.   She'd never in her life felt so lost and alone, and part of her badly wanted to reach out to someone – to Lauren or Julia or even one of her sisters – but she felt too frozen inside to make the attempt.

She worked ridiculously long hours and would have spent even more time at the office had the constant temptation to try and see Nick not been present.   She filled the empty hours without him by running, sometimes more than three hours in a session, and had lost even more weight as a result.

She'd dropped so much weight, in fact, that she had to begin wearing some of her older clothes.   When Nick had ruthlessly plowed through the contents of her closet and they'd filled several large garbage bags with stuff to give away, she had stored the bags temporarily in the basement of her apartment building. She'd become so obsessed with Nick, so caught up in their relationship, that she had forgotten all about the bags until recently.   One by one she dragged each one back upstairs, leaving them smack in the middle of her apartment, and pulled things out as she needed them.

Angela had always been a fairly meticulous housekeeper, but now the apartment was quickly becoming a mess. She didn't bother changing the sheets or making the bed any longer, had let the laundry pile up as well as the few dishes she used, hadn't swept the floor or dusted the furniture or even taken out the trash.

And she would probably forget to shower each day if she wasn't always so cold. Even with the warm Indian summer weather in San Francisco as of late, Angela was cold all the time. She'd stand beneath the shower for long minutes, the water almost blisteringly hot, and still had trouble getting warm. When she was at home she kept the heater on continually, and more often than not was huddled beneath the bedcovers, shivering even with sweats on and several blankets piled on top of her.

And she cried at what felt like the drop of a hat. Almost anything, it seemed, would trigger an hours-long weeping jag – a sad song on her iPod, a romantic show on TV, looking at all the beautiful things Nick had bought her – the clothes, shoes, jewelry, even the locking display cabinet he'd bought for her early on in their relationship so that she could keep her medals and trophies secure. She'd considered boxing up all of the things he'd given her and either donating them to charity or storing them in the basement, but every time she gave the matter serious consideration she'd decide she couldn't bear to be parted from them just yet.

On one of the weekend trips he'd taken her on, a T-shirt of his had wound up in her suitcase and she'd kept it carefully hidden away. But since the break-up she'd pulled it from its hiding place and had begun to sleep with it beneath her pillow. The scent of his body no longer clung to the soft cotton fabric, but if she closed her eyes and focused hard enough she could still smell his clean, masculine essence.

She'd forgotten to call home the past couple of weekends, too dazed and distraught to remember, but it hadn't seem to concern Rita overmuch since there'd been no communication from her end. Under normal circumstances Angela might have felt hurt – or angry – that her mother cared so little about her that she couldn't be bothered to check in after not hearing anything for two weeks. But right now the only thing Angela cared about was Nick, and how she continued to hope and pray that he'd come back to her any day now.

At the office she hadn't received any new referrals since the break-up, and knew instinctively that this was one more way he was cutting off ties with her. It was fortunate that she was so far ahead of her goals and the thresholds she needed to meet, because the last thing she was capable of doing right now was networking and cultivating new clients. A few days ago, when she'd been able to focus her attention long enough to work it out, she had calculated that it would probably be several months yet before she'd have to concern herself about bringing in new business. But she simply couldn't think ahead that far right now, couldn't bear to imagine the empty loneliness that stretched ahead of her.

As two weeks became three, Angela became increasingly obsessed with seeing Nick again, telling herself that if he caught sight of her surely that would make him realize how much he missed her and wanted her back. She'd wait outside their office building, staying discreetly out of sight, and wait for him to exit or enter. When that failed to produce results, she started driving by the restaurants and clubs she knew were his favorites, searching the nearby streets for a glimpse of one of his cars, but again to no avail. She toyed with the idea of calling one of the few friends he'd introduced her to – in particular Dante Sabattini whom Nick considered his closest friend. She wondered if Nick had mentioned their break-up to Dante, if he'd ever discussed his feelings about her with his friend. She didn't have Dante's personal phone number but knew where he worked, and even went so far as to look up the contact information for the venture capital firm he co-owned. But even as her fingers hovered over the keypad of her phone, ready and willing to dial the number, she set the receiver down with a resigned sigh. Even if Nick had talked about her to his best friend, there was no guarantee Dante would consent to take her call, much less share details of a private conversation. And, of course, he'd be certain to tell Nick she'd called, which would not only anger him but also drive the point home even further that he'd made the right decision to end things.

It was on a Thursday, nearly four weeks since Nick had broken things off, when the final blow was dealt. She was sitting at a little outdoor table at the coffee shop across the street from the office when she saw him. Her heart began to beat rapidly, and she smiled for the first time in nearly a month as he exited the building. He looked as fit and strong and gorgeous as ever, wearing a navy pinstriped suit. His hair had been cut recently and his skin was darkly tanned. It didn't matter in the least to her at this moment that the break-up hadn't seemed to have had any sort of impact on him whatsoever, that he looked just the same as always while she was a complete mess. Self-consciously, she tucked a loose strand of hair back into the untidy braid she'd clumped it in this morning, wished that she wasn't wearing one of the old trouser suits that Nick hated with a passion, and that she'd made some effort to slap on makeup. But none of that really mattered as she drank in the sight of him hungrily, as though she was virtually starved for it, memorizing each beloved feature of his face and body. She began to rise from her seat, fully intent on dashing across the street just so she could talk to him for a minute.

And then she sank back down again abruptly, her legs suddenly threatening to give out from under her. Because instead of glancing across the street to where she sat, Nick was greeting the beautiful blonde he had obviously arranged to meet. She was tall and shapely, wearing a black sheath dress and towering heels, her glossy hair falling to her shoulders in thick waves. And as Nick bent his dark head to give her a kiss, Angela made a little sound of distress, her hand fluttering up to her mouth. She knocked over her coffee but didn't even notice until the hot liquid spilled onto her lap. Even then she didn't bother to blot it up, staring instead in mingled horror and despair as Nick slid an arm around the blonde's waist and they began to walk off in the opposite direction.

Angela remained frozen in place for long minutes, shivering despite the warmth of the day and the hot coffee that had stained her suit trousers. She was oblivious to the stares she received from other patrons or from passers-by, oblivious to anything but the heartbreaking realization that Nick had well and truly moved on, forgotten her. He was seeing someone else now, fucking someone else, and for all she knew the blonde was only one of several women he'd been with over the past month. While she'd been grieving so deeply, had longed for him constantly, he'd already replaced her.

Somehow she managed to stumble back to the office, long enough to gather her things and mumble to her assistant that she didn't feel well and was headed home. The bus ride back to her place was a blur, and she'd marvel at a later date how she'd ever managed to get aboard the correct one. She was half a block from her apartment before she turned around and backtracked until she reached the small neighborhood liquor store she'd been frequenting more and more as of late. The clerk on duty wasn't the one she normally saw, given that it wasn't even two o'clock, and she ignored the quizzical look he gave her when she plunked her purchases down on the counter.

"Uh, will that be all?" he asked dubiously, eyeing the half dozen assorted bottles of vodka, tequila, and whiskey.

"For now." She held out her credit card, silently daring the clerk to comment further.

Back at her apartment, she tossed off her suit and shoes and dug items out at random from her trash bag stash. The paint-stained, holey sweat pants and worn out monkey slippers felt like old friends, as did her high school sweatshirt. But her new best friend quickly became the bottle of vodka that she broke open and began to steadily work her way through as the afternoon faded into evening.

＊＊＊

Lauren figured she was just about the only person on the nearly ten hour flight arriving in San Francisco from Tokyo who was wide awake and refreshed. And that included the other members of her crew, all three of whom still had an additional connecting flight to make before reaching their respective homes.

The four of them had left Vietnam some eighteen hours ago, changing planes in Japan, having spent ten days on their most recent assignment. As usual, she'd fallen into a deep, restful sleep almost immediately upon takeoff from Tokyo, and had woken up about ninety minutes ago, just in time for breakfast and several cups of heavily creamed and sugared coffee. Her co-workers – all men – looked like they'd been through the wringer by contrast and all three were glaring at her as they stumbled off the aircraft.

"Okay, boys, don't dawdle now or you'll miss your next flight," she chirped cheerily. "Meanwhile, I'm going to go bail my car out of long term parking and have myself a nice leisurely drive home."

Chris, the crew's videographer, glared at her. "Bitch," was all he muttered, though in a good-natured, teasing tone. He, like the others, knew better than to ever use a derogatory term in Lauren's presence and actually mean it.

She chuckled evilly and pressed a quick kiss to his stubbly cheek. "Maybe you can get some sleep on your flight to New York," she offered innocently.

Chris mumbled something unintelligible beneath his breath, but Lauren knew it was something he'd never dare to repeat out loud. Grinning, she gave her other crew members – Karl and Stefan – a hug good-by. All three men looked even worse under the harsh lights of the airport terminal, like they'd been drop-kicked by an especially angry mule.

"Ah, come on, ladies," she teased. "Just console yourselves with the fact that we have a whole ten days off until we have to reconvene for our next assignment. Take care of yourselves – Christina, Karla, and Stefanie!"

Within the first few weeks of her joining the crew, she'd chided them about how much they tended to whine at certain times and had not so teasingly referred to them as a bunch of high school girls. From there, the feminine versions of their names had quickly evolved, and she was merciless about using their nicknames when the occasion called for it.

Lauren was still chuckling to herself as she sauntered leisurely to baggage claim, pulling out her phone as she did so. There were a few texts from Julia, an email from her parents, and three new voice mails. The first she deleted immediately since it was from a guy she'd been stupid enough to give her number to last month; the second was an appointment reminder from her dentist; and the third was from Angela.

At least the number was Angela's. She wasn't quite so certain about the garbled, nearly incoherent voice, and had to replay the message three times before she could understand even a portion of it.

"Hi, it's Angie. Sorry I've blown you off so much lately. I – been busy – it's – ah shit, it's all over now, he's got someone new. Doesn't matter. Sorry, I know you're pissed, don't blame you. Bye."

Lauren frowned as she stuck the phone in the pocket of her cargo pants, grabbing her overstuffed duffel off the baggage carousel easily with one hand.   Angela had sounded ill, confused, almost incoherent. She'd sounded, Lauren realized with a sigh, stinking, falling down drunk.

'Damn you, Angie,' she cursed beneath her breath as she walked outside of the terminal toward the parking shuttle. 'And here I was counting on spending a few peaceful days back at the cabin. Now it sounds like I've got to pull your drunken head out of your ass. What the hell have you done to yourself?'

***

It was worse, much, much worse than she could have imagined, as Angela's very irritated landlord – a grouchy old Italian guy who reeked of garlic and cheap red wine – grudgingly let her inside the apartment. When Angela hadn't answered her phone or responded to the persistent ringing of the outside doorbell, Lauren had all but threatened the recalcitrant old fart into letting her in, telling him in no uncertain terms that if her friend was sick or hurt it would be his responsibility.

But Lauren had never envisioned this – this chaos, this total disarray, this – stink. She wrinkled her nose as she shut the apartment door behind her and more closely surveyed the scene in front of her.

Smack in the middle of the room were half a dozen large black trash bags, from which a variety of clothes and shoes were spilling out. The tiny kitchenette looked like it hadn't been cleaned in weeks, with dirty dishes and empty wrappers littering every available surface. The smell of rotting garbage was vaguely nauseous, even for someone like Lauren who normally had a cast iron stomach. Among the debris, she noted with a grimace, was an alarming number of empty liquor bottles.

As for Angela herself, Lauren assumed that the lifeless lump sprawled out beneath a pile of bedcovers was her friend. She was snoring rather loudly, the only part of her visible a few straggly locks of black hair. As Lauren drew closer, she was repelled by the combined odors of sweat, booze, and vomit, and puzzled when she noticed one of Angela's hands clutching what looked like a man's black T-shirt.

"Okay, it's bad enough you've got trash bags filled with old clothes in the middle of the room, and that your apartment smells like a beer hall. But, honey, no offense. You really, really need a shower," drawled Lauren. "Time to wake up now and get your ass in gear."

Angela groaned as Lauren gave her a firm shake, burrowing her head deeper under the pillow and pulling the bedcovers up over her head. "Go 'way," she mumbled. "Leave me alone."

Lauren glared down at her. "I should do exactly that, you know. It's what you deserve after blowing me off so many times over the past year so you'd be available to go fuck that asshole whenever he snapped his fingers. But from what I could interpret from your message, I'm guessing he's not in the picture any longer?"

As Angela began to sob loudly and uncontrollably, Lauren cursed – first in English, then French, and finally, for good measure, in Spanish. And even though she'd always been a firm believer in tough love, she found herself comforting her best friend as Angela cried her heart out over the louse who'd broken that same organ into a million tiny pieces.

Between crying jags, Angela managed to stutter out what had happened with the cold-hearted bastard whom she'd devoted the better part of a year to. Maddeningly, she still refused to reveal his name or any other details, and Lauren forced herself to stay calm and not scream at her friend to stop being such an idiot over a guy who'd treated her like scum on the bottom of his shoe. She was seldom tactful, and had spoken what was on her mind since she'd been a small child, but for once she held her tongue, knowing that her usual candor would only make Angela cry harder.

Then, when she couldn't handle the incessant weeping – or the rank body odor – a minute longer, she half-pushed, half-dragged Angela into the bathroom, shoved a towel and a robe into her hands, and forced her to take a long, hot shower. Hot evidently being the operative word, since it took mere minutes for the tiny room to fill up with steam.

Lauren didn't waste any time after that, carrying out bags of trash and recycling to dump down the chute in the hallway. By then she was wiping sweat off her brow and opened up the single window in the apartment to get some fresh air. She frowned to notice the heat had been cranked up to eighty, and quickly dialed it down to a reasonable temperature. As she heard the water shut off in the bathroom, she stripped the sheets from the bed and pulled open the drawer built into the bed frame to get clean ones out.

She froze when she saw was else was stored in the drawer next to the spare set of sheets. "Holy shit!" she exclaimed, shaking her head in disbelief as she spied several sets of silken cords, a variety of scarves, and even a couple of blindfolds. There were other items, too, some of which she recognized and others she wasn't sure she'd ever want to become acquainted with.

"What are you doing?" asked Angela in alarm.

She emerged from the bathroom clad in a robe and a frayed pair of slippers, her hair wrapped up in a towel. She hurried over to the bed and pulled the clean sheets out of the drawer before shutting it firmly. But Lauren knew what she'd seen and wasn't about to ignore it.

"So in addition to letting him control every second of your

life, you also let this prick tie you up?" she asked incredulously. "What the fuck, Angie? Did you lose your mind along with your free will?"

Angela glared at her darkly. "It's not what you think. He never hurt me or did anything I didn't consent to."

Lauren shook her head. "Jesus, this is like a David Lynch movie or something – all this dark, twisty, bizarre stuff. And getting weirder by the minute." She pointed a finger at Angela. "The one thing you'd better *not* tell me is that you ever let this bastard hit you. Am I going to find any other kinky shit lying around if I keep poking – you know, like whips and chains?"

Angela shook her head vehemently. "No, nothing like that. He – he wasn't into any of that stuff. You know, like Erika's parents used to keep in that strange dungeon room. And he never hit me, not even close."

"But he did hurt you," Lauren murmured quietly. "Maybe not physically but in a whole lot of other ways. At least if the number of empty booze bottles I just threw away is any indication. When did the sonofabitch break things off anyway?"

Tears welled up in Angela's bloodshot eyes again. "About a month ago," she whispered. "But I kept hoping he'd change his mind, that he'd call me and say it was all a mistake."

Lauren stared at her, aghast. "You've been like this for a month?"

Angela shrugged. "Not – quite this bad. I mean, not - "

"Not on a bender and passed out drunk?" finished Lauren. "When did that start and why?"

The tears started to stream down Angela's gaunt cheekbones, and for the first time Lauren noticed how much weight her friend had lost since the last time they'd seen each other. Admittedly, Angie had packed on a much needed ten pounds or so and had looked terrific, but Lauren was guessing she'd lost at least that much now and maybe more.

"Thursday," whispered Angela brokenly. "Two – two days ago I – I saw him with someone else. He was meeting her for lunch and when I saw him kiss her, that's when - "

"When you really lost it." Lauren shook her head. "I'm sorry, honey, sorry that you had to see that. Do you think he intended for you to see him?"

"N-nno." Angela sank down onto the bed, heedless of the fact that there weren't any sheets on it. "He didn't know I saw him. I'd, uh, been hoping to run into him so I was hanging out at a coffee shop near his office when he walked out of the building."

"Christ." Lauren ran a hand over her face, suddenly feeling in dire need of more coffee. Or some tequila. "So you were basically stalking this guy is what you're saying."

The towel wrapped around Angela's head began to slip off. "I guess a little," she admitted in a small voice. "I just wanted to see him, that's all. I don't think I would have had the nerve to actually go up to him. But I guess this proves you should be careful what you wish for, doesn't it?"

Lauren sat down on the bed next to her, wrapping a comforting arm around her shoulders. "More often than not, yes. So you saw him with his new bimbo and went off the deep end. Does that about cover it?"

Angela's long, wet hair fell about her face as she gave a little nod. "More or less. That's when I knew – when I realized it's over. Really and truly over. He's not coming back to me and I have no idea how to go on from here."

She curled herself up into a fetal position as she began sobbing again, and Lauren rolled her eyes heavenward.

"Oh, this is *so* not how I wanted to spend my down time," she grumbled as she went in search of coffee making supplies. "I should have waited until I was home before checking my messages. Sometimes I think I should just stamp a big ole S on my forehead for Sucker."

She unearthed some crumpled paper filters and found a package of ground coffee in the fridge. The pot had almost finished brewing when Angela dashed into the bathroom, a hand over her mouth, and a decidedly green cast to her features.

"Aw, fuck," groaned Lauren. "And I really, *really* didn't figure on holding anyone's head over the toilet this weekend. Someone in this apartment is going to owe me big time."

***

Lauren ended up staying for four days, bossing Angela around the entire time and refusing to let her feel sorry for herself. Between the two of them order was restored to the apartment, starting with the discarded sacks of clothing. They went through them again, pulling out suits and other items that Nick had hated but that were perfectly all right for the office. This time Lauren carted the actual giveaways directly to Goodwill, not allowing Angela the opportunity to re-stash the bags in the basement. At some point Lauren had rummaged through the extensive wardrobe Nick had bought, emitting a low whistle when she'd realized just how much there really was. She'd offered to get rid of the whole lot, but Angela had stubbornly refused to let go of anything just yet, even though all of it was at least a size too big after her sudden weight loss.

"I'll, um, go through everything soon," she'd promised. "When I'm in a better frame of mind to deal with it."

Lauren had scoffed. "Oh, bullshit. You'll hang on to every single thing. Just like you sleep with that stupid T-shirt of his like it's a damned security blanket or something. I'd be burning it in effigy if it was up to me. After I'd sliced a couple of dozen holes in it first."

"Don't," Angela had warned. "I know it's unhealthy but I'm not ready yet."

In the time she'd hung around, Lauren had forced Angela to eat, shower, go for long walks, and go out to the movies. By the time Lauren headed home to Big Sur, Angela felt marginally calmer and more in control, even though she was always freezing now and never felt hunger pangs. Lauren had made her promise to keep in close touch, vowing to return and move in if she didn't hear from her at least three times a week.

"I don't care if it's a phone call or a text or an email," Lauren had stated. "No matter where I happen to be, I always have access to my messages. So don't make me try and track you down while I'm in Borneo or Kenya because my office manager gets pissy if I rack up too many roaming charges."

"Okay, I promise." Angela had given her a fierce good-by hug. "And – thanks. For everything. I'd probably be sleeping in a pool of my own vomit right about now if you hadn't badgered Mr. Musante to let you in."

Lauren had wrinkled her nose at the mental image. "Eww. Really gross visual there, Angie. But I'm glad I was here, glad you drunk dialed me when you did. And I'm always here, understand? Even if I'm half a world away I'll always be there for you. You might have forgotten that fact over the past year but it was always true."

Angela had felt tears begin to well up in her eyes until Lauren had given a firm shake of her head.

"Uh, uh. No way are you going to cry again. I swear I don't understand why you aren't completely dehydrated by now considering how much you've cried over the past four days. So stop it," she'd ordered sternly. "Nobody is worth that much grief. *Nobody.*"

And as the next couple of weeks passed, Angela tried – really tried – to remind herself of that fact. She attempted to throw herself back into her job, even going so far as to make cold calls to a list of prospective clients.

She started calling her parents again on the weekends, and was surprised when Rita scolded her for making them worry when they hadn't heard from her for over a month. And when she broke down crying over the phone, her mother had been uncharacteristically sympathetic.

"It's that man you were seeing, isn't it?" she'd asked baldly. But there had been no scorn or condemnation in her voice for once. "What's the matter? He didn't hit you or anything, did he?"

Through her tears, Angela had wondered wildly why everyone seemed to think Nick had been physically abusive to her.

"No, Mom," she'd sniffled. "He would never do that. And we're not seeing each other anymore. It's been over for more than a month."

"Good." Rita's voice had been firm, non-nonsense. "He wasn't good for you, Angela, wasn't the right man. What kind of man doesn't want to meet a girl's family, lets her go to her cousin's wedding all alone? I hope you got rid of those things he bought you or gave them back to him. And I hope you have enough sense not to take him back if he calls you again."

"He won't be calling again, Mom," she'd murmured brokenly.

It was as though saying those words out loud to her mother had made her realize once and for all just how true they were. Nick had quickly and thoroughly locked her out of his life, and had very obviously forgotten all about her with the same sort of arrogant ease that he sailed through life with.

She'd had another good, long cry after that conversation with her mother, and then, despite her half-hearted vows to Lauren, had made a trip to the liquor store. But she did force herself to keep the drinking under control, limiting herself to just enough shots to dull the pain and enable her to fall asleep.

She couldn't, however, drink at work and thereby block out the hurt and misery she felt each time she overheard the renewed gossip about Nick. During the long months they'd been together, the gossip mill had pretty much ground to a halt, the overall conjecture having been that Nick finally had a steady girlfriend, though her identity had always remained a mystery. But once it had passed the four or five month mark in their relationship, any talk about Nick and his unknown amour had pretty much dried up.

Until now, that is. Apparently he was back on the market in a big way, if the gossip could all be believed, and Angela felt like another piece of her heart was being crushed each time someone shared a new tidbit of information about him.

"There was a picture of him in the newspaper the other day at some charity auction, and he had this gorgeous blonde with him. I think the paper said she was a model or an actress."

"Manning is definitely back to his old ways from the sound of it. He was seen with three different women in one week. And I'm guessing each one was hotter than the last."

"I saw him at that cocktail party at the Four Seasons – you know, the one to celebrate the engagement of two of his staff members. He had a redhead with him and it sure looked to me like they couldn't wait to go have a private party of their own."

Each time she was forced to hear about yet another new woman Nick had been seen out with, the pain was more than she could handle. She took to keeping her office door closed, to shunning contact with the worst of the gossips, and to leaving the room the moment she heard his name mentioned.

But it was when she saw him again in person – at one of those mandatory, all-hands-on-deck meetings, the very same kind where they'd first connected – that Angela began to realize she needed to start her life over. And that, unfortunately, included finding a new job.

She'd known he'd be at the meeting, of course, given that the firm's top market analyst would be speaking. In one of the limited number of conversations she and Nick had had about business, he'd spoken highly of this particular analyst, calling him one of the few people in the financial industry who knew what the hell he was talking about.

Knowing that she'd be seeing Nick, she had actually taken care with her appearance for the first time in weeks – making sure her hair was clean and falling in the long, loose style he preferred; applying enough makeup to conceal the pallor of her skin and the near-permanent dark circles under her eyes; digging out one of the dresses he'd bought her – a slim fitting sheath of dark green that wasn't quite as loose on her as most of her other things. Quite intentionally, she'd also worn one of the choker necklaces he'd given her, as though to send him the silent message that he could still own her if he desired, that all he had to do was crook a finger and she'd come running to him at full speed.

But the only thing Nick did when he happened to glance her way at the meeting was to look right past her as though she wasn't even there. Angela stood there in stunned disbelief that after all they had shared, all the months she'd spent devoting herself to him, that he could ignore her so completely. Especially since the mere sight of him was making her feel alive in a way she hadn't felt since that awful night when he'd all but dumped her on the sidewalk. Her eyes drank in the sight of him, how sexy and powerful he looked in his black pinstriped suit, and she longed to rush over to him, fling herself into his arms, and beg him to come back to her.

It was then, when she realized how low she'd sunk, how desperate and pathetic she'd become, that she quietly made her decision.

* * *

Lloyd Raskin stared at her in shocked disbelief. "I don't even know what to say, Angela. I would have never in a hundred years expected this. Are you – I mean, I thought you were happy here. You've certainly been one of the most successful young brokers we've ever had. Is it about money? I can't increase your payout until you've been here two full years but - "

"It's not the money," she assured him quietly. "I know I get paid fairly, no complaints there. And I am – have been – happy here."

He shook his head. "Then why the hell are you leaving? Let's talk this through, okay? See if we can't find a way to convince you to stay. Unless," he added in a stern voice, "you've already got another job. Is that it, Angela? You got recruited away from us with the lure of a big bonus? If that's the case - "

"No. That's not it either," she confirmed. "It's – well, it's personal, Lloyd. There's some stuff I'm working through right now, and being here makes it impossible to get past it."

Lloyd frowned. "Personal, huh? Well, I know that no one is harassing you, because you're too strong a person to take that kind of crap. So it's got to be a man. And tell me if I'm wrong, but I believe that man is none other than Nick Manning."

Angela's jaw dropped open in alarm, but she could tell from the expression on her manager's face that there was no point in denying it. She looked down at her lap, wringing her hands in agitation. "No," she whispered. "You're not wrong."

"Damn it," Lloyd cursed angrily. "I should have known. Some of those accounts that came your way – I knew they'd asked for Nick first but that they didn't meet his criteria. I should have put two and two together then. But I convinced myself that he was just doing what you'd claimed – helping out a fellow Stanford alum."

"I never asked him for help," she declared defensively.

"When we were together we rarely even discussed business. And I've brought in plenty of my own accounts."

"I know that," Lloyd replied firmly. "No one would ever accuse you of not working your ass off, Angela. You deserved those accounts. Especially since it seems that Nick's done a real number on you."

She glanced up at him in alarm. "What does that mean?"

"No offense, but you look like hell these days," Lloyd told her bluntly. "Like you haven't had a good night's sleep in weeks. You're a bundle of nerves and I'm betting you haven't eaten a decent meal since he broke up with you."

Angela gave a little shrug. "You're assuming he's the one who broke things off."

Lloyd hooted. "Yeah, and rightly so. Women don't say no to guys like Nick Manning. Ever. And if you'd been the one to end it, you wouldn't be looking like a ghost right now. Or be resigning from a job you're damned good at. Tell me what I can do to convince you to stay."

"Nothing." Her voice was barely audible. "I just can't handle it any longer, Lloyd, being in the same office as Nick. Not that I actually see him all that often, but, well, the gossip is flying around fast and furiously since he's been back on the dating scene. I try to block it out but it isn't always possible. And knowing that he's in the same building, so close and yet I can't see him. It's just – too hard."

"Here." He handed her a wad of tissues as she started crying. "I won't even ask how badly that bastard hurt you. Nick's a great guy in a lot of ways – one of the best football players of his generation, a hugely successful broker, a very generous benefactor to several charities. But he's also a number one asshole most of the time. Damn him to hell," cursed Lloyd. "What was he thinking of anyway? You're too young for a shark like him, and he had no business messing with you."

"I'm – I'm sorry," sobbed Angela. "I should have never gotten involved with him. I'd heard all the gossip, knew he wasn't a forever kind of guy. But I couldn't help myself. The first time we met – it was like touching live flame."

"Don't blame yourself," consoled Lloyd. "If Nick wants something he goes after it with no holds barred. You never had a chance, kid. That's why I blame him for all of this. He should have left you the hell alone." He picked up her letter of resignation again and sighed. "So, no chance I can talk you out of this?"

"No. I need to move on and make a clean break. This is the only way that's going to happen."

"You realize you won't be able to take any of your accounts with you, right?" asked Lloyd. "Standard industry rules, except maybe for some family accounts or if the clients insist on following you."

Angela nodded. "I know. It doesn't matter. Besides, it's not like I honestly earned most of those accounts anyway. I'm prepared to start over – in every way."

"Hell of a waste," said Lloyd in disgust. "Christ, I wish I had the guts to march into Manning's office right now and give him a piece of my mind. Or punch him."

"No!" Angela protested. "Lloyd, please. You can't say a word. He can't ever know that I told you about us. He – I promised him."

Lloyd's gaze narrowed. "I'd say he can shove those promises up his arrogant ass. But don't worry, I won't say anything to him about you. I may be a manager here but Manning's got a hell of a lot more power. And I happen to like my job."

"Thanks. I appreciate it. And please don't say anything about my leaving," she begged. "The last thing I need is for everyone to start asking me why. Or, God forbid, to throw me a going-away party. I just – want to leave quietly."

Lloyd nodded. "Agreed. Do you have any idea of where you're going, what you're going to do next?"

"Not really," she admitted. "I've got some money saved so there's no huge rush. I'd like to stay in the brokerage business, of course, but I'd consider banking, venture capital, financial planning."

He hesitated. "I might have an idea. I had lunch with an old buddy who works at Morton Sterling now. Although, you might hate my guts within a week just for suggesting this."

Angela smiled at him. "I can't imagine doing that. I'd be grateful for a referral."

Lloyd grimaced. "Hold onto that thought until you've met Barbara Lowenstein for the first time. There's a reason why her nickname   is   the   She-Wolf   of   Wall   Street."

Chapter Thirteen

Four Months Later

"Close the door behind you. The last thing I need is for any of those nosy bastards out there to overhear us. And, Jesus, hurry it up, will you? I swear for someone as skinny as you are you sure as hell move at a snail's pace at times."

Angela shut the door to her boss's office as instructed and took a seat at one of the chairs facing Barbara's desk. The chair, she noted without surprise, was practically the only surface in the entire office not covered with untidy stacks of papers, file folders, magazines, and binders. Barbara's desk was unquestionably the messiest area, with empty food containers and wrappers and half-full cups of coffee joining the piles of papers.

And Barbara herself was a mess, though Angela knew her tough as nails boss didn't give a rat's ass about her appearance and never had. At sixty one years old, Barbara Lowenstein had been a stockbroker for more than thirty-five years, and had had to fight and claw her way up the ladder of success in what she'd often referred to as the "good old boys club". There had been very few female brokers when she'd been hired at Morton Sterling over three decades ago, and certainly no successful ones. Barbara prided herself on being the one who'd not only broken the mold but shattered it in the process. Aspiring young brokers of both genders looked up to her with awe, and many had tried over the years to cultivate her as a mentor. But Barbara had neither the time nor the patience to share her considerable expertise with any of them, and she'd developed a well-earned reputation as a scary, temperamental old witch.

She was a short woman, whose lifelong plumpness had now spread into borderline obesity. Her fashion sense was non-existent, evidenced by the out-of-date, ill-fitting burgundy suit that clashed badly with a light blue blouse. She had short, frizzy hair dyed an odd shade of red that was closer to purple. Barbara didn't bother with makeup, except for an occasional slash of lipstick, and the only jewelry she ever wore was a plain, masculine looking watch.

Years of being both a heavy smoker and drinker had taken their toll on her features, leaving her skin saggy and wrinkled, her teeth yellowed, her voice raspy with a perennial smoker's cough. She was also mean as a snake, insulted everyone in the office – including the managers – and went through assistants almost as quickly as she did a carton of cigarettes.

But, as Angela had discovered during the four months she'd worked for the so-called She-Wolf of Wall Street, Barbara also had possibly the most brilliant financial mind she'd ever been exposed to. And in between being screamed at and having insults hurled her way constantly, she had also learned more in the past months about stocks and financial planning and market trends than she had during her four years at Stanford.

Barbara glared as Angela took a seat. "You look like crap this morning, missy.   Got another hangover? And don't try bullshitting me. I've been hungover way too many times not to recognize the signs."

Angela shrugged. "Not exactly hungover, no. Just a bad night is all. What's up?"

Barbara chuckled, though with her hacking smoker's cough it sounded more like a witch's cackle. "Getting right to the point, are you? Or are you just avoiding the question? Doesn't matter, I've always appreciated the fact that you never try to waste my time with worthless chitchat. So here it is, missy. I have never even considered doing something like this in my career but I realize I'm not getting any younger. I need a partner, Angela, and you're the only person I've ever even thought about asking. So what do you think?"

Angela seldom showed emotion these days, her face a permanent, carefully controlled mask of unsmiling indifference. But the news her boss had just shared was more than enough to get a reaction out of her.

"You're really serious?" asked Angela haltingly. "I mean, the way you're always yelling at me or telling me I'm stupid and incompetent - "

Barbara waved a hand impatiently. "Jesus, I talk to everyone that way. Always have. And unfortunately most people I've had the misfortune to work with in this industry *have* been stupid and incompetent. You at least have potential, someone I think I can actually work with. Besides, you've never once tried to answer me back no matter how awful I was to you. Or worse – cried."

Angela looked down at the floor, her hands clasped quietly in her lap. "I don't cry. At least, not any longer."

"Got all that out of your system when that bastard Manning dumped you, huh?" asked Barbara with her usual candor. "I'm glad to hear you don't cry anymore over that worthless piece of shit. It's bad enough he turned you into some sort of zombie woman. I'd hate to think you were wasting even one more minute of your life on him."

Angela had been startled when her boss had confronted her a couple of months after she'd begun working here. Barbara had grown increasingly frustrated when, no matter how loudly she yelled, or how nasty the insults she flung became, that none of it seemed to phase Angela even a little bit. She did her work like a robot, never smiling or showing any sort of reaction, and definitely never crying. Barbara's current admin assistant – a woman in her late forties named Ginger – had marveled at Angela's ability to take the verbal abuse.

"I swear there are some days I want to wring the evil old bitch's neck," Ginger had confessed. "They warned me about her when I transferred here from Salt Lake City, but I never expected it to be this bad. And let me tell you, I worked for some real assholes in my old office. But she makes them look like a bunch of puppies. You must have to recite the Serenity Prayer like ten times an hour in order to put up with everything she dishes out."

No one really understood just how frozen Angela was inside these days. When she'd made the decision to leave Jessup Prior, she'd ruthlessly shut down her emotions at the same time. It wasn't so much about achieving a state of serenity or even calmness as it was about simply not allowing herself to feel anything. She'd found it was much easier to get through each day that way, and she'd become an expert in a very short period of time at not caring about anything.

But Barbara's curiosity had been piqued about this young, rather waifish looking girl who never smiled, never got upset, never seemed to change expression, and she'd called Angela into her office for an extremely rare personal chat. Barbara had never allowed herself to become friendly with her staff, fearing that to do so might actually make her seem human. And she'd worked too damned hard over the years to cultivate a reputation as a ballsy, cold-hearted bitch to ease up in her old age.

With a rapid-fire series of questions, Barbara had finally managed to pry the truth out of her new associate – that the reason for Angela's complete lack of emotion was because of a man.

Barbara had given a "humph" of disdain at this revelation. "Figures," she'd said with mild disgust. "Bunch of bastards, every single one of them. But I'm surprised that someone as tough and smart as you are would let a man fuck her over so badly. I know some of the guys at your old stomping grounds. You don't spend almost forty years in this business without getting to know your competition. So who was it?"

When Angela hadn't replied, Barbara had begun to toss out names of the dozen or so male brokers she knew at Jessup Prior. And when Angela's spine had stiffened at the mere mention of Nick's name, Barbara had known instantly that she'd struck pay dirt.

"Nick Manning, huh?" Barbara had shaken her head in bemusement. "What were you thinking of, missy? He's a shark, that one, and you must have been awfully easy prey for someone like him. And he's an even bigger dickwad than I thought if he messed you up this badly. How long were you together – couple of months?"

Angela had given a brief shake of her head. "Almost a year, actually."

Barbara's small, deep set eyes had bugged out as much as

was physically possible. "Are you shitting me? From what I've heard Manning's the ultimate love 'em and leave 'em kind of guy. You must have a magic snatch or something to have kept him interested that long."

The stark pallor of Angela's complexion had flushed a bright shade of pink at her boss's extremely frank way of speaking. "Uh, actually, if you don't mind, I'd really rather not talk about him."

Barbara had shrugged. "Fine with me. I've never been one for girly gossip, as you've probably guessed by now. Just answer me one question, though – is Manning the reason you gave up everything at Jessup Prior to come here?"

Angela had given a brief, curt nod. "Yes. That's why I left. I – well, couldn't handle knowing he was in the same building. I was afraid that one day I wasn't going to be able to stop myself from barging into his office and groveling at his feet to take me back."

Barbara had made a disgusted sound. "You're an even bigger idiot than I first thought, then. To sacrifice a year's hard work for a man? All right, you can take your bony ass back to your desk now, I've got clients to call. But a word of advice, missy – don't ever, ever let a man control you like that again. Men always look out for their own interests first, so don't forget that."

Now, Angela gave a shake of her head. "No, you were right, what you told me a couple of months back. Men *are* out for themselves, and I'm not about to let one ruin my life ever again. Especially not – Nick."

His name was difficult for her to speak out loud, and she hadn't done so in a long time. But with each day that passed she thought about him a little less often, ached for him a teeny bit less; and what she'd told Barbara was entirely true – she hadn't shed one more tear for him, didn't know if she would ever be able to feel enough to cry over anything again.

"Good. Glad to hear it," replied Barbara firmly. "Because if you agree to the terms of this partnership – and goddamn, girl, you'd have to be a half-wit not to – then you're going to work harder than you ever have in your life. There won't be time for you to weep and wail over a man who kicked you to the curb like last week's recycling."

Angela listened intently as her boss laid out the relatively simple terms of the proposed partnership. A fifteen percent cut the first year, twenty five by the second, and then increasing in gradual increments over the next few years.

"By then I'll have either retired or dropped dead," Barbara stated dispassionately. "I've already got emphysema, you know, not to mention high blood pressure, clogged arteries, and diabetes. My doctors are constantly nagging me to lose weight, stop smoking, start exercising. But fuck them all – I've worked too hard to live like some monk eating brown rice and broccoli all the time. No one's going to tell me how to live my life, I don't care how many degrees they have. So, what do you say, missy?"

"I say yes," agreed Angela impulsively. "You're absolutely right – I'd have to be a moron to refuse. Even aside from the percentage, just the opportunity to learn from you is enough to help me decide."

Barbara gave a hoot of laughter. "Oh, honey, that's awful pretty but you don't have to flatter me. I'm already impressed by your smarts and how tough you are. Anyone that can take the crap I've offloaded on you these past few months is worthy of being my partner. Let's go tell McReynolds, shall we? He'll shit his pants, but he almost always does that anyway when he sees me coming."

***

If Angela had thought she'd worked hard during her year at Jessup Prior, she quickly realized how wrong she'd been. And while she'd certainly had a staggering workload during the months she'd spent as Barbara's associate, it was nothing compared to what the older woman expected of an actual partner.

But Angela never complained and certainly never regretted her decision. Becoming Barbara's partner had been a stellar career move – the opportunity to be mentored by one of the most brilliant financial minds on the West Coast a once in a lifetime break.   She was pleasantly surprised at just how much responsibility Barbara had delegated to her, and how she'd begun to meet and work with clients right from the start. And while Barbara continued to work insanely long hours herself, it seemed to Angela that her boss was at least a little less stressed and didn't fly off the handle quite so often.

She had also discovered that Barbara had both a wicked sense of humor and a rather odd maternal streak. In her own, gruff, tough love manner, Barbara took more interest in Angela's life and wellbeing than Rita ever had.   Barbara nagged at her constantly to eat something, made tactless comments about how skinny she was, and advised her not to wind up a bitter, dried up old maid the way she had.

"I got married to my job thirty years ago," admitted Barbara. "But you're just a kid, so take my advice – work hard now, be a success and make a bunch of money, but don't wind up alone. And if you do get married one day, remember two things – get a pre-nup and make damned sure you keep your money in a separate account. Don't ever give a man control over you ever again, and especially not over your money."

Predictably, the news of Barbara's new partnership with Angela had sent shockwaves reverberating through the office. Any number of the brokers had come up to Angela, most offering congratulations, others commiseration, but all of them had given off vibes of professional jealousy. Over the decades that Barbara had been a fixture in the office, many aspiring young brokers had been brave enough to approach her with the idea of taking on a partner, only to be banished from ever setting foot in her office again. Even older, more established brokers had proposed the idea of a partnership to her, largely to give their sagging careers a much needed boost. She'd sent every one of them away with their tails tucked between their legs as well.

Angela's income also reaped the benefits of her new partnership, enough that she was able to buy a new car and move to a bigger apartment. It was a flat, actually, located in trendy Lower Pacific Heights, and boasted a separate bedroom and a real kitchen. Not that she actually cooked or even ate a real meal these days, but it was nice to have so much space after her cramped studio apartment.

The flat was somewhat sparsely furnished, since she'd only had a few pieces in her old place, and it was rare for her to have either the time or the inclination to go shopping. Lauren had forced her to buy a futon so that she'd have a place to crash when she was in town, and Julia, who was an interior designer, had promised to go furniture shopping with her the next time she came out from New York for a visit.

Her relationship with her family was as strained and distant as ever, though she didn't seem to care as much these days, an unexpected benefit that came with closing off her emotions. She still called her mother dutifully each Saturday, attended all the important family functions, but merely went through the motions each time. She said little when she was with them, kept to herself as much as possible, and left for home as soon as she was able. If Lauren was at home, she would drive up from Big Sur to spend the night at her parents' house so that she could spend a little time with Angela.

And when Deanna had exclaimed in alarm about how skinny her younger sister had become, Angela made sure to pile on extra layers each time she visited her family in order to disguise her extreme weight loss. The ten pounds she'd lost during the first few weeks after Nick had broken things off had rather quickly become twenty, and was now approaching thirty. She'd had to use some of her increased earnings to buy several new suits, everything in a size zero, and even then she'd had to have the waistbands taken in a few inches. She ate the bare minimum of calories needed to subsist, and usually had to force food down.

But despite what everyone who looked at her must certainly think, Angela wasn't anorexic or bulimic. She didn't intentionally starve herself, didn't think she was overweight. She knew very well that she was too thin, didn't think she looked at all attractive this way, and realized her lack of appetite was both dangerous and unhealthy. She didn't eat because she simply didn't care, because food was unimportant, and she couldn't summon up enough effort most days to remember to eat.

She'd also upped her running miles significantly, especially on the weekends when she didn't have work to fill in the empty hours. On a dare from Lauren, she had entered a half marathon race the previous month and had enjoyed it enough to set her sights on running a full marathon in a few months' time. Angela quickly discovered that running for fifteen or twenty miles helped her get into a zone where she could easily block out anything besides her workout. She'd pop her headphones in, crank up the hard rock mix on her iPod, and then it was just her and the road or the trail. She ignored the other runners, walkers, and cyclists around her, just as she shunned most people these days. She had zero desire to run with someone else, and was an admitted loner.

And dating was definitely off the table. Even all these months after things had disintegrated with Nick, the very thought of going out with someone else – much less sleeping with them – made her shudder in revulsion. The wounds he'd inflicted on her were still raw and oozing, and there was no possible way she was going to willingly let herself be hurt again. Nick had damaged something deep inside of her, had made her wary and unable to trust or open up to anyone.

And then, of course, there was the stark realization that any other man would forever pale in comparison to Nick. How could she ever be happy or satisfied with someone else when Nick had been so – so much? He'd had everything a woman could possibly want in a man – fantastic looks, an incredible body, wealth, power, intelligence, success, sophistication, an often wicked sense of humor. And she knew that there would never be anyone to compare to his mind-boggling sexual prowess. He was a God, incomparable, one of a kind. He'd ruined her, spoiled her, for other men, and she was destined to spend the rest of her life knowing she would never come close to what she'd had with him ever again.

It was odd, really, that everyone seemed to have assumed she'd moved on, had put her eleven months and five days with Nick behind her. Her family, Lauren, Barbara – they all thought that because she worked so many hours, ran so many miles, that she must simply fall into an exhausted slumber each night, too worn out to even think. No one knew that it was the nights that were the worst – that the nights were when the memories would flood in and threaten to drown her each time. And because she'd vowed to never cry over a man again, that was when she reached for the bottle of vodka or tequila and drank until the numbness began to seep back in.

But there were nights when no amount of alcohol could ease her pain, and those were the times she was forced to do the unthinkable – feel.

***

Thirteen Months Later

Angela was vaguely surprised at how many people were in attendance today, the chapel at the cemetery nearly full, though mostly with co-workers and clients. Barbara hadn't had much of a family, just a nephew she hadn't seen in years and a couple of distant cousins. It made Angela sad to realize that she'd likely been closer to her boss than almost anyone else here today.

Barbara's sudden death from a massive heart attack shouldn't have been such a shock, given her steadfast refusal to obey any of her doctor's orders. Up until her dying day she'd continued to smoke several packs of cigarettes a day, eat a greasy, calorie-laden diet, and rarely take her prescribed medications. She'd collapsed at her desk just after lunch, and had been dead before the paramedics could arrive. For once Angela had been grateful she'd mastered the ability of shutting off her emotions, as it had helped her get through the trauma of seeing her boss – and her friend – die before her very eyes.

It was less than a week after the funeral when Angela was called into her manager's office, a summons she'd been expecting, and had mentally prepared herself for. In the thirteen months she'd been Barbara's partner, the older woman had taught her well and Angela was more than ready to fight for what she knew she was entitled to – namely fifty percent of Barbara's clients.

"You're a very lucky young woman, Angela," began Paul McReynolds as he closed the door to his office.

Angela arched a brow at her manager. "Really? Is that what you'd call watching someone drop dead right in front of you?"

Paul had the good graces to look vaguely ashamed. "I'm sorry for what you had to go through that day. I can't even imagine how upsetting it must have been. Still, you seemed to keep your head on straight and not fly into a panic."

She shrugged. "Sometimes you just operate on auto pilot in these situations, do what has to be done. Not that my remaining calm helped poor Barbara in the end, did it?"

"No. Look, Angela, I don't mean to sound insensitive. I realize that you were probably one of the few people in this world who actually liked Barbara. But there's also no denying the fact that you stand to benefit from her death."

According to the firm's policies, so long as a partnership between two brokers had been in existence for at least a year, then the surviving partner was entitled to fifty percent of the accounts upon the death of the other. The surviving partner was also entitled to choose exactly what accounts they wanted to keep from that fifty percent.

Knowing this meeting with Paul was imminent, Angela had gone through the client lists with a fine tooth comb to identify the most desirable and lucrative accounts. She quietly handed Paul the list of those clients now.

"This is approximately fifty percent of Barbara's account book," she told him matter-of-factly. "The ones I've chosen to keep as my entitlement. Let me know who the rest of the accounts get distributed to and I'll make sure everyone gets their client files."

Paul glanced at the list and gave a low whistle of admiration, no doubt having recognized a good many of the names. "Well, you certainly knew what you were doing when you made your choices, didn't you? You sure you're going to be able to handle some of these, Angela? Barbara had a lot of high profile clients, you know."

"I'm sure." It had been a long time since Angela had felt this self-assured about anything. "Barbara had faith in me and she taught me a lot. Plus, I've already met all of these clients and they like me. My decision is final."

Paul chuckled. "She did teach you well, didn't she? Just don't turn into a ballbreaker like she was, okay? You're too young and have too much potential to become a cranky old shrew like your partner was."

Angela gave a casual lift of her shoulder. "My personal life has nothing to do with my professional one. But I fully intend to make Barbara proud of me and do the right thing by these clients."

Paul sighed. "Fine. Now, I can't let you have her office, unfortunately. *That* would really set off fireworks around here. I'll warn you that a lot of people are going to be royally pissed off about the percentage of her book you're getting – not that you're not legally entitled to it, of course."

Up until now, Angela had been sitting at a cubicle just outside of Barbara's office, but with her acquisition of half of the book she was now well within her rights to get a private office.

"I don't care about her office," replied Angela. "In fact, I don't think I could work in there without reliving the day of her death over and over. What other spots are open?"

Paul hesitated. "Right now the only other one is at the very end of the hallway, the one in the corner. It's not very big or - "

"I'll take it," interrupted Angela. "It will be fine for me. I don't need much space and I like the idea of being a bit isolated. I don't like a lot of distraction when I'm working."

"Well, that was easy," said Paul in relief. "I wish I could tell you that it's going to be as easy for you these next few weeks. Watch your back, Angela. Legally entitled or not, you're bound to get a lot of backlash, a lot of petty professional jealousy from people who don't think you earned it."

She gave a short, bitter laugh. "Didn't earn it? Did anyone else work eighteen hour days, plus take work home at night and on weekends? Did any of them get called an idiot twenty times a day, or have to tiptoe around a boss who could fly into a rage at a moment's notice? I sure as *hell* earned every one of those accounts, Paul, and I'll gladly tell that to anyone who thinks otherwise."

Paul grinned. "I think my warning has come too late – you're already   turning   into   a   ballbreaker."

Chapter Fourteen

Thanksgiving, two and half years later

It was a cold, foggy morning in Carmel, typical for this time of the year, but once she'd completed five miles or so of her planned twenty mile run, Angela finally began to warm up a bit. Doing these long runs not only provided her with the solace and peace of mind she needed so badly, but also helped to dispel the perennial chill that at times seemed to seep into her very bones. Running made her blood pump faster, warmed her up, so that her extremities didn't feel quite so icy.

And today this early morning run through the streets of her old neighborhood, and then connecting to a new bike path, also provided her with an excuse to get out of the house. She never liked coming home, and a big family dinner such as today's Thanksgiving celebration was one of her least favorite occasions. So she welcomed these next few hours when she could be blissfully alone and not have to be confronted with the unhappy memories being inside her parents' home invariably dredged up.

She bumped up the volume on her iPod at some point, as though she could drown out the voices in her head that always threatened to distract her. But the song that came on next did nothing to help the cause, and she cursed softly, belatedly recalling that she'd meant to delete this particular entry from her playlist months ago. And yet, even as her finger hovered over the forward button, she continued to listen to the heartrending lyrics of O.A.R.'s *Shattered*. She'd listened to this song so many times after the break-up with Nick that she'd half-jokingly begun to think of it as her theme song.

As she listened to it now – for the first time in months – Angela wondered if she would ever feel whole again. As the singer asked the question of how many times he could break until he shattered, she knew exactly how he felt.

But when she felt the unwelcome shimmer of tears begin to

well up behind her eyes, she ruthlessly advanced the iPod to the next song, gratified to recognize the throbbing beat of a Papa Roach song. There was nothing the least bit sad or sentimental about a song like *Last Resort*, and once again she was able to push any depressing thoughts from her head and just run.

She hit the ten mile mark, her turnaround point, and stopped to take a long swig from her handheld water bottle, taking a brief walk break as she did so. She'd learned over time to take these little breaks during her long runs, especially since she'd moved into ultrarunning over the past year. She'd taken to the marathon distance easily, and after completing three of them within six months, she'd sought out bigger challenges – fifty kilometers, fifty miles. In the coming year, she had plans to run a couple of hundred kilometer races, with the goal of completing a hundred miler after that.

She was about four miles from the end of her run when another runner pulled up beside her. As was her norm, she ignored the person to her left, remaining focused on her music and her running. But the guy she could glimpse from her peripheral vision evidently wasn't taking the hint easily, keeping pace with her as they ran side by side. Her first impression was that he was unusually tall, something she typically noticed about a man since she tended to tower over so many people. The second thing she noticed was that he seemed to be keeping up with her easily, though she'd admittedly had to slow down over the last few miles due to increasing fatigue. And the third thing she noticed, as she stole another sideways glance at him, was that the somewhat goofy grin he gave her seemed oddly familiar.

She pressed the pause button on her iPod and gazed at her uninvited running companion quizzically. "Um, do I know you from somewhere?"

He brushed a lock of his shaggy, sandy brown hair out of his eyes and grinned even wider as he nodded enthusiastically. "I didn't think you'd remember me, Angela, but yeah, we went to high school together. I'm Dwayne Conroy. Uh, it's been a long time, hasn't it?"

Angela's eyes widened in surprise. "Dwayne? Ah, yeah, it has definitely been a long, long time."

The Dwayne Conroy she remembered from high school – the same guy Lauren had caustically nicknamed Dwayne the Dweeb – had always been – well, a real dweeb. Astonishingly tall – at least half a foot taller than she was – he'd also been skinny as a rail, incredibly clumsy, and quite possibly the goofiest guy she'd ever seen. Back in high school his jeans had always been too short, his glasses too thick, his braces too shiny. He'd hung out with the other nerds and geeks, and Angela couldn't recall ever associating with him during their school days.

But the years since their senior year had been kinder to Dwayne, as her quickly assessing gaze took note of. The glasses were gone, and his light blue eyes twinkled at her merrily. Gone, too, were the braces and he grinned at her with a set of straight, gleaming white teeth. He was still incredibly tall, of course, but not nearly so skinny and seemed to have finally grown into his height. No one would ever call him built or muscular, but he was certainly lean and fit and wore his workout clothes well. He might never fit anyone's opinion of a cool guy, but he was definitely not a dweeb any longer.

"I never knew you were a runner," he was telling her now. "From what I remember in high school, you played a lot of other sports, though – soccer, basketball, volleyball."

She nodded. "You've got a good memory. And, no, I didn't really run in high school, at least not seriously. I started running about three years ago. What about you?"

As they ran along at a comfortable pace, Dwayne chatted happily about his college days at Texas A & M, where he'd been a national collegiate champion in the high jump. Somewhat guiltily, Angela realized she'd never took notice of the fact that Dwayne had also been a standout on their high school track team, good enough to have been recruited by several colleges.

She told him about her own years at Stanford on the volleyball team, the NCAA titles they'd won, and her Olympic experience.

Dwayne gave a low whistle. "Wow. That's my goal, you know. To make the next Olympic team. My coach thinks I've got a great shot, especially since I took the silver medal at this year's national championships."

"Oh, so you still compete?" she asked in surprise. "I mean, it wasn't just something to get you through college?"

Dwayne shook his head. "Nope. That's what I always figured, too, but my college coach was the one to suggest I stay the course awhile longer. He knew some people at Nike and helped me to get a sponsorship deal after graduation."

Angela gazed at him in amazement. "Wow, that's fantastic, Dwayne. I guess I never paid much attention to the track team back in high school, never - "

"Never paid much attention to *me*," he finished. "Hey," he added soothingly when she flushed with embarrassment, "don't worry about it. Hardly anyone noticed me back then. Or if they did it was to laugh because I walked into a door or tripped over my shoelace. I never expected a girl like you to notice me."

Angela quirked a brow at him. "Huh?"

Dwayne chuckled. "You never knew I had a huge crush on you back then, did you?"

She was instantly flustered. "Um, I, ah, never noticed, no. But in all fairness I didn't really date much in high school, didn't pay attention to guys in general. I was so much taller than most of the guys that I always felt - "

"Awkward? Ungainly?" finished Dwayne. "Yeah, I know the feeling. Still do, matter of fact. But that was one of the things that attracted me to you. I figured we had our height in common."

"Yeah," she mumbled, not sure what else to say. She'd had zero idea that Dwayne had been attracted to her, and guiltily acknowledged that even if she'd known it would never have amounted to anything back then. He'd been far too much of a dweeb, and she'd been too screwed up to even consider dating someone.

They were now two houses down from Angela's parents' house, and had stopped running as they continued to chat.

"So where do you live these days?" inquired Dwayne. "You're not still here in Carmel, are you?"

Angela shuddered. "God, no. Oh, I like Carmel just fine, just not living – here." She indicated the house. "I'm only home for the holiday. I actually live and work in San Francisco now."

She told him about her job and her flat, and he nodded in acknowledgment.

"You always were really good at math as I recall," he replied. "I'll bet you're incredibly successful at what you do. I'd, uh, love to discuss it with you sometime – the stock market, that is."

"Sure, we could do that. Where are you living now?" she asked, feeling oddly at ease with a guy she hadn't seen in over seven years, and whom she hadn't exactly known very well in school.

Dwayne looked a bit uncertain. "Eugene, Oregon, actually. That's where Nike has a big training facility. I share a house with a bunch of other track people, but I also travel a lot during track season – mostly in Europe."

"So you don't get down this way very often?"

He shook his head. "A few times a year to visit my family is all. But, ah, I usually always fly into San Francisco when I do, so maybe we could meet up for coffee or lunch sometime?"

The polite but firm brush-off Angela usually gave to the few men who tried to ask her out these days froze on her lips. The hopeful puppy dog look on Dwayne's face touched something in her, made her smile in a way she hadn't done in a very long time. He was such a nice, genuine guy, clearly still awkward and goofy, that she found herself replying, "I'd really like that, Dwayne."

The grin he gave her threatened to split his face in half and made him look oddly appealing. "Wow, that would be great, Angela! In fact, how long are you staying in Carmel this weekend?"

She'd had more than half a thought about leaving early tomorrow morning, even though she knew such a decision would be met with disapproval from the family. Now, she impulsively told Dwayne, "Sometime on Saturday, I think. I'm not exactly sure when."

His grin grew even wider. "Would you – that is, how about if we met up sometime tomorrow? Like for coffee or lunch? We could even do another run together in the morning and then have breakfast. Unless," he added soberly, as though the idea had just occurred to him, "you're here with a boyfriend or something. Or have other plans with your family."

Angela gave him a reassuring smile. "No, to both questions. No current boyfriend and no plans with the family. I'd love to meet up for another run and then maybe grab coffee afterwards. I'm, uh, not much of a breakfast eater."

His gaze traveled quizzically, assessingly, up and down the tall, skinny length of her body, and, rather amazingly, he blushed. She wasn't sure when the last time a guy had actually blushed in her presence – if ever – had been but if so it had surely been way back in grade school.

"Yeah, you're, uh, slimmer than I remember from high school," Dwayne replied tactfully. "Guess you must run an awful lot of miles. You're about the same build as a couple of the female marathon runners in my training group."

"I've actually taken it to the next level and started running ultras," she told him. "Kind of crazy, huh? At least, that's what most peoples' reaction is when I tell them I've run a fifty mile race."

Dwayne shrugged. "Not crazy, just different. But, seriously, Angela, if you're doing that sort of mileage you really need to keep up your calorie intake. I, uh, majored in nutritional sciences at school, figure on becoming a dietician when this high jump thing eventually ends for me. We could – that is, if you want to – discuss a good nutrition plan for you sometime."

She scuffled the heel of her shoe against the curb, gazing downward. Discussing her drastic weight loss was never easy for her and usually put her on the defensive. But once again Dwayne sounded so sincere, so caring and just so *nice* that it was downright impossible to feel any sort of annoyance or anger at him.

"Maybe," was all she mumbled in reply. "And, well, that's nice of you to offer. It's just – food and I – we have sort of a weird relationship these days. But I'm not anorexic, despite what everyone thinks. I just – well, it's complicated."

Dwayne gave her shoulder a quick, reassuring squeeze. "Okay. Maybe you'll feel like talking about it one of these days.

In the meanwhile, why don't you give me your number?"

Angela hesitated briefly before reciting her cell phone number and email address, watching as he entered both into his phone. She told herself firmly that agreeing to meet Dwayne for a run and coffee didn't constitute an actual date. This was Dwayne Conroy, after all, "Dwayne the Dweeb" that she'd known in high school. He was just a guy, an old school mate, and it was just coffee. There was no need to panic, she reminded herself, no cause to be alarmed despite the fact that she hadn't been out with any male in more than three years.

Oh, Lauren and Julia had both done their damndest to, as they'd so succinctly put it, "get her out there". Julia had moved back to San Francisco almost a year ago and was occupying the flat just below hers. She was also dating a seriously gorgeous guy – the co-owner of the firm she worked at – and had tried on numerous occasions to fix Angela up with one of Nathan's friends. Julia, who was admittedly a fantastic cook, also tried on a regular basis to make Angela eat more. Thus far, her efforts on both counts had been largely unsuccessful.

And Lauren, whenever she happened to be in San Francisco, practically manhandled her – not an easy feat, considering the eight inch difference in their height – to go out to dinner or dancing or drinking – usually all three. She continued to bully Angela to move on, find someone else, enjoy life again.

Thus far, however, Angela had continued to resist getting involved with another guy, whether it be a full-fledged relationship or simply a meaningless one night stand. She was surprised – given her gaunt frame and total indifference to her appearance – when men still approached her at clubs or bars, leading her to wonder just how desperate some of them were.

But now she sensed it wasn't like that with Dwayne, that his intent in befriending her wasn't solely to get her in bed. He was just, she realized with something of a shock, being a good guy.

And as she let herself inside the house, a rare smile crossed her features as she realized it had been a long, long time since she'd felt like this – like maybe, just maybe, life could be worth living   again.

Chapter Fifteen

April, Present Day

The view of the San Francisco Bay and Sausalito harbor from the back deck had been one of the primary reasons Nick had bought this grand home nearly a decade ago. There were other reasons, of course – its size and spaciousness; the clean, sleek lines of its design; the complete privacy it afforded him; and its close proximity to San Francisco, just a quick drive across the Golden Gate Bridge. But if pressed to pick the one thing that had really sealed the deal for him when it had come time to make a final decision, the view had very likely been the deal maker.

He stood at the deck railing now, cradling a glass of merlot in his hand as he watched the sun begin to set over the harbor. The dozens of houseboats and other sailing craft moored there were all beginning to turn their lights on, creating something of a fairytale atmosphere, and from a distance he could glimpse both tourists and locals alike as they strolled along Bridgeway, the main thoroughfare in town where most of the shops and restaurants were located.

He had felt an affinity with this house the moment he'd walked inside accompanied by the real estate agent, and knew he had to have it. Over the years the house, with its stellar waterfront views and sheltered back deck and garden, had become far more than a home to him. This was his private place, his sanctuary, and he could count on one hand the number of people he had ever invited inside – just his parents and a couple of very close friends. And he'd never, ever, brought a woman here, refusing to share his sacred space with any of the ones he'd had brief, fleeting relationships with. And, even though they'd been together for nearly a year, he'd never brought Angela here, either.

"Fuck."

His breath expelled in a sigh of frustration as he realized where his thoughts were taking him once again. Ever since he'd seen her earlier today it had been nearly impossible to get her out of his head. A whole gamut of emotions had been twisting him into knots for hours now, emotions that he'd rarely if ever allowed himself to feel. For the most part, Nick had lived his life without a single regret, had never permitted himself to look back and wish he'd done something differently, and he'd certainly never felt the least bit guilty about the choices he'd made. With one exception to all of these things – namely, Angela Del Carlo.

He'd struggled with the guilt for years now, ever since the night he'd cruelly broken things off with her, had practically pushed her out of his car. He had forced himself to harden his heart on that awful night, to block out the sounds of her pitiful sobs and desperate pleas to give her another chance. It had been the only way he'd been able to actually go through with it, to end the relationship he should have never entered into in the first place.

But the guilt and regret he'd experienced during these past few years were nothing compared to the overwhelming remorse that he'd felt the moment he had seen Angela again today. She'd born little resemblance to the sultry, sexy beauty who'd more or less been his sexual slave for nearly a year. Little by little he'd deliberately molded her to fit his picture of the ideal woman – urging her to put on weight so that she'd have curves in exactly the right places; picking out the sort of clothing for her that he found the most alluring; teaching her exactly how to please him in bed. The image of how she'd looked that last night was burned into his memory banks, never to be forgotten – the way her long, dark hair had fallen in shimmering waves nearly to her waist; how that white dress had clung to her sleek, toned curves and bared a great deal of those gorgeous, shapely legs; how her beautiful dark eyes and wide, full-lipped mouth had been perfectly made up, not overdone or flashy, but just enough to enhance her natural beauty.

But the woman he'd seen today was nothing like the beautiful, passionate woman who'd been his lover once upon a time. The woman who'd stood across that desk, staring at him with an empty, soulless expression, was a shadow of her former self – in more ways than one. Painfully thin now, practically a goddamned walking skeleton, her ugly pantsuit had hung loosely on her emaciated frame. Her once glowing complexion was sallow, her cheekbones hollowed out and her big eyes sunken in. She hadn't worn a scrap of makeup, and there had been dark circles under her eyes. Her hair had been ruthlessly scraped back into a knot, and at first glance he hadn't noticed her wearing any jewelry at all, not even a watch.

But it had been the look in her eyes – or lack thereof – that had really disturbed him. Her voice had sounded hollow and lifeless, and Angela herself looked like all the life had been sucked out of her.

And then there had been her hands – their extreme iciness startling - and he'd had to force himself not to flinch when he'd touched her. She'd always had such soft, warm hands, and he'd loved the feel of them as they'd caressed every inch of his body. Now they were as pale and bony as the rest of her, and their coldness made him worry that she was sick. Or anorexic.

Nick reached for the bottle of wine he'd left on the deck table, grimacing slightly when he noticed how much of it he'd already consumed. But, what the hell, he thought in disgust. He needed something to help numb these feelings of guilt that were threatening to choke him. He'd never imagined that Angela wouldn't get over him, wouldn't have moved on a long time ago. She'd been so young, had so much going for her – beauty, brains, ambition. He'd been shocked to learn she had pretty much just up and left Jessup Prior, leaving behind an impressive book of clients – many of whom he'd directed her way – and started from scratch at Morton Sterling. And then to learn she'd chosen to work with a soul-sucking bitch like Barbara Lowenstein rather than remain in the same office as himself – well, that had really made him feel like shit. He had never meant to drive her away, to make things so painful that she'd had no other choice but to leave her job.

Nick gave himself a mental kick in the ass when he recalled

the last time he'd seen Angela before today – at another of those useless office meetings. He'd known she would be there, had been half afraid that she would try to approach him, and had wanted to avoid an awkward scene at all costs. So he'd been even more of a prick than he'd already been to her and looked right past her as though she hadn't existed. It was ironic that he'd never had a problem blowing off women in the past, but when he'd had to do the same to Angela he'd felt like the biggest asshole in the history of the world.

In fact, he realized in disgust as he took a slow sip of wine, he'd been a total, complete, and revolting asshole to her during the entire duration of their relationship. When he'd laid out his admittedly ridiculous conditions to her that night at the Biltmore, he had never really believed she'd accept. And when she had agreed, he had certainly never expected it to last for more than a month or two. The fact that she'd hung in there for so long continued to amaze him, and made him realize just how strong willed she really was.

But there was almost nothing left of that woman now – the one who looked like a strong wind would blow her over, whose arm had felt alarmingly thin and frail beneath his fingers, whose eyes looked dead. *He* had done that to her, he realized now with a groan. She'd devoted herself to him, had given him everything he'd asked of her, had *loved* him for God's sake, and he had thrown all of it away – he'd shoved her out of his life just as he'd shoved her out of his car that night.

When he'd finally accepted the offer to join Morton Sterling, it had been with the knowledge that Angela worked for the same firm. The decision to leave Jessup Prior – and all that he'd built up there – had been a tough one, a decision he'd thought about and planned for nearly a year. He had grown increasingly concerned about the company's financial stability over the years, was dissatisfied with its earnings and cash reserves, and had begun to hear mounting rumors of potential buy-outs or takeovers. But when he'd shared his concerns with fellow brokers or upper level managers, they had all brushed him off, either unwilling to believe the cold hard facts or choosing to ignore them for reasons of their own. Nick had been determined not to go down with a sinking ship, and to leave on his own terms. He'd discreetly met with three different rival firms, carefully weighing what perks and bonuses each one offered, and taking his time to plan his ultimate departure. Management at Jessup Prior had been in shell-shocked disbelief when he'd rather casually announced he was leaving, and though he hadn't been able to outright take his accounts with him, he was supremely confident that nearly every one would follow him to his new firm. He had also taken three of his team members with him, and had the guarantee of being able to hire a fourth as part of his signing package.

Even before his new manager – Paul McReynolds – had brought him to "meet" Angela, he'd heard grumblings from a few of the other brokers about the "ice queen in the corner" and "Ballbreaker Barbara's protégé". After leaving Angela's surprisingly small corner office – surprising given the level of production she'd achieved – he had casually asked Paul about her. Nick had felt immensely proud to learn how she'd built up her portion of Barbara Lowenstein's client base into a truly impressive book. True, she'd received something of a lucky break but, given what he'd known of the older woman, there was little doubt Angela had more than earned those accounts.

And seeing Angela again today after all this time had definitely sent him on a little trip down memory lane. In the years since he'd ended things between them, he hadn't allowed himself to think of her very often, largely to avoid the guilt that invariably accompanied such thought. He'd moved on, of course, easing back into his old routines without blinking an eye. But while there had certainly been other women, none of them had lasted more than a week or two, and he couldn't honestly remember any of their names by now. And for the last eighteen months or so, he'd been without a woman altogether, had been celibate for perhaps the first time since his teens.

He'd told himself the reason for his self-induced celibacy was simply because he'd been too focused on transitioning his business to another firm, getting everything in order, and making sure he took the best possible offer. But a big part of his abstention was because he was tired of the whole dating scene at this point in his life, weary of all the work involved, and the inevitable nasty scene that occurred when he told a woman he wouldn't be seeing her again. During the year he'd been with Angela, it had been a tremendous relief not to have to engage in all of the various dating rituals, to know that for once he had a steady woman in his life. It had really been the perfect arrangement, especially since she'd been so completely keen to obey his rules and had never tried to ask him for more than he was willing to give. And as each month of their relationship had passed, Nick had been increasingly surprised that he hadn't grown bored or dissatisfied with her, or that he hadn't felt the restless need to move on to someone new.

Yes, everything had been near to perfect until she'd come home from that damned family wedding looking like she'd been emotionally tortured and drained. He'd silently cursed her total bitch of a mother, had wondered how a woman could say such awful things to her own child, and had felt tremendous empathy for Angela. Granted, his own mother and father would never win any awards for Parent of the Year, but at least he'd never felt unwanted or unloved.

Nick had sensed all along that Angela secretly wanted more from their relationship – even though she'd been extremely careful, almost paranoid about voicing such needs – and had seen the hurt on her face that she couldn't always hide when he'd left her bed after several hours of hot, intense sex. The air of casual sophistication she'd always assumed in his presence had begun to ring false, and by the end she'd started clinging to him in near-desperation, as though she knew the end was near for them.

It had been on the night of her birthday when he'd realized things had to end once and for all. When, at the very height of passion, she'd let the words slip out, the three words that had felt like an electric shock to his system. And he'd realized then he had known all along that she'd fallen in love with him, and had deliberately chosen to ignore that fact. He'd continued to take advantage of her willingness to be with him under any conditions – conditions that any other woman would have balked to even consider. But Angela had wanted him badly enough, had loved him that much, that she'd put up with his neglect, his control, the deliberate way he always kept her at a distance. And he'd decided that he couldn't keep leading her on, couldn't live with himself another week under such conditions, so he'd done what he believed to be the right thing and cut her loose.

In the weeks following their break-up, Nick had resisted the urge to call and check up on her, and make sure she was okay. He'd told himself over and over that this break was the best thing for Angela, and that now she'd be free to find a nice guy who could treat her right and with whom she could form a normal, healthy relationship. God knew after the way he'd been brought up, and after what he'd seen firsthand of so-called normal relationships, that he had zero idea of how to have one himself.

Nick had thought many times over the years that a list of the more unfortunate twists of fate in the history of mankind most assuredly had to include the day his parents met. There was no other logical explanation for why two people who were almost polar opposites, and who had nothing even remotely in common with each other, would have met, hooked up, conceived a child – accidentally, of course – and then muddled things up even more by deciding to get married. But fate eventually corrected itself when his parents got divorced less than three years later, going their separate ways to live the sort of lives they had always been intended to. All would have been right with the world from that point on except for one major complication – the child they had conceived together, namely Nick.

It was hard for Nick to imagine how his stern, uptight, and by-the-book father had ever let his hair down long enough to get involved with his fun-loving, amoral, and irresponsible mother. But, having seen photos of the two of them when they'd still been in their twenties, he'd had a fairly good idea of the one thing that had brought them together – sex.

Roger Manning's own father – Nick's paternal grandfather – had made it very clear to his only son from a young age about what would be expected of him – just as several prior generations of Manning men had done with their own sons. Roger attended a prestigious private high school, obtained his undergraduate degree at the family alma mater Yale, and then enrolled in law school at the same university. After passing the bar exam, he'd be expected to join the family firm in Boston, and perhaps eventually become a judge or a member of the Presidential cabinet. There was no question of Roger not obeying or going against his father's wishes, and until he met the gorgeous Sheena Sumner during spring break of his final year of law school, he wouldn't have even considered doing so.

Sheena – blonde, buxom, and beguiling – had been a young, up and coming TV actress when she'd met the darkly handsome but rather prudish Roger. She'd been visiting the same Florida beach town where Roger was enjoying spring break with several of his school friends, even staying at the same resort. His friends had dared him to approach her, having found it hilarious that he was possibly the one man in America who didn't know who the sexy, provocative actress was. After several drinks to bolster his courage, Roger had asked her to dance and the rest was history – tawdry as it was.

They had fallen in instant love/lust and spent the rest of the week together. With her TV series having wrapped for the season, Sheena had followed Roger back to New Haven where they'd continued their steamy, passionate affair. And then two things happened almost simultaneously that changed everything – Sheena's series was cancelled and she discovered she was pregnant.

She'd begged Roger to marry her, vowing to give up acting to become a full-time wife and mother. They'd eloped, choosing not to break the news to his parents until after the fact. Very predictably, his father had hit the roof but none of his threats or insults could convince Roger to annul his ill-advised marriage. Time and the course of nature would wind up taking care of that matter instead.

Extremely ambitious and intent on advancing his career as quickly as possible, Roger had grown impatient and intolerant of Sheena's lack of formal education, her unwillingness to play the part of devoted wife, and her careless, irresponsible attitude. For her part, Sheena swiftly became bored with being a stay-at-

home wife and mother, missed California and all of her celebrity friends, and longed for a more exciting, glamorous life. So when Nick was barely two years old, his parents divorced, and none too amicably. And while Sheena left her marriage with a considerable financial settlement, the shared custody arrangements for Nick were far less generous to her.

Nick remained in Boston with his father, who wasted little time in remarrying – this time to a fellow attorney, an ambitious, intelligent woman who understood and supported Roger's rapidly advancing career. Nick was left largely in the care of nannies, sent to the same elite private schools that his father and grandfather had attended, and had been subjected to the exact same sort of rules and controls that they had had to endure as well. But from the time he'd been old enough to think and speak for himself, Nick had rebelled against those rules, had chafed against the controls. Roger had blamed his son's continual defiance on the bad genes he'd inherited from Sheena, and dealt with Nick's rebelliousness by imposing still more rules. By the time Nick had entered his senior year of high school, he'd been counting the days until he turned eighteen and would finally be free to make his own decisions and control his own life.

The very first thing he'd done in preparation for his liberation had been to rather calmly inform Roger that he had no intention of following in the family footsteps, either by attending Yale or becoming an attorney. Roger had stared in speechless shock when his only child had announced very matter-of-factly that he would be attending Stanford instead, courtesy of the athletic scholarship he'd been offered, and would be majoring in finance. Roger had protested, of course, had shouted and threatened and had very nearly taken a swing at the son who now towered over him by several inches and outweighed him by more than thirty pounds. But all of his yelling and theatrics had been of no avail in the end, because Nick had intimidated his father in more than a physical way and Roger had thrown up his hands in exasperated surrender.

From that point on, Nick had immediately begun to make his own rules, control his own life, and for the past twenty-odd years no one had ever tried to defy him or bend him to their will. Not his teachers, his coaches, his employers. It helped, of course, that Nick had always come to class or football practice or the office more than fully prepared, having thoroughly studied the lesson or the game plan or the investment, and by doing so had gained the respect of his superiors and colleagues along the way.

Roger had certainly tried many times over the ensuing years to re-assert his control over his son, but had not so graciously conceded defeat each time. As for his mother – well, that was a whole different story, wasn't it? Because if his father had been an uptight control freak who lived his life according to an archaic rule book, then Sheena had delighted in breaking every single one of those same rules and then some.

Had it been under Roger's – and the rest of the Manning legal team's – complete control, then Nick would likely never have been allowed to see his mother at all. But even though Sheena was something of a fluttery birdbrain with little common sense, the same could not be said of the sharp, streetwise attorney who managed her business affairs and contracts. It had been due to his influence that Sheena had set her stiletto-shod foot down and insisted on having summers and holidays with Nick. Roger hadn't been able to block his ex-wife's access to their son, and thus Nick had spent his summers and most holidays in various parts of the globe with his glamorous, fun-loving mother – in Monte Carlo, Buenos Aires, St. Bart's, Mallorca. And Sheena had more than lived up to her well-earned reputation as a free-spirited party girl. Wherever they happened to be staying for the summer – a rented villa in the south of France; on her current boyfriend's yacht sailing around the Greek Islands; in the luxury condo in Acapulco that belonged to her agent – there were always lots of other people hanging about, always a party of some sort happening. Sheena's vibrant personality attracted an entourage wherever she went, and Nick never knew who he'd find sleeping in a guest room or passed out cold on the living room sofa. Sheena had a constant parade of husbands, boyfriends, and lovers, was always in love, always happy, and had never learned the meaning of the words privacy or discretion. Whenever Nick stayed with his mother, it was a sure bet that the paparazzi was also close by. He'd still been a young boy when he had become repelled by their persistence and intrusiveness. His own image had been plastered all over the tabloids, usually next to a photo of Sheena drinking and dancing with the current man in her life – men who had gradually become younger and younger as the years passed. Nick had been angry and upset at this gross invasion of his privacy, especially when he returned to school in the fall and had to bear the brunt of jokes from his friends who'd seen one or more of the photos.

So when he'd left for Stanford at the age of eighteen, it had been with the intention of never allowing anyone to either control or exploit him ever again. He would no longer be pushed and pulled between a father who tried to enforce rules that controlled every aspect of his life, and a mother who lived with no rules whatsoever. Nick quickly found a happy medium to exist in, one where there were certainly rules but only ones of his own making and where he was always the one calling the shots.

When he'd become a professional football player, he had tried his best to avoid interviews and press conferences, and more often than not was photographed in his full uniform – helmet included – in order to conceal his face as much as possible. And he'd learned early on how to steer clear of women who craved the spotlight, who adored the idea of dating a professional athlete and all the media attention that went along with it. He was scrupulous about keeping his private life private, one of the reasons he rarely dated the same woman more than a few times.

And the control he insisted on was never more present than it was in his business dealings. Almost from the very start of his career as a stockbroker, Nick had made it very clear to his clients that he expected them to follow his recommendations to the letter. Those who had disagreed or resisted had been politely referred to a different broker. He hadn't cared much who he turned away, either – CEO's, business owners, celebrities, pro athletes. More often than not those who had initially refused his proposal had wound up opening an account with him anyway, especially when they heard from friends and associates just how gifted Nick was at the art of making money.

Yes, Nick liked his life just fine, liked the fact he had no obligations, no one to dictate to him or make demands, no one to answer to. His schedule was entirely his own, he could decide how and where to spend his leisure time and with whom. But here he was, approaching forty in less than three years, and exactly what did he have to show for it? Certainly a staggeringly large bank account and stock portfolio; a fantastic waterfront home here in Sausalito; several expensive cars. Then there was the Super Bowl ring, the MVP trophy, years and years worth of other trophies and awards accumulated during high school, college and his time in the NFL. He had a wide network of friends and acquaintances, though he considered less than a handful of them to be in his so-called inner circle; and he had managed to forge a distant but acceptable relationship with his parents. Roger was a federal appeals judge, still living in Boston but now with his third – and much younger – wife. Sheena still flitted from one glittery locale to another, in between making movies and TV appearances. After her fourth marriage had ended in a very predictable divorce, she'd sworn off getting married again and simply took lovers. The last one, Nick recalled with disgust, had been several years younger than he was.

By almost anyone's point of view, Nick had it all – the perfect life, certainly everything he had ever wanted for himself. But he was honest enough to admit that it was a lonely, solitary existence, and that he had a great deal of difficulty in allowing anyone to get close to him. It was why his relationships with women never lasted very long, and why he'd pushed Angela away so hurtfully when she'd gotten too close.

He missed her. And now he wanted her back.

Nick grabbed the bottle of wine and poured the rest into his glass, resisting the urge to bolt it down as he grappled with the truth he'd just admitted to himself.

During the years they'd been apart, he hadn't allowed himself to think of her too often – half-afraid that he'd give in and call her up, and even more afraid that she would tell him to go fuck himself if he did. But he recognized now that the time they'd spent together had been one of the best of his life. He'd enjoyed her company – her wit, her mildly sarcastic sense of humor, all of the things they'd had in common. And the sex, of course, had been phenomenal. She'd always been eager, hot, and willing to do anything he asked, always anxious to please him. He'd taken other women out after the break-up with Angela – to dinner or a party or for drinks – but it had been several months before he'd actually felt the need to take any of them to bed. And the sex had always been casual, impersonal, even meaningless, strictly a normal physical release with zero emotional involvement. Sex had become so unsatisfactory, in fact, that his self-enforced celibacy had been due at least in part to the strange ennui that had overcome him in the last few years.

He hadn't realized until he had seen her today exactly how much he needed Angela back in his life and in his bed. *Her* bed, technically, since he still wasn't ready to bring a woman here to his sanctuary. And now, seeing how skinny and pale and despondent she'd become, he vowed to do whatever it took to make her snap out of her ghost-like existence. He'd bring her back to life, and then he'd bring her back to *him*.

Nick knew without being told that things would have to be different between them now. He'd hurt her badly, used her, broken her. There would have to be some compromises made on his part, while still retaining control over the relationship. But one way or the other, he was going to claim his angel again, and this time he wouldn't be so foolish as to let her go.

Chapter Sixteen

Late May

"O kay, looking great there, Angela!
"You got this, girl!"
"Three miles until the finish. You're killing it!"

Angela gave a brief little wave of acknowledgment to the aid station volunteers as she headed back out onto the trail towards the finish line at Stinson Beach. Today's fifty kilometer race had been a challenging one, with some of the steepest climbs and rockiest terrain that she'd ever run. But she felt strong, even after twenty eight miles out here, and knew from reports she'd been given at the various aid stations along the way that she was one of the top women in the race right now.

She was virtually alone on the trail as she left the aid station, entering a section of the course than ran through a rainforest-like environment. It was cool and shady, overgrown with ferns and moss, and at this point largely downhill. She glided over rocks and tree roots with relative ease, but remained cautious, having suffered more than a few nasty scrapes or a twisted ankle from falls on trails like this.

Today, in particular, she'd badly needed the release that running always brought her, had needed it more than ever before during these past few weeks. Ever since Nick Manning had arrogantly swaggered his way back into her life and started chipping away at the impenetrable walls she'd erected around herself.

When they'd both worked at Jessup Prior, it had been an extremely rare occasion when she caught a glimpse of Nick at the office – a chance encounter in the elevator, seeing him across the room at a meeting. She'd longed for such rare moments, had had to constantly fight the temptation to walk past his office just for a brief glimpse of him. But now, when he was the last person she wanted to see, it seemed he was hanging around constantly. Scarcely a day went by when he wasn't poking his head into her office and making some sort of half-teasing, half-caustic comment that never failed to make her blood boil. And Nick, the evil bastard, would merely chuckle when she made a cutting remark in response, or asked him in her very best ice queen tone to leave her the hell alone.

And, after each of his annoyingly unwelcome visits, Cara would almost always pop her cheerful but meddling little head inside her office, either to sweetly inquire if everything was okay or to gush once again about how smoking hot Nick was. And Cara, forever the caregiver, the "little mother" that Angela had dubbed her, would invariably find a way to offer her a package of cookies or a candy bar, or plop a sandwich or a donut left over from an office meeting right in front of her. More often than not, Angela would find herself reaching blindly for whatever Cara brought in, and had, to her astonishment, somehow managed to pack on almost ten pounds over the last month.

She'd gained so much weight, in fact, that she'd had to dig out her size two wardrobe and even some of those things were getting a bit snug now. It was a good thing that her otherwise modest sized bedroom boasted a sizeable walk-in closet, because Angela wasn't one to get rid of things easily. Lauren liked to call her a packrat or tease that she was going to become like one of those pathetic people on *Hoarders*, but it really wasn't all that bad. Admittedly, though, she did have a lot of clothes, and in four different sizes ranging from the tiny size zeroes that had recently become too tight up to the fabulous size six designer wardrobe that Nick had bought her several years ago.

Despite her repeated assurances to Lauren, Angela had never been able to summon up the will to get rid of all the things he'd given her. She would resolve to do just that, would grab a box of extra-large trash bags and march into her closet, prepared to fill the entire box of bags up. But then it would only take one fleeting memory of the night she'd worn a particular dress for her to abandon the clean-out project yet again. At least she'd finally gotten around to covering all of the things he'd bought her with zippered garment bags, so that they didn't serve as constant reminders whenever she had to grab something from her closet.

"Crap!"

Her thoughts a million miles away, she'd lost focus for a moment and stubbed her toe on a rock, causing her to wobble precariously for a bit before she regained her footing. She couldn't afford such distractions, she told herself angrily, and blocked everything out of her mind as she covered the last mile or so of the course. Normally she'd have her ear buds plugged in, letting the music drown out her troubled thoughts, but headphones weren't allowed at most races for safety reasons. So for the final mile of the race she tuned everything out, an ability she'd honed to a fine point these past few years, and just let the pure joy of running take her over.

She could hear the sounds and voices coming from the finish line before she could actually see it, and the adrenaline rush she always experienced at the end of a race allowed her to sprint the final few yards. The trail and ultrarunning community was a tight-knit one, and even though Angela was still an aloof loner for the most part, a lot of the other runners and volunteers had come to know and recognize her. Their shouts of encouragement as she crossed the finish line actually brought a rare smile to her face, and she high-fived several of the finish line crew as they offered congratulations.

Someone handed her a bottle of water, and she was drinking it down thirstily when a familiar voice sounded to her right.

"Congratulations, Angel. That was a pretty impressive sprint to the finish, especially after a thirty mile race. I never knew you were that tough."

Angela whirled to face the very last person she'd expected – or wanted – to see here this morning. Nick was grinning at her wickedly, and he looked so damned sexy her already weary legs grew even weaker at the knees. Unshaven and wearing a pair of oversized aviator sunglasses, he looked dark and dangerous, his neatly pressed dark wash jeans and pristine white cotton shirt making her acutely aware of her own sweaty, disheveled appearance in running shorts and short-sleeved top. The sight of his powerfully muscled forearms, bared by the way his sleeves were rolled up to the elbow, made her eyes widen, and she couldn't help but recall exactly how strong those arms were, and how much she'd loved to have them wrapped around her.

But then another image came to mind, that of the night he'd all but shoved her out of his car – and his life – and she glared at him fiercely.

"What in the world are you doing here?" she hissed. "And please don't tell me you've suddenly become a fan of ultrarunning because I won't believe you."

Nick chuckled. "Not really much of a spectator sport from what I can see. And not quite as exciting as a basketball game or a tennis match, is it? I actually happened to be meeting with a client who has a weekend house here in Stinson Beach, and was passing by this way as I was leaving. Thought I might as well check it out while I was in the neighborhood."

She took a drink of water, gazing at him warily. "Why is it I don't believe a word you just said? But, hey, it's a free country, isn't it? Now, if you'll excuse me, I need to get some dry clothes on."

But, to her chagrin, Nick didn't take the hint and ambled alongside her as she walked to her car. As she unlocked the door to pull out her sweats bag, he ran a hand admiringly over the hood of her Toyota 4Runner.

"Nice wheels," he commented. "I see you finally upgraded from that rattletrap you used to drive around in."

She nodded, reaching inside her bag for a towel and a clean T-shirt. "It was time. A present to myself when I went into partnership with Barbara."

Nick grimaced. "How the hell did you put up with that bitch anyway? From everything I've heard about her, she was merciless, mean as a snake, and never let anybody get in her way."

Angela gave a mirthless little laugh as she briskly toweled off her arms and face. "Sounds an awful lot like most of the men I've met in this business, yourself included. Except that just because Barbara was a woman in a man's world, everyone called her a bitch for working hard and going after what she wanted. You know what they'd call a man who did the same thing? Successful."

Nick held up a hand in defeat. "I know, I know. I sound like the biggest chauvinist ever. But it wasn't Barbara's ambition I was dissing. It was her personality. I just hate to think of you having been subjected to all her insults and tirades."

She shrugged as she pulled her damp running top off over her head. "Her temper tantrums never bothered me. I knew most of it was only for show so I'd just try to block - "

His sharply indrawn hiss interrupted what she was going to say next, and she frowned as he stared at her in shock. His darkly tanned skin paled a little as his gaze raked over her upper body, now clothed only in a black exercise bra.

"Jesus Christ," he rasped. "How the hell much weight did you lose anyway? I can count your fucking ribs, Angela."

Her cheeks flushing in anger, she ruthlessly pulled her clean shirt on, covering up her admittedly bony torso. "Leave me alone, Nick," she told him angrily. "That shouldn't be too hard for you to do. In fact, I'd say you're awfully good at that, wouldn't you?"

"Angel." He went to take her by the arm but she wrenched it out of his grasp.

"Don't call me that," she spat. "I've told you over and over not to use that name again. And stop pretending that you give a damn when we both know you don't. You made it very, very obvious how little you cared about me and I got the message loud and clear."

This time she couldn't step away fast enough as he took her by both arms, his dark eyes glittering down at her fiercely.

"I care enough to want to know why you thought starving yourself was a good idea," he bit out. "You have to know this isn't healthy, that you look - "

"Like a skeleton. Or an anorexic. Yes, I'm well aware of how I look," she retorted. "After all, everyone in my life nags me about it constantly. And I'm not trying to be skinny or lose weight. I don't have a poor body image or think I'm fat. Eating is just – hard." The last word was a whisper, causing Nick to grimace.

"How much weight did you lose and when?" he prodded.

She rolled her eyes. "God, some things never change, do they? You're still demanding all the answers but never giving any in return. Well, maybe you should just butt out of things that don't concern you from now on, Nick. Like me."

He gave her a little shake, his mouth set in a tight, angry line. "But you do concern me. So, I'm asking again. Exactly how much weight did you lose and, more importantly, why?"

Angela tried to wriggle free but his big hands were like shackles around her frail upper arms. Angrily, she lashed out, "Fine, if you insist on knowing. At my lowest weight I was down a total of thirty pounds, but I've gained almost ten of those back recently. And I lost weight because food just didn't seem very important anymore." She closed her eyes, desperately fighting to stem the tears she could feel beginning to well up. "Not much of anything seemed important for a really long time."

Nick uttered a low, succinct curse before releasing her carefully. "Because of me," he stated flatly. "You stopped eating when we broke up. So this," he gestured at her ultra-thin frame, "is all my fault."

She scowled. "Don't flatter yourself. Hard for you not to do, I know, but at least try. I told you a long time ago that I've always been thin and never had much of an appetite. When we – used to date, you'd practically force feed me. I'm just back to my natural weight now is all."

He shook his head. "Uh, uh. Not buying that one. Granted, you packed those ten pounds on when we were together and looked fantastic as a result. But you were never this thin to begin with." His gaze dropped to her tiny waist and the concave curve of her tummy before traveling down to her narrow hips and long, skinny legs. "And you never had this before, either. I noticed it when you were finishing the race."

She made a little squawk of protest as he lifted the hem of her shirt and flicked the jeweled blue dragonfly that pierced her navel. She slapped his hand away and yanked her shirt back down.

"Do you mind?" she asked in indignation.

"I do, actually," he drawled. "I'm not sure I like the body jewelry, not sure it suits you. What made you do something like that anyway?"

She began to pull on a pair of nylon track pants. "It was an impulse," she admitted. "Actually, more of a drunken dare from one of my friends."

Nick crossed his arms over his chest and shook his head. "Don't tell me, let me guess – the infamous Lauren. From everything you've told me about her, that sounds like something she'd do. Did she get her belly button pierced, too?"

"Not that night, no. But she did get another tattoo."

His eyes narrowed dangerously. "Please tell me that your so-called friend didn't talk you into getting inked as well as pierced? Frankly, the more I hear about this woman the less I like her."

Angela smirked. "That's okay. Because she really, really doesn't like you, even without knowing your name. You should actually hope you never meet her in person because she's usually got a switchblade with her."

"Nice company you keep," he replied sarcastically.

She reached inside her bag for the bottle of recovery drink she forced herself to consume after each workout. Unfortunately, the chocolate variety didn't taste much better than the vanilla.

"Lauren might have a few rough edges but she's the best friend anyone could ever ask for," Angela said soberly. "She's held my head over the toilet plenty of times to prove it."

She'd meant the words as a joke, as sarcasm, but Nick apparently didn't think it the least bit funny, given the way his eyes glittered darkly in response.

"Been drinking a lot, have you?" he asked almost menacingly. "I thought we got that under control, Angel."

She uncapped her drink and took a sip, refusing to let him intimidate her, reminding herself that he had no rights over her any longer, no business butting into her life. "I really don't see how that's your business," she replied tartly. "Especially since the only rules I obey these days are my own."

"Is that right?" he drawled in a deceptively lazy tone. And then, without warning, he grabbed hold of the long, thick braid of her hair, wrapping it around his wrist and yanking her flush against his body. She gasped in alarm, one hand reaching out to brace herself against his heavily muscled shoulder.

"Thank God you still had enough sense left not to cut your hair," he muttered, giving the braid a sharp tug. "But as far as I can see that's about the only sensible thing you've done in the last four years. Looks to me like someone needs to be reminded of the rules she once agreed to obey."

Anger and indignation blazed through her, and she slapped furiously at the hand that held her braid captive. "Fuck you," she spat, in a tone she would never have dared to use in the past in his presence. "I'll tell you one thing, Nick. The days of me obeying anything you tell me are dead and buried. So let go of me and then go piss off."

He only snickered and pulled her even closer against him. She was startled to realize that he was aroused, and bit her lip to stifle the groan that threatened to escape as she felt the thick ridge of his erection brush against her thigh, felt the heat of his body pressed against her chest.

"I'm not used to this feisty side of you," he said half-jokingly. "But I think I like it. For now, though, I want you to do what I say and come out to breakfast with me. And you're going to eat whatever I order for you – a full stack of pancakes with a side of scrambled eggs and bacon, plus a protein smoothie. For starters."

Angela would have sooner died than admit the super-sized meal he'd just described actually sounded delicious, and her tummy rumbled automatically in response. But, determined that he would never have the opportunity to order her around again, she held up the bottle of recovery drink.

"I've actually got my breakfast right here, thanks. And if you don't mind letting me go, I need to get home."

Nick gave the bottle's label a quick, scornful glance. "You consider that a meal? Christ, no wonder you look like a scrawny chicken. Where did you buy this crap anyway? It's not a brand I've ever heard of before."

Defiantly she took a long swig. "It's not crap. It's a very healthy, high protein recovery drink, specially formulated for endurance athletes. And I got it from my – my boyfriend."

Nick scoffed. "Right. The boyfriend. The guy with no name that you keep mentioning. I'm far from convinced this so-called boyfriend even exists."

She finished off the drink. "He definitely exists. And his name is Dwayne Conroy. I went to high school with him and we met up again last Thanksgiving."

"So, he was your high school sweetheart or something?" asked Nick sarcastically.

Angela smiled, recalling just how big a nerd Dwayne had been back then, and how she hadn't even given him the time of day. She'd been touched – and felt more than a little guilty – to have learned he'd had a crush on her for a long time.

"No, we didn't date back then," she replied shortly. "And he happens to be competing in a track meet back in New York today that's going to be on TV in an hour or so. So, sorry to cut this scintillating conversation short, but I need to leave now if I want to catch the broadcast in time."

But Nick had very deliberately positioned himself to stand in front of the driver's side door, effectively blocking her entry to the car. His expression looked thoughtful, almost bemused. "So this Dwayne guy – he's a runner, too?"

Angela shook her head. "High jumper. He won the U.S. indoor title in February, and just missed making the podium at the world championships. He's got a great shot at making the next Olympic team."

"How sweet. Maybe you'll have his and hers matching medals," smirked Nick. "But tell me – does Dwayne think you're too skinny? Or maybe he's into women who have the body of an eleven year old boy."

Her face burned with indignation at his very intentional insult. "It's none of your fucking business what he's into," she flung back. "Just like I'm not your business. But if you must know, then yes. He does think I'm too thin. And unlike everyone else who's so quick to nag or insult me about it, Dwayne has actually taken the time to discuss the problem rationally and try to help me with my diet. He's also a clinical dietician, has a degree in nutritional science. And this recovery drink you just dissed – it's actually very calorie dense so it's an easy way for me to try and pack on a few pounds."

"Fine," he conceded reluctantly. "But it's still no substitute for a real meal. You'd probably have to drink a case of this shit a day to get back to a decent weight. Tell Lover Boy he needs to figure out a way to put some meat on your bones in a hurry."

"Stop nagging me," she warned. "You're beginning to sound just like everyone else. I'll eat when I feel like it and nobody is going to force me to do otherwise. Especially not you. Now, can I please get inside my car?"

"In a minute." Nick seemed in no hurry whatsoever to move and was deliberately ignoring her growing agitation. "So, are you living with this guy?"

Angela sighed. "Really, Nick? I find it hard to believe that this is the most interesting thing you've got to do on a Saturday – quiz me about my private life. And, no. Dwayne and I do not live together, he doesn't even live in the area. He's based up at the Nike training facility in Eugene."

"Hmm. So you don't even see this guy half the time?" replied Nick scathingly. "Doesn't sound like much of a relationship to me."

Her fingers curled into tight little fists, her nails digging into her skin as she fought the urge to ram her fist into his rock hard gut. Or his jaw. Or, better yet, his balls.

"You've got some nerve," she told him through tightly clenched teeth. "As though what you and I had was any sort of relationship, huh? I may not see Dwayne all that often but at least I can call or text him whenever I want to, I don't have to lie about him or keep him hidden away from my family and friends, and he doesn't expect me to obey his asinine rules like I'm his property or something. I'd take a long distance relationship with him any day over what your warped idea of one is."

Nick's face was darkly flushed, and his eyes blazing with anger as he yanked her hard against him, his fingers biting painfully into the bony protrusion of her hips. "You agreed to obey those rules, Angel," he bit out. "No one ever held a gun to your head. And I think it's way past time for me to start imposing those rules again, telling you how to do things. After all, it doesn't look like you've done a very good job at taking care of yourself these past years, does it?"

This time she did hit him, or at least tried to, but her palm barely grazed his cheekbone before he clamped his fingers around her wrist. Wincing in pain, she nonetheless continued to glare at him furiously.

"The day I let you order me around again will be a cold one in hell," she snarled. "And considering how long it took me to crawl out of there the first time, there's no way I'm ever going back in."

Nick's tight, angry expression softened then, and she could swear she saw something resembling real tenderness in his eyes.

"It wouldn't be like that this time, Angel," he murmured soothingly. "I was a prize winning jackass to you, I admit it freely. And I realize things would have to be different between us, that I'd have to – well, compromise."

"Compromise?" Her tone was scornful. "Wow. A word I never thought was even in your vocabulary. But it doesn't matter, Nick, not even a little. You could go so far as to let *me* set down all the rules and it wouldn't matter."

"I don't believe that for a minute, Angel," he told her with a smug grin. "What we had together was too good, too special, for us not to give it another shot."

Angela stared at him. "Are you high? Or having a serious mental breakdown? What we had, Nick, was a one-sided relationship where you had absolutely everything your way all the time. Granted, the sex was hot, but since you're far from the only guy in this world with a big dick and a dirty mouth, I'd say you don't have a hell of a lot going for you these days."

For a minute he looked so furious that she was half-afraid he was going to shake her again, and then tightened his fingers around her wrist so fiercely she was convinced it was going to snap in two. Gradually he regained his composure and loosened his grip some, but still didn't release her completely.

"We had a lot more than just good sex," he replied tersely. "Only I was too much of a self-centered prick to admit it. And I realize now that I'm going to have to earn your trust again after the way I treated you. But just so we're clear, Angel – you *will* be mine again. I don't care about the high jumper. You don't belong to him because you've never stopped being mine."

"I don't belong to anyone," she snapped. "And if you think I'd ever willingly go back to you, then you've gone completely off the deep end." She closed her eyes, fighting back the tears once more as she mumbled, "It almost killed me, Nick, losing you. I won't go through something like that ever again. So just stay away from me, please? I realize that by some fucked up twist of fate we're stuck working in the same office, but I'll transfer to a different branch if I have to. So, please – leave me alone."

He was silent for long seconds, his face almost devoid of expression, and Angela wondered wildly what kinds of thoughts were running through his head right now.

When he finally spoke, his voice was somber, almost hollow. "I'll leave you alone for now. But this isn't over, Angel. *We're* not over, and I'm going to do whatever it takes to make you realize that."

She tugged futilely at the wrist he still held imprisoned between his fingers. "Can I go now?"

He let go of her wrist only to take her by surprise and bring her palm to his cheek instead. "Just answer me one more question before you leave." At her nod, he gave her hand a quick squeeze. "Why are your hands so cold now? One of the things I remembered was that your hands were always so warm and soft. What happened to change that?"

She tried valiantly to ignore how good it felt to touch him again, even just his cheek, and replied in a cool, impersonal voice. "You know that old saying about cold hands, warm heart? Well, that's just a stupid old wives tale because my heart is covered in ice, too."

This time when she jerked her hand away he didn't try to hold her back, simply standing there and watching as she drove off.

***

"Good morning, Cara. How's everything going so far today?"

Cara Bregante glanced up from her computer monitor at the sound of the deep, masculine drawl and gulped. She wasn't sure she'd ever get used to the effect the tall, dark, and ultra-intimidating Nick Manning had on her. Of course, she assured herself hastily, it seemed like he had that same effect on nearly every other woman in the office so she was hardly alone in her weakness. And while Nick did seem to pay far more attention to her than he did to any of the other females, Cara knew it wasn't because he was hitting on her. No, she knew exactly why he stopped by so often, and why she'd so willingly joined forces with him.

She grinned up at him, trying not to feel dwarfed by the way he towered over her. "Really well, Mr. Manning. She was so ticked off after you stopped by earlier that she ate a whole bagel. With extra cream cheese."

Nick grinned back, giving her a wink. "Atta girl. One way or another we're going to pack some more weight onto that boss of yours."

"She already looks a lot healthier than when I first started working here," chirped Cara. "Though I've got to admit it's a little weird that she tends to eat more when she's angry or irritated."

"Emotional eating," declared Nick. "It's a well-documented fact. Admittedly most cases are when someone is stressed or depressed but apparently the key with Angela is when she's pissed off at me."

Cara giggled merrily. "You really made her mad this morning. When I went in there after you left, she'd thrown a book against the wall. And then she ate that whole bagel without even being aware she was doing it."

"Happy to oblige," he replied. "Now, tell me. Anything interesting on her schedule this week?"

Cara glanced behind her nervously, making sure the door to her boss's office remained closed. If Angela had any idea that Cara was not only secretly conspiring with Nick to get her to eat more, but was also letting him know about her personal appointments, she'd be throwing more than just books against the wall.

Nick had told her in strictest confidence that he and Angela had been together a few years back – a fact that Cara had begun to suspect the first time she'd seen them together and observed how hot and fast the sparks had flown. Nick had also begged for Cara's help in convincing Angela to give him a second chance, and Cara, who'd always been a starry-eyed romantic, had willingly agreed to do whatever she could. She would secretly let Nick know about any weekend plans Angela might have mentioned, or certain meetings or appointments where he could contrive to "coincidentally" be in the same area.

"Um." Cara hesitated now, not at all certain if she ought to be telling this particular bit of news to Nick. "Not really. I mean, no social engagements or races this week. Except, well, I'm not sure - "

Nick placed his hands on her desk and leaned over a little further, bringing his darkly handsome face to within inches of hers. She gulped again as he very deliberately smiled at her, and she wondered weakly if it was really possible to drown in someone's eyes.

"Cara." Her name sounded like a purr on his lips – the purr of a huge, menacing lion, that is. "You know you can trust me."

Cara shook her head. "It's not that. It's just, well, this particular appointment is different. It's – more personal. Like - "

"What?" asked Nick teasingly. "A pap smear? Bikini wax? Or some other type - "

"Lunch with Dwayne," she blurted out. "He's meeting her here today at one o'clock."

Nick straightened suddenly, his grin fading. "I see. Well, things are going to get very interesting around here in a few hours, aren't they?"

Cara fought down a paralyzing sense of alarm. "What – you aren't going to approach him, are you? Angela will go ballistic if you do anything."

Nick gave her another wink. "Didn't you know I'm a huge track and field fan? I'd love nothing better than to meet a medal winning high jumper. Hey, no worries, Cara. I just want to size up my competition a bit is all. Everything will be just fine."

As Nick sauntered off with his usual careless swagger, Cara couldn't help sighing in reaction. God, she thought, it was a real pity he was way too old for her, way too tall, way too out of her league, and way too interested in Angela. And, having met Dwayne Conroy more than once or twice, Cara thought rather smugly that Nick definitely didn't have to worry about any potential competition coming from that end.

**

Nick scowled as he read over the limited amount of information he'd been able to pull up on Dwayne Conroy. It was basically just his athletic bio and results from his college and professional competitions. There was an official photo posted on the U.S. Track and Field website that revealed a guy of average looks, large, squarish features, a shock of sandy brown hair, and a decidedly goofy grin. Aside from that, there was really no other information he could find.

As he closed out the website and returned to the financial report he was *really* supposed to be checking out, Nick wondered what the hell he was doing anyway. When had he ever bothered to check out the competition, so to speak? Christ, he'd never *had* competition before now, never had to worry about wooing a woman away from another man. Women flocked to him automatically, ignored other men in the hopes of attracting his attention. So why the hell was he bothering to try and get Angela back again, especially when she continued to make it very obvious that she didn't give a shit about him any longer?

But it was precisely because he didn't really believe that fact that he kept on trying. He refused to accept the reality that the blazing attraction that had existed between them four years ago had burned out and couldn't be re-lit. And he wasn't going to give up on her without a fight. He *knew* that she still cared for him, could see it in the way she reacted to him. Granted, her reactions right now consisted of alternately cursing at him or threatening to throw something his way, but, hey – wasn't hate just one step away from love?

Nick was grinning as that old saying came to mind just before one o'clock, and he started walking towards the elevator lobby. But the grin froze on his face as he saw Angela and Dwayne approaching from the opposite direction.

Today had been the first time since he'd started working here that Angela had actually worn something other than one of those god-awful tailored pantsuits. And while the crisp, khaki-colored belted shirtdress wasn't exactly sexy, it was a vast improvement over any of the other outfits he'd seen her wearing the past couple of months. It showed off the long, slender length of her legs, which, he was relieved to notice, didn't look quite so scrawny these days. In fact, Angela was slowly beginning to gain a bit more weight, and while she was still a long way from where she needed to be, her cheekbones didn't look so gaunt and she actually had a hint of cleavage.

She'd also, Nick noticed grimly, bothered to do something with her hair and makeup today, and was even wearing a pair of earrings and a gold bracelet. And, he realized with a pang, she was smiling, *really* smiling, for the very first time since he'd seen her again. The fact that she was bestowing that smile on another man made his fists clench in mingled fury and frustration.

Dwayne Conroy was every bit as goofy and somewhat nerdy as his photo had hinted at, but from initial appearances he also seemed like a genuinely nice guy. There was nothing the least bit pretentious about his appearance, dressed as he was in jeans, a red polo shirt, and athletic shoes, the latter two items both emblazoned with the signature Nike logo. He was exceptionally tall, perhaps even an inch or so taller than Nick, who certainly wasn't used to having to literally look up to other men. But Dwayne was as lean as a greyhound, as opposed to Nick's heavily muscled form, and Nick guessed the younger man had been skinny as a beanpole until just a few years ago.

But, he acknowledged reluctantly, Angela didn't seem to give two figs about how Dwayne looked, or that her current boyfriend wasn't exactly stud material. And somehow or other, the tall, awkward looking guy had managed to work at least one miracle – getting the so-called ice queen to thaw out enough to actually smile.

Angela glanced up first at the sound of Nick's footsteps on the tiled floor of the elevator lobby, and the smile froze on her face, her dark eyes suddenly furious. Dwayne followed the direction of her gaze, but his own reaction at seeing Nick was vastly different. His eyes practically bugged out of their sockets, and his jaw dropped open in disbelief.

"Oh, my, God," Dwayne murmured in awe. "Are you really Nick Manning? *The* Nick Manning from the 49ers?"

Nick gave his so-called rival his best "gotta keep the fans happy" smile. "Guilty as charged. Angela – introduce me to your, ah, friend."

Angela gave him a look that said she'd much rather introduce his crotch to the pointed toe of her shoe. Dwayne beat her to the punch by eagerly extending his hand in greeting.

"Dwayne Conroy. Wow, this is unbelievable, such an honor to meet you, Nick. Uh, that is, can I call you Nick?" he babbled excitedly.

Nick couldn't help returning Dwayne's grin. "Yeah, it's all good. And – wait. Dwayne Conroy. Why does that name sound familiar?" He pretended to think for a few seconds before snapping his fingers in recollection. "I know. I watched you compete at the indoor track and field championships. You won the high jump, didn't you?"

By now Dwayne was almost leaping out of his size fourteen shoes in excitement. "Come on! No way does *the* Nick Manning watch indoor track. Or remember the name of the high jump guys. I'm being punked, right? Angie, did you put him up to this?"

Angela crossed her arms over her chest, giving Nick the most evil glare he'd ever seen. He could almost feel the ice pouring off of her, and he half-expected to feel sharp little icicles stabbing into his skin any moment now.

"No," she replied flatly. "I most certainly did not."

But Dwayne was too excited about meeting Nick to notice his girlfriend's own unenthusiastic attitude towards the famed football star.

"And why didn't you tell me a big star like Nick Manning

worked here?" Dwayne asked her. "Especially since you know what a huge 49ers fan I've always been."

Angela gave a careless little lift of her shoulder. "I guess I didn't give it a second thought."

Nick dared to give her a cheeky grin and a flirty wink, letting her know that he wasn't fooled by her apparent indifference. And then he ignored the evil eye she kept focusing his way while he chatted casually with Dwayne for several minutes about football, track, basketball. It was only when he was sure he saw steam rising from the top of Angela's sleek raven head that he backed off his very intentional antagonizing.

"Angela looks hungry," he told Dwayne. "I'd better let you two head out for lunch."

Dwayne looked crestfallen for a moment, then brightened again as he asked, "Hey, why don't you join us, Nick? Man, that would be the greatest! You wouldn't mind, would you, Angie?"

Angela looked like she minded a great deal, but before she could voice her objections, Nick shook his head.

"I appreciate the offer, Dwayne, but I'm afraid I already have a lunch engagement."

Angela sniffed disdainfully. "Another new girlfriend, I assume?"

He gave her a knowing smile, quite certain that was jealously he heard in her voice. "A client, actually. I've, ah, been out of the dating game for quite some time now. It's tough meeting the right girl these days."

Angela made a very undignified snort of disbelief, while Dwayne was all too eager to offer his assistance.

"Oh, I could probably introduce you to someone, Nick," he chimed in. "There's a whole group of single women who train with me up in Oregon. Or Angela's got this friend she could introduce you to. Her name's Lauren."

"No!"

Angela and Nick both uttered the exclamation simultaneously, causing Dwayne to stare at them in bewilderment.

"Ah, I don't think that's a very good idea, Dwayne," Angela mumbled hastily. "I mean, Lauren travels so much and she's so independent that I don't think she'd appreciate anyone setting her up."

"Yes, thanks for the thought, Dwayne," Nick told him amicably, "but I'm not much into blind dates at this point in my life."

"Sure. Okay." Dwayne nodded, still looking a bit bemused. "Probably all for the best, anyway. I mean, you're a big, tough dude, Nick, but Lauren – well, she can be kind of scary. Some of the stories Angela has told me about her are hard to believe."

Angela took Dwayne firmly by the arm. "We should let Nick go meet his client, Dwayne," she said, not even trying to sound tactful. "Besides, he was right before. I'm starving."

"Okay, let's go. Hey, great to meet you, Nick," enthused Dwayne. "I hope we meet again soon."

Angela practically yanked Dwayne into the waiting elevator car, not giving Nick a chance to reply.

But it didn't matter, thought Nick in a very satisfied manner as he walked back to his office. Because, having seen Angela and Dwayne together now, he had all the answers he needed. And knew what his next step in luring her back into his life was going to   be.

Chapter Seventeen

Late June

Angela had been trying – really trying – all evening to get into the swing of things. It was, after all, Julia's bachelorette party and a night to just let loose, have fun, and drink until she got shit faced. But so far she had only been able to achieve one of those goals – namely, the latter one. And, as she sipped at another tumbler of lemon infused vodka, she wondered if part of her problem was because she was secretly jealous of Julia, or that she wasn't wishing it was her own bachelorette party being celebrated tonight, or her own wedding scheduled for a week from now.

She shook her head angrily, finishing her drink and motioning to the bartender for a refill. Julia had been considerate enough to hire a stretch limo to pick up and drop off all her guests tonight, so no one had to worry about driving home drunk. Though admittedly she hadn't been drinking much at all as of late – part of the so-called healthy eating plan that Dwayne had designed for her. He was thrilled that she'd gained a full twelve pounds, was feeling stronger, and laying off the booze. What he didn't know was that she'd gained most of the weight by stuffing her face in angry reaction each time that jackass Nick popped his arrogant head inside her office.

She refused to think about that heartless bastard tonight, and instead focused her thoughts back to Dwayne. Angela couldn't help but smile as the goofily grinning image of her – exactly what *was* Dwayne to her anyway – came to mind. He really was the sweetest guy – kind, considerate, funny. She'd laughed more in the past few months than she had in years, and most assuredly during the past four years – a time when she'd feared she had forgotten how to laugh. Dwayne had been a great friend to her, they'd had a lot of fun together, and he was one of the few people in her life that she genuinely liked.

But, she realized with real regret, what she felt for him would never be anything more than friendship. There was zero physical attraction on her part, and aside from some friendly hugs and a few awkward kisses, there'd been no intimacy between them. Dwayne had never once pressured her about having sex, and frankly, she'd had her doubts for some time that he'd *ever* had sex with anyone. Via a couple of somewhat uncomfortable conversations, she'd learned that he was not, after all, a virgin but he was most definitely still very awkward and inexperienced with women. As for herself – well, after spending nearly a year as Nick Manning's lover there wasn't much she *hadn't* done in bed.

She'd kept that knowledge to herself, however, and had never fessed up to Dwayne that Nick had been the man responsible for the deep funk she'd fallen into. She preferred, in fact, not to talk about those eleven months with anyone, be it Dwayne, Lauren, or Julia. And while Dwayne knew there had been somebody, she'd never told him any details, whereas the twins at least had some vague idea of what her ill-fated relationship with Nick had been like.

Angela grimaced as reluctant thoughts of her annoying ex-lover came to mind now. Nick continued to make a pest of himself, sticking his head inside her office door almost daily and saying something to get under her skin. By now her suspicions that he and Cara were in cahoots to get her to eat more were well founded, and if either of them thought they were continuing to fool her then they badly needed a reality check. Oddly, though, it didn't irritate her any longer and she almost looked forward to both Nick's deliberately antagonizing comments as well as whatever tempting treat Cara would oh so subtly plunk in front of her. It felt good to actually have something of an appetite again, and she even found herself eating dinner most nights of the week now. And by now she'd put on a few more pounds, enough to necessitate wearing her size four wardrobe and even some of the slimmer cut size six pieces.

Like, for example, the dress she wore tonight. It was one of the first things Nick had bought her and had always been one of her favorites – a strapless Dolce and Gabbana with a pleated bodice and full skirt. The black background was relieved by the pale pink and green floral print. The fine, silky fabric felt luxurious against her skin while the fuller skirt helped to hide how slender her lower body still was. Almost defiantly she'd added a pair of strappy black sandals with a towering heel, so that she stood well over six feet tall. And so far this evening – both at dinner, the first bar they'd hit up, and now this place – Angela hadn't spotted even one guy who might be taller than she was. Not that trolling for men was even close to being on her agenda this evening, especially not on the night of Julia's bachelorette party where almost a dozen other semi-inebriated women were along for the ride.

Lauren, of course, had organized the whole thing, though she'd consulted with Angela about what places they ought to hit up. Lauren didn't venture up to San Francisco all that often, and had never been a big city girl, unlike her twin. But Lauren certainly seemed to be in her element tonight – daring one of the other women to order a dangerously potent sounding drink; asking the DJ to play a certain song; bullying several of the others in their group to get up and dance; openly flirting with one good looking guy after another. Angela, who'd watched her best friend in action at bars just like this one far too many times to count, knew that the vast majority of Lauren's flirting was all for show. She was extremely picky about the men she dated, much less slept with, and Angela couldn't recall the last time Lauren had actually gone home with a guy.

As she remained seated on her barstool, ignoring Lauren's attempts to cajole her onto the dance floor, she had the oddest sensation of being watched. But a quick glance around the dimly lit bar revealed nothing amiss, and she told herself she was just being paranoid. Someone as tall as she was got a lot of curious stares, from men and women alike, and she should certainly be used to it by now.

It had been Angela's idea to come to this particular bar, even though it was more on the subdued, darkly sophisticated side than some of the others on Lauren's schedule for the evening. This place had always been one of Nick's favorites, and the owner was an old friend of his. They had always been assured of their privacy here, had always been given a secluded little booth in a darkened corner where they could talk, touch, kiss.

She bit down on her lip to stifle a groan as she recalled one of the times he'd brought her here, and, if memory served her correctly, she'd been wearing this exact dress. The full skirt had allowed Nick easy access to her, and he'd taken quick advantage of that fact by finger fucking her to a heart-stopping orgasm. He'd made her suck on an ice cube the whole time, cautioning her not to make even the slightest sound or else he'd stop what he was doing. It had been one of the many, many ways he'd enjoyed exerting his control over her, and she'd loved it.

Angela shuddered, forcing her thoughts back to the present, and bolted down the rest of her drink quickly. As she shifted slightly on the padded leather barstool, she realized her panties were now soaking wet – the mere recollection of what Nick had once done to her in this place more than enough to arouse her. Gingerly she eased herself off the stool, catching Lauren's eye and mouthing that she was headed off to the ladies room.

Lauren frowned as she mouthed back, "Hurry it up. Time to move on to the next place soon."

Angela sighed as she made her way to the restroom, for she should have guessed that a sleek, classy place like Orphus wouldn't have been happening enough for Lauren. It had been a stupid decision on her part to suggest this place, particularly when it was chock full of memories she had no business recalling.

She made quick work of her visit to the ladies room, but the hairs at the nape of her neck prickled with awareness again as she walked down the long, darkened corridor on her way back to the bar area. She was just about to the end of the corridor when a slow, lazy drawl – an achingly *and* annoyingly familiar drawl – stopped her dead in her tracks.

"Funny you should have worn that particular dress tonight. Were you by any chance remembering what happened the last time you wore it? And in the very same bar, too. Quite a coincidence, wouldn't you say?"

Telling herself that it couldn't possibly be him – that she'd had more to drink tonight than she'd thought and was starting to hear things – Angela turned around slowly, disbelievingly, and found herself staring into Nick's dark, wicked eyes.

"You have got to be kidding me," she muttered in revulsion. "Please tell me that I just can't hold my liquor anymore and that you're a really bad figment of my imagination."

Nick chuckled and shook his head. "'Fraid not, Angel." He reached out and grabbed her hand, jerking her flush against his big, hard body before she could protest or resist. And with the ridiculously high heels she'd stupidly chosen to wear tonight, escaping him wasn't going to be easy.

"But," he added sternly," the mere fact that you think you've had that much to drink doesn't please me one bit. I know you're here for your friend's bachelorette party, Angel, but that doesn't give you automatic leeway to get plastered. How much have you had to drink anyway?"

She was so furious that she was almost shaking in her stilettos. "You don't seriously think I'm going to answer that question, do you?" she retorted scathingly. "Or that you've got any right at all to ask it?"

Nick smiled, but it was one of those icy cold smiles he gave when something displeased him mightily. "Oh, I've got every right in the world, Angel," he replied harshly. "And once you stop playing these pointless little games with me, you'll realize just how many rights I still have over you."

She gave him a futile shove with her free hand. "You've got no rights over me at all. Not-a-single-one." She enunciated each word with careful precision. "And this really annoying tendency you have of showing up in places where I happen to be – if it keeps happening, Nick, I'm going to file a restraining order against you."

He gave a shout of laughter. "Oh, that would be a good one, Angel! Speaking of which, I can just see the reaction on some judge's face when I talk about all the different ways you used to love being restrained – scarves, cords, cuffs. The cuffs were your favorites as I recall. Tell me – did you keep all that stuff? Though I honestly can't see Dwayne being the sort who'd get much of a kick out of - "

As a group of giggling, half-drunk, forty-something's – all wearing far too much makeup and far too little fabric – stumbled past on the way to the ladies room, Angela placed her free hand over Nick's mouth, her gaze furious while he was wildly amused. And, in spite of how angry she was at this particular moment, she didn't miss the way the drunken pack of cougars were checking Nick out very thoroughly, and for some reason that really, *really* pissed her off.

When the women – who were all wearing dresses far more suited to someone half their age – had tottered noisily into the restroom, Nick took her firmly by the arm and began steering her back towards the bar. But instead of escorting her over to where Lauren and the others were waiting, he continued to walk her towards a back corner of the room – towards a secluded corner she was all too well acquainted with.

"Stop right here."

She latched onto a corner of the bar and held on for dear life, refusing to take one more step. Nick attempted to drag her along in his wake, only to frown at her when she wouldn't budge.

"We have things to discuss, Angel," he informed her in that haughty, know-it-all tone she'd come to resent and despise. "*Private* things. When I saw you here a few minutes ago I had Eddie clear out our favorite table so that we could have a drink together. Though I'm seriously considering changing your order from vodka to coffee."

If she hadn't been afraid of making a scene, especially when the ten other women in her party were little more than a stone's throw away, Angela would have gladly spit in his face. Instead, she just stared at him in stunned disbelief.

"You know, the more nonsense I hear you spout these days, the more I'm convinced you're having a full mental breakdown," she told him. "Even if I wasn't here for my best friend's party, there's no way on earth I'd consent to sit at that – that table with you ever again."

Nick stepped in close, wrapping an arm around her waist and pulling her flush against his body. Her breath caught in her

throat as she realized he was aroused again, and making very sure
that she was very aware of that fact. She struggled not to notice
how good he smelled, that all-too-familiar scent she'd always
loved so much. Unable to bear the burning intensity of his gaze,
she glanced downwards, focusing instead on the strong, tanned
column of his throat. He was wearing all black, typical for those
occasions when he didn't wear a suit, and was simply but suavely
attired in an open-necked shirt and tailored trousers. And, she
thought weakly, he looked even better than he smelled. Or felt.

"What's the matter, Angel?" he whispered suggestively in her
ear, making sure none of the other patrons gathered around the
crowded bar could hear him. "Afraid that one or both of us will
wind up underneath the table if we sit there? It certainly
wouldn't be the first time, would it?"

Angela felt the sweat begin to trickle down between her
breasts, at the same time that other bodily fluids began to dampen
her thighs – again. His wickedly taunting words forced her to
recall erotic images she hadn't permitted herself to think about
for years – that of Nick discreetly sliding down beneath the table,
his big body barely concealed by the tablecloth as he spread her
legs wide and buried his face in her soaking wet pussy. Or of
other times when she was the one kneeling beneath the table,
unzipping his fly and taking him between her lips.

"That's never going to happen again," she told him faintly,
willing herself not to whimper as she realized how hard her
nipples were. "Whether it's here or any other place. You blew
whatever chance you had with me four years ago, Nick, and I
don't know how else to get the point across that I'm not
interested in being your slave again."

He nuzzled the side of her neck, his tongue tracing an arousing
little circle around her ear. "And I told you it wouldn't be like
that again. We'd sit down, talk about this calmly, compromise."

She couldn't suppress the shiver that rippled up and down her
spine as his fingers traced along her bare arm and shoulder.
Desperately fighting not to lose herself to his seductive mastery
again, she heard herself asking him in a voice that barely sounded
like her own, "Okay, let's start compromising right now. Come
with me and I'll introduce you to my friends. You've heard me

mention the twins often enough. It's about time you met them, don't you think?"

Nick froze, his lips still pressed to her throat but his hand stilled on her shoulder. He slowly took a step or two away from her, his mouth turning up at one corner in an unwilling smile.

"You've made your point, Angel," he conceded. "For now."

She rolled her eyes. "Figures. You talk about wanting to make compromises, that things will be different. So far, though, sounds like the same old Nick to me. The one I've got no intention of taking up with ever again."

"Well, we'll see, won't we? Obviously this isn't the right time or place but make no mistake, Angel – there *will* be a right one and very, very soon."

"Humph." She gave a little shake of her head. "And you still haven't told me how you just happened to be here tonight – once again, very coincidentally where I happen to be."

Nick smiled mysteriously. "Or we could look at it from a different angle. Why are *you* here at a place you know very well I patronize frequently? Maybe you're the one stalking me, Angel."

"Seriously?" She gaped at him, appalled by his arrogance. "I'll have you know this is one of several places we're hitting up tonight and almost all of them are located within a mile of each other. And that's another thing – how did you know I was here for a bachelorette party?"

"That's easy." He nodded across the bar to where the other women were still gathered. "That sexy little thing in the coral dress – the twin I assume is Julia – is wearing some ridiculous sash tied around her that reads "Bride to Be"."

"Oh." Angela had forgotten about the silly party gift one of Julia's co-workers had insisted she wear, despite Lauren's caustic remark that it made her sister look like a pageant queen. "Lucky for you she's still wearing that stupid thing. Lauren's threatened to cut it off of her about five times already."

Nick's gaze narrowed in irritation. "Don't tell me, let me guess – with that switchblade she likes to cart around. Where is the bloodthirsty little wench anyway?"

It only took her a moment to locate her best friend, but then it usually wasn't hard to locate Lauren – even in a crowd.

"The one in the jeans and tank top. With six empty shot glasses in front of her."

Nick chuckled. "*That's* Lauren? The ballsy chick you've told me about? The one Dwayne said is scary? Jesus, I could pick her up with one hand."

Angela gave him a falsely sweet smile. "And she'd used the opportunity to stab you in the other one. Excuse me, but I need to get back to my friends now. And if you just happen to coincidentally show up at any of our other stops this evening, I'll definitely call the cops and tell them you're a psycho stalker."

Nick's chuckle morphed into full-fledged laughter as she walked away briskly, and if Lauren hadn't caught her eye at that precise moment, Angela wouldn't have hesitated to turn and flip him off.

***

The unexpected encounter with Nick, however, ruined the rest of the evening for Angela, despite her best efforts to put on a brave face for Julia. She brushed Lauren off every time her friend demanded to know what the hell was wrong, and wound up drinking a lot more than she'd originally planned on doing – an action that only made things worse. Angela wasn't a happy drunk – like Julia's co-worker Courtney who was currently being the life of the party. Neither was she a sloppy drunk like Julia's friend Jada, who was weaving around and looked like she was going to toss her cookies any minute now. And she wasn't a mean drunk, either, like Lauren could be sometimes when she'd had a *whole* lot to drink and was in a bad mood to boot.

No, Angela was just a plain old depressed drunk, the sort who got quieter and more withdrawn the more she drank. And that was precisely what happened as the evening wore on, as she rather morosely followed the others from bar to bar.

Except, of course, when Lauren got involved in a bar fight and Angela felt the need to jump in and help her out. She'd watched the scene unfold, had sighed while predicting what would happen next. A guy – good-looking, well-built, well-dressed – had been flirting rather outrageously with Lauren and Angela had rolled her eyes when she'd observed how her friend was deliberately toying with him.

And then the guy had done the unthinkable and put his hand on Lauren's ass. But it was whatever he'd whispered in her ear after that when she'd erupted – landing a roundhouse kick solidly in the guy's gut, causing him to stumble and crash into some nearby tables, which in turn caused the disrupted patrons to yell and scream. Meanwhile, the guy's companions rushed over to join in the fray, and Angela found herself hurrying over to defend Lauren by tossing her drink into someone's face.

And when Jada really screwed things up by puking all over the bouncer's shoes, well, that was when the group of "ladies" was promptly ordered to vacate the premises and they all moved on to the next bar.

By the time the limo arrived to take everyone home at the end of the evening, Angela was more than ready for the party to be over. As each of Julia's guests was dropped off at their place of residence, Angela shrank further into the corner seat she'd appropriated, uncommunicative and lost in thought. She was very reluctantly pried from her corner, however, when it was Courtney's turn to be dropped off, since Julia's hipster co-worker had passed out cold. It took Angela plus three others to drag the tall, gangly girl up to her apartment and deposit her on her bed.

As soon as she was back inside the limo, she retreated to her little corner and stared out the window without really seeing anything. The encounter with Nick had shook her up more than she'd initially realized, more than she was willing to admit, and she began to tremble in delayed reaction.

She closed her eyes, pressing her flushed cheek against the cool glass of the window, and willed herself to calm down. Because, despite her brave, defiant words to the contrary, she knew deep down that letting Nick back into her life was exactly what she craved more than anything. It was, after all, what she'd dreamed of for years, the dream that had given her hope, kept her going for so long. But now that the dream could very easily become reality, she was terrified to let it happen. She didn't believe for a minute that Nick could really change, could ever willingly compromise on anything. And she was afraid, so afraid, that she'd wind up not caring about any of that and fall back under his control the next time he snapped his fingers.

The second to the last stop of the night was to let Julia's friend Tessa off at her boyfriend's palatial Pacific Heights mansion, and Angela found herself whistling along with Lauren as the limo pulled up to the curb.

"Hot damn girl, you really landed yourself a winner," said Lauren in admiration as she patted Tessa on the arm. "Hold on to that man for sure. Better yet," she added with a wink, "use those handcuffs Jules put in everyone's goody bag and chain him to your bed."

Julia had spent weeks assembling the pretty pink, white, and black striped party bags, filling them up with all sorts of girly little trinkets. Angela had been commandeered into helping her put them together last week and recalled that a few of the items included semi-naughty gifts like a silk blindfold, a bottle of massage oil, and a pair of flimsy, fluffy pink handcuffs.

The shy, pretty Tessa blushed furiously at Lauren's bawdy suggestion and could only stammer a rather flustered good night as she exited the limo. Lauren was chuckling wickedly as they pulled away.

"Did you see the look on her face when I mentioned chaining her man to the bed? And when I made a little joke earlier tonight about Ian tying her up, she had the exact same reaction. Trust me," she nodded with confidence, "those two get up to some kinky shit every so often."

Julia eyed her twin with a scowl. "Honestly, Lauren? I mean, you've met Ian. He's the most conservative, proper English gentleman you'll ever want to meet, while Tessa blushes at the drop of a hat."

Lauren shrugged. "Everybody's got a bit of a dark side, sis. Even those two. Trust me, I'll betcha Ian trusses her up in not only the handcuffs but the blindfold and the thong, too."

"Except those particular cuffs are really just for show. They aren't meant for BDSM play," murmured Angela quietly. "Way too flimsy."

The moment the words left her mouth she would have done anything to take them back, especially when she saw the way Julia and Lauren were staring at her in stunned silence. She hadn't meant to say something like that, was now kicking herself mentally for having blurted it out, and knew Lauren at least wouldn't let it alone for hours now.

Lauren found her voice first. "Uh, would you be speaking from experience there, Angie? Or have you just been watching too much porn?"

Angela gave Lauren a playful shove. "I haven't watched porn since our senior year of high school at Erica Lyman's house. Now *her* parents were really into some kinky shit."

Julia shuddered as she recalled the sordid tales Lauren had whispered to her about the various DVD's and sex toys Erica's parents had *tried* – most unsuccessfully – to hide from their daughter and her very inquisitive friends. "Okay, already feeling a little queasy over here. Let's not talk about Mr. and Mrs. Lyman's, uh, quirks tonight."

Lauren kept her gaze steadily focused on Angela. "Fine. But I still want Angie to answer the questions about the handcuffs."

Angela's dark eyes glittered dangerously. "Tough. Not going to happen. In fact, just forget I said anything."

"Oh, like hell I will," laughed Lauren. "You know me, girlfriend. I'll keep at you like a dog with a bone until you answer me. Was it seeing that big hunk of studly goodness tonight that finally loosened your tongue?"

Angela gasped, her eyes widening in alarm as both she and Julia stared at Lauren, who was looking way too smug for anyone's liking.

"I, um, don't know what you're talking about," Angela replied defiantly.

Lauren just looked amused. "Bullshit. You just think nobody noticed you arguing with Mr. Dark and Dangerous when we were at our second stop of the night. What's his name, Angie? Did you know he was going to be there tonight? And is he the reason you've been so out of it all evening?"

Angela's lips tightened into a hard, mutinous line. "Back off, Lauren. I'm not talking about it. Ever."

But Lauren was a long, long way from being deterred. "He's the one, isn't he? The fucker who broke your heart three – no, it's almost four years ago now, isn't it? The one who broke *you*, Angie. Tell us his name. And, more importantly, why he's suddenly showing up in your life again."

"He's *not* in my life again," snarled Angela, her anger a blazing hot force to be reckoned with. "At least not that way. And his name isn't important. *He's* not important."

Lauren gave a careless shrug. "Sure didn't look that way to me. Jules – you should have seen this guy. Tall – even taller than Ian – and built like a tank. Dark hair, dark eyes, dark clothes. He reminded me of the devil – a really well built, really good looking devil."

Angela's mouth was trembling now. "He *is* the devil," she whispered brokenly. "And he's trying to lure me back into hell."

As the twins stared at her in mingled shock and horror, Angela gave herself a little shake and struggled to regain her composure. She pointed a warning finger at Lauren.

"And the subject is now officially closed. *Closed*," she emphasized when Lauren started to speak. "If you try talking about it again, I'll call a taxi and go stay at a hotel. I mean it, Lauren. You need to butt out, okay?"

Angela's voice was so filled with repressed rage that Lauren for once didn't dare argue back and merely nodded. The remainder of the drive back home was passed in uncomfortable silence, save for the occasional drunken hiccup that escaped Julia's mouth despite her best efforts to suppress them.

As soon as the limo pulled up in front of their building, Angela wasted little time in exiting and then briskly climbing the two sets of stairs to her flat. She barely even mumbled a good night to Julia and her fiancé Nathan, who'd been waiting at the curb for their arrival. Fortunately Lauren had been enlisted to help guide her very tipsy twin inside her own flat, giving Angela a few precious minutes to make herself scarce and hopefully escape more of Lauren's prying.

But despite getting undressed, throwing on some ratty old

PJ's, and diving under the covers in record time, Angela couldn't completely avoid the doggedly stubborn Lauren. Never one to let a closed door deter her, Lauren ignored it to poke her head inside Angela's bedroom.

"Hide all you want to, Angie," she called out. "But I'm on to you now. More importantly, I know what that devil looks like and I won't stop until I figure out who he is. Then the fun is really going to begin. Sweet dreams now."

But Angela had neither dreams nor nightmares as she fell – surprisingly quickly – into a deep sleep. Maybe it was all the booze she'd consumed, or maybe there was some other underlying reason, but it was one of the most restful sleeps she'd had in years.

***

When, right on schedule, Cara poked her beaming, perky little head inside the doorway on Monday morning, Angela refused to let her resolve weaken, no matter how adorable the younger woman looked. She'd been far too lax with Cara recently, she realized, and needed to lay the law down on a few things.

"Cara, could you close the door and have a seat, please?" asked Angela in her most businesslike tone. "There's something we need to discuss."

Her admin assistant's big eyes grew even wider, and Angela was secretly pleased to see a hint of fear in their depths. She wasn't planning on yelling at Cara, but the girl definitely needed to realize how displeased Angela was with her at present.

"O – okay," murmured Cara uncertainly, even as she shut the door and perched nervously on one of the guest chairs. "Is, um, something wrong?"

"Depends on your answer, I suppose." Angela lounged back slightly in her chair, tapping her pen on the surface of the desk.

Cara clasped her hands in her lap in obvious agitation. "Answer to what? Did I do something wrong? What is it? Whatever it is, I'm so sorry! I'll do whatever I have to in order to fix it. I - "

Angela held up a hand to stop the babbling. "Just answer me truthfully. Have you been giving Nick Manning information about me? Specifically, what my personal appointments are and where he might be likely to run into me?"

Angela knew immediately – from both the way Cara's mouth dropped open in shock and how her eyes grew even rounder – that she'd found her culprit. There really hadn't been any other suspects so far as she was concerned, because no one else besides herself and Cara would have known about some of the appointments.

Cara's full bottom lip began to quiver and there was a sheen of tears in her big eyes. "I – I'm sorry, Angela," she stammered. "I know it was wrong to tell him. But – well, he's so charming and has this way of getting you to tell him things without even being aware you're doing it. And, well, it was *sooo* romantic, I thought – how the two of you had been together once and then how he'd stupidly let you go and how he's trying to get you back again. And, well, you know me – I'm a sucker for a good love story, a hopeless romantic, and - "

Angela held up her hand again, thinking that Cara talked even faster when she was agitated. "Okay, enough. I get the picture. And, yes, unfortunately I'm all too aware of just how persuasive Nick can be when he turns the charm on full force. I'm guessing a babe in the woods like you never stood a chance against a wolf like him. But I want you to promise me now that you aren't going to tell him even one more thing. Do we understand each other?"

Cara nodded frantically. "Yes, yes, I promise, Angela! And, honestly, I didn't mean any harm, I really didn't. I guess – well it's hard to imagine anyone not wanting to be with someone like Nick. He's *sooo* gorgeous and sophisticated and dreamy. I thought – well, I thought I was helping you. I figured you'd had a lover's spat or something when you knew each other before, and that you were still mad at him over whatever happened to break you up."

"Mad doesn't even begin to cover it," replied Angela dryly. "And while I appreciate your concern for me, it ends now, okay? Including all of your not so subtle attempts to get me to eat.

Though I had that one figured out quite some time ago."

"Oops." Cara giggled. "Busted, guilty as charged! But at least that seems to be working. You really do look great, Angela, so much healthier. And if I promise not to shove cupcakes under your nose, will you promise to keep on eating more?"

Angela regarded her overeager young assistant dubiously, though Cara reminded her so much of a loveable, cuddly puppy right now that it was impossible not to offer up a faint smile. "All right, I'll try. And you don't have to stop completely. I'm particularly fond of that crumb cake you bring in sometimes."

"Isn't that the best?" gushed Cara. "I get it at this bakery a couple of blocks from here. And you should see the other stuff they make. Do you like lemon bars? Or blackout cake? And their peanut butter - "

"Just the crumb cake," interrupted Angela. "And once in a while, not twice a day. Now, as long as we're on the same page about this issue, let's get to work, hmm? And if that wily bastard Nick stops by, tell him the two of you have been made. The information leak stops now. Are we perfectly clear?"

Cara nodded. "As glass. I promise not to tell him about any more of your plans. Uh, oh."

Angela frowned at the note of concern in her assistant's voice. "What now?"

Cara worried her bottom lip, her eyes holding a decidedly guilty expression. "I, um, may have shared details about one other appointment with him. But don't worry. I really, really doubt he'd just show up *there*."

Angela sighed. "Go on, tell me. What appointment did you tell him about?"

"Not so much an appointment, really. But I may have, ah, mentioned the date and location of your friend's wedding this Saturday."

Angela shook her head in disbelief. "Really, Cara? Why in the world would you have told him something like that? God, that's all I'd need – Nick deciding to crash Julia's wedding just so he can mess with my head for a few more minutes."

"Relax," replied Cara, her voice sounding a hell of a lot more confident than Angela felt at the moment. "I mean, all of the other places he showed up at were around San Francisco. What are the chances Nick would actually drive all the way to Pebble Beach just to see you for a few minutes?

Chapter Eighteen

"Well, you're looking mighty pleased with yourself this afternoon. What's her name?"

Dante Sabattini gave Nick a very satisfied smile as he lifted his glass of red wine. "You know me too well, my friend. And her name is one you've heard me mention enough times over these past couple of years to drive you crazy."

Nick sighed. "Please tell me you are not still obsessed with nailing that actress who's got your balls in a vise."

Dante winked suggestively. "Nope. Because I've already nailed her. Multiple times. And that's just for starters. I'm happy to say this is the start of a beautiful and lasting relationship."

"Great. I'm very happy for you and – what's her name again? Keely? Krista?"

Dante shook his head. "Come on, Nick. How many times over the past year and a half have you heard me talking about her? It's Katie. Gorgeous, sexy, Katie who can do things with that mouth of hers that are probably still illegal in some countries."

"Sorry. And, yes, it's all coming back to me now. I'm not sure how I could ever forget the name of a woman who had you jacking off like a twelve year old boy over the new swimsuit edition of *Sports Illustrated*."

Dante's dark olive skin flushed in embarrassment. "Hey, I never did that. And wait until you meet her in person, Nick. You'll be trying to figure out how to make a move on her yourself without pissing me off in the process."

"No." Nick toyed with his grilled swordfish, his usually robust appetite off today. "First of all, I never, ever poach on another man's woman. Second, your Katie isn't really my type. I prefer my women to be all natural, and from what I can tell not much about yours is real – dyed hair, fake tits, veneers."

Dante stared across the table in appalled disbelief. "And how the hell can you tell any of that? You've seen her in person like, what – once? Twice? And both of those times were from a distance."

Nick swallowed a mouthful of fish, rice, and grilled vegetables, washing it all down with a healthy swallow of wine. "What can I say, my lovestruck friend? I've got certain – talents where women are concerned, can pick out the real thing from a poor substitute with just a glance."

"Hah!" smirked Dante. "Big surprise, considering how many women you've banged over the years."

"You're kidding, right?" asked Nick, chuckling. "Let's not start comparing numbers, Dan, because that might just be one category where you passed me up a long time ago. Especially considering the fact that I've been living like a damned monk this past year and a half."

"Well, whose fault is that?" declared Dante. "You could have fresh pussy every night of the week if you want. And you've been off your game for way longer than eighteen months, my man. You haven't been your old self since – well, since before you were with Angela."

Nick's hand froze halfway to his mouth with another forkful of his lunch. Quietly, he set the fork down. "You might be right, Dan," he admitted soberly. "I never even realized it when we were together, but she got under my skin in a way nobody else has ever been able to do. I'm not sure why I never saw that clearly until she came back into my life."

Dante snorted, his own healthy appetite not in the least affected as he swallowed a heaping forkful of seafood linguine. "You never realized it the first time because you were way too busy being an asshole," he declared. "You treated Angela like shit back then, took advantage of how young she was and how she was willing to do fucking anything for you. And, hey, I know exactly what you're going to say next – you laid out the rules, told her what to expect, and nobody twisted her arm to get her to agree. It still doesn't excuse the fact that you didn't treat her right. Especially when you broke things off. You were cold, Nick. Ice cold."

Nick scowled, ignoring his food but finishing off his wine and then motioning to the waiter for a refill. He seldom drank more than a glass at lunch, and oftentimes didn't have any alcohol during his midday meal, but he allowed himself the indulgence today. He'd been in a rotten mood since he'd woken up – hell, most of the week – and Dante's rather blunt criticism wasn't helping to make things better.

"You know, Dan," he drawled, using the abbreviated form of Dante's name as most of his close friends did. "You aren't exactly a shining example of how to treat a lady, either. Rumor has it that your middle initial really stands for Player instead of Pietro."

Dante grinned. "Hey, I'm the first to admit I've gotten around. A lot. But whether it's for a month or a night, I've always treated my ladies like royalty. That's why they all still love me, why I have to block so many phone numbers, de-friend so many of them on Facebook. You, on the other hand," he shook his head in disapproval, "usually treat women with less regard than you do a bottle of good Bordeaux. And you treated Angela even worse – like a six-pack of cheap malt liquor."

"I'm well aware of how badly I handled things," admitted Nick in resignation. "You think I haven't lost sleep over it, haven't beaten myself up a hundred times? And now that I want to do the right thing by her – have a real relationship – she won't give me the time of day."

Dante looked at him scornfully. "Well, duh, *stupido*. Did you really think she was just going to fling herself back into your arms and beg you to pick up where you left off?" When Nick didn't reply, he only stared at him harder. "You did, didn't you? God, I always knew you were an arrogant bastard, but for you to honestly believe something like that – I think you're having some serious mental health issues, my friend."

Nick smiled faintly. "Odd, that's what Angela keeps telling me – that I'm off my rocker if I really believe she's ever going to take me back. But it wouldn't be like – like it was before. I've told her over and over that I'd be willing to compromise."

"Honestly?" Dante arched a skeptic brow. "I've known you now for what – eight, nine years? I've never once seen you back down on anything, or not insist on having your own way all the time. I don't blame Angela for not believing you. Frankly, my friend, you've got a really shitty track record."

"I can change," Nick replied reluctantly.

"Can you? Can you really?" challenged Dante. "Let's put that theory to the test, shall we? Are you willing to let Angela visit your house? Or, hey – wait for it – actually sleep over?"

Nick didn't answer, his mouth tightening mutinously as he glared at his friend.

But Dante was just getting started. "Okay, let's see what else you're supposedly willing to compromise on. Can she call you whenever she feels like it? Send you a text or an email? Oh, and will you let her pick the restaurant where you're going for dinner – I mean, at least every so often?"

"Yes," conceded Nick. "The restaurant part is fine. Within reason, of course. I don't care who it is, I'm not eating fast food or greasy takeout or anyplace that offers a Monday Night Football special of Budweiser and hot wings."

"Snob," chided Dante. "You barely condescended to eat at my family's restaurant, even though you admitted later it was some of the best Italian food you ever had. But what about the first part of the question, Nick – the phone calls and such?"

Nick hesitated. "I honestly don't know. I guess I'd have to agree to allow contact, but only up to a point. You know how I am about my privacy."

Dante sighed. "Yeah, you're a pain in the ass and paranoid to boot. Okay, next question. Are you willing to meet her parents? Angela's a nice Italian girl, after all, and I'm sure her folks would insist on meeting her – uh, boyfriend? Man friend?"

"I'm not really sure she gives a crap about what her family wants. From what I know, they have kind of a complicated – no, make that a fucked-up – relationship. They don't treat Angela very well, especially her mother."

Dante shook his head. "Avoiding the real question again, Nick. If she asked you to – say, go with her to a family wedding or her father's birthday party, something like that – would you go?"

Nick tried to avert the question by re-posing it to Dante.

"Would you? If Katie asked you to meet her parents, take her to her best friend's wedding – would you do it willingly?"

"Hell, yes," declared Dante without hesitation. "But then I'd go just about anywhere Katie asked me – to the movies to see a chick flick, to the drugstore to buy tampons, to watch her try on shoes for three hours straight."

Nick shook his head in disgust. "My God, this girl really has you good and pussy whipped, doesn't she? All I can figure is that she either had some sort of voodoo hex cast on you, or else she's got a gold plated honey pot."

Dante grinned. "Well, she definitely has the latter, she's for sure got me under some kind of spell, and if I'm whipped then I don't care because it's the best kind of pain in the whole fucking world. But, hey, this is about *you*, man, not me. I've already told you I treat my women like they're someone special. The real question is – how far are you actually willing to compromise in order to get Angela back? Because so far, if I'm her, I'm not hearing anything new, just the same old song you're always singing."

"Yeah, I know." Nick blew out a breath in frustration. "It's called being caught between a rock and a hard place, Dan. I want her back, I know I've got to change my ways in order to do so, but, well, old habits die hard, you know? I guess I'm still selfish enough and too set in my ways to willingly change. At least enough so that she'll concede to talk about it, if nothing else."

"Well, here's a thought," offered Dante. "If you don't think she's ready to listen – and, more importantly, you're not willing to compromise – then stop talking and start acting instead. From what I used to observe, things were pretty hot between the two of you a few years ago. Just – uh, give her a sample of what she's been missing. Unless, of course, she's not really missing it."

Nick's eyes narrowed dangerously. "What the hell is that supposed to mean?"

"You did tell me she's dating some other guy, didn't you? What is he – a pole vaulter or a javelin thrower or something?"

"High jumper. And there is *no* way," insisted Nick, "that a nerd like that is capable of satisfying a woman like Angela."

Dante grinned merrily. "So what are you waiting for then?

Ah, but you'd be breaking one of your rules, wouldn't you? Like the one you just brought up a few minutes ago – how you don't poach on other men's women."

"Fuck that." Nick pounded his fist on the table hard enough to start the plates and cutlery shaking, and forcing Dante to grab wildly at his wine glass. "She doesn't belong to him. Angela was mine first and I've decided to re-claim my property."

"Uh, uh." Dante was shaking his head emphatically. "See, that's part of the attitude adjustment you need to make, Nick. You don't fucking own people. Angela is not nor has she ever been your property, your possession, even though that's how you treated her four years ago. Relationships are all about equal give and take, and not these one-sided affairs that are all you've ever known. And until you're ready to accept that – and actually do something about it – Angela would be a hell of a lot better off if you just left her alone."

The look on Nick's face was grim. "I know that. Damn it, why do you think I left her four years ago? Of course she'd be better off without me in her life. The problem is, she hasn't been, at least not from what I've seen. And the even bigger problem is now that I've seen her again, I can't stand the thought of not having her with me."

"Well, then, you'd better get your shit together, Nick. Nobody's saying that relationships aren't a lot of hard work. But you at least need to be willing to try and *do* the work. From where I'm sitting, it sure as hell doesn't look like you've reached that point yet."

Nick heaved a sigh of frustration. "I've always admitted to being a fucked-up bastard. And the real issue is I don't even know where to start if I decide to change things."

"Maybe you should try following my advice – stop analyzing, stop talking, and just fucking take her to bed. Maybe a week or two of nonstop sex will somehow magically fix everything."

He regarded Dante dubiously. "Uh, huh. And you really think that's going to just make all of the other issues disappear?"

Dante's dark eyes twinkled mischievously. "Well, it's a helluva good place to start, isn't it? And it's always worked for me in the past. Look at it this way, Nick – a week of hard, dirty sex might not make things better but at least you'll have a lot of fun trying."

***

Angela couldn't help herself. No matter how many times she'd tried to convince herself over the past week that Nick wouldn't *dare* show his face at Julia's wedding, she hadn't been able to keep from looking over her shoulder every so often just to make sure. She was furious that she'd allowed him to make her act all paranoid, on top of everything else he'd done, and she was still more than a little peeved at Cara for giving details about her personal life to that controlling bastard.

She peeked over her shoulder so often, in fact, that Lauren had finally snapped, "Who the hell are you expecting to see back there anyway – Freddy Krueger? A swarm of angry bees? Knock it off, Angie, would you? You're starting to freak me out a little."

So she'd tried not to keep sneaking furtive little glances wherever she went, tried to fight off the fear that Nick would actually have the nerve to drive all the way down here to cause trouble. God, that would be *all* she'd need this weekend, with not just Lauren and Julia constantly nearby but Dwayne flying down for the wedding, too. And Dwayne, of course, knew exactly who Nick was and wouldn't hesitate to clue Lauren in if she inquired. And then – well, then all hell would definitely break loose.

Angela breathed a sigh of relief when a discreet inspection of the banquet room at Casanova – the trendy Mediterranean restaurant in Carmel where Julia and Nathan had chosen to hold their rehearsal dinner – revealed no unwanted guests were present. But her paranoia wouldn't go away quite so easily, and when she had to make a trip to the ladies room she all but dragged Lauren along with her. If anyone could defend her from Nick, it would be her best friend. Lauren would never –

'God, stop it!' she told herself angrily. "You don't need to be defended from anyone. Nick is not going to just pop out of some

corner and maul you. And even if he did, you're a big girl,
Angela, and you sure as hell can take care of yourself!'

She felt better, more confident, after the little pep talk she
gave herself, and was able to relax and enjoy the rest of the
evening.   Both Julia and Nathan had wonderful families,
everyone seeming to get along and enjoy each other's company.
There didn't appear to be any of the gossip, bickering, and petty
jealousy that always seemed to be going on at her own family
gatherings. And since she'd always felt closer to Julia's parents
than her own, it wasn't so surprising for her to pretend for this
one night that she was an actual member of the McKinnon
family.

Dwayne seemed to fit right in with everyone, especially
Nathan's younger brother Greg, who had also competed in track
during his school years.   Dwayne, in fact, got along with
everyone she'd introduced him to so far, including her own
family.   Her parents had declared him a "nice young man",
though admittedly her mother hadn't been thrilled to learn he was
an athlete by profession – and a poorly paid one to boot. Dwayne
was good natured enough not to mind when her aunts and sisters
gave him the third degree, and had quickly bonded with the
sports-crazy male members of the family.

It was just too bad, thought Angela with regret, that Dwayne
was more like the brother she'd never had than her boyfriend.
And that, despite her mother's not so subtle hints, he would never
be her fiancé, much less her husband.

Dwayne dropped her off at her parents' house after dinner
before continuing on to his own family home. He'd begun to hint
lately that maybe they ought to consider taking their relationship
to the next level – namely, sleeping together. Angela had been
startled and completely caught off guard, and had only been able
to stammer and stutter in response.

And even though her parents were out of town at present – this
time on a cruise to Alaska – Angela had discouraged Dwayne
from staying at the house with her as he'd initially suggested.

"It's just – well, that place doesn't hold very good memories
for me," she'd explained. "I wouldn't want – well, I'm sure you

get the idea. Besides, you don't get to see your own family all that often these days so I'm sure they'd be disappointed if you didn't stay with them."

And while Dwayne had readily agreed with her rationale, Angela had been guiltily aware that she'd been almost desperately scrambling for delay tactics. But she simply wasn't ready to become intimate with him – or with any man. Even though it had been nearly four years now since she'd had sex – since that fateful night of her twenty-third birthday – she had no intention of ending her self-imposed celibacy until she was good and ready. And since the affection she felt for Dwayne was strictly on an emotional level, there was really no chance of him ever being the man to end her four year drought.

There was, in fact, only one man she'd met over the last few years who'd touched her on any sort of physical level – the only man who'd ever truly done so in her entire twenty-six years.

'Damn that Nick. It always comes back to him, doesn't it?' she thought bitterly. 'He's definitely ruined me for anyone else. And apparently the only way I can deal with that fact is to either give in or get out.'

Get out of the office, that was. She'd given the matter some serious consideration as of late, had even done some very casual checking into rental property and real estate around both the San Jose and Oakland areas. Both of those cities had a large branch office of Morton Sterling, and she'd be able to transfer to either of them while still retaining all of her clients. Such a move would remove her from Nick's path and allow her to return to a life without him in it, a life where he wasn't constantly tormenting her and tempting her to come back to him, to be under his control again.

And there was no way he'd consider following her. Not when he had really just settled into his new offices with a new firm, was even now still assembling his team. Angela knew he had two associate brokers – who happened to be a married couple – along with an admin assistant, and all three had made the move with Nick from Jessup Prior. And, according to what she'd learned from Cara, a second assistant had just been added to the team. Rumor had it that Nick was still looking for a third associate and possibly another admin assistant, and that nearly every up and coming broker in the office was vying to join his team.

Angela snorted in derision as she got ready for bed. She couldn't imagine working for someone like Nick, and assumed that he insisted on complete control of everything having to do with his business, just like he did in all other aspects of his life. Even with a boss as tough as Barbara had been, at least Angela had been free to take her own path, make her own decisions. Barbara might have pushed her hard, might have made most work days a living hell, but she'd always had complete faith in Angela and had encouraged her to think for herself.

And, Angela was pleased to note, that very same sort of self-sufficiency Barbara had drummed into her had spilled over into her personal life. It had helped Angela take control of her life again, had made her into a stronger person, and given her the strength she'd needed to stand up for herself – to her bosses, her family, and, more recently, Nick.

Just before falling asleep, she smiled to herself as she imagined how loudly Barbara would have laughed to realize it had been her influence that now gave Angela the guts to stand up to Nick, to resist his potent allure, and not allow herself to fall back under his spell. In fact, thought Angela sleepily, if Barbara was somehow watching all of this unfold from up above, she was more than likely having a very satisfied drink or two while she did.

***

Nick figured he'd been nursing the same drink for the better part of a half hour now, but given that it was only the middle of the afternoon he wasn't about to overindulge. His table was tucked into a discreet corner of the lobby bar here at the Gregson Resort in Pebble Beach as he waited – none too patiently – for Angela to make an appearance. That he felt like the worst sort of stalker wasn't sitting very well with him. In fact, he'd asked himself at least a dozen times already what the hell he was doing here.

He hadn't been at all surprised when cute, gullible little Cara had informed him rather haughtily that she would no longer be able to keep him apprised of Angela's personal appointments. They'd been found out, and the only real surprise was that it had taken Angela this long to figure things out. Nick had assured Cara it didn't matter, that she'd been a big help, and that he appreciated her efforts up to this point. He'd been confident that if he had kept at her a little while longer Cara would have caved in to his very deliberate charm and found some way to continue conspiring with him. But he genuinely liked the girl and had no desire to get her in more trouble with Angela – who was becoming more and more like her former mentor Barbara Lowenstein with each passing day – and not in a good way.

He'd been surprised – and reluctantly admiring – of how Angela had stuck to her guns thus far. Given how deeply she'd fallen under his control four years ago, Nick had rather arrogantly assumed that all he'd have to do was sweet talk her a bit in order to lure her back. But his Angel had most definitely developed claws during the time they'd been apart, and she wasn't even attempting to keep them sheathed. Claiming her again was proving to be far more difficult than he'd imagined, and was causing him to do things he'd never, ever considered before just to get a woman.

Like driving two and a half hours to Pebble Beach under the pretext of meeting a client, just so he could catch a glimpse of Angela and possibly have an opportunity to approach her. He had, in actuality, played a round of golf earlier this morning with his client Alec Glover – a client who just happened to be the manager of this hotel. The same manager who'd quietly given him the details he'd asked for about the wedding this afternoon.

"It's out in the garden chapel, with the reception on the outdoor patio," Alec had told him. "But if you want to, let's say, keep a low profile while you keep an eye on all the comings and goings, the best place to do that is from the lobby bar. All of the guests will have to pass by that way, including the bridal party."

Alec, who owed Nick big time for the many donations of autographed football memorabilia made to an annual charity auction he oversaw, had also discreetly informed him that neither Angela nor Dwayne were registered guests at the hotel. Nick assumed that they were staying with their families, adding an unforeseen glitch to his plans.

Though to call his actions thus far today an actual plan was really stretching it, he thought. He had no fucking clue what he was going to do when and if he saw Angela, had no idea why he was even here. Up until today he'd fully believed that only women – desperate ones, at that – did this sort of shit – lying in wait for someone, arranging to "accidentally" run into them. He was beginning to think that both Angela and Dante were right – he was, in fact, having some sort of mental breakdown. He knew for sure that Angela was driving him mad with her continued refusal to resume their relationship, and that something had to give – very, very soon.

Nick's patience – which was usually in short supply to begin with – had very nearly reached the end of its limits when a stream of elegantly attired wedding guests finally began to filter past the bar in a slow but steady stream. It wasn't difficult to pick them out – the men in suits, the women in varying lengths and styles of cocktail dresses – especially since the guests at the hotel were mostly garbed in "resort casual" clothing at this time of the day.

He recognized one of the guests as being none other than Ian Gregson himself – part of the family who owned not just this hotel but hundreds of others around the world. Ian was the Managing Director of all the hotels in North and South America, and was one of the very, very few people that Nick had actually attempted to solicit as a client. And while Nick did manage accounts for several of the Gregson hotel managers, plus members of Ian's management staff, rumor had it that the Brit had quite the financial acumen himself and preferred to manage his own personal investments.

Nick toyed with the idea of approaching Ian, even if it was just to say hello, but thought better of such an action when he noticed the breathtaking blonde by his side. Ian had eyes for no one but the gorgeous woman tucked against him, and Nick wisely stayed in his seat, continuing to keep his gaze peeled for a very different woman.

Four men garbed in formalwear, whom he assumed to be the groom, his father, and groomsmen, crossed the lobby next, and Nick checked his watch with barely concealed impatience. Fifteen more minutes until the wedding and still no sign of the bride. Or, more importantly, a particular bridesmaid.

His patience was finally rewarded a short time later when a white stretch limo pulled up to the porte-cochere. One by one the bridal party emerged from the vehicle – the bride, her parents, her sister and Angela. Nick smiled in appreciation at how beautiful she looked today. God knew he despised weddings for the most part, and all of the pageantry that went along with them. But there was no denying how striking his angel looked in her green floral print bridesmaid gown – the deep V-neck and long floaty skirt a perfect style for her tall, slender body, and the color ideally suited to her skin tone and hair.

Her subtle but expertly applied makeup did a lot to enhance her big, dark eyes and wide, full-lipped mouth, as well as highlight cheekbones that were nowhere near as hollow as they'd been almost three months ago. Her long, shiny hair – which he knew was too stick straight to hold even the slightest curl – had been pulled back from the sides and held in some sort of clasp at her nape. The smile she gave the bride – her friend Julia – made her whole face light up, and Nick's breath caught a bit in his throat as he took in her glowing beauty.

He hadn't expected anything more than this – the opportunity to get a fleeting glimpse of her dressed up in that beautiful gown. But today was evidently going to be a lucky one for him, as fate presented him with an unexpected bonus when Angela murmured something to her friends before hurrying off in the direction of the restrooms.

Nick waited until the others had left the lobby area to continue on towards the wedding chapel before he stood. A wicked smile teased the corners of his mouth as he ambled leisurely towards the restrooms, seemingly in no hurry whatsoever. He ignored the looks he received from both men and women – the former likely wondering if he was really *the* Nick Manning, the football player, while the latter group was sizing him up for vastly different reasons. He didn't think he'd ever get used to the attention he attracted, a holdover not just from his days of being a professional athlete but of being the son of the world famous – and infamous – actress Sheena Sumner. And while his mother thrived on such attention – lived for it, in fact – he still hated it with a passion, and belatedly wished he'd thought to wear a pair of dark sunglasses and maybe even a hat.

Fortunately the hallway outside of the restrooms was deserted, and he was quite alone as he waited for Angela to emerge. Still not entirely sure of what he was going to say to her, it turned out he didn't have to ponder the matter for very long.

She stared at him in ill-concealed shock as she exited the ladies room, and he could have sworn he glimpsed fear in her eyes. But that expression was swiftly replaced by anger, and if looks could kill he'd be drawing his dying breath at this moment.

"I can't believe you had the nerve to show up here," she whispered. "God, Nick, you can't be here. Please don't - "

He held up a hand. "Relax, Angel. I'm not going to crash your pretty little friend's wedding. I wouldn't do that to you."

Angela shook her head. "Then why are you here? And I won't believe for one second that it's some sort of bizarre coincidence."

Nick offered up a weak smile. "I actually did play a round of golf this morning with a client – a client who also happens to be the manager of this hotel. I was going to use that as my excuse until I realized just how flimsy it sounded. So, to answer your question honestly – I have no idea why I'm here, Angel, except that I'd go to most any length to see you, I guess."

She glared at him. "This is beyond belief, even for you. You've got way bigger balls than I would have ever believed."

He laughed. "Well, honey, you ought to know exactly how big they are, considering how many times you've been up close and personal with them." In one swift moment he was by her side and pulling her against him, his lips teasing her ear. "Not to mention the other, ah, oversized body parts you're very well acquainted with."

She flushed hotly and tried to squirm out of his grip. "Sorry I don't have time to discuss the size of your manly equipment right now. In case you've forgotten, I do have a wedding to attend."

Nick caressed her cheek, his thumb brushing over her full, trembling lips. "You make a beautiful bridesmaid, Angel," he murmured. "And if I was going to the wedding you can be damned sure I'd be staring at you the entire time instead of the bride."

She rolled her eyes. "I'm sure the groom would be relieved to hear that. But fortunately for all of us you don't like weddings, do you, Nick? Avoid them like the plague, don't you? In fact, I'm surprised you're not breaking out in a rash being this close to one."

"Which just goes to prove what I'm willing to do so that you'll come back to me, Angel," he rasped, his arms tightening around her waist as he pulled her even closer against his rapidly hardening body.

Angela glared at him, and if he hadn't sidestepped at that precise moment, she would have driven the stiletto heel of her sandal into his instep. "Why won't you listen, Nick?" she pleaded. "There is nothing you can say that's going to change my mind."

"I wasn't planning on talking, Angel," he whispered, just before taking her mouth in a blistering kiss.

She struggled against him for no more than ten seconds before he heard her groan and then melt against him, her hands no longer trying to push him away but pulling him closer instead, her slender arms twining around his neck.

Nick was too aroused, too consumed with pleasure, to feel triumphant. He turned her around, shoved her up against a wall, heedless of her dress or the fact that she was supposed to be walking up the aisle at her friend's wedding in just a few minutes. He needed her too badly, wanted to luxuriate in the feel of her body rubbing up against his, longed to bury himself as deep inside of her as he could get. He ran his hands over her hips, her ass, holding her still as he ground his hugely engorged cock against the notch of her thighs. He kept on kissing her, one deep, drugging kiss after another, as though he was starved for the taste of her – which he most definitely was. She whimpered as he cupped her breast, flicking over the hard point of her nipple with his thumb.

He reluctantly broke the kiss, but only held her tighter, murmuring huskily in her ear, "Jesus, Angel, you're on fire for me, aren't you? And I'm burning up for you. I want to take you to bed, fuck you for about a week straight, until you pass out from the pleasure." He kissed his way down her throat, his fingers still plucking at her engorged nipple. "I'll get a room while you're at the wedding, text you the number, and then you can meet me there afterwards. How quickly do you think you can get away?"

She froze in his arms, her hand slapping his away from her breast. "Let go of me, Nick," she told him in a cold, horrible voice. "Otherwise I'm going to start screaming, and since Julia knows the owner of this hotel very well, his security people aren't going to give a damn who you are."

Reluctantly, he released her and stepped back, watching as she smoothed down her skirts and tried valiantly to still the quivering of her kiss-swollen lips. She looked shell-shocked, furious, and incredibly aroused all at the same time.

"Angel, we – " he began, only to be cut off as she lifted a hand in warning.

"No. Stop it," she ordered. "Just don't speak right now, Nick. What you just did – what *we* just did – was wrong. I'm here with Dwayne, you know, he's my *date*, for God's sake. So I sure as hell don't appreciate you lying in wait for me and then – *molesting* me - "

He gave a shout of laughter. "Oh, Angel. You and I have very different definitions of molestation, don't we? I wasn't exactly forcing you just now, was I? In fact, I'll bet if I slid my hand up under that pretty dress of yours, you'd feel juicier than - "

She clapped a hand urgently over his mouth as a hotel employee rounded the corner at that moment. "You've made your point," she hissed. "Yes, you can still turn me on, Nick. Yes, you're still an amazing kisser. But not much else has changed about you, either, from what I've seen. And until it does you need to leave me alone."

Nick shook his head. "Not after what just happened. Not after you've proved how much you still want me."

Angela caressed his cheek, the gesture surprisingly tender. "You don't get it, Nick," she whispered sadly. "I've never stopped wanting you. But it can't be like it was before. Because the last time – you broke me, broke me into a hundred little pieces, and it's taken me all this time to become whole again. And I won't ever let anyone break me again – not you or any other man. So until you're ready to do a hell of a lot more than just compromise, leave me alone."

Nick let her go, watching with mingled fury, admiration, and desire as she hurried away. But that kiss – that one earth shattering, wildly erotic kiss – had given him all the answers he needed, and he was smiling broadly as he walked out of the hotel.

Chapter Nineteen

Late July

Angela had read at least half a dozen internet articles so far this morning and was still incredulous at the breaking news. The very idea that a firm as old and established as Jessup Prior was now essentially bankrupt and in the process of being taken over by a commercial bank was beyond shocking. But the more she read, the more it became apparent that the firm had been in trouble for quite some time, and that the signs of their imminent financial demise had all been there, clear as a bell. Except that no one had bothered to pay attention to them – no one, that is, except for the brilliant Nick Manning. She now knew exactly why he'd jumped ship, had given up everything he'd achieved at Jessup Prior to start over. He had been one of the very, very few people who'd been able to correctly interpret the signs of impending doom, and had very wisely bailed at the exact right time. The lucrative deal he'd struck with Morton Sterling was locked in tight, and he'd most certainly guaranteed himself the best possible terms by changing firms when he'd done so in April.

Angela smiled in reluctant admiration, and her opinion of Nick – at least her *professional* opinion – shot up by several more degrees. Leave it to him to come out of this disaster smelling like a rose, while his former co-workers were very likely scrambling around frantically at this moment, their futures up in the air.

She closed out the article she'd been reading and returned her focus to work. It had been a busy month, somewhat unusual for the summer as that was typically a slow time in this business. And she'd been grateful for the unexpected surge in business, since it was keeping her distracted from other – well, issues in her life.

After the encounter with Nick at Julia's wedding, she'd been jittery and on edge for the rest of the day, terrified that he wouldn't stick to his work and not crash the reception. Dwayne had noticed her edginess, but had tactfully not said a word about it until he'd driven her back to her parents' house that night. And then, it had all come out.

Dwayne hadn't looked in the least surprised when Angela had confessed that the man who'd broken her heart so thoroughly four years ago had been Nick. In fact, Dwayne had merely nodded in acknowledgment.

"Yeah, I sort of figured that it was him for a while now," he'd commented matter-of-factly. "Ever since that day we ran into him at your office. I mean, I'm not the brightest when it comes to picking up those sort of vibes, but you and Nick were really giving off some serious sparks. And you had told me once that the guy was someone you used to work with. I remember reading an interview Nick gave to Sports Illustrated right after he retired from football and he mentioned there he was joining Jessup Prior. So, I put two and two together and came up with old boyfriend."

Angela had sighed. "You won't say anything, will you? Lauren's just chomping at the bit to figure out who he is, and she can, uh, be something of a troublemaker when she's in the mood."

Dwayne had chuckled. "Lauren? A troublemaker? I'd have never guessed. Actually, back in high school I did see her take down Sam Patterson once with a kick to the head. And while Nick's a lot bigger than Sam was back then, she could still do some damage – especially if Nick underestimates her. So, don't worry, Angie. Your secret's safe with me."

She'd squeezed his hand gratefully. "Thanks. You're – you've been such a good friend to me. I'd pretty much forgotten how to laugh, how to have fun, until we met up on Thanksgiving. And I - "

"Can't find a way to tell me that all we'll ever be is friends," finished Dwayne. "You don't have to, Angie, because I've pretty much always known that."

Her jaw had hung open in surprise. "Dwayne – I don't know

what to say except – I'm sorry. You're a great guy, truly you are, and I like being around you so much. I like you. But, well, I think that everything I went through after the break-up with Nick – it, well, it damaged something in me and I'm not sure if I'll ever be able to have that sort of relationship with anyone again."

He'd shaken his head. "I think what you're not seeing clearly is that Nick is still the one that you want. And if he's going to all this trouble just to see you for a few minutes, I'd say it's pretty clear he feels the same way about you."

"It's not that simple." She'd shut her eyes, trying to find the right words. "He does want me back, but only on his terms, in spite of what he says otherwise. And our relationship – it was very one-sided. Nick's an extremely controlling man and I'm not prepared to let him call all the shots any longer."

Dwayne had given her a fist bump. "Good for you. I can tell in just the few months we've been hanging out how much stronger you've become – physically and emotionally. And I can just imagine how stubborn a guy like Nick could be. So, please, promise me – for your sake, Angie – that you won't give into him again. That if you do decide to take him back, it will be on your terms and not his."

"I promise." She'd given him a quick, affectionate hug. "God, I wish I wasn't so hung up on that bastard, because you're such a good guy, Dwayne. You've been good to me and good for me. I'm just an idiot, I suppose."

"Nah, not in the least," he'd assured her. "Besides, now that I know for sure that Nick was the guy there is no way I'd ever want to try and follow in his footsteps. I don't imagine there are too many men in this world who would willingly want to follow an act like that."

"Don't think that way," she'd protested. "Sure, Nick's sexy and sophisticated and he could sweet talk the pants off a nun if he wanted to. But he's also self-centered, selfish, and an emotional fuck-up. You, on the other hand, are a genuinely nice guy and any woman would be lucky to have you. I'm just sorry I'm still too screwed up to fully appreciate that."

Dwayne had wrinkled his nose. "Honestly, I think if you took an opinion poll of most men in this country, the vast majority would rather be a self-centered jerk like Nick than a nice guy like me. But I knew from almost the very beginning that you and I would never be more than friends. I'm just glad I could make you laugh again. That's one thing at least I've got over Manning."

They'd talked after that for hours, until it was the middle of the night and both of them were yawning. Dwayne had fessed up to having a bit of a crush on one of the runners in his training group, and Angela had encouraged him to go for it, especially since the girl would be doing the same European track circuit that he was about to embark on.

"Well, there's your opportunity," she'd pointed out. "Traveling together, staying in the same hotels, going out for meals. And you'll be gone – what? Six, seven weeks? I fully expect that when you and – Maggie, right? – return to Oregon in August that you're going to be an official couple by then."

Dwayne had smiled. "Maybe it will be the same for you and Nick. Just think – we could double date."

Angela had shaken her head sadly. "I wouldn't hold out much hope of that happening. As set in his ways as Nick is, it's completely unrealistic to think he's ever going to change enough for my liking. And I can't go back to the way things were before, I just can't. I don't think I'd survive a second time."

But it seemed that she didn't really have to worry about that happening, because Nick had pretty much left her alone since the wedding. It had been weeks since he'd popped his head inside her office, and she didn't like admitting to herself how much she missed those annoying little visits. He seemed to have reverted back to his old ways, that of sequestering himself inside his office and having little to do with anyone besides his team. And since she rarely left her own office, there was very little chance of running into him during the day.

She tried to tell herself it was for the best, that she'd been fooling herself to believe that Nick could ever truly change, that he would even *try* to change for her sake. No, leopards definitely didn't change their spots and Nick Manning would never learn how to compromise. It hurt to accept the truth, to realize that she didn't mean enough to him, but at least she'd recognized the facts before she'd done something stupid – like have sex with him, for example.

And when she wasn't at work, she was running – a *lot*. The hundred kilometer race she'd been training for all year was this weekend, and she worried constantly that she wasn't ready, hadn't prepared enough, despite having followed to the letter the program a fellow ultrarunner had helped her design. She'd even gained some more weight, so that she was now right around where she'd been when she had first met Nick. Admittedly, she did feel stronger during her runs, was sleeping better, and thankfully didn't feel nearly as cold these days. And, even better, most of the people in her life had stopped nagging her about how skinny she was, or trying to find ways of getting her to eat more. Though as busy as she'd been these past couple of months, she'd seen almost nothing of her family and friends.

Julia and Nathan were back from their honeymoon in Bora Bora, both looking tanned, well rested, and extremely well fucked. Julia had blushingly confessed that they'd spent more than half of their tropical vacation being naked, and the new bride was absolutely glowing with happiness. The newlyweds were now busy getting caught up at work, and also overseeing the construction of their new home in Tiburon, due for completion at the end of December.

Lauren, too, had been crazy busy, having jetted off to another exotic locale for a work assignment right after the wedding, and then spending a week in New York at the magazine's head office. But she was flying back to San Francisco later this week, and planning to stay through the weekend. She'd promised to hang out at the race on Sunday, waiting to cheer Angela on as she completed each loop of the course. Absurdly, Angela found herself half-wishing that she hadn't forbidden Cara from feeding Nick information about her schedule so that he might have chosen to be there at the race himself. She'd denied it for days afterwards, but had finally admitted that she'd been thrilled to find him at the finish line that day in Stinson Beach. No one else had ever come out to watch her compete – her friends, Dwayne, certainly not her family. So it had meant more to her than she'd ever let on that he'd been there that day. Only now she doubted if he'd ever show up anywhere for her again. She'd defied him, set down her conditions, and evidently Nick had decided he couldn't – wouldn't – change his ways.

She should feel relieved, really, that he'd made his choice. Because she knew Nick too well, knew that, in spite of what he might say in order to get her back, what he might be willing to compromise on at first, that deep down he'd never change. If she had made the fatal mistake of going back to him, sooner than later she would have regretted it – because it would have meant losing herself to him a second time. And this time around she'd have had no chance of finding herself again.

***

The elegantly appointed banquet room at the Gregson Hotel on Nob Hill was the chosen venue for this evening's retirement party. Stan Wagner, the retiree, was the longest tenured broker at Morton
Sterling, with over fifty years of employment to his credit. And since Stan had always been kind to her, had frequently offered her advice and given her encouragement, Angela had agreed – albeit reluctantly – to attend his party tonight. Normally she shunned most office events – Christmas parties, summer picnics – but she did have a soft spot for Stan. He'd always been the complete opposite of the hard-edged, tough-talking Barbara – a real, old-fashioned gentleman, but one who fully supported and approved of women in their business. Stan had also been one of the very, very few people in the office that Barbara had liked, and he'd even managed to coax a raspy laugh from her once in a while.

Stan's dainty, exquisitely feminine wife Felicity apparently adored lavish parties and dressing up, and thus formal attire had been specified on the invitation for tonight. And since Angela had been so pressed for time these past few weeks, she hadn't had the opportunity to shop for something new. Instead, she'd reluctantly selected one of the beautiful designer gowns that Nick had bought for her to wear this evening. The formal dresses she owned had been pushed to the very back of her closet, but she'd known even before unzipping the garment bag which one she'd choose.

The only other time she'd worn this particular dress had been to a party Nick had brought her to – a party given by a former teammate of his and one where he'd felt assured of their privacy. She'd felt like both a princess and a siren in the gown, and the way Nick had looked at her – well, that had made her feel like the most ravishing woman on earth.

And ravish her he had that night – during the limo ride to the party; in a bedroom of the sprawling mansion set high in the hills above Palo Alto that they'd snuck off to midway through the party; and then for hours and hours upon their return to her apartment. She'd been sore and wrung out for days afterwards, walking with a definite hitch in her step, but glowing each time she recalled their wild night of passion.

Julia had helped her get dressed tonight, as well as doing her hair and makeup, while Lauren had lounged back on Angela's bed instead, drinking a beer while making little critiques here and there. At one point, blusher brush in hand, Julia had turned on her sister in exasperation.

"And how exactly would you know that I'm not applying the blush to the right part of her cheekbone?" she asked in annoyance. "Frankly, I wasn't sure you'd even know what kind of brush to use, given how seldom you wear makeup."

Lauren shrugged and took a swig of her Stella Artois. "Come on, Jules. How many times did I watch you put on makeup while we were growing up? I think you started glopping the stuff on when you were eleven."

Julia's cheeks flushed with natural color. "I was *not* that young," she protested weakly. "I mean, sure, I experimented with makeup then. But Mom would never let me leave the house with it on so that doesn't count."

"The point I was trying to make is that I pay attention," drawled Lauren. "I listen, even when you think I'm not. So believe me when I tell you that you're putting the blush too high up on the cheekbones. You're going to make Angie look like a clown."

"Impossible," declared Julia as she whisked one final bit of sparkly blusher on Angela's right cheek. "Because Angie looks drop dead gorgeous tonight. And more like her old self than she has in years. Stand up, now, and let us give you one more lookover, hmm?"

As Angela stood and obediently made a slow 360° turn, Julia sighed in envy.

"God, I wish you weren't eight inches taller," she bemoaned. "Otherwise I would *so* be borrowing that gown. It's stunning, Angie. And you're stunning."

Lauren gave a very unladylike belch, belatedly covering her mouth. "Oops. Sorry, chugged that last bit down too fast. But Julia's right, girl. You look hot."

The Marchesa gown was simple and elegant, but also incredibly alluring, the teal silk shade a perfect foil for Angela's olive skin and dark hair and eyes. The gown was Grecian in style, leaving one shoulder bare, while the pleated bodice and long, draped skirt flattered the tall, slender lines of her body. With it she wore towering silver metallic evening sandals, her only jewelry a dangling pair of diamond and aquamarine earrings.

Julia had arranged the heavy mass of her hair into a low, thick chignon and her makeup was dramatic – eyes shadowed and lined in smoky gray; her complexion glowing with the shimmery, gold-flecked blusher; her mouth looking sinfully lush with its application of dark mocha gloss.

As she inspected herself in the full length mirror hanging on the back of her closet door, Angela thought wryly that most of the attendees at the party tonight wouldn't recognize her. The gorgeous silk gown and stiletto heels were a far cry from her boring pant suits and nondescript shoes, while she rarely wore either makeup or jewelry to the office.

But more than that, she realized, was that tonight she looked and felt like *Angela*. Not Angie, the name her family and friends had always called her – Angie, who'd been the somewhat awkward, often rebellious girl she'd been growing up. And certainly not Angel, the impressionable young woman whom Nick had plucked out of a crowd and molded into his ideal of the perfect lover. No, tonight she was finally Angela – a confident, successful woman capable of making her own decisions and taking charge of her life. A woman who no longer needed her family's approval or attention in order to be happy, who had resisted the temptation of falling back under her former lover's control, and for whom the future was finally beginning to look bright.

"I still wish you'd have let Nathan fix you up with his friend Jonathan," lamented Julia. "I mean, the guy's kind of a tool and it would have definitely been a one-time deal for you. But at least he's tall and good looking, and he can even be kind of charming if he works at it hard enough."

Angela gave her friend a pat on the shoulder. "Gee, thanks. He sounds like a real prize. But I've got no problem going alone, honest. I probably won't even stay that long. I mean, the guy who's retiring is close to eighty years old so I doubt this is going to turn into some wild party."

"See, you should have held on to Dwayne a little longer," chided Lauren. "I mean – I can't believe I'm actually saying that but at least he could have been your date tonight."

Angela shook her head. "Don't forget he's been in Europe for almost a month now, and he'll be there another couple of weeks at least. Besides, based on the last email he sent a few days ago it sounds like he and that runner he likes have been hanging out more and more."

Julia gave her a little hug. "You did the right thing by being honest with him," she insisted. "Dwayne's a nice guy but I could tell things were never going to get serious between the two of you. And you'll meet the right guy one of these days. Watch – it'll happen when you least expect it."

Lauren smirked. "Meanwhile, us single girls can still hang out and have some fun. I figured you won't want to go out drinking tomorrow night since you've got your big race the next morning, but maybe on Sunday we can get into some trouble."

Angela grimaced. "I've got a feeling after running more than sixty miles on Sunday morning the only thing I'm getting into that night is a hot bath."

"You're a little nuts, you realize that, right?" asked Lauren calmly. "And coming from me – the girl who's rocked climbed in Portugal, bungee jumped in New Zealand, and swam with sharks in Ecuador – that's saying a lot. Exactly how long is it supposed to take you to finish this race anyway?"

"If all goes according to plan, around eleven hours," replied Angela. "So with a five a.m. start that would have me finishing around five thirty p.m."

Lauren brightened. "Well, then. Plenty of time for you to take a shower, catch a quick nap, and then hit a few bars. Or," she conceded grudgingly when she glimpsed the scowl on Angela's face, "I could get some Chinese takeout and chill a couple of bottles of wine."

"Even better," piped up Julia, "I'll cook. You'll need to replenish about ten thousand calories after a run like that, so I'll have tons of carbs – lasagna, garlic bread, salad. And definitely something yummy for dessert!"

Angela smiled gratefully. "I don't want you going to any trouble, Jules. Chinese would be fine."

Julia waved a hand in dismissal. "It's no trouble at all. Besides, I don't have to cook tonight since the three of us are headed to the Giants game in a bit. And Nathan's brother got us club level seats, which means the food will be a bit more upscale."

Julia's new brother-in-law Jared was a professional baseball player for the Colorado Rockies, who were in town to play the San Francisco Giants. Angela had been more than a little speechless to learn her friend – who was far more interested in shopping, the theatre and yoga – was actually attending a sporting event.

Angela gave a dubious glance at Julia's floral print, multi-tiered sundress and cork heeled wedge sandals. "Are you, ah, wearing that to the game?"

Lauren hooted. "You should know by now, Angie, that this is Jules' idea of dressing down. Did you think she'd be wearing jeans and a T-shirt instead?"

Angela was saved from further comment by the honking of a horn outside, signaling the arrival of her taxi. She gave each of the twins a hug. "Gotta run. Well, not in these shoes, maybe, more like walking very, very carefully. Thanks, you guys, for getting me all girly."

Julia straightened the single shoulder strap of Angela's gown. "You know how much I love doing stuff like that. I had fun. And it was so worth it to see how gorgeous you look right now. I just wish you had a hot date so that all of this gorgeousness could be better appreciated."

Angela picked up her silver clutch and pale gray pashmina. "Forget about it, okay? It's just an office event, after all, and probably going to be boring as hell. I'd much rather be wearing jeans and flats right now and going to the baseball game with you guys instead. But I'd better dash now. Love you guys!"

Knowing that the twins would lock up after her – and that Julia at least would do some tidying up – Angela made her way carefully down the stairs and into the waiting taxi. She hadn't been fibbing just now when she'd told the twins that she would much rather be going to the baseball game instead of this party. Because she'd always been such a loner at the office, there were very few people she knew well enough to actually socialize with. Cara, of course, hadn't been invited – it was likely that just the older brokers and a few of the more successful younger ones plus management would be attending tonight. Angela just hoped that Felicity hadn't stuck her at a table with that jackass Jay Corcoran. There was *no* way she could sit through an entire meal having to listen to the sales manager spouting out company propaganda.

And thank God she wouldn't have to worry about running into Nick tonight. Not only did he hate these sort of office functions worse than she did, but he scarcely knew Stan Wagner, having only worked at the office for three months or so. And the only thing worse than seeing Nick tonight would be having to see him with a date clinging to his side. She shuddered as she exited the taxi, the smartly uniformed doorman ushering her inside the lobby of the luxuriously appointed Gregson hotel, as the image of Nick with a glamorous blonde or redhead came to mind. She might not be willing to concede to his terms again, but that didn't

mean she wasn't still horribly jealous of all the women he must
have fucked over the past four years. And she most certainly
wouldn't be able to handle seeing him up close and personal with
one.

Once inside the banquet room, she accepted a glass of
champagne from a passing waiter, her gaze swiftly taking in the
other guests already assembled. She was relieved not to see the
annoying Jay among them, at least not yet, and made her way
over to greet the guest of honor and his wife.

Stan, a slim, dapper man in his late seventies, gave her a flirty
grin as he pecked her on the cheek. "I almost didn't recognize
you, my dear, " he told her. "Quite a change from those very
businesslike suits you wear to the office. You look exquisite,
young lady, absolutely exquisite."

Smiling, Angela bent to press her cheek against Felicity's, the
older woman more than a foot shorter than she was. "Your
lovely wife is the one who's exquisite," teased Angela. "Thank
you both for inviting me tonight. It's truly an honor."

Felicity, her frosted blonde hair arranged in an elaborate twist,
and her dainty, petite figure clothed in a long cream chiffon skirt
and sequined hot pink jacket, beamed up at Angela. "Ah, but
Stanley is quite right. You're stunning, dear, just stunning. I'm
surprised your young man has let you out of his sight for this
long."

Angela was puzzled at her hostess' words. "What young man?
I'm here alone this evening."

Felicity looked confused. "Your date didn't make it? Why,
he just called me a few days ago to apologize and beg my
forgiveness for RSVP'ing so late. He said he hadn't been able to
confirm his plans before then and that you were too peeved at
him to call me yourself. I must say, Angela, he's quite a
charmer. And I'm dying to meet him. Stanley says he's caused
quite a stir around the office."

Angela shook her head, bemused. "Honestly, Felicity, I don't
know what's going on but - "

"Sorry I'm late, Angel. One more sin you'll have to forgive
me for. Ah, and this beautiful lady must be Mrs. Wagner. I have

to thank you once again for accepting my inexcusably late RSVP."

Angela stared in horror as Nick took Felicity's tiny hand and brought it to his lips. He was wearing a beautifully cut black tuxedo that had most certainly been custom made for him, and Felicity was staring up at him in stunned disbelief, yet another gullible victim of his charm.

Angela was still shell shocked as Nick shook hands with Stan, congratulating him on his retirement and thanking him profusely for inviting him to the party. And then, before she could utter a word of protest, he was grasping her by the arm and steering her away, grabbing two champagne flutes as he did so.

"Here, you look like you could use this. Not," he added with a chuckle, "to throw in my face, though. Drink up, Angel, and don't even think about making a scene. We both have to face most of these people on Monday morning, you know."

Not sure whether to scream, laugh hysterically, or throw a punch, she followed his advice and bolted the entire contents of the flute down at one time. Nick must have sensed the anger beginning to boil up inside of her, and wisely guided her to a somewhat secluded corner of the room. Only then did she lash out.

"What the hell are you doing here?" she hissed. "And what's this bullshit about being my – my *date*? My God, you've done some ballsy things before, Nick, but this one really wins the prize. How dare - "

He cut off the rest of her fiery diatribe by bending his head and kissing her – not one of his usual domineering kisses but a light, almost sweet brush of his lips against hers. She gazed up at him in bewilderment when he lifted his head.

"What – what was that all about?" she asked dazedly. "You – everyone just saw – they'll all be talking - "

Nick shrugged. "Good. Let them talk. I guarantee that by Monday morning it will be all over the office that I kissed you and that we're a couple. You got a problem with that, Angel?"

"No." She shook her head, then paused. "I don't know. Maybe. I mean – what? God, you're driving me nuts here, Nick. Why are you doing this?"

He didn't answer for long seconds, merely sliding his hand to the small of her back as he continued to guide her around the room. "I'm trying, Angel," he replied in a low voice. "Trying to – well, to compromise, I suppose. And I know how much it always bothered you before to have to keep our relationship a secret. This – tonight – is my way of showing you that's one of the ways I'm willing to give."

Her spine stiffened as she glared at him. "Except that you're *not* my date. You lied – blatantly – to poor Felicity. And apparently charmed the socks off of her in the process."

Nick grinned wickedly. "I heard through the office grapevine that you were invited tonight. And that you weren't bringing a date. And, no, I didn't wheedle that information out of Cara. The person I charmed it out of," he added with a mischievous smile, "was Stan's assistant. And since the Wagners belong to the Biltmore Club, I was able to – let's say, *obtain* – their phone number. Felicity was more than delighted to learn you were bringing a date after all."

She pursed her lips, wondering if she looked as pissed off as she felt. "You've really got a nerve, Nick, I'll hand you that. I've got half a mind to walk out of here right now."

He shrugged. "Fine with me. This hotel has an excellent restaurant where we'd have a lot more privacy and probably a much better meal than what we'll have here. I'm ready to go whenever you are."

Angela glared at him, resisting the urge to flip him off. "I didn't mean walk out of here with you."

Nick snickered, capturing her hand in his and drawing it to his lips. "Now, why would you do something like that, Angel? It's not polite to stand your date up."

She tried to tug her hand free. "Except you're really not my date, are you? And being polite to you is the last thing I care about."

He slid an arm around her waist, hugging her close against him as he nuzzled the side of her neck. "Was there a particular reason you chose this dress tonight? Feeling sentimental, perhaps?"

"Hardly," she scoffed, trying really, really hard to ignore how good he smelled and how tempting it would be to lean her head against his broad shoulder. "I didn't have time to go shopping and just pulled the first thing I saw out of my closet."

He brushed his lips against her temple. "You always were a really bad liar, Angel," he murmured in amusement. "You chose this dress because it held some incredible memories for you. Just as it does for me. Do you remember the limo ride up to Pete's house? Your pussy tasted ten times sweeter than the chocolate fondue he served for dessert."

"Jesus, Nick." She felt her cheeks flame in reaction. "For God's sake, keep your damned voice down."

He smiled wickedly, running his knuckles over her flushed cheek. "But as beautiful as you looked that night, you're even lovelier tonight, Angel. Normally I like your hair loose but fixed this way it really shows off your gorgeous face. Did you spend the whole afternoon at the salon?"

"No. My friend Julia – you must remember her, given that you tried to crash both her bachelorette party *and* her wedding – did my hair and makeup."

Nick took her lips in another soft kiss, leaving her breathless. "She did a good job," he told her huskily. "You're glowing, Angel. You looked beautiful at your friend's wedding but tonight – you're a siren. And I'm falling a little deeper under your spell with every minute."

She was saved from having to think of a reply – a very good thing, considering he'd just rendered her speechless – by the call to dinner. And throughout the meal, Nick continued to act the part of devoted date – showering her with attention; making sure her wine and water glasses were refilled; asking how she liked her food. He found little ways to touch her at frequent intervals – a hand on her arm, the brush of his lips against her temple, his thigh rubbing against hers beneath cover of the table. He even chatted pleasantly with the other guests at their table, suavely fending off questions about the nature of his relationship with Angela, and managing to steer the conversation back to more neutral territory when a question got too personal for his liking.

After dessert and coffee were served, he drew her out onto the dance floor, and she finally sighed in surrender as his arms closed about her. He'd rarely taken her out dancing when they had been together in the past, and she exulted in this rare pleasure.

"I see we fit together as well as ever, Angel," he murmured against her ear. "Though I would have never doubted that fact."

Angela lifted her head from his shoulder to give him a warning look. "I wouldn't push your luck, Nick. I'm still not sure I shouldn't be royally pissed off at you right now. And you haven't even considered Dwayne in all this."

"Ah, yes. The boyfriend," replied Nick lazily. "How is your young man anyway? More importantly, why isn't he here with you this evening?"

Angela considered lying, then thought better of it, knowing Nick could sniff out an untruth faster than a bloodhound. "Dwayne's in Europe right now, competing in a series of track meets. He'll be back in the States in a few weeks. And, well, we're not – seeing each other anymore. We're still very good friends but we decided that's all it will ever be between us."

Maddeningly, Nick didn't look the least bit surprised at her news. "Correction, Angel. *You* decided that's all it would be. I'm guessing good ole Dwayne would have gladly taken whatever scraps of attention you chose to throw his way."

She refused to admit that he was right. "It wasn't like that. Dwayne and I – it was never really more than friendship. We never even - "

"Fucked?" As usual, Nick never held back but at least he'd kept his voice pitched low. "Yeah, I figured that. He's a nice enough guy for a nerd, but there was no way he'd have been able to handle a woman like you, Angel. After all," he whispered, his teeth nipping at her earlobe, "it takes a man with certain talents to keep you satisfied. And I really doubt Dwayne would know how to - "

He yelped as she stomped on his instep with the stiletto heel of her shoe. "Don't you dare," she hissed. "Just – don't."

Nick laughed as he wrapped both arms around her waist, twirling her around the dance floor. "I knew he'd never been your lover," he told her in a hushed tone. "Because you'd never have responded to me the way you did at the wedding if he had. In fact, I'd wager a guess and say that you haven't had a lover in a very long time."

"Unlike you," she replied in a hollow voice. "And don't you dare try and bullshit me, Nick. There's no way I'll believe you've been a monk for the last few years."

"I haven't. At least not for four years. But would you believe me when I tell you there hasn't been anyone for almost two years now?" he asked quietly.

She hesitated, wanting with all her heart to take what he said as truth, but finding it hard to accept, given what she knew of his immense sexual appetites. "No, not really," she acknowledged.

"It's true," he assured her. "Part of it was because I'd been working so hard to prepare for changing firms. But most of it was because I just got tired of it all, of how empty I felt. Of how," he added in a husky voice, "I never came close to feeling what I did with you."

"Nick." Her voice was breathless, wispy, and she felt like swooning beneath his intense regard.

"Let's get out of here," he urged. "I want to be alone with you, Angel. Will you come with me?"

He took a step back and held out his hand. She hesitated, knowing that if she placed her hand in his she'd be falling back into more than just his arms. He would own her again, become the center of her universe, and she'd be risking far more than just her heart – her very sanity would be on the line as well.

Taking a deep breath, she placed her hand in his.

***

The elevator doors had barely closed behind them when Nick shoved her up against one wall, kissing her like a starving man. Angela groaned beneath the ferocious demand of his kiss, by the way his tongue plundered her mouth almost brutally. She slid her arms inside his unbuttoned tuxedo jacket, pulling him even closer against her as she clutched fistfuls of his dress shirt. He was already hard and ready, grinding the enormous swell of his erection against the silk of her gown, and she thought faintly that she could come very easily if he just kept that up a few more seconds.

She was barely aware when the elevator doors slid open and Nick guided her out, his arm wrapped around her waist as he walked her down a long, carpeted hallway. He stopped half a dozen times on their way, pushing her against the nearest wall or door as he kissed her again, each time a little more aggressively than the last. It was only when he paused to pull a card key from his pocket and open a door that she realized he was tugging her inside a hotel room. She'd just assumed they'd be leaving the hotel, to get his car or a cab, and then go – where? To her flat – the same flat where Lauren was bunking for the weekend? Surely not to Nick's place, especially since she still didn't even know where he lived.

But then none of those details mattered, that he'd evidently planned all of this out and had counted on seducing her tonight. Because all she wanted was to give in, to stop fighting this wild attraction that had never really died. She was finally being honest with herself – completely, totally honest – and admitting that she'd never stopped wanting him, that she'd only been fighting herself and not him these past months.

As Nick closed and locked the door behind them, she stood in the middle of the room, her arms crossed over her chest as she suppressed a shiver. But for once she didn't feel in the least bit cold; rather, an all too familiar heat was suffusing her body and the shiver was pure reaction, nothing else. Her eyes drifted shut as she felt him step up behind her, his broad, hard chest pressing against her back, while his long fingers trailed slowly, arousingly, up and down her bare arms.

"It's been so long, Angel," he whispered, his breath tickling her ear. "I wanted to take this slowly, to savor you, seduce you. But all I can think about right now is how hard I am, how much I need you. Can you feel how much I want you, Angel?"

She trembled as his arms wrapped around her waist and he pulled her even closer against him. The hard bulge of his cock rubbed suggestively between her buttocks, in the place he'd sworn never to take her because it would be too much. "Yes," she gasped unsteadily. "I can feel you, all of you. And I – I want you, too, need you just as much."

His hands began to search along the side of her dress. "As I recall," he murmured huskily, "this particular garment has a hidden zipper somewhere. Ah, there it is. Careful now, we don't want to tear this."

He unzipped the fragile silk easily, then helped her slide the garment off her body, leaving her clothed in just her lingerie and high heels. Nick turned her to face him, his big hands gripping her hips as he did so, and he looked his fill. His eyes grew darker, his skin ruddier, as he drank in the sight of her in a strapless bra of pale blue lace and a matching pair of panties.

He trailed a long finger over the exposed upper curves of her breasts, his breath starting to hitch a little faster as he observed the taut peaks of her nipples straining against the lacy bra. "Beautiful," he rasped. "Every bit as beautiful as I remembered. Still too thin but we'll get to work on that quickly enough." One of his hands slid around to squeeze her ass cheek, half-bared by the high cut of her underwear. "I should really be spanking you right now, for neglecting yourself that way, for not taking better care of this beautiful body. But not now. Right now all I want to do is this."

Angela cried out in surprise as he slipped his hand inside her panties, thrusting two fingers deep inside of her soaking wet slit before hooking them against the front of her pelvis. It took a ridiculously brief amount of time – half a dozen deep thrusts of his fingers, a few whisks of his thumb over her clit – for her to come.

"Ohh! Ohh!" she whimpered, her body bucking against his hand as the orgasm continued to ripple through her. It had been so long, she thought wildly, so very long since she'd felt this way. She'd never been tempted to make herself come, knowing it would be a poor, unsatisfying substitute for the real thing. The last time she'd felt this sort of bliss had been the night of her twenty third birthday, and her long starved body rejoiced at the pleasure that had been denied to her for so many months.

Nick slowly, carefully, withdrew his fingers from inside of her, deliberately licking the wetness off. "Even more delicious than I remember," he purred. "Now, get on the bed, Angel. And get naked. I can't wait any longer to have you."

She was too dazed to resist, and climbed onto the plush king sized bed as Nick undressed with uncharacteristic haste. She watched him with unabashed interest, her eyes starved for the sight of his powerfully muscled body, and especially the thick, heavy girth of his cock. She'd almost forgotten just how huge he was, how long and intimidating, and she shivered in anticipation, hoping that her out of practice body would still be able to accommodate him without too much difficulty.

And then Nick was splendidly, majestically nude, and he was kneeling in front of her, spreading her legs wide. Without another word, he took hold of that almost ruthless looking cock and began to slowly, inch by inch, guide it inside of her.

He was just about halfway in when his control snapped, and she cried out in alarm as he rammed himself the rest of the way in, buried inside of her now from tip to root. She froze in shock as her body struggled to accept him, her head thrashing against the pillow as she whimpered in distress.

"Shh. Easy, baby," he soothed. His hand stroked the side of her hip, gentling her, letting her get used to the unfamiliar feel of him filling her, stretching her. "It *has* been a long time, hasn't it? You feel tight as a virgin," he groaned. "And – Christ – I don't want to hurt you, Angel, but I need this more than I need to breathe right now."

She hooked an arm behind his head and pulled his mouth down to hers, a move she would likely never have dared to try before. "You won't hurt me," she urged. "And I need it as much as you do. I need – to be fucked."

Nick swore roughly as he pulled her legs up to wrap around his hips. "Then hold on tight, Angel, because that's exactly what you're going to get."

"Ah, God," she sobbed, her back arching off the mattress as he began to thrust powerfully, pounding that big, hard cock inside of her without mercy. And quickly, all too quickly, her body remembered him, opened for him, welcomed his fierce, primitive possession. Their arms and legs tangled together, their mouths fused tightly in a never-ending series of hungry, desperate kisses as they fucked like a pair of wild beasts. She came once, twice, was still shuddering in reaction as Nick, too, found his release. Never before could she remember him bellowing that loudly, his body shaking that hard as he emptied himself inside of her, filling her up with his cum until she could feel it trickling down the inside of her thighs. He collapsed on top of her, his body still twitching, as she struggled to breathe with his heavy weight crushing her into the mattress. Finally, he heard her gasping for air and hastily slid off of her, his arm draped limply across her stomach.

"Your hair's a mess," he mumbled against the side of her neck. "Sorry."

She laughed, the sound distinctly hoarse. "Like I really care. Besides, you prefer it loose, don't you?"

Nick pulled the remaining pins out of her hair, then spread the long raven strands out on the pillow. "You didn't cut it," he marveled. "In fact, it seems longer than ever."

She gave a small shrug. "I didn't pay much attention to my appearance these past few years, didn't always bother with things like haircuts. It just didn't seem important."

"I could tell," he replied quietly. "Looks to me like we'll need to start from scratch, Angel – putting that weight back on you, ditching those butt ugly pantsuits and shoes. Not to mention - "

"Hush." She placed two fingers over his lips and shook her head. "Not now. Please. I can't, Nick. I just can't deal with your rules and demands right now, okay? Just don't – spoil this."

"All right." He wrapped her in his arms and kissed her forehead. "And I know I need to back off on some of that stuff, know that I can't dictate to you the way I used to. Things need to be different. *I* need to be different."

Angela caressed the damp skin of his stomach, kissing a path across his chest. "Well, not with everything," she teased. "For example, I always liked the demands you made when we were in bed."

He snickered, giving her a light smack on her bare ass. "Good. Because I'm going to be very, very demanding tonight. Good thing I planned ahead and booked this room. I don't think I could have waited until we got to your place."

Angela's hand stilled as she fought off a sudden sense of unease. "That wouldn't have worked anyway. Lauren's crashing at my place this weekend." She took a deep breath before adding quietly, "We could have gone to your place instead, you know. After all, that's one of the ways you're going to need to compromise if we're going to make this work between us."

His body tensed up immediately, and she could feel him beginning to withdraw, both physically and emotionally. "Angel, don't. I agreed not to push you, so why don't you agree to return the favor?"

"Favor?" She sat up abruptly, easing herself away from him. "For God's sake, Nick, you've never even told me what city you live in, much less invited me to see your place. How is this relationship ever going to work if you can't do something as simple as that?"

He growled, pushing himself to a sitting position and reaching for her. "I'm trying, Angel," he bit out. "It's not easy for me, but I'm trying. But you're going to have to give me space, realize that it's going to be baby steps all along the way."

"Baby steps?" she repeated in disbelief. "Are you kidding me? If you're really serious about making this work, Nick, then you need to be taking leaps right now. Great, big flying leaps."

"That's not going to happen," he argued. "You're asking too much of me, Angel, more than I can give you right now."

Angela felt her heart begin to sink, along with all the hope she'd begun to feel this evening. She eased herself off the bed and began to gather up her clothes. "What I'm asking for, Nick," she corrected, "isn't anything out of the ordinary, isn't anything that every other normal couple doesn't accept automatically. But I'm beginning to see that you're still not ready to change. Worse, I'm doubting if you ever will be."

He bounded off the bed, splendidly nude, and she forced herself to avert her gaze while dressing hurriedly. If she kept looking at him, she'd be tempted to touch him again, and if she touched him she'd be back on that bed within seconds, with Nick buried inside of her.

"Where the hell do you think you're going?" he demanded. "Get back in that bed right now. I'm nowhere near done with you tonight."

"No." She shook her head as she zipped up her dress. "But I'd gladly go back with you to your place, spend as many hours there with you as you like. It's your choice, Nick. Either we continue this at your place or I leave right now. Alone."

His mouth tightened in mutinous anger. "Are you threatening me, Angel?"

"I'd prefer to think of it as an ultimatum," she corrected, buckling her sandals. "But whatever you want to call it, I'd say it's pretty obvious you aren't ready to do your part to make this work between us." She picked up her clutch and wrap, pausing with her hand on the doorknob. "You know where to find me when you finally decide you're ready."

And even as he began stalking towards her, she fled, heading for the elevator as quickly as possible before she lost her nerve and ran back in the opposite direction.

Chapter Twenty

"Jesus, Nick. Are you trying to kill yourself this morning? Or maybe avoid murdering someone else? Take it down a notch or two, man."

Isaac Ochoa had been Nick's personal trainer for more than a dozen years now, dating back to his days in pro football, and it had been a long time since he'd seen his client – and friend – work out with this much intensity. Isaac had arrived at the private gym around eight a.m. this morning, and from the looks of things Nick had already been hard at work for at least an hour. The trainer had watched Nick with mingled concern and awe as he put himself through a grueling workout, one that would have dropped any other man within the first twenty minutes or so – lifting weights, doing pull-ups, sit-ups, push-ups, back to the weights, then a round with kettle bells and medicine balls before heading to the punching bag. Nick, who was usually always controlled and deliberate about his workouts, was instead like a maniac today, unfocused and filled with raw power.

When Nick forced himself to do another fifty pull-ups, then dropped to the mat to start another series of push-ups, Isaac placed a restraining hand on his arm.

"Okay, that's enough, man. I don't know what the hell is bugging you this morning but you need to take a break. Even an ironman like you needs to back off once in a while. Here, drink this."

Nick scowled as Isaac handed him both a towel and a bottle of Gatorade. He reluctantly mopped up the sweat pouring off his face before twisting the bottle open and drinking it down thirstily. "I'm fine," he grit out between tightly clenched teeth. "And if you don't approve you can get the hell out. It's not like I need anyone telling me what to do around here."

"You're right," agreed Isaac calmly. "Frankly, sometimes I think you just keep me around because you think I need the paycheck. Which is totally inaccurate, by the way. I've got plenty of clients who actually need my help, not someone like you who probably knows more than I do about working out anyway. But today, right now, you do need to listen to my advice and finish this, Nick. Go grab a shower and some food and then put your feet up for the rest of the day. I know you won't listen to a word I say, but at least I'm covering my ass by suggesting it."

Nick shook his head. "No, you're right. As you can probably tell I needed to work some shit out. Life is – complicated at the moment."

"Hmm." Isaac was puzzled, because in all the years he'd known Nick he had rarely seen him stressed about much of anything. Nick simply didn't tolerate things like stress, and if something didn't sit well with him he merely removed it from his life. "Can't imagine what that would be. You're the most footloose guy I know – no obligations, no commitments. So it's either work or, well, I don't know what else it could be."

Nick finished off the bottle of Gatorade and tossed it into a nearby recycling bin. "It's a woman," he acknowledged reluctantly. At the look of shock on Isaac's face, he shrugged. "Yeah, I know. I'm still in disbelief about it myself. But, damn, this one – she's wriggled her way under my skin, got inside my head. Not to mention constantly finding ways to really, really piss me off. And I'm afraid I could work out for another six hours and still not get her out of my head today."

Isaac shook his head in amazement. "I've known you a long time, man, and have *never* seen you rattled over a woman. So this one must be something special, huh?"

Nick hesitated for long seconds before giving a reluctant nod. "Yeah, apparently so. I can't think of any other logical explanation for why I'm putting up with this kind of shit at my age. Hey, I'd better get going. Thanks, dude. For stopping me from killing myself today. Or, worse, passing out. My reputation would have never been the same if anyone had seen that happen."

Isaac grinned and gave his longtime friend a fist bump. "So am I ever going to meet this chick?"

Nick smiled wryly. "Yeah, one of these days I'll bring her

around. That is, if she's still speaking to me after the – ah, disagreement we had last night. I've got a feeling I have some major kissing up to do this weekend."

"Now *that* I'd pay *you* good money to see."

Nick was still chuckling to himself as he made the short drive from his gym across the bridge to Sausalito. The weather was foggy and cool this morning, so typical for summer in San Francisco, but he knew that by early afternoon the sun would be out and his incredible view of the bay from his back deck would be as clear as ever. Though given the condition he was in right now, he might very well be taking a nap by then.

He'd been *furious* after Angela had stormed out of that hotel room late last night, and had pulled his clothes on hurriedly, determined to chase after her and drag her back with him. But as he was lacing up his shoes, he thought better of the idea, especially since he would likely only make things worse given the black mood he was in. Both of them needed to calm the hell down and then talk things out when they were in a more rational frame of mind. And, admittedly, trying to have a serious conversation right after a round of especially frantic sex was not the best timing in the world.

He pulled the Ferrari inside his garage before entering the kitchen through the side door. He started a fresh pot of coffee brewing before heading for the shower, badly needing both the caffeine and the pounding of the hot water to revive him this morning. After Angela had ditched him last night, he had left shortly afterwards, not caring that the four hundred dollars he'd casually dropped on the hotel room would be wasted. But sleep had evaded him once he reached home, and he'd had a restless night, tossing and turning, and finally giving up on the idea altogether around five a.m. It was then he'd headed to the gym, arriving when it opened at six, and putting himself through the workout from hell. If Isaac hadn't intervened, he'd probably still be there, punishing his body until he finally dropped from exhaustion.

He fixed himself breakfast, his culinary skills fairly basic but adequate, and ones that had been learned out of necessity during the summers he'd spent with his mother. Back then, after a night of partying, his mother and her guests would sleep until the noon hour or later, and Nick had realized early on that if he wanted to eat before then he'd have to figure out a way to feed himself.

And, oddly enough, it was his mother that he thought about after finishing his breakfast. He was sitting out on the deck that was still encased in fog, sipping what was probably his fifth cup of coffee that morning in an attempt to keep himself awake. He asked himself what the hell he thought he was doing, even as he scrolled through the list of contacts on his phone. He had no idea where his mother was at this particular moment, what time zone or part of the world she was in, and only hoped it wasn't the middle of the night somewhere as he placed the call.

He was relieved when Sheena answered on the third ring, and more so when she sounded wide awake. She was also positively joyous to receive such an unexpected call from her only child.

"Nicky, honey, this is such a nice surprise!" she gushed. "Is everything okay? I mean, I hear from you so seldom these days that I can't help but worry that there's a bad reason for your call."

He fought off the guilt he felt at her words, knowing full well that he neglected his mother in spite of what he considered very good reasons for doing so. "There's nothing wrong, Mom," he assured her. "I just – well, need a bit of advice is all. Female advice. And you're the ideal person to give it to me."

"Well, of course, honey," Sheena replied. "I know I haven't been the most ideal mother in the world to you, but I hope you know I'm always, always here for you, Nicky. You're the most independent man I've ever met, and you'd rather cut off your arm than ever admit you need help, but you can always call me if you ever need anything. So, now, what's this advice you need?"

Haltingly, hesitantly, Nick began to tell his mother about Angela – about their relationship four years ago, how he'd broken things off when she'd grown too close, and how they were working together again now. He left out some of the more intimate details, of course – his mother did *not* need to know *that* much about his sex life, after all. But when he told her that he truly cared for Angela, wanted her back, but was obviously going about it the wrong way, Sheena interrupted him.

"Okay, honey, I'm getting the picture here," his mother told him. "You had a relationship with this girl four years ago. She was young, naïve, and let you call all the shots. Then you broke up with her – and probably broke her heart in the process. Now you've met up again and you've decided to take up where you left off. Except from what I know of you, Nicky, you probably still want everything your own way and just assume this girl is still so crazy about you that she'll just take whatever you give her. Am I still on track here so far?"

"More or less," he grumbled. "But I've told her I'm willing to make some compromises, that I know everything can't be all my way. It's just – well, I don't think things are progressing along quickly enough for her liking and she's asking for more than I can give her right now."

Reluctantly, he told his mother about last night's blow-up – again leaving out the part about the really hot sex – and how he feared Angela wasn't going to give in this time, that *he* was going to have to make the next move.

"You're damned right you are, Nicky," Sheena replied firmly. "And it's going to have to be a major move when you do. If you care about this girl as you claim to, then it can't be like it was with all the other women you've had in your life. And unfortunately for you, as controlling as I know you are, that means you're going to have to do a lot more compromising that you think. Starting with inviting this girl – Angela, right? – over to your hideaway there. Dinner, I think, and then spending the night."

Nick closed his eyes, massaging the back of his neck which felt like a mass of bunched nerves. "That's not as easy as you think it is, Mom."

"Oh, baloney," exclaimed Sheena. "Now, I know exactly why you never invite anyone over there, Nicky, why you like your damned solitude so much. I'm well aware of how much you hated the complete lack of privacy you had growing up with me as your mother. I'm a social butterfly, need to have tons of people around me all the time, while you're just the opposite. But if you want to have a real relationship with your Angela, you're going to have to open up to her, share your life with her.

And inviting her to see your house is the first step."

"Fine." He shook his head in frustration, not in the least surprised that his mother would be taking Angela's side in this, even though the two women had never met. "I'll invite her over. I'll call her up tomorrow, maybe even go see her in person, and ask her to come over."

"There you go again, Nicky. Putting things off. Why not just call her up now, have her come over tonight?"

"No." He didn't want to admit to his mother that he needed some time to emotionally prepare himself for something like this. "That is, I had a lousy night's sleep, can barely keep my eyes open right now. I'd be rotten company for anyone today, much less a woman I'm trying to appease. Besides, she's probably too pissed off at me right now to agree. Best to let her simmer down another day."

"Fine." Sheena heaved a sigh. "But don't put it off another day, Nicky. And don't let this girl slip away. Because if you're not careful, if you don't start changing your ways, I'm sorry to say you're going to wind up a bitter old man like your father. Oh, I know he's on marriage number three, that he's not a bachelor like you are. But trust me on this – no matter how many wives your father might have, he's always going to be alone. Because he'll never let anyone get close enough to him to make a difference. So please promise me that you won't let yourself turn into your father, Nicky. That would be a terrible, tragic thing to let happen."

Nick was touched by his mother's passionate plea, and he realized that she was right – he could very easily become as bitter and distant as his father if he didn't do something about it soon. "I promise," he told her quietly. "And I also promise to keep in touch more often, Mom. Because you're right. My summers with you might have been completely unorthodox but I never doubted that you loved me. I've been a lousy son to you all these years, but I can try to work on that, too."

Sheena started weeping after that, and Nick silently cursed himself for saying such sappy stuff to his admittedly dramatic mother. He tactfully changed the subject, inquiring where in the world she was at the moment, and then breathing a sigh of relief as Sheena began to prattle on cheerfully about how much fun she was having this summer in the Florida Keys. He ended the call a few minutes later, but not before Sheena got in the last word.

"I've always loved you more than anyone else in the whole world, Nicky," she told him. "I know I could have been a better mother, a *different* mother, but I doubt I could have loved you more than I do. Now, you do what your mother tells you for once and do the right thing for your Angela. And don't wait so long in between phone calls next time, hmm?"

Nick was rather appalled to feel the shimmer of tears at the back of his eyes as he hung up, and scowled as he set his phone back down. Reluctantly, he figured he'd better straighten his place up a little – and make a trip to the grocery store – since it looked as though he was actually going to have a guest here tomorrow evening.

And then, as he stood to go back inside, the sun finally began to break through the fog.

***

It was pitch dark outside, the streets quiet and deserted, when Angela pulled her car out of the garage very early on Sunday morning. With a five a.m. race start, she was allotting herself plenty of time to drive to the staging area in the Marin Headlands, park, check in, and warm up a bit. She hated getting to a race at the last minute, even if it meant rising at the unholy hour of three a.m. to get there.

It was another foggy morning and she cranked the heater up a little higher as she drove towards the Golden Gate Bridge. Lauren had still been fast asleep when she'd left a few minutes ago, snoring softly as she'd burrowed deeper into the mattress of the futon. And Angela had thanked her lucky stars that Lauren had been way too sleepy on Friday night to quiz her about the retirement party. By the time she'd arrived home from the Gregson Hotel around midnight, Lauren had already been curled up on her pillow and yawning broadly, not even noticing the way Angela's hair had been falling in tangled strands down her back.

Or how her makeup was all smudged. Or, most important of all, how badly her legs had been shaking after the totally unexpected encounter with Nick.

She'd slept poorly Friday night – little wonder considering everything that had happened – but had managed to pull herself together enough by Saturday morning so that Lauren hadn't guessed something was off. At least not right away. But as the day wore on, and more and more memories of Friday night had continued to haunt her, it had become increasingly difficult to pretend that nothing was wrong. And after the first three tries, Lauren had stopped believing Angela's excuse that she was just nervous about the race on Sunday.

"Nice try, Angie, but I'm not buying it," her friend had insisted. *"I've seen you right before much bigger sporting events than this – when our senior year team was playing for the conference soccer title, before two of your NCAA volleyball championships, when you were waiting to hear if you got chosen for the Olympic team. You had ice in your veins every single time, never let your nerves rattle you even once. So while you might be a little worried about this race – hell, I'm worried about your sanity for even thinking about doing it – that's not what's bothering you right now. So fess up."*

Angela had considered fobbing Lauren off with another lie, but had just sighed and told her the truth. At least, some of it. She still wasn't prepared to reveal Nick's identity, fearful that Lauren would lose no time in figuring out how to locate him and give him a piece of her mind – not to mention the tip of her boot.

"It was – him. You know who I mean. After all, you've seen him twice now, haven't you?"

Lauren had picked up her mug of coffee – they'd been having a late brunch at a café not far from the flat – and regarded Angela thoughtfully. "Ah, so the lying has finally stopped, has it? Good, because you're without a doubt the shittiest liar I've ever known."

"Yeah, that's what he tells me, too," Angela had sighed. "So, the night of Julia's party – you called it right. He is back in my life, though not like it was before. He – well, he's working at my

firm now, moved over there in April. And he's been making it pretty clear since then that he wants me back."

"Not a shocker. What would shock me – no, make that infuriate me – would be to learn that you're his pet again, obeying his orders like he's some fucking king or something. After all the times I nursed you through hangovers, Angie, listened to you wail and held your head while you puked – I will kick your ass all the way down to the next county if you've gone back to him that way." Lauren's voice had quivered with barely repressed rage.

Angela had shaken her head. "No. Not like that. Never again like that, with him or anyone. He swears it will be different this time, that he's willing to compromise. But I'm not sure I can really believe what he says."

Lauren hadn't replied for more than a minute, taking a long, slow chew of her blueberry muffin and calling the waitress over for more coffee. When she finally spoke, she was almost unnaturally calm. "Have you fucked him again?"

Angela had stifled a chuckle, thinking how much alike Lauren and Nick were in certain ways. Neither of them believed in beating around the bush when it came to getting information. "I could try and lie to you, but I won't. Yes, I went to bed with him last night. He, ah, got himself invited to the party, unknown to me, and, well – he looks extremely hot in a tux. And it's been a really, really long time since I've had any and champagne always loosens my inhibitions and – well, you get the picture."

"Yeah, I think I do." Lauren had heaved a sigh. "So this guy – Mr. Whatisname – he's your big weakness. I get that. I also get that you've had a longer dry spell than the Sahara Desert. But, Jesus, Angie – what the hell were you thinking of? More importantly, what happens from here?"

Angela had blown out a tense breath. "Hell if I know. I walked out on him afterwards, Lauren. He'd booked a room at the hotel, planned on me staying overnight with him. But when I happened to bring up the topic of maybe going to his place instead, he froze up like a clam. So I left a gorgeous, stark naked and really horny guy in a lux hotel room and got a cab back here. Am I an idiot or what?"

"No." Lauren had been grinning. "You're brilliant. Because that's exactly the sort of thing I would have done under the circumstances, and of course I'm the smartest person I know. So, good for you, Angie. Not," she'd added sternly, "that I'm condoning what you did. In fact, I ought to be shaking some sense into you right this very second. But if you are going to get involved with this clown again, then at least stand your ground and make him follow your orders for a change. At the very least, take turns ordering each other around. Starting with introducing him to your very best friends in the whole world. Knowing Julia she'll make enough food tomorrow night to feed three city blocks, so invite your mystery man over to join us. I'll even promise to leave my knife behind at your place."

Angela smiled now as she recalled that conversation, and at how relieved she'd felt to get it all out in the open. She'd balked at giving Lauren any more information, however, begging for her friend's understanding for a just a little while longer. She hadn't known when Nick would try to contact her again – or if she'd pushed him too far this time and he'd decided she wasn't worth the trouble. But when Saturday had come and gone with no word from him, she began to worry that she'd ruined it all and that he wouldn't be calling or seeing her again. And that was when the doubts had started creeping in again, the thought that maybe she was being too demanding, asking for too much too soon, and that she really ought to let Nick dictate the pace of their newfound relationship. She'd gone back and forth in her head on the matter so many times last night that sleep hadn't come easily, and she'd unfortunately be starting off this morning's race with a rather bad case of sleep deprivation.

She flipped around through several different radio stations during the drive, searching for some music to help relax and calm her mind. She finally settled on an alternative rock station, listening to the final few notes of an old Green Day song that she'd always liked. But when the next song came on, her finger froze over the pre-set buttons, knowing she should quickly change stations but unable to resist listening to Christina Perri's haunting ballad *Jar of Hearts.*

This had been another of those songs she'd played constantly on her iPod following the breakup with Nick. It had suited her mood back then perfectly, the lyrics about a former lover who was going to catch an cold because of the ice inside his soul. But now the lyrics took on something of a different meaning – especially the ones about the girl who'd been living half a life, the one who was no longer anyone's ghost, but also the one whose lover now wanted her back. And as she continued to listen to the song, unable to turn it off, her resolve returned even stronger – the resolve that she wouldn't fall back under Nick's control, that she was stronger now, and was determined to never return to that ghostlike state she'd existed in for far too long.

It was still dark when the race began at five a.m., and nearly all of the five hundred runners were wearing headlamps and some sort of reflective gear. Angela had figured that she would ditch both after completing the first lap of the course. Each lap of the rugged, rocky terrain was a little less than ten and a half miles, allowing the runners to pass by the main staging area at the end of each lap. This was where Lauren would be meeting up with her – in theory sometime around the end of lap number three, provided Lauren got up in time and didn't get lost on the drive over. Angela had tried to give her directions but Lauren had stubbornly insisted she'd find her way over and rarely paid attention to maps anyway.

She felt strong and focused during the first lap, especially after the sun came up. The Marin Headlands were still her very favorite place to run, even if today the trails were more crowded than usual with so many race participants. But the crowd began to thin out noticeably midway through her second lap, and she would go for half a mile or more at a time without seeing anyone else. She paid close attention to her intake of both fluids and food, even though her stomach rebelled at the thought of eating very much during an endurance event like this one. She forced herself to eat a little, however – a handful of pretzels, a couple of chunks of watermelon - especially since her lack of sleep the past two nights began to tell on her much earlier than she'd feared. Twice she lost her footing and wobbled precariously, catching herself just in time before doing a face plant on the trail.

The weather, too, was turning out to be quite a bit warmer than she'd hoped for, especially since the previous day it had been cool and foggy.   Her stomach began to cramp up as she completed the second lap, but after she drank two cups of the electrolyte beverage they offered at the aid station she started to feel a little better.   And of course the cheers and encouragement of the volunteers and other runners helped boost her spirits, and she began the third lap with a renewed burst of energy.   She knew Lauren would be there at the end of this next lap, and that her friend would certainly think of something motivational to call out as she ran past.

But the third lap didn't prove quite as easy as the first two. Two miles in Angela began to struggle with both nausea and dizziness, and had to take walk breaks several times.   The hot sun was beating down on her and her legs began to feel wobbly.   She was determined to see this through, to finish this race that she'd trained so hard for, but her body was definitely having other ideas.   She forced herself to keep moving, to jog for a bit longer each time, and remain focused on her goals.   She blamed her lack of energy and focus on missing out on her sleep the past couple of nights, which in itself was a direct result of being upset about what had happened with Nick.

And it only took the most fleeting thought of him to distract her further.   As she struggled along the trail, images of Nick began to crowd her mind – of how charming he'd been at the party on Friday; how wonderful it had felt to dance with him and be held close against his big body; the sensual pleasure of his possession that she'd known once again in that hotel room; the hope that had filled her heart that this time it could really work between them, could really turn into something meaningful and lasting.

But then other, less pleasant images of him took over – of the night he'd broken up with her four years ago, forcing her out of his car and his life; of the smug look of satisfaction on his handsome face after he'd kissed her at Julia's wedding, confident that he now had her exactly where he wanted her and that she would fly back into his arms willingly; and the taut anger she'd been met with after issuing her ultimatum on Friday.

She was confused, uncertain, both about Nick's true feelings for her and what her next steps should be in whatever sort of relationship they were attempting to form. Sweat was pouring down her forehead and into her eyes, making them burn, and she cursed the heavy length of her braid that felt like it weighed fifty pounds today. Something wasn't agreeing with her stomach – perhaps the sugary electrolyte drink that she'd been guzzling down thirstily at each aid station – and she fought the urge to retch with each step she took. If she could just get through this third lap – the halfway point of the race – she would sit and rest at the staging area for a few minutes, regain her bearings, and then hopefully continue on with renewed strength.

But barely a mile from the end of the lap, a wave of dizziness caused her to lose her balance, catching the toe of her shoe on a rock and falling hard onto the rocky trail. And as the side of her head made contact with the unforgiving terrain, she slid into total darkness.

***

Nick had made it his business soon after joining Morton Sterling to learn the address of Angela's new home. That it had been obtained dishonestly – by telling that diehard little romantic Cara that he wanted to send Angela flowers – hadn't bothered him in the least. But now, as he parked his SUV down the street from her building, he felt renewed guilt at how easily he'd duped the naïve little admin assistant. He just hoped that Cara had a fiercely protective father or older brother looking out for her, because her gullibility would certainly make her an easy target for a guy looking to score.

As he climbed the outer stairs to the flat, Nick thought that Angela had definitely traded up in the world by moving to this neighborhood. It was a much nicer and more desirable area from where she'd lived four years ago, and he assumed her flat was a hell of a lot bigger than her old studio apartment.

He'd thought about calling her first – hell, he'd almost dialed her number a dozen different times yesterday – but figured the element of surprise would be on his side under the circumstances. If he had to strong arm her into his car and over to his house, he'd do exactly that. This wasn't going to be easy for him, but he was determined to prove his willingness to change for her – for *them*. He took a deep breath and rang the doorbell.

Long seconds passed without an answer, and he wondered grimly if she was out on one of those ridiculously long runs she apparently did on a regular basis. He was about to ring the bell again when the door to the landing opened and he found himself looking down at the petite, tawny haired woman that he recognized from the night at Orphus – the one who reportedly carried a switchblade on her person at all times. Nick's spine stiffened, and all of his defenses rose up at once as he and Lauren McKinnon stared at each other as though they were mortal enemies.   And even though it was absurd to feel even the slightest bit unsettled about a woman who was nearly a foot and a half shorter than he was, Nick began to understand what Dwayne had meant about Lauren being kind of scary.   Because the look in her green eyes told him very clearly that she knew exactly who he was, and that he was going to have an awful lot to answer for.

"So, we finally meet," drawled Lauren, leaning casually against the door frame. "Except I think you might have a slight advantage over me – Mr. I Don't Have a Name."

Nick grinned in spite of himself, realizing that Lauren's laidback, seemingly casual attitude was anything but and he looked over her curvy, petite figure assessingly, trying to figure out where she might be carrying the knife given how tight her jeans were. "Based on the stories Angela has told me about you – *Lauren* – I'm amazed you haven't managed to pry that information out of her by now."

"Humph." Lauren made a sound of disgust. "That Angie can be revoltingly stubborn at times.   Even drunk off her ass she didn't cave in.   So since I assume you came here looking for her, the price of entry involves information."

Nick held out his hand. "I'm Nick.   Nick Manning.   A pleasure to finally meet you, Lauren."

She snorted. "You'll probably be taking those words back

once I'm finished with you. But come on in. Angie's flat is the upstairs one."

Nick followed Lauren up the staircase, trying not to stare at her ass while still searching for any potential hiding places for that knife. He'd just stepped inside the flat, heard the door shut behind him, and then somehow he found himself on the floor, sprawled on his back and staring up at a very smug looking Lauren.

"It's the big ones like you that never see that little trick coming," she bragged. "And that particular trick never gets old."

Nick glared at her darkly as he got to his feet, refusing to give her the satisfaction of rubbing his sore posterior. "Angela told me you're some kind of martial arts fanatic. What the hell was that – judo? Kung Fu?"

"Nah. That was just good old dirty street fighting. And nothing less than you deserve for the shitty way you've treated Angie over the years. You're lucky I didn't go for the roundhouse kick. I've knocked men out with that one a few times."

He crossed his arms, leaning against the wall as he watched her with renewed concern. "And you're lucky nobody's spanked your ass in return. Or maybe they have. You like that kind of stuff, honey?"

She winked at him suggestively. "Well, now, that's getting a little too personal. Especially since we've just met. Generally speaking, though, I usually prefer to be the one doling out the punishments."

"Yeah, why is it that doesn't surprise me in the least?" asked Nick caustically. "Now, am I permitted to speak to Angela or are you going to make me jump through hoops first?"

Lauren plopped herself onto a chair. "Angie doesn't need my permission to speak to anyone. Unlike you, Mr. Manning, I don't impose rules on her. But she actually doesn't happen to be home at the moment, I'm afraid."

He glared down at her darkly. "Okay. So you want me to play twenty questions, is that it? Where is Angela and when is she expected back?"

"Well, that depends," replied Lauren in a deceptively calm

voice.

When she didn't elaborate further, Nick's glare turned to a scowl. "All right, I'll bite. What does it depend on – *exactly?*"

She shook her head. "Uh, uh. That domineering thing doesn't work on me, Nick. Never has, never will. So I suggest you ask your questions *nicely* if you want answers."

"You know, *Lauren*, I've known you exactly three minutes and you're already the biggest pain in the ass I've ever met. But I sense you can play this game as well as I can so I'll ask again – *nicely* this time. Where is Angela and when is she going to be back?" Nick bit out.

"Why do you want to know?" inquired Lauren innocently. "You see, Angie hasn't always made the best choices where you're concerned so I'm afraid you're going to have to go through me to get to her. And unless you can convince me that your – let's call them intentions – are above board, you can go jump in the bay. So, why exactly are you here right now, Nick?"

"None of your business," he growled. "Hey, babe, I get that you're protective of your friend. That's admirable, especially considering how shitty her family has treated her over the years. But Angela's a big girl now and she doesn't need her little friend butting into her life."

Once again the aggravating little witch caught him completely off guard, though this time it wasn't with one of her dirty fighting tricks. In fact, she remained seated and he was the one jumping out of the way as a wicked looked knife sailed with precision through the air, imbedding itself into the wall about three inches from his head.

"What the fuck?" he yelled. "I swear to Christ you are insane. Totally, over the top, fucking insane."

Lauren stuck her tongue out at him as she very calmly sauntered over and pulled the blade out of the wall, sticking it back inside her cowboy boot where she'd evidently been hiding it. "I've been called worse things," she replied. "But the one thing you do *not* call me is babe. Got it, big guy? And calling me Angie's little friend is pushing it as well. So, now that we're square on all that, let me get a few things off my chest. And then, based on your answers, I might just tell you when Angie's due back."

Nick's gaze dropped automatically to Lauren's chest, which was very impressively showcased in a snug fitting cropped T-shirt, and forced himself not to smirk, well aware that she could pull that nasty looking knife out in the blink of an eye. "Fine," he muttered tersely. "Say what you have to. But I've got a pretty good idea of what you're going to get off your chest. Unfortunately, it's not that shirt that's doing a piss poor job of - yeah, never mind," he added after spying the murderous look in her eyes.

"Hah, hah. Why do you men always think that dirty talk turns a woman on? Some of the bullshit my brother-in-law spouts – and my sister falls for it every single time." Lauren shook her head. "So, have a seat, Nick. Way past time for you and I to get acquainted, don't you think?"

He sat down on the futon, careful to keep his distance from Lauren. "I suppose," he answered grudgingly.

"Relax." Lauren waved a hand in dismissal. "I'm not going to start asking you a bunch of personal questions. Especially since Angela herself doesn't seem to know a whole lot about you. I think she'd be pretty ticked off at me if I managed to pry facts out of you that are still deep, dark secrets to her. The only thing I'm really interested in finding out about you is this – what the hell are your intentions towards her this time around? Because you just about destroyed her during the last go round, and I'll tell you now – if you screw around with her like you did the last time I'll bury that knife of mine somewhere besides the wall. Like your chest cavity. Or your left testicle."

Nick suppressed a shudder, and bit down on the inside of his mouth to keep himself from delivering a scathing retort, especially since he had no desire to serve as Lauren's target practice again today. "My intentions, as you call them," he began tersely, "are between Angela and myself. But they are – let's call them *honorable* – this time around. I know I hurt her badly four years ago."

"Do you?" asked Lauren somberly. "I'm really not sure you know just how badly, Nick. Obviously bad enough to make her stop eating, to lose so much weight that my sister and I actually discussed kidnapping her and forcing her to enter a clinic for those kinds of disorders. But we realized that she wasn't actually anorexic, that the reason she didn't eat was because she'd just stopped caring. About food, about herself, about living."

He nodded. "The first time I saw her again, back in April – I was shocked. She looked like a completely different person. And her hands – they were so cold, like she was frozen from the inside out."

"That's because she was. Emotionally, at least. She shut everything down inside, cut off her feelings, and just went through life like some sort of ghost all the time. Even drinking didn't help, because Angie's one of those people who just gets quieter and more depressed the more she drinks."

Nick glared at Lauren. "And I've got little doubt after some of the wild stories I've heard that you encouraged her to drink. Angela's got a problem with the booze, you know, she likes it a little too much. And you sure as hell didn't do her any favors by egging her on."

Lauren's green eyes were furious. "Fuck off," she spat. "You've got no idea what went on these last four years, no idea at all. For example, after Angie saw you kissing one of your new sluts outside your office building she went on a total bender. She drunk dialed me, left me some sort of garbled message, and I had to force her landlord to let me in her apartment. The place was a total shit hole, she hadn't eaten or bathed or gotten out of bed in three days, and she'd gone through at least ten bottles of booze already. If I hadn't found her when I did, she might have died of alcohol poisoning. So if you're looking for someone to blame for her drinking problem, asshole, you might want to start with yourself."

It wasn't often that Nick found himself rendered speechless, but he could only stare at Lauren in horror after her outburst. He'd had no idea that Angela had seen him with one of the women he'd dated casually after their break-up – *dated*, not fucked – and that she had taken it quite so hard. He shoved a hand carelessly through his hair, the information he'd just learned too upsetting to deal with properly right now.

"What else?" he asked quietly. "What else happened to her after that?"

Lauren shrugged. "You must know some of it. She left your old firm, even though she'd worked like a slave for over a year to get as far as she did. But she couldn't handle the thought of seeing you again with another woman, and didn't trust herself enough not to run into your office and beg you to take her back. So she split and started over again, working for that nasty old woman who called her names and screamed at her all day long. And Angie took it, she just took whatever that bitch dished out, because she didn't care anymore. When you left her, something inside of her broke and even after four years I can't really say for certain that she's completely healed up. She's better, that's for sure, and thank God she's put some weight back on. But deep down there's still a part of her that's really messed up, and I've finally come to terms with the fact that you're the only one who can fix her for good."

Nick's mouth quirked up at one corner at this reluctant admission from Lauren. "And I'll bet it just about killed you to admit that," he taunted.

"More than you'll ever know," she returned sharply. "But it is what it is, you know? Angie's a smart girl, always got straight A's in school, always aced exams, got into Stanford and graduated top of her class. But she hasn't always been smart about other things – namely, some of the choices she's made in her life. And getting involved with you was probably the worst decision she's ever made. However, it's done now and there's no going back. You're the one for her, and as much as I'd love that to not be the case, it's a fact."

"What about Dwayne?" asked Nick. "Did you approve of him?"

Lauren scoffed. "You're joking, right? I mean, when Angie told us she was finally dating someone after so long, Julia and I were ecstatic. And then when she told us who he was, I seriously thought she was fucking with me, pulling a practical joke the way she used to back in high school. You know what Dwayne's nickname was back then – a nickname I gave him, by the way?"

"No idea, but I'm guessing it wasn't a flattering one."

She snickered. "It was Dwayne the Dweeb. He was tall, skinny, awkward as hell. He wore these big, thick glasses, his jeans were always about three inches too short, and I swear he bumped into every wall and door he came near. And when Angela told us he was the new guy she was seeing, all I could think about was the time Dwayne tripped over his own feet in chemistry class. He knocked over half a dozen beakers, and then cut his hand on the broken glass."

Nick couldn't help but smile at the image Lauren created. "Well, it seemed that he grew out of the awkward stage eventually. At least the one time I met him in the office he wasn't tripping over anything. And even though he seemed like a nice enough guy, I hated him a little, too. Because he'd actually made Angela smile for a change, something I hadn't been able to do for two months."

Lauren nodded. "I admit when I saw the two of them together a few months ago that she seemed happier than she had for a real long time. But I also knew it wouldn't last. There was zero chemistry there, especially on Angie's part, and, well, once a dweeb always a dweeb. But you're avoiding the real subject, Nick. I'm guessing you're good at that sort of thing."

His gaze narrowed in annoyance at her persistence. "What else do you want to know before you tell me exactly where Angela is?"

"What I want," Lauren told him softly, "is your guarantee that this time around things will be different with Angie. That you open up more, agree to meet her friends and family, and treat her right. That you let her spend the goddamned night at your place once in a while. Because I know who you are now, know where to find you, and if you break her heart again I'll break your nose. For starters."

Before he'd met the fiery hellcat a few minutes ago, Nick would have laughed scornfully at the idea that any woman – much less one of her petite stature – could have inflicted anything more serious than a scratch on a man of his height and bulk. But having been on the receiving end – twice, now – of Lauren's anger, he kept his mouth shut and merely nodded in agreement.

"I won't break her heart," he assured her soberly. "I'm not saying any of this is going to be easy for me, but I'm willing to try. Because – shit, I'm really not good at this sappy stuff – I care about Angela a lot. And if I knew what it felt like to be in love with a woman, I think maybe – well, I think that could be what I'm feeling."

Lauren grinned broadly. "Okay. You've convinced me. For now, at least. But mark my words, Manning, I'll be keeping a very close eye on you."

Nick checked his watch none too patiently. "If I've finally managed to reassure you sufficiently, do you mind telling me when Angela's due back?"

"Oh, not for hours and hours," replied Lauren airily. "Didn't she tell you? She's running some kind of crazy person race today, one that involves doing ten mile loops on this rocky, dusty trail. She won't be finished until dinnertime at the earliest."

"Dinnertime? But it's barely ten in the morning," Nick replied incredulously. "How long is this race anyway?"

Lauren shrugged. "A hundred kilometers. I forget what she said that was in miles. Regular math was never even my thing much less all that metric system stuff."

"Sixty miles, give or take." Nick shook his head. "And it's supposed to get into the eighties everywhere today. She is crazy, isn't she? So exactly where is this race taking place?"

"Oh, didn't I mention?" asked Lauren innocently. "Hmm, well, I was planning on driving over there in a few minutes, catch her at the end of her third lap and throw some water on her, whatever the hell you're expected to do. I suppose, if you ask very nicely, that you could come along for the drive."

Nick glared at Lauren with ill-concealed impatience. "You're suggesting we, ah, go together? Fine, but I'll drive. We can take my car."

Lauren shook her head. "Uh, uh. No way. If you want to come along, then I'm doing the driving. And since I'm the only one of us with directions, I'd say you don't have much choice in the matter."

***

Half an hour later, Nick was thanking his lucky stars that he'd had such a light breakfast this morning. Otherwise, given Lauren McKinnon's very questionable driving abilities, he'd have certainly chucked the contents of his stomach a good five miles ago.

"Jesus Christ, will you watch where you're going?" he yelled as Lauren took a treacherous hairpin turn at what was surely a very unsafe speed.

"Relax," she assured him arrogantly. "I've got this, big guy. I drive much narrower, steeper roads all the time in Big Sur. Even have to use the four wheel drive on most of them. This is nothing. And you really don't have to keep holding onto that roll bar for dear life. After all, aren't you supposed to be this big, tough macho football player?"

Nick didn't answer her, looking out the passenger window instead, and immediately regretted his action. Lauren's big, sturdy Jeep Wrangler might be able to handle these sort of narrow mountain roads just fine, but that didn't mean he had the same sort of confidence in her erratic, rather careless driving skills.

"Just get us there in one piece, okay?" he bit out. "I knew I should have driven. How much further is it?"

She reached over to pat him on the arm, and he cringed to notice she was now only driving with one hand – around a hairpin curve. "Less than three miles, tough guy. So if you have to barf, please try to hold it in until then. God, and I thought the guys in my crew were a bunch of wimps. At least they don't complain when I do most of the driving during assignments."

Nick shuddered to think of Lauren driving in a foreign country, and most likely not in a vehicle as new or well-maintained as her Jeep. And he felt nothing but pity for any man who had to work with her, much less travel with for days and weeks at a time.

Fortunately, her estimations were right on the money and they were pulling into a dusty parking lot just a few minutes later.

The staging area of the race was a beehive of activity, with runners finishing one lap and heading out for another. There were all manner of volunteers scattered about - some manning a water and food station; others offering medical care to runners who looked in need; still others whose job it seemed was keeping track of all the runners' progress and making note of how many laps they'd completed and what their total running time was.

Nick took charge of the situation before Lauren could butt in, and asked the volunteer who looked like they were in charge of the lap counting about Angela's progress.

"Del Carlo?" The volunteer squinted as he consulted his laptop. "Yeah, here she is. Finished lap number two right around the four hour mark, great pace for this course. If she's still maintaining that kind of pace, then she ought to be finishing up lap number three within the next fifteen, twenty minutes. Just keep watching for her."

But when twenty minutes passed without any sign of Angela, both Nick and Lauren grew impatient. And when forty five minutes had gone by, they grew concerned. They took turns nagging the race officials, inquiring about Angela's status, and wondering what could have gone wrong to throw her that far off pace. And when it was a full hour past the time she ought to have shown up, Nick was preparing to head out on the trail in search of her.

Lauren eyed his designer jeans, expensive Italian leather loafers, and white shirt with disdain. "Uh, no offense, but those aren't exactly ideal hiking duds you've got on. Why don't you let me go out instead? I'm not the runner Angie is but I put in enough miles to get by."

Nick arched a brow as his gaze scanned over her own tight jeans, cropped tee, and cowboy boots. "You aren't exactly dressed for a run right now either."

And then, whatever scathing comment Lauren was about to fire back with froze on her lips as a runner dashed towards the staging area, looking harried and frantic as he completed his loop.

"Runner down on the trail!" he yelled. "Less than a mile from here. Looks like she fell and got knocked unconscious. We need the medics out there pronto!"

Lauren clutched at Nick's arm for support. "Oh, my God! Do you think that's Angie?"

Nick fought off the immediate sense of panic that rose up. "I don't know," he replied tersely. "Let's see if we can get more information."

But the paramedics on site weren't waiting for clarification, and had already headed out on the hot, rocky trail with a collapsible stretcher and a medic bag. Nick, meanwhile, managed to work his way over to the runner who'd made the discovery and ask the visibly shaken young man more specific questions.

"Look, I'm sure you're upset about this, but we think the runner you found is our friend," Nick began. "Can you describe her at all?"

The runner nodded. "I didn't notice her bib number because she was sprawled face down on the trail. But she's tall, really tall, with a long black braid. And she was wearing - "

But Nick and Lauren didn't wait around to hear anymore, since they both knew now that the injured runner was most definitely Angela. They headed out together on the trail, neither one content to wait around for the paramedics to re-emerge. As they strode along at a brisk pace – fear evidently giving both of them an adrenaline surge – Nick cursed softly.

"Why the hell is she even doing something like this anyway?" he asked out loud, though not necessarily addressing his question to anyone in particular. "Why so damned many miles, and on terrain like this? And it's got to be close to eighty out here already, maybe even hotter. She's probably passed out from heat stroke, probably didn't eat enough. Goddammit!"

"Hey, chill out up there, okay?" called Lauren, who was struggling to keep pace with Nick's much longer-legged stride. "And don't blame Angie for this. She knows what she's doing, prepared for this race for months. She's been doing long distance running for a long time now, ever since – well, a long time. And given how rocky it is out here she probably just tripped or something, maybe sprained an ankle. Don't jump to conclusions, hmm?"

Nick shook his head as he shouldered on. "I just don't get why she feels the need to do something this extreme. I mean, a marathon is way more than most people ever attempt. Why did she feel like she had to run this far?"

"Because it was her way of dealing with things," replied Lauren bluntly. "She'd tell me that when she would go on these really long runs – twenty miles, longer even – that it was easy for her to block stuff out. She'd plug in her iPod and just run for hours and hours. It became a coping mechanism for her, a way to forget how much she was suffering inside. It helped – even for a little while."

He nodded. "Okay, I get it. So this is my fault, then? The fact that she could be sick, injured now. Because if I hadn't hurt her so badly, hadn't broken up with her, then she wouldn't have felt the need to put herself through this sort of physical challenge. Wouldn't have had the need to deal with so much pain."

Lauren scoffed. "Don't flatter yourself that much, Manning. Angie's always been an athlete, always played sports. Way before she ever met you she had a bunch of other crap in her life to deal with. She played four different sports during the school year, and joined three leagues in the summer just so she'd have an excuse not to be at home. This ultrarunning stuff – it's a different sport but the exact same sort of coping mechanism she's always used."

Nick felt a bit better at Lauren's reassurance, but that relief was short-lived as he and Lauren reached the site where Angela had gone down. The paramedics had already lifted her onto the stretcher, and were just about to pick her up when Nick rushed over to her side. She was pale and unresponsive, covered in dirt and blood. Her knees and shins were scraped and bruised, her eyes closed and her breathing shallow. Impatiently, he brushed aside one of the paramedics and took her hand, alarmed at how cold it felt while the rest of her skin was burning up.

"Angel," he called out to her, touching the side of her cheek carefully. "What's the matter with her? Did she faint? Is it heat stroke or something else?"

"We're not sure yet, no way to tell until we get her in the ambulance," replied one of the paramedics. "It looks like she hit her head hard, given the size of the bruise on her temple. And from the way she was clutching her side a minute ago, she's probably got a few cracked ribs as well. But, sir, you need to get out of the way so we can get her out of here as quickly as possible. Every minute counts right now, okay?"

Despite the protests of both paramedics, Nick insisted on carrying one end of the stretcher, pointing out that he was a lot taller and stronger than either of them and could bear the weight much easier. Rather grudgingly, the slighter of the two gave in and it quickly became apparent that was the right decision, as Nick's superior strength proved a godsend in transporting Angela back to the staging area as fast as possible.

Nick was arguing heatedly with the ambulance driver, insisting that he wanted to ride along with them, when Lauren took him firmly by the arm.

"They'll need room back there to work on her," she pointed out. "And, well, you're a big dude, you'll take up too much space. Besides, Angie's car is here and you'll need to drive it back for her. One of the volunteers already brought over her bag from the sweats check, so I'm guessing the car keys are in here somewhere."

He gave a reluctant nod, and took the bag from Lauren's outstretched hand. "You're right. Besides, I'd probably end up pissing these guys off even more than I already have. I'll get her car and meet you over at the hospital. *After* I get to see her one more time."

The paramedics had already inserted an IV into one of Angela's arms, and were getting ready to strap her in for the ambulance ride. She was drifting in and out of consciousness now, her head lolling to one side, and whimpering in pain. But this time, instead of roughly shoving the paramedic out of his way, Nick asked for what he wanted instead.

The paramedic gave a brief, reluctant nod. "Make it quick. We need to get her in ASAP, get a CT scan for that bump on her head."

Nick stuck his upper body inside the ambulance and took her hand gently in his, wincing when he saw the bits of dirt and drying blood on her scraped palm. He brought her hand to his lips, and gave her a reassuring smile as her eyes fluttered open weakly.

"Nick?" she rasped, her voice barely audible. "What – am I hallucinating? How – why are you here? What – what happened?"

"You fainted, Angel," he told her gently. "And then you just took a little fall, that's all. You're going to the hospital now to get checked out, and Lauren and I will be waiting there for you. Just take it easy now, baby, and let these guys fix you up, hmm? Everything's going to be all right, I promise."

She tried to draw a breath to speak, but cried out weakly from the pain in her ribs. "Nick, I'm scared," she whispered.

But even those three little words proved too much of an effort for her, and she drifted into unconsciousness again. Nick reached over and pressed a kiss to her forehead, murmuring to her even though he knew she couldn't hear him.

"Don't be scared, Angel," he told her. "Because I'm here for you, and this time I won't leave. Ever again."

And as the paramedics shooed him out of the ambulance and finished strapping Angela in, Nick could only stand there helplessly, especially when he realized that *he* was the one who was truly scared right now.

Chapter Twenty One

"What the *hell* is taking so long? I knew I should have insisted they brought her to University Medical Center instead of this place. We would have had answers half an hour ago if we'd gone there. This place – who the hell knows when we'll hear anything."

Lauren sighed, having heard this particular tirade from Nick at least four times already. "I'm going to go out on a limb here, Manning, and guess that patience isn't one of your better virtues. And do you think you could maybe sit down for a few minutes, hmm? I swear you're going to grind a hole in the linoleum otherwise."

Nick glared at the floor. "That actually wouldn't be very hard to do, given that this crappy stuff has got to be at least thirty years old."

"Look, I realize this isn't the fancy-ass private hospital you wanted them to bring Angie to, but it is the best trauma center in northern California. They know what they're doing here, Nick. Honest. Now sit the hell down or I'll do it for you."

"In your dreams," he grumbled as he reluctantly took a seat next to Lauren. "You got lucky, that's all, caught me unawares. Now that I know how dirty you fight, you won't pull that little trick on me again."

Lauren gave him a cheeky little grin before toasting him with the giant cup of coffee she was sipping. "We'll see. That's far from the only trick I know, after all. And sometimes these things happen when you least expect them."

Her words were far more significant than she realized, thought Nick as he tapped his foot impatiently. The very last thing he'd expected this morning - when he'd made the drive over to Angela's to invite her to his place in Sausalito- was that they'd wind up in the ER at San Francisco General Hospital instead. And that he'd now be beside himself with worry about what could possibly be wrong with her. The best case scenario was that she was just suffering from heat exhaustion, not to mention some sore ribs, scrapes and bruises, that they would re-hydrate her, check her out, and release her in a few hours. But Nick couldn't forget the concern the paramedics had voiced – not once, but twice – about some bump or bruise on the side of her head, and the urgency of having a CT scan done. *That* was the part that was leaving him with a very unsettled feeling.

"Are you going to call her parents?" he asked Lauren abruptly. He couldn't help feeling annoyed that she seemed to be taking all of this in stride, remaining calm and composed as she sipped from that monstrous cup of coffee. While he, on the other hand – the one who was always cool and unemotional – could barely sit still for five minutes at a crack.

Lauren gave a somewhat disinterested shrug. "Not yet. Let's wait and see what the doctor says about her condition. If it's nothing major and they're going to release her today or even tomorrow, I probably won't call them. I don't think Angie would want that, and frankly, they probably wouldn't give a shit anyway. She's, uh, told you about that whole situation, I assume?"

Nick nodded. "Yeah. They sound like a charming family, especially the mother."

Lauren gave a short, bitter little laugh at his obvious sarcasm. "You've got no idea. Rita is a heartless, selfish bitch, always has been. And while Gino's a nice enough man, he's got zero backbone, lets himself be bossed around 24/7 by that bitch he's married to. He'd have to sneak away to watch Angie's games in high school, tell Rita he was working when he was really at one of our soccer games. She would have made his life even more of a living hell if she'd known the truth. So, no, I don't think Angie would want either of them here right now. If it turns out to be something more serious, I'll call them up. But don't hold your breath – it would take an awful lot for Rita to come running all the way up here, and there's no way I want to imagine this situation getting that serious."

"I agree."

There was a somewhat uncomfortable silence between them for a few minutes, until Lauren stuck her cup of coffee in his face.

"Sorry, I didn't think to offer you any. That's one reason I grabbed such a big cup, figured you might want some. Help yourself."

Caffeine sounded like an excellent idea, so Nick took the cup from her and tilted it up to his mouth. He shuddered as he swallowed and shoved it back in her direction.

"Jesus Christ, how much sugar did you put in there?" he wheezed. "It barely tastes like coffee."

Lauren shrugged. "I lost count. Usually I throw about four packets in, plus a bunch of cream, but since this is the jumbo sized cup I might have doubled that."

Nick shook his head. "Unreal. You must have one of those metabolisms that burns too fast."

She looked pensive for a moment, then gave a brief nod. "Something like that. I do drink a lot of coffee, probably way too much, but when you travel as much as I do, and as far as I do, caffeine becomes a necessary evil."

He was about to quiz Lauren about her job, figuring the wild stories she must certainly have to share would help distract him from worrying about Angela, when two other people hurried inside the waiting room. The woman he knew to be Julia, Lauren's identical twin, and he assumed the dark haired man with an arm wrapped around her waist was her new husband.

"Jules, Nathan. Thanks for getting here so fast." Lauren sprung to her feet and embraced her sister and brother-in-law.

"How is she? Any word yet?" asked Julia anxiously.

Lauren shook her head. "Nothing yet. Though if someone doesn't come out and update us soon, I think it's going to take all three of us to hold this one back."

Julia and Nathan were staring at Nick, and he realized they both recognized him – though for vastly different reasons.

"Damn. Nick Manning," said Nathan in stunned disbelief. "This is – a huge surprise. What are you doing here – and how do you know Lauren?"

But Julia had quickly drawn her own, very different conclusion as to why Nick was here. "He's not here with Lauren," she told her husband. "He's here for Angela. Aren't you?"

Nick glanced down at Julia, relieved to see the gentle smile on her stunningly beautiful face as well as the look of understanding in her eyes. It was rather obvious that the twins were as different as night and day, both in the way they dressed and in their personalities.

"Yes," he answered. "I am. I'm, uh - "

"You're the one," replied Julia simply. "The one she was so wrapped up in four years ago. The one," she added, "that she never got over."

"Yes."

Nick didn't know what else to say, but he sensed with Julia that there was no need to speak further, at least not right now. And then, even though it was obvious that Lauren was by far the more controlling and outspoken twin, it was Julia who quietly took charge of the situation. She and her husband had brought along containers of food and drink which she now disbursed among the four of them.

"I wasn't sure how you took your coffee," she told Nick. "There's cream and sugar in one of these bags if you don't like it black."

He shook his head urgently. "Black is fine, thanks. I still haven't gotten the taste of your sister's disgusting brew out of my mouth."

Julia nodded in understanding. "Lauren has a huge sweet tooth, practically lives on sugar and caffeine. She should have warned you before offering you a sip."

Lauren shrugged, unconcerned. "Or maybe he should have asked first."

Nick's gaze narrowed as he studied Lauren. "Are you always like this?"

Nathan chuckled. "You mean a pain in the ass? Lauren doesn't know any other way to behave."

"Don't." Julia laid a hand on her husband's shoulder and shook her head. "Not now, not today. Especially not when we're waiting for word on Angie. Let's all agree to play nice."

Lauren munched on a container of soba noodles and grilled

chicken, wielding a pair of chopsticks with careless ease. "Nathan started it," she mumbled accusingly. "But I'll ignore him for now. Be warned, though, bro – this isn't over."

Nathan rolled his eyes, spearing a forkful of shrimp tempura. "It never is." He glanced over at Nick, offering an apologetic smile. "Lauren's actually harmless, you know. Way more bark than bite."

Nick glowered. "Except when she's sweeping your legs out from under you. Or using you for target practice with her nasty little knife."

Julia's mouth dropped open as she lowered her spoonful of chicken udon back into the takeout container. "She didn't. Lauren – you promised Dad you'd stop carrying that knife around with you everywhere. It's one thing when you're on assignment somewhere, I realize you need to protect yourself. But not here. You don't need - "

Whatever further admonition Julia was about to give her sister was interrupted by the arrival of a rather agitated-looking young doctor dressed in light blue scrubs. And when he asked if anyone was there for Angela Del Carlo, all four of them rose to their feet. The doctor – who looked barely old enough to be in college, much less practicing medicine, at least in Nick's opinion – glanced uncertainly from one to the next.

"Well, looks like you're all here together, so I'll give you a quick update on Angela's status," began the young doctor, who belatedly introduced himself as Cole McIntyre. "Your friend – uh, excuse me, unless either of you gentlemen are her husband? Fiancé?"

"I'm her – significant other. Boyfriend. Whatever the hell you want to call it," muttered Nick darkly. "We're – together."

Nick ignored the three startled glances sent his way and prodded young Dr. McIntyre to continue.

"Well, Angela has got a few different things going on," he stated. "I'll start with the more minor issues first and then discuss the most serious of her injuries. She definitely exhibited all the classic symptoms of heat stroke – dizziness, drifting in and out of consciousness, hot, dry skin but very little sweating, rapid heartbeat. We were able to get that under control fairly easily, pumping her full of fluids and cooling her body temperature off. She was competing in an endurance event when this happened, correct?"

Lauren nodded. "A hundred kilometer trail race. I told her she was nuts to even think about it but she's a stubborn one. But I'm sure she took precautions, drank plenty of fluids, that sort of thing."

Dr. McIntyre shook his head. "Sometimes it doesn't matter in cases like this. In fact, drinking too many electrolytes can wind up throwing them off balance. In any event, the heat stroke has been dealt with and shouldn't cause any additional problems. Next, we took an x-ray which revealed three cracked ribs. Not much to do for that except wrap them up a bit, restrict her movements, and give her something for the pain. There are also a number of scrapes and bruises, again relatively minor compared to the real issue."

"That bump on her head," Nick stated flatly.

"Yes," agreed the doctor. "We did a quick CT scan, which revealed a subdural hematoma. In other words, Angela has bleeding between the layers of tissue surrounding the brain. And it's a very good thing we got her in here and were able to make the diagnosis so quickly, because time is of the essence in treating an injury like this. Ironically, suffering from heat stroke and passing out is probably what's going to save her life. If she'd simply tripped and hit her head, she might not have lost consciousness. Often times with this sort of condition the patient falls and bumps their head, feels fine and just walks away, not realizing that the bleeding going on beneath the surface is quietly killing them."

"So what happens next?" Nick asked, trying to stay calm, though it was growing increasingly harder to remain so with each passing minute.

Dr. McIntyre took a deep breath before continuing. "She needs to have a procedure done. It involves drilling what we call a burr hole into her skull, and then draining the blood out. She's being prepped for that surgery right now."

"And that will take care of the problem, get rid of this

bleeding?" demanded Nick. "Any other problems or complications that you haven't told us about?"

The doctor hesitated before replying, rather obviously intimidated by Nick's size and the ferocity of his expression. "It's a fairly common procedure, sir. And very low risk. However, I will tell you that this is an acute hematoma, so it's a very, very good thing we're treating it this quickly. As far as the complications – I will warn you there is always the risk – a low one, mind you – that this doesn't fix the problem. She could need additional surgery, possibly a craniotomy where part of the skull is removed. Or, in some cases, depending on the severity of the bleeding, a patient can suffer a stroke or sometimes paralysis. But that's a relatively small risk, and again, the fact we're catching this so quickly is a huge plus. Now, do you have any other questions? Otherwise, I should get back to help them prep her."

Lauren and Julia glanced at each other worriedly, before Lauren gave a quick nod and asked the doctor, "Should we – that is, in your opinion – do you think her parents need to be called? We haven't contacted them yet until we knew more about her condition."

Dr. McIntyre paused for several seconds, and Nick could tell the young physician was trying to maintain an air of calmness, whether it was for his own sake or for theirs.

"Yes," he replied decisively. "I think that would be a good idea. I need to go now but someone will be out when the surgery is finished to update you. It will be a few hours before it's over and she's in recovery. Stay positive, okay? Chances are very good that everything will be just fine."

"Wait.'

Dr. McIntyre gazed at Nick inquiringly. "Yes? You have another question?"

Nick glanced around the waiting room, taking in not only the worn floor but the peeling paint on the walls and the old fashioned furniture. "Not a question so much as an opinion. Two of my clients are considered top of their field in neurosurgery. Do you think it's worthwhile to call one of them, maybe both, and get their opinions on this? I mean, no offense,

Doctor, but the facilities here look a little on the shabby side. I just want to make sure Angela is getting the best possible care."

Dr. McIntyre shook his head. "I understand your concern – you *are* Nick Manning, aren't you?" At Nick's brief acknowledgment, the doctor continued. "At this point, Mr. Manning, it wouldn't do much good to bring in another doctor, no matter how qualified or highly regarded they are. Angela needs to get into surgery without delay, and we simply can't wait for a consult at this time. And, look – I know this place isn't as spruced up and plush as some of the private hospitals in town, but we are a very highly ranked trauma center. And the surgeon who'll be performing the procedure on Angela is extremely experienced with traumatic brain injury. Trust me, she's in very good hands. Now, forgive me, but I really need to go check on our patient."

Nick shoved his hands inside his jeans, his fists tightly clenched as he debated whether to call his clients and get their opinions anyway. He felt a slight tug on his shirt sleeve, and glanced down to find Julia gazing up at him in understanding.

"Hey, I get it," she assured him gently. "You're really worried about Angie and I don't blame you. But the doctor's right, this place isn't the fanciest but they have the most experience with trauma cases. I should know – I was one of them."

As Nick regarded her quizzically, Nathan put a comforting arm around his wife's shoulder and explained. "An ex-girlfriend of mine – a *crazy* ex-girlfriend," he clarified, "blamed Julia for my breaking things off with her. And she, uh, sort of shot her. Fortunately, it was just a deep graze but last year I was the one standing where you are right now, Nick – worried sick about my girl and feeling helpless."

"Angie's condition sounds a lot more serious than my little bullet graze, Nathan," admonished Julia. "Which is why we'd better place that call to her parents. Lauren – do you want to do the honors or should I?"

"Hmm. Let's think about that for a minute here," replied Lauren carefully. "On the one hand, I've got no doubt I can bully the two of them into getting their butts up here pronto. But on the other hand, I might piss Rita off too badly and that could, uh, complicate matters."

Julia sighed. "Hand me Angie's phone, would you? I'd better make the call."

***

"Marisa, I'm very sorry that this happened right in the middle of your son's birthday party. But I think it's pretty important that your parents at least are here. What? No, we don't know exactly when she'll be out of the surgery. Ah, no, I don't think it's a good idea to wait until she's out before you tell your parents. Omigod, are you really trying to suggest that all of this is Angela's fault? I can't believe you're even thinking such a thing. Now, please, can I speak to one of your parents? Honestly, Marisa? Don't you think *they* should be the ones to make that decision?"

Nick was just about at the end of his rope with what he was overhearing from Julia's end of the conversation. She'd first tried calling Angela's parents at their home, and when the call went to voice mail she'd dialed Marisa, the older sister. And from what Nick could make out, there was some sort of child's birthday party going on, and Marisa was balking at the idea of ruining the brat's celebration by putting her mother or father on the line. Poor Julia was struggling to be polite and remain calm, but Nick could see her growing angrier and more frustrated with each passing minute. Lauren, who was perched on the arm of her sister's chair, looked ready to burst a blood vessel and at one point Nathan actually laid a restraining hand on her arm.

"Marisa, I swear that this is important – *really* important. For God's sake, if it was just some cracked ribs and bruises I wouldn't have even called. But Angela is about to go into surgery - "

Nick had had enough, his tolerance at the very end of its limits, and he plucked the phone from Julia's hand impatiently. "Let me take it from here," he mouthed to her, and Julia nodded gratefully.

"This is Nick Manning," he announced brusquely. "I'm Angela's – let's call it her significant other. She's had an accident and your parents need to get up here as quickly as possible. So I'd appreciate it if you could put your father on the phone."

There was silence on the other end of the cell phone for several seconds, and then a woman's high pitched voice squeaked, "Is this some sort of prank? How does Angela know someone like Nick Manning? She's never mentioned it to any of us before."

Nick swore beneath his breath and counted to ten before replying acidly, "She can catch all of you up on that some other time. Put your father on the line now."

"But we're just getting ready to cut the cake! Didn't Julia tell you it's my son's eleventh birthday? Can't I have my father call you back in, say, fifteen minutes?" whined Marisa.

Nick thought it was a very fortunate thing that Angela's sister wasn't here at this very moment, because, while he'd never been violent towards a woman in his life, he'd have been sorely tempted to slap Marisa's face – hard. "I don't give a shit about your kid's cake," he bit out. "Frankly, I wouldn't care if your father's about to have an audience with the frigging pope right now. Put – him – on – the – fucking – phone – now."

Marisa's voice was much more subdued as she stammered, "O – okay. Hang on a sec, I'll get him for you."

Nick glanced over at the twins, both of whom were giving him the thumbs up, and he couldn't resist grinning in return. And then a man came on the line, sounding completely confused.

"Hello? My daughter said you were calling about my Angie. Is she all right? What's happened to my baby?"

Nick forced himself to remain calm as he quickly introduced himself, then filled Gino Del Carlo in on the situation. "She's about to go into surgery, Mr. Del Carlo, and they weren't very clear on how long it might take. But I suggest you and your wife leave Carmel as quickly as possible so you can be here when she wakes up. I've got Angela's cell phone with me, so you can call as often as you like for updates during the drive."

Gino sounded upset, his voice raspy as he assured Nick they would be on the road within the next few minutes. "My wife – she can be a little stubborn sometimes, so it might take me a few minutes to get her out of here. But we'll be there as soon as we can. Just – don't let anything bad happen to my Angie, please? I – I know I've been a lousy father to her, haven't been there for her when she needed me. But I love her more than anything else, Nick, I always have. Would you tell her that for me, please?"

"I will," assured Nick gently. "Though I really think she'd prefer to hear that from you."

He ended the call, but kept the phone with him. And then he was completely taken aback when Lauren – who just hours earlier had thrown a knife at his head – got up and gave him a hug.

"You're even more of a badass than I am," she admitted. "And whether you know it or not, Manning, you just proved to all of us that you're in love with Angie. And as soon as she wakes up, you'd better tell her that yourself or you'll wind up on your ass again. Deal?"

Nick laughed in spite of himself. "Yeah, deal."

***

It was already past the dinner hour, but Nick wasn't the slightest bit hungry and thus far had resisted all of Julia's pleas to eat something. Nathan, who was clearly infatuated with his gorgeous wife and seemed reluctant to leave her side even for a minute, had advised Nick to give in gracefully since eventually Julia would get her way. But he'd been spared the ordeal of having to once again refuse both the sandwich and the bowl of soup she'd been trying to force on him by the arrival of the surgeon who'd operated on Angela.

The news, so far, was positive. They had drained the blood that had pooled up inside her brain tissue and everything looked clean. But the surgeon had warned that they really wouldn't know for sure if the procedure had been successful until Angela woke up and they could perform a few simple tests. There was still the very real possibility that she would need additional surgery, or that complications could arise, and the next dozen hours or so would tell the story.

And when the surgeon had said that one of them could sit with Angela once she was out of recovery, Nick and Lauren had had something of a face-off, each one stubbornly insisting that it ought to be them. It had been Julia – sweet, calm Julia who Nick already liked a whole lot better than her very difficult twin – who had placed a hand on her sister's arm and murmured quietly, "Angie would want Nick there with her. We both know it. So let him go in first and then you can sit with her after a bit, okay?"

"Fine." Lauren had pouted sullenly. "But if he's not going to eat that sandwich you bought him, I call dibs."

Nick had been all too happy to sacrifice the sandwich he didn't even want in exchange for getting to see his angel first. And the exact minute the nurse had beckoned him inside the hospital room, he was sitting by her side, picking up the hand that wasn't punctured with the IV needle.

There was a white bandage on the side of her head where the burr hole had been drilled, but Nick was grateful to see that they'd only had to shave a very small patch of her beautiful hair. The rest of the long raven tresses were tumbled over her pillow, and he carefully smoothed them out, running his fingers through their silky length. Her face was almost as white as the bandage but she looked peaceful and pain free as she continued to sleep off the effects of the anesthesia. The scrapes on her hands had been cleaned up, and to look at her now it was hard to believe how bad off she'd been a few hours ago.

He placed a soft kiss on her palm before bringing it to his cheek. He cleared his throat a couple of times, but his voice still sounded raspy and uneven when he finally spoke.

"I know you can't hear me right now, Angel, and maybe that's a good thing," he began. "Because I've got a feeling I might need to rehearse this little speech I'm about to make a few times before I get it right. As you know, I'm not very good at this stuff – talking about my feelings, sharing secrets. I've always dismissed it as sappy and sentimental, but the truth of it is that it scares the shit out of me to open up to anyone."

He talked to her about his parents, how he'd been tossed and tugged between them growing up like some sort of beach ball. About how cold and distant his father had been, and how much Nick had hated all the rules set down for him. And then he told her about his mother – his sweet, slightly loony mother and how every day had been a party for her. He explained about how his need for privacy, for secrecy, had stemmed from all the summers he'd spent with his mother and her celebrity friends, and how his own privacy had been violated too many times to count.

"And when I saw how unhappy my father was with his second – and now third, wife – and how my mother's idea of a long term relationship encompassed a few months – well, it pretty much turned me off on the ideas of love and commitment," he admitted. "So I was determined that I'd never end up in the same sort of situation myself, avoided getting serious with a woman like it was the plague."

Angela's eyes fluttered weakly and he paused, hoping that she would wake up now and that the doctors could confirm everything was okay. But she merely gave a tiny sigh and kept sleeping, and Nick continued on haltingly.

"And then I met this beautiful, smart, funny and very, very sexy young stockbroker. And I knew from the minute I looked into her gorgeous eyes that we could have something good together. Except I was still scared to death about having a long term relationship, so I deliberately made things as difficult as possible for you, set down ridiculous conditions that no sane person would ever agree to. And I did that to scare you off, so that you'd go running away and I would just forget you and move on to the next woman, same as I always had. "

He squeezed her hand a little tighter. "But you surprised me, Angel. *Shocked* me, more like it. I never, ever expected you to actually agree to what I demanded of you, and I sure as hell never dreamed you could continue to go along with it for so long. And I knew – I always knew, I think – how you felt about me. Because the only reason anyone would have tolerated the way I treated you was because you loved me."

Nick took several deep breaths before continuing, knowing that she couldn't hear him but not certain he could deal with hearing himself admit this next part out loud. "When you came home that day from your cousin's wedding, all upset because of the fight you'd had with your mother, I knew then that things couldn't go on between us the way they had. No matter how many times you told me you didn't care about getting married, I knew it wasn't the truth. So I forced myself to act like an unfeeling asshole, to break things off with you, and tell myself in the process that I was doing what was best for you in the long run. Except that was a lie, Angel. I ended things because *I* was the one who'd gotten too close to *you*. I'd found myself starting to care about you, *really* care, and that sent me over the top."

He kissed each of her fingers carefully, then brushed an errant strand of hair from her forehead. "Staying away from you after that was one of the toughest things I've ever done. You have no idea how many times I started to call you, or stop by your place. I never gave you back your keys, and there were at least ten times I parked outside your building and thought about going up. Strictly to check on you, I told myself, but that was a lie, too. And then I heard through the grapevine that you'd quit your job, went to another firm, and I knew that was your way of moving on. So I left you alone and hoped that you'd find the right guy for you someday, a guy who wasn't all screwed up like I was and who could offer you a nice, normal sort of relationship."

The monitors that Angela was hooked up to kept up their steady little rhythm of beeps as he continued to talk in a low, soothing voice. "When I saw you again in April, I was torn apart. I never imagined that you would have taken our breakup so hard, that it would have hurt you so badly. I never imagined," he added hoarsely, "that you loved me that much. So I've been stumbling along these last few months, trying in my usual take charge fashion to make it all up to you. Except that I've got no fucking clue about how to have a real relationship, so of course I've screwed everything up in the process."

He gave a short, bitter laugh. "I was even jealous of Dwayne, you know? Oh, not because of his incredible good looks or anything. Like your pal Lauren told me earlier – once a dweeb, always a dweeb. No, I was jealous of him because he made you smile. *Really* smile. And I'm not sure you ever smiled like that for me even once. It made me realize just how big of a jerk I'd been to you when we were together, and how much I still had to learn about making you happy."

Nick brushed his knuckles against her cheek, relieved to find her skin cool to the touch. "But when I kissed you that day down in Pebble Beach just before Julia's wedding, I knew I still had a chance with you, that you still cared about me. And yet I kept fighting it, knowing full well that I'd have to change my ways if I wanted to get you back. And it scared the crap out of me, Angel. Me – big, bad Nick Manning, who'd terrorized some of the best quarterbacks in the NFL, the same guy who once told a billionaire that I wouldn't take his account because he wanted too much control over it. I faced all of that stuff without the slightest hesitation, no fear whatsoever. But compromising my rules in order to have you back in my life – that fucking terrified me, backed me into a corner and so I kept away from you for a few weeks."

Angela continued to lay motionless, her long, dark eyelashes resting like plush fans on her cheeks, her breathing steady but controlled. Nick squeezed her hand a little tighter, as though willing her to wake up so that the doctors could assure him that everything was fine now, that she'd come out of the surgery like a champ. She *had* to be okay, he thought despairingly, just *had* to. After everything he'd put her through over the past years, everything her family had put her through since birth, Angela deserved to be happy, deserved to be treated like a princess. Deserved, he acknowledged with a sigh, to be loved.

"I should probably be writing all of this down somewhere," he said jokingly. "Because I really doubt I'll be able to remember it again. More than that, I hope I don't chicken out and lose my nerve to actually tell you when you're fully conscious. Because you deserve to know the truth, Angel, and the truth is that I care about you – a lot more than I've let myself believe until recently. And, honestly, I don't know what it feels like to be in love with someone, because that's never happened to me before. So maybe when you wake up we can talk about this love thing, and you can help me figure out if that's what I'm feeling right now. All I know is that I need you in my life again, Angel, and that I'm willing to do whatever it takes to make that happen. And that if anything happens to you – well, I can't even think about dealing with that right now. So if all that put together means that what I feel for you is love – well, hell. Then, yeah, I'm guessing I love you."

As Nick continued to watch her carefully for any signs of awareness, the corners of her mouth began to twitch upwards in a semblance of a smile. And then those long, luxurious lashes of hers blinked twice, three times, and she slowly opened her eyes.

"Yeah," she whispered, her smile broadening. "I would say that's love. Because that's exactly how I feel about you, Nick, and I've been in love with you for years."

He laughed just before bending over to press a soft kiss on her lips. "Fess up now, Angel. How long have you been awake and how much of all that did you really hear?"

She gave the hand that still held hers a gentle squeeze. "See, that's the thing," she murmured in a barely audible voice. "I could hear everything, but I was so out of it that I didn't know if it was real or just a dream. And if it was a dream," she added softly, "I didn't want to wake up. Ever. Because everything you just told me – you have no idea how many years I've waited to hear it all."

Whatever he was going to say in response was interrupted by the arrival of a nurse, who looked equal parts relieved that Angela was actually awake, and annoyed that Nick hadn't immediately summoned her. And then he was being shooed out of the room with the arrival of the doctor and a couple of other staff members, despite his protests to the contrary. But he managed to catch Angela's eye just before leaving, and grinned as she blew him a kiss. Reluctantly, he made his way back to the waiting room to share the news about Angela waking up and found himself standing in the middle of what sounded like a battlefield.

***

Lauren glared at Deanna as she took a seat next to Rita. "Hey, I've made the drive up from Carmel plenty of times over the years and no way does it take *this* long, even in traffic. So what exactly was the hold-up, hmm? Angela's been out of surgery for almost an hour now."

Deanna had the good graces to look guilty. "Well, Dad was too upset to drive and Mom refuses to drive in San Francisco. So they asked me to take them and, well, I had some arrangements to make first."

Lauren pursed her lips in disapproval. "Like what? What sort of *arrangements* take precedence over the fact that your sister was undergoing potentially life-threatening surgery?"

Rita frowned. "There's no need for that sort of tone, Lauren. Deanna was good enough to miss her daughter's swim practice this afternoon to bring us here. And of course all of us had to leave poor little Giovanni's birthday party early. We got here as soon as possible, so don't you dare criticize us."

"You're kidding, right?" gaped Lauren. "Swim practice and a birthday party were more important than brain surgery?" Beneath her breath she whispered to Julia, who was standing right beside her, "And are they joking about the kid's name? Shit, he must get beat up at least once a day with a pussy name like that."

Julia, always the peacemaker, gave her sister's arm a warning squeeze as she explained to Angela's family, "Lauren's been here with Angela the whole time, was at the race when she got injured, so it's understandable that she's a little stressed. And worried."

"I am stressed. *And* worried," agreed Lauren. "But I'm also ticked off that Julia and I are the ones who have been here the whole time, instead of Angie's family. By my calculations, the three of you should have been here at least two hours ago. And – oh, my God – is that a fresh Starbucks cup you're carrying, Deanna? Your sister's just had brain surgery and you stopped to get a fucking latte on the way here?"

Deanna cringed at the threatening tone of Lauren's voice. "It was – I needed the caffeine. And it just took a few minutes. Besides, it's not like any of us could have done anything here. She was already getting prepped for surgery when Julia called my sister."

"Sister. Funny you should mention that word," drawled Lauren, crossing her arms over her chest. "Because you and Marisa have been the shittiest sisters ever to Angela. Julia and I are more her sisters than the two of you will ever be. Today just went and proved that point all over again, didn't it?"

Deanna gasped, one hand drifting up dramatically to clutch her chest. "How dare you? You've got no right to say those things to me, you don't know anything about it."

"Wrong." Lauren was in Deanna's face now, pointing a finger at her, and noting with satisfaction that Angela's sister was quivering in fear. "Julia and I know everything. Every time Angie was upset or sad or lonely growing up, who do you think she ran to? Not you or Marisa, that's for damned sure. And certainly not her own mother." She turned accusingly to Rita. "When Angie got her period for the first time, it was *my* mother who explained it all to her. When she got the flu and couldn't keep any food down for days, it was *my* mom who took care of her and nursed her back to health. And when she got the news that she'd been chosen for the Olympic team, it was *my* mom and dad who threw her a little party, who cooked food and baked a cake and made a big deal out of it. All of you," she pointed in turn at Deanna, Rita, and Gino, "have done nothing but let her down her entire life. Including today. Deanna and Marisa have been lousy sisters, and you – Rita and Gino – you've been really, really lousy parents. On second thought," she finished bitterly, "maybe you should have all just stayed down in Carmel, eating little Giovanni's birthday cake. Angela's *real* family has been here with her the entire time."

Deanna was sobbing by now, her mouth quivering as tears ran down her cheeks. Rita stood up, her mouth a thin, angry line and her face pale and taut.

"You have no right to say things like that to my daughter. Or to me," she hissed. "You were always a rude, wild little girl who's grown up into an ever ruder woman. I should never have allowed Angela to be friends with you and your sister. Both of you have been bad influences on her."

Lauren, who had faced far more intimidating people than

Angela's petite, sixty-seven year old mother in her life, wasn't about to start backing down. "Are you joking? You were all too happy for Angie to hang out at our house as often as possible. After all, that pretty much gave you a free babysitter to go do all the things you wanted to do, didn't it? When we were kids and even in high school, she ate dinner at our house five out of seven nights, did her homework there, slept there a lot, too. And I'm guessing you didn't even notice she was gone half the time."

Rita's eyes were filled with rage and her hands shook. "Our family is none of your business. So stop making trouble where there isn't any and - "

"Enough!"

Six pairs of eyes turned to stare in astonishment at Gino. He'd been silent up until this point, watching all of the drama unfolding – Lauren getting in Deanna's face and making her cry, then standing up to Rita as she'd tried unsuccessfully to intimidate her. Julia, meanwhile, had tried valiantly to keep the peace, while Nathan had wisely stayed in the background and hadn't interfered. As for Nick, no one had even noticed that he'd walked back into the room and remained hidden in a corner, unobserved.

But Gino was definitely making himself heard now, his face ruddy with angry color, and his dark eyes – so like Angela's – were blazing with fury.

"Now, all of you –" he pointed accusingly at his wife, daughter, and then at Lauren. "Be quiet, will you? This is a hospital, for God's sake, not a soccer match."

Rita glared warningly at her husband. "Don't tell me to keep quiet, Gino. This little troublemaker here is the one who started all of this. Tell her to shut up, not me."

Gino shook his head. "No. Because everything Lauren just said is the truth. You and I were lousy parents to our Angie, and I can't think of one person who would say otherwise. And Marisa and Deanna haven't been very nice to her, either. But all of that, every bit, is *my* fault. Because I should have stood up to the lot of you a long, long time ago. And now my baby girl is hurt, just had major surgery, and I wasn't even there when it happened. I'm the worst father in the whole world."

Rita and Deanna were staring at him in shock, too flabbergasted by his uncharacteristic outburst to think of a reply. Lauren was trying very hard not to smile in satisfaction, while Julia kindly patted the visibly upset older man on the shoulder.

"No, you're not," she assured him gently. "Angie always knew you loved her. And you're here now, that's all that matters."

Gino nodded, his eyes suspiciously damp. "Thank you, Julia. I know you and your sister, not to mention your parents, have always been good to my Angie. You were there for her when I wasn't, when I should have been. But I was too afraid of upsetting Rita, of making her angry, and then she'd take that anger out on Angie."

"I never did that!" screeched Rita. "Gino, don't you dare discuss our private affairs in front of all these people."

Gino shrugged, for once not caving in to his wife's anger and demands. "It's not much of a secret, Rita. We all failed our daughter over the years, but that ends right now. I don't care how mad you get, or what other plans you make, from now on I'm going to see my baby as much as possible, call her on the phone every day if I want to. I just hope it's not too late for her to forgive us. To forgive *me*. It's a father's duty, after all, to protect his children, and especially his little girl. And I'm going to try and make it all up to her, whether you care or not."

Rita opened her mouth to protest, but no words came out and she sunk defeatedly back into her chair. Deanna had retreated to a corner, tears still streaming down her cheeks, and Nick couldn't tell who she appeared more afraid of – Lauren or her suddenly assertive father.

"Angela's awake. The doctors are in her room now running some tests, but so far she seems fine."

Everyone turned now to watch Nick as he walked slowly inside the waiting room. He turned first to Gino, extending his hand.

"We spoke on the phone earlier today, Mr. Del Carlo," he told the older man. "I'm Nick Manning. And I'm sure as soon as the doctors say it's okay to go back in her room, that Angela would really like to see you."

Gino nodded, though he looked more than a little awestruck as he shook hands. "I thought my daughter was pulling my leg when she told me you were the one who called," he confessed. "I've been a 49er fan since I was a little boy. And I was actually there at the stadium when you recorded five sacks in one game. One of the best games I've ever seen. This – this is an honor, Nick."

Nick shrugged, never terribly comfortable when he received accolades from his old fans. "We can talk football some other time, if you don't mind. I think our focus now should be on your daughter."

While Gino nodded in agreement, Angela's sister and mother started advancing on Nick as though they were sharks scenting blood in the water.

"Wow, Marisa really was telling the truth," said Deanna in amazement. "Why in the world didn't Angela tell us she was dating someone like you? I mean, I thought she was still with that Dwight guy she went to high school with."

"Dwayne," her mother corrected. "And when has your sister ever kept us in the loop about what goes on in her life? It's all a big mystery with her. I'm Angela's mother, Rita. And this is her sister, Deanna. And you say you're Angela's boyfriend, but if that's the case, how come this is the first any of us are hearing about it?"

Nick grinned. "Because we used to date a few years ago and just officially got back together – oh, about ten minutes ago."

Deanna gasped. "Oh, God, *you* were the one, weren't you? The guy she was seeing back then, the one who bought her all those expensive things. And she never said a word, never even hinted who you were."

"No one knew," Lauren interjected. "Not even Julia and I. We just met Nick earlier today ourselves. But it's been obvious to us for a long time now that Angela never got over him, that he was always the one for her." She gave Nick a saucy wink. "And now, lucky for him, he's finally realized that, too."

Nick was about to offer up a somewhat scathing retort when Angela's nurse popped her head inside the waiting room, giving a thumbs up.

"Okay, it's all good," she said cheerfully. "Passed all of her tests with flying colors and the doctor said she's going to make a full recovery. You can go in and see her now. *One* of you," she added sternly, as several people got up at once.

Nick shook his head at Lauren and placed his hand on Gino's shoulder. "I think that Angela would very much like to see her father at this moment," he said firmly. "Come on, I'll show you the way."

And as much as he wanted to continue the conversation with his angel that had been interrupted by the nurse's intrusion, Nick was more than content to watch from outside her room as Gino embraced his daughter, his tears mingling with hers. After all, they had time – all the time in the world now – to talk.

Epilogue

November

"Go back to sleep, Angel. It's pouring cats and dogs out there, and if you think I'm going to let you go run some crazy trail race in this weather, think again. But if you really want a workout later this morning, I can definitely oblige."

Angela smiled sleepily and cuddled up against Nick's warm body, more than content to stay put in the big, plush bed when she heard the wind and rain that pounded against the bedroom window. "Hmm, that was a half marathon I was going to do this morning," she complained. "Thirteen point one miles. I figure I would have burned off more than a thousand calories. Think you can match that?"

Nick growled as he tumbled her onto her back, looming above her as he stretched her arms above her head. "You don't need to worry about burning calories. In fact, you're still too skinny for my liking. We've got a few more pounds to go before you pass inspection."

She gave him a playful shove, knowing she wouldn't be able to budge him even an inch. "I'm only two pounds lighter than when I was at my heaviest a few years ago. And with the holidays right around the corner, and all the events we've committed to, I'll probably have to go up another dress size."

"Good. I'd love nothing better than an excuse to buy you a whole new wardrobe. Though I'm not looking forward to some of these social events we agreed to attend," he grumbled.

She caressed his heavily stubbled cheek tenderly. "I know," she acknowledged with a smile. "And I love you for making the effort. Both of us have been alone too much in our lives, and it's way past time for that to change."

He gave a gruff nod before rolling onto his side and pulling her close against him. "Hush now, okay? It's still dark outside, it's a Saturday morning, and we could both use some extra sleep."

"Okay."

She nestled her head willingly beneath his chin and sighed in contentment. Nick fell back asleep within two minutes but it took her a bit longer, and she spent the time gazing at him in wonder.

It was still hard to believe sometimes how far they'd come in their relationship in just a few months. A relationship that was a world apart from what they'd had the last time. This time, it was far more of an equal partnership, a give and take, even though Nick still struggled with his need for ultimate control a little too often. But he was trying, really trying, to be the sort of man he wanted to be for her, and if things weren't always perfect – well, this wasn't some sort of fairy tale, after all, but real life.

A life that was good, really, really good, she realized with a smile. A life that made her happier than she'd ever been, and where she couldn't imagine ever needing or wanting anything more than what she had right now.

After her accident and subsequent surgery this past summer, Nick had insisted she stay with him during her recuperation. He'd gone ahead and hired a nurse to look after her while he was at work, even though she'd protested she could take care of herself. Shockingly, her mother had actually offered to remain in San Francisco for a few days and look after her, but Angela had gently refused, sensing that this was a crucial time in the development of her relationship with Nick and feeling the need to be with him as much as possible. That hadn't, however, stopped the daily phone calls from her father, anxious to know how she was feeling and warning her not to overdo. Most of the time her mother had come on the phone as well, and Rita had even made an effort to sound concerned about her. Her sisters had sent flowers and a fruit basket, and had each called a couple of times to check on her. Angela hadn't been able to say for sure, but she'd strongly suspected her father's influence had been behind all of that.

Her eyes grew a little misty now as she recalled the rather heart wrenching conversation she'd had with Gino in her hospital room. She'd never seen her dad cry before, but that day he had wept almost inconsolably onto her pillow as she had assured him everything was going to be okay now. Gino had told her over and over how sorry he was for everything she'd gone through over the years, that he should have been a better father and stood up to Rita far more often, while Angela had told him it didn't matter any longer and that she'd always known he loved her.

"After all," she'd murmured, "if it wasn't for you sticking up for me all those years ago, I wouldn't even be here today. You loved me before I was even born, Dad, and I'll always remember that. And you and I are going to make a pact with each other right now that things will be different from here on. Whether Mom and my sisters are on board with that, I don't really care."

And while things were far from perfect with her mother and sisters, Angela admitted that the situation was slowly beginning to improve. She didn't know whether to credit the tongue-lashing that Lauren had given Deanna and Rita that day at the hospital (which both Nick and Julia had recounted to her afterwards), or the fact that Gino was now asserting himself for once, or whether it was because everyone in her family was all goo-goo eyed over Nick. He'd accompanied her on two visits to Carmel thus far, and both times everyone – parents, siblings, brothers-in-law, nephews, nieces - had more or less tripped over themselves in order to talk to him. Nick had taken it all in stride, even though Angela could tell how much he disliked all of the socializing, and he'd managed to win everybody over within the first hour of their arrival.

He was trying, she told herself with a smile, *really* trying to make things work. The first step he'd made in that direction had been to ask her to move in with him, to not automatically go back to her flat once she'd fully recovered. She'd been shocked speechless, never having imagined that they could make quite so much progress in their relationship that fast, but had quickly accepted. Her lease had been up anyway in October, so the timing of her move had been ideal.

Nick had admitted that asking her to move in hadn't been an

easy choice for him, and that he was probably going to piss her off at least twenty times a day while he adjusted to having someone live with him after so many years of going solo. But both of them had been pleasantly surprised at just how easily Angela had fit into his life, at how well they got along and how Nick hadn't felt the least bit threatened that his privacy was being encroached upon. They had fallen into a routine with astonishing speed, and Nick told her frequently how much he loved having her here, how empty his life had been before she moved in.

And then, barely a month ago, he'd given her another shock by proposing that they go into partnership together at work.

"You know I've been looking to bring another member into my team," he'd told her. "And I can't think of anyone else in the office – hell, the entire business – that I'd rather have working with me. You're smart as hell, work harder than I do most of the time, and with you on board we could take on even more clients. Besides, it would force you to move out of that corner office you've buried yourself away in for so long and join the real world."

They were still finalizing everything at this point, getting paperwork drawn up and hammering out all the details, but as soon as they returned from visiting Nick's father over Thanksgiving, Angela would be moving into the empty office adjacent to his. Cara, too, would be joining the team and had told her boss more than once what a great opportunity this was for both of them.

"Not many people can make a go out of working and living together," Cara had cautioned. "But I think after all you've been through that you and Nick know what it's going to take in order to make this work. Just don't let him think he's your boss or anything. Stick up for yourself when he starts getting too pushy, okay?"

Angela had laughed at the irony of her young assistant's advice. "You're a fine one to be telling me that. Especially since all he has to do is give you one of those famous smiles and you melt like a stick of butter at his feet."

Cara had sighed. "I know. I told you I've got a problem with hot guys. I've really got to work on that one of these days."

Life, thought Angela sleepily, couldn't get much better right now. She was moved in, bag and baggage, with her dream man; was about to go into a very lucrative partnership with the very same man at work; was closer to her father than ever before and gradually beginning to mend fences with the rest of her family. She was healthy and fit, eating normally, and while she was still running had cut back on the extreme ultrarunning for the time being. She was too busy, after all, between work and Nick to put in those sort of miles right now. And she no longer needed to run for hours at a time to forget or block things out, because those years when she'd lived half a life were long gone now.

She wasn't naïve enough to believe that everything was going to be all sunshine and roses from here on end. Nick was still a stubborn bastard more often than not, and it was going to take some time to loosen up someone who'd been set in his ways for such a long time. But he'd been doing a lot more than compromising these past few months – inviting her to share his home; making an effort to meet her family and friends; going public with their relationship. They were flying back to Boston soon to spend Thanksgiving with his father and current stepmother, though Nick had warned her it wasn't going to be a particularly enjoyable holiday.

"My father's an ass and he and I butt heads constantly," he'd cautioned. "And his current wife is a doormat, almost thirty years younger than he is, and probably only with him for the money and prestige that comes with being married to a federal judge. But thank Christ that Thanksgiving only rolls around once a year. *And* that my father keeps a very well stocked liquor cabinet. We'll all need it before the long weekend is over."

They had agreed to attend the office Christmas party for once, having acknowledged that they both needed to work on their social skills. Added to that was Dante's annual holiday bash, a party being hosted by one of Nick's former NFL teammates, and Julia and Nathan's combination New Year's Eve/housewarming party being held at their brand new, nearly completed home in Tiburon.

Christmas would be spent at her parents' house, and they had already made their plans to fly out to Tahiti and spend a week with Sheena right after New Year's. Nick called his mother dutifully once a week now, and she usually demanded he put Angela on the phone for a few minutes each time.

But the one thing Nick hadn't changed his mind on, and wasn't willing to compromise on, was the subject of marriage. He'd been upfront and honest with her from the very first about that, but she could truly, sincerely, accept the fact that it didn't bother her in the least.

"Look," he'd told her within the first week of her moving in with him, "I've never bullshitted you before and I'm not going to start now. I love you, Angel, and I will do everything in my power to make sure you know that. I want you with me always, can't imagine a life without you in it. But this marriage thing – that's not me and I'm not sure it ever will be. I promise I'll always take care of you, will damned sure always be faithful to you, and I'll work real hard on not being too much of an asshole. But marriage – I'm just not sure that will ever be for me."

"It's okay," she'd assured him with a kiss. "I don't need that from you, Nick. I don't need the rings or the priest or the piece of paper that the law says binds us together. And I really, really don't need the white gown or eight bridesmaids or the reception with rubbery chicken and barely palatable wine. All I need," she'd added, wrapping her arms around him tightly, "is you."

He had hugged her fiercely, burying his face in her hair. "Well, that, Angel, you've definitely got. For life, baby. That's the honest truth, and I'll even write it down for you if you want."

She'd shaken her head. "No. Because it's already written on my heart."

She must have fallen asleep after that, because the next thing she knew Nick was waking her persuasively, kissing his way down her body until her eyes fluttered open with a groan. She gasped as he nuzzled his face between her thighs, his tongue rimming the opening to her body that was suddenly wet with need.

He wrung two stunning orgasms from her, making sure she was fully prepared for him, expertly using his tongue, lips, and fingers to arouse her and allow her to open completely. But when it finally came, his first thrust inside of her pliant body wasn't the savage, almost brutal possession she'd grown accustomed to, grown to crave. Instead, he slid in almost gently, a little at a time, and then just rocked his hips back and forth carefully a few times before holding himself still.

"Something wrong?" she asked breathlessly, unable to look away from the dark eyes that held hers captive.

He shook his head, a slow grin materializing. "Not a damned thing, no. It's pouring rain outside, while I'm tucked up all safe and warm inside my bed. Not to mention," he purred, bending down to nuzzle her neck, "inside of you. So I would say that everything is just about perfect right now."

She ran her hands up over his bare, broad chest until her arms were closely entwined around his neck. "Mmm, except that I couldn't possibly be burning up that many calories just being still this way. And you did assure me that I wouldn't regret skipping that race earlier."

Nick grinned, his hands sliding beneath her buttocks as he got to his knees, still deeply imbedded inside her body. "And I am a man of my word, Angel. So if it's a workout you're after, you're definitely in the right place."

She thought wildly that Nick's idea of physical activity was a hell of a lot more fun than slopping through muddy trails and skirting tree roots with the rain pounding down on her the whole time. And that the way he was twisting and contorting her body, pulling her on top of him one minute, and then flipping her over onto her belly the next, must surely be burning up a thousand calories at least. And when it was over, when he'd made her come more times than she could keep track of and he'd collapsed on top of her in a heavy, sweaty heap, her heart was pounding so fast that she felt like she'd just run a marathon at world record pace.

Nick's hand caressed her bare back soothingly as their breathing gradually returned to normal. "Still regretting sleeping in and missing that race, Angel?" he murmured to her teasingly.

"Hmm, maybe just a little," she teased back. "But then, I tend to forget sometimes that I'm sleeping with the devil and that he constantly tempts me to do naughty things."

He laughed, capturing one of her hands and interlacing their fingers together. "While having my angel back in my life is saving my soul."

She grinned at him. "So while you're corrupting me I'm saving you? I guess as long as there's a happy medium that will balance itself out in the long run."

"Speaking of runs, you've still got several hundred calories to burn off here if you want to make up for that half marathon, Angel," he reminded seductively, his hand cupping her breast. "Not to mention the huge breakfast I'm going to insist you eat in a few minutes."

She made a sound of pleasure deep in her throat as he licked her nipple. "No rush. We've got the rest of the day to burn off those calories, don't we?"

Nick shook his head. "No, baby. We've got the rest of our lives."

About The Author

Janet is a lifelong resident of the San Francisco Bay Area, and currently resides on the northern California coast with her husband Steve and Golden Retriever Max. She worked for more than two decades in the financial services industry before turning her focus to producing running events. She is a former long-distance runner, current avid yoga practitioner, is addicted to Pinterest, likes to travel and read. She has been writing for more than three decades, and is the author of the Inevitable series – six interconnected but standalone books, and the Splendor trilogy. Her writing genre is steamy contemporary romance, specializing in what she likes to call "romance for romantics".

Email – janetnissenson@gmail.com

Website/Blog - http://www.janetnissenson.com

Facebook - https://www.facebook.com/janetnissensonauthor

Twitter - https://www.twitter.com/JNissenson

Goodreads - https://www.goodreads.com/author/show/7375780.Janet_Nissenson

Pinterest - http://www.pinterest.com/janetnissenson/

Instagram - https://www.instagram.com/janetlnissenson/

TITLES BY THIS AUTHOR

The Inevitable Series:

Serendipity (Book #1 – Julia and Nathan's story)

Splendor (Book #2 – Tessa and Ian's original story)

All You Need is Love (Book #1.5 – the Serendipity sequel)

Shattered (Book #3 – Angela and Nick's story)

Sensational (Book #4 – Lauren and Ben's story)

Serenity (Book #5 – Sasha and Matthew's story)

Stronger (Book #6 – Cara and Dante's story)

The Splendor Trilogy

Covet (Book #1)

Crave (Book #2)

Claim (Book #2)

Printed in Great
Britain
by Amazon